A Petal in the Wind

Book 3

The

Great War

OTHER BOOKS BY MIKO JOHNSTON

A Petal in the Wind

A Petal in the Wind
Book 3

The

Great War

Whidbey Writers Group Press

Cover Design by Audrey Mackaman
Edited by Kitty Kladstrup

This is a work of fiction. Names, characters, places, brands, media, and incidents are either the product of the author's imagination or are used fictitiously. Any resemblance to similarly named places or to persons living or deceased is unintentional.

Print ISBN 978-1-944215-24-8

EPUB ISBN 978-1-944215-25-5

Second Edition

DISCOUNTS OR CUSTOMIZED EDITIONS MAY BE AVAILABLE FOR EDUCATIONAL AND OTHER GROUPS BASED ON BULK PURCHASE.

For further information please contact wwgpress@gmail.com

Whidbey Writers Group Press is a d/b/a of

DEDICATION

To Jakob, who fought valiantly for his country.
Wounded in the Great War, murdered in the Shoah.
You deserved better.

PART ONE

A FACTORY TOWN
NORTH OF PRAGUE
August 5, 1914

CHAPTER ONE

Relief washed over Lala Hafstein as the taxi laden with trunks and valises came to a stop in front of her family's house. Lala stepped out first, cradling her satchel, while her father Jakob helped her mother Sarah from the vehicle. As she inhaled the scent of roses warmed by the afternoon sun, Lala looked over the property. The two-story stone cottage perched on a hill, overlooking rolling plains sectioned by thickets of forest. The cherry tree was bare of fruit, but the walnut tree was full of nuts, the plums needed harvesting, and apples and pears would soon ripen on their respective trees. To her surprise, everything looked the same, for absolutely nothing else was remotely so.

Her parents entered the house as the taxi driver went to fetch the luggage from the vehicle's boot. As he bent over to remove a trunk, Lala asked him, "What was it like here when it began? How did you know?"

The driver understood, for he answered without hesitation, "Church bells, Miss. The church bells rang out." He stood up and with head bent, took off his cap and held it against his heart as if facing a coffin. "Not just our church bells, but you could hear them ringing off in the distance, from every town and hamlet in the region, ringing for a long,

11

long time. We knew then our empire was at war."

As he described that moment, Lala could almost hear church bells clanging from near and far. She'd been in Berlin since July twenty-eighth, when her family traveled there to celebrate her fiancé Armin Smetana's first art exhibit. In that brief time, war had erupted and grown rapidly, engulfing many European nations. It delayed their trip home for two fitful days and nights. It also retriggered nightmares from her childhood in a Russian shtetl, of the Cossack pogrom that left her orphaned and homeless until the Hafsteins adopted her, a secret no one outside her family knew. The first of many secrets.

The driver lifted two trunks and carried them to her house. Lala followed him inside, pausing at her reflection in the entryway mirror. Only then did she notice she hadn't been carrying her satchel. She'd been clutching it against her chest as if ready to bolt straightaway.

Déjà vu, she thought. Déjà vu.

Footsteps echoed on the stairway as the driver came back downstairs with Lala's father close behind.

"I'll help you with the last trunk. It's quite heavy." Her father swept his handkerchief across his brow, likely in anticipation of the effort as much as in protest of the heat. The driver nodded and the two men went outside.

Lala went upstairs to her bedroom and opened both windows to refresh the room. She unpinned her coif and let her walnut brown hair tumble down her back, then removed her shoes and stockings. Her travel trunks had been stacked next to the dowry chest at the foot of her bed, but the arduous overnight trip left her too exhausted to unpack. They'd wait until morning.

From her satchel she removed the drawings she'd made while in Berlin. She'd spent days sketching the lavish rooms and lobby areas of the renowned Hotel Grande in Berlin, partly as a drawing exercise but also to study the art of furniture arrangement, which she sought to pursue as a career. Her enduring dream, to study at the Art Academy in Prague, had been dashed when the school rejected her application. Only marriage to Armin, the Academy's most talented and wealthiest student, would have qualified her to attend, but the price proved too dear.

While in Berlin Lala had seen firsthand what she'd wondered about for months—the true nature of her fiancé's relationship with his friend Karel. Germans called them 'uranists'; others used worse names. The two men were lovers. Upon learning their secret, she convinced Armin to end the engagement in a way that would evade the true reason. With Karel's blessing he agreed, but instead he enlisted in the German army. Worse, he'd asked her to wait for him, in front of family and friends, denying her the chance to say no without seeming heartless. When she asked him why, he said it was to keep her connected to his family; he knew his father Josef was in love with her and suspected she felt the same. She tried to deny it…

She blanched. "What did you see?"

"The two of you kissing in the street. How long have you been in love with him?"

"I'm not—"

"As long as he's been in love with you?"

"What a ridiculous thing to say."

"Is it? Then of all the great works of art he owns, why does he have your portrait hanging in his office?"

"I've told you before, he thinks it's a masterpiece."

13

"Not my painting, Lala, you. You are the masterpiece…."

She could not allow herself to fall in love with Josef Smetana. Having an illicit romance with a married man, father of her "fiancé" and her father's employer, would violate societal mores and, worse, her integrity. Just because they shared a kiss, one thrilling, passionate kiss….

With practiced ease, she pushed the thought from her mind and returned to her drawings, singling out one of a shop in the hotel lobby. Her friend Paulina Sipek recently started a clothing business with financial backing from Josef's wife Romy. Paulina had given Lala a free hand in designing the shop and was thrilled with the results. Unfortunately, the outbreak of war undermined their prospects, casting doubt on their business succeeding.

"Lala," her mother called out from her bedroom down the hall. "Would you be a dear and check the mail? I had Hilde leave it on the kitchen table."

"I'll tend to it right now." Grateful for the diversion, she went to the kitchen and found where the maid had left a stack of cards, most of them addressed to Lala. She opened one and found a note from an acquaintance of the Smetanas congratulating Armin and her on their engagement. The official announcement, along with reportage in the society page of the newspapers, had gone out shortly before their departure for Berlin.

The sound of an automobile rumbling along their driveway sent a disquieting tremor through Lala; unexpected noises had that effect on her since the war began. She hurried to the hallway to peer out a front window as the Smetanas' Rolls Royce parked in front of her house.

Lala rushed to the door. She wondered if something had happened, perhaps a message from Armin. Maybe Romy had sobered up after last night's drinking binge and decided Lala wasn't worthy of her newfound affection.

She opened the door to find Josef, his arm raised, about to knock. Tall and distinguished, he appeared lost in thought. As his gaze turned from the door to her, his grave expression melted away, his lips parted silently like a starving man confronted by a feast that was out of reach. Years ago, in a Russian city, Lala had seen that look reflected in a restaurant window as she stood helplessly outside. It was her face, after days of hunger, pining for what she needed but could not have.

"Good afternoon, Jos—Mr. Smetana," she said as coolly as she could despite the excitement coursing through her. Merely being in his presence, close enough to inhale the distinct scent of him, to reach out and run her hands over his trim body, was enough to disrupt her ability to speak with clarity, to think beyond the desires that his nearness brought out.

"Hello, Lala. I, um, trust I didn't wake you?" Josef sputtered and then flushed in response to his odd question—it was mid-afternoon. Normally at ease and in command, he seemed flustered before her, which Lala attributed in part to her unpinned hair and bare feet, as she looked in Armin's portrait of her. She found Josef's reaction alluring.

She assumed the same pose as in the painting, with her head tilted to accentuate the length of her neck, bow lips slightly parted, but her umber eyes focused on him. "No, we're quite tired after our journey home, but we're all awake."

Her father had come downstairs, having changed into a fresh suit. When he saw his employer standing in the doorway, he waved him inside.

15

"Josef, please excuse my daughter's lack of manners. Come in."

Mortified, Lala stepped aside and allowed him to enter the house.

"I trust nothing untoward has happened," her father said as he invited Josef into the parlor.

Josef's chauffeur Smolak, a tall, stocky man, with kind eyes and a fleshy nose anchored by a handlebar moustache, appeared at the doorway with a satchel.

"All is well," Josef said. "Apparently, after our train arrived at the Central Station, a porter placed one of your bags with ours."

With Jakob's approval, the chauffeur brought the bag into the house and carried it upstairs.

"I didn't want you to be concerned that the bag was left in Prague, so I brought it to you immediately."

"Thank you, Josef. With everything we've been through in the past few days, we might not have noticed it was missing for a while."

The chauffeur returned and stood behind Josef, waiting for further instructions.

"May I offer you a drink?" Jakob asked. "I still have some of that fine Scotch you gave me."

"Perhaps another time." His dark eyes swept discreetly over Lala. "I should return home now. Good day, Jakob. Good day…Lala." He followed his chauffeur to the car.

Jakob closed the door and turned to Lala, looking baffled. "I wonder why he came here to bring our satchel."

"You heard what he said, Father. He didn't want us to worry about it being lost."

"But his chauffeur could have brought it. Why did he personally make the trip?" Jakob wondered. "It's not like him to be that solicitous."

The scent of him lingered. "We're family now."

CHAPTER TWO

Lala slept and dreamed, as she had since returning home two weeks earlier. Dreaming not of what had been, but of what might be. Arms wrapped around her waist, lips pressed to hers, the earthy smell of the man who—

A sharp noise snapped her awake just after dawn. Startled, she sat up in bed and listened, and was about to chalk it up to her dream…a heartbeat…a gasp of passion….

A pebble hit her bedroom window. She leapt out of bed to see who had thrown it, hoping it was Josef in secret pursuit, desiring a rendezvous.

Paulina stood below her bedroom window next to the linden tree. Why was she wearing a coat over her nightclothes?

Lala wrapped her robe around her and hurried downstairs, barefoot, to let her friend in.

"What happened?" she cried, knowing her fashion savvy friend, who took great care in her appearance, would not be dressed like that unless it was an emergency.

Paulina rushed in, breathless, trembling despite the warmth of a late August morning, the rims of her eyes red.

"Ivo's been conscripted and is being sent off to war. He had to leave early this morning." Fresh tears flowed down her cheeks. "I don't think I could bear to lose him, Lala."

Paulina's life had been filled with tragedy. Her father and brother died when she was young, leaving her mother so morose she eventually committed suicide. Shortly thereafter, Paulina met Ivo Chytry, a friend of Armin's, and they fell in love.

Lala wrapped her arms around her friend in a sympathetic hug. "Ivo is a strong man, and very clever," she reminded Paulina. "He'll manage to get by."

"But they're sending him to the Eastern Front. How can they expect him to fight against his own people?"

Ivo, like many in Bohemia, was half Czech and half Serb. His mother's family still lived in Russia, the main adversary of their empire at war.

Lala hustled Paulina into the kitchen. After stoking the stove, she set a kettle of water on it to boil. "Stay and have breakfast with us."

Paulina nodded. "Shall I prepare something for you?"

"No need, my friend. Mother has finally agreed that I should learn to cook. She's been teaching me." She fetched a wedge of cheese and the butter crock from the icebox. "I'm not very good yet, but I can manage something simple like breakfast."

Any household duties had been off-limits to Lala since childhood, when her mother assumed she would marry Armin. But when his unsuitability for marriage became evident, Sarah changed her mind and decided it would be practical for Lala to know how to cook and keep house.

Lala cut slices of bread and cheese on the chopping block, artfully arranging them on a platter with the butter crock and a jar of cherry jam. She directed Paulina to the cupboard that held dairy tableware and asked her to set the table for four in anticipation of Lala's parents joining them.

Sarah wandered into the kitchen. She tugged on the front of her blouse, which fit snugly over her full bosom and stout figure.

"Lala, why aren't you dressed?"

Then she noticed Paulina standing behind the table. "Paulina, how nice to see you. Did you spend the night?"

"No, Mrs. Hafstein, I just arrived."

Sarah's look of puzzlement prompted Lala to explain the circumstances of her friend's appearance.

Sarah patted Paulina's hand, Sarah's version of a hug for anyone of stature due to her elfin height. "I'm so sorry, dear, for both of you. I could try to tell you not to worry about him, but of course you will."

The sound of water boiling drew Sarah's attention to the stove. "My husband should be ready to come down for breakfast. I'll make coffee."

Jakob soon joined them, dressed in a suit befitting his recent promotion to vice president of the factory, his honey-colored hair slicked back so that not too much scalp showed. He bent over to kiss his wife; although below average height, he stood half a head taller than Sarah.

Lala brought him up to date as they sat down to eat. Lala passed the platter around the table. Despite the adequate portions, everyone ate meagerly. Their restraint stemmed from a fear that if the war didn't end soon, food shortages and rationing would follow. Each had witnessed long lines outside the markets and shops in Berlin during the opening days of the war.

Jakob kissed his wife and daughter goodbye as he

prepared to leave for work. "Paulina, I would be happy to drive you home to change. You won't want to go to work dressed like that."

"Thank you for offering, Mr. Hafstein, but I'm not going to work today, I'm too upset. Besides, hardly anyone is buying dresses now, maybe another heartbroken woman to see off her beau, or husband. That and one rush wedding." She blinked back tears. "Once the men are gone, there may be no business."

Her position in Paulina's venture had become a lifeline for Lala when she needed a way out of her engagement to Armin. Paulina would have to terminate Lala's position if sales didn't increase.

"What will you do?" Lala asked.

Paulina grimaced. "I'm going to have to ask Mrs. Smetana for another loan. Lala, would you be a dear and talk to her first? She'll be more likely to say yes to me if you rally her spirits."

Romy Smetana assumed Lala was in love with her son. Having blamed herself for Armin's enlistment, Romy became bereft in his absence. She began clinging to Lala during their trip home from Berlin, believing only Lala understood her sorrow.

"Tell her about Ivo's conscription," Lala suggested. "She'll understand and sympathize."

"I thought about doing so, but wouldn't it be taking advantage of her? What would that make me, then?"

Lala's words caught in her throat. She had considered using her budding relationship with Romy to get closer to Josef, Romy's husband. What did that make her?

CHAPTER THREE

"Welcome, my dear," Romy Smetana's voice reverberated in the cavernous grand hall of the mansion. Although the woman had suffered from various ailments over the years, Armin's engagement seemed to have had a wondrous effect on her, putting a rosy glow in her cheeks and bolstering her appetite, which had long been birdlike. With her beloved son gone, her lean body appeared more fragile, her face ghostlike against her dark hair.

Romy left her half-empty snifter of cognac on the lacquered Venetian credenza and rushed over, arms extended, to hug Lala, her expression a volatile mix of joy and sadness. The embrace lasted longer than Lala expected, or preferred.

When Romy broke away, her eyes brimmed with tears. "Have you received any mail from Armin?"

"No, Romy, not yet."

She wilted. "I had so hoped you would have by now. It's been nearly a month and I haven't heard from my son, not a word."

"He probably hasn't had a chance to write."

Romy retrieved her snifter and finished its contents in one swallow. She didn't offer any to Lala. Not that it mattered. Lala didn't drink spirits in early afternoon. "I suppose there is some comfort in knowing he hasn't written to you, either. At least I need not assume he's ignoring only me."

Romy had become more open and intimate with her since Armin left for battle. Lala issued a cool smile. Although blunted when aimed at Lala now, Romy's habit of lobbing insults was as ingrained in her as salt in the ocean, as she admitted on the night they returned from Berlin...

"I've been unfairly harsh toward you, my dear, for which I must apologize, for you haven't deserved it."

Lala shook her head. "That's not necessary——"

"But it is." Romy leaned forward as if sharing a confidence. "I can be very harsh with people, but it is because I demand the best from everyone." She tapped her finger against her chest. "Myself included."

But her pallor startled Lala. She rarely saw Romy without a glass of spirits in her hand now, another striking change from their Berlin trip.

Romy took Lala by the hand. "Come and sit with me in the parlor." She waited for her butler to open the door. The Smetanas never did anything as menial as open doors.

Lala bit her lip as shame swept over her. Being critical of Romy was not the way to ease her guilt over having fallen in love with Josef. Unfortunately, that shame did not extend to her passionate feelings, but then again, she hadn't acted on them since that spontaneous kiss, that magnificent, life-altering kiss.

A rush of heat rose within her as the moment replayed in her mind, how his arms surrounded her body, how his lips felt against hers, their bodies crushed together, the warm scent of bergamot and leather....

Lala pressed her knees together and tried to push such thoughts away, as she'd taught herself to do with horrors from the past. Resisting the arousing images of that memory proved to be more difficult.

"You're smiling, dear. What has you so happy?"

Romy's question reeled her back. A harmless explanation came to her. "I've learned that the best way to overcome sadness is to think about something happy."

"How clever of you. Whatever it is, it seems to be working. You keep having those happy thoughts, my dear. It's good to see you smile."

The irony would have been funny if she hadn't grown fond of Romy; now it felt sordid. "Perhaps you might give it a try," she suggested.

Romy appeared to consider it. "All right." She sat perfectly still, her eyes raised to the corner of the room, but moments later she shook her head. "No, it doesn't seem to be working for me, but then, I don't deserve to be happy like you do. What were you thinking about, dear?"

Lala hesitated before answering. "A kiss. A very special kiss." She felt her face redden.

That seemed to delight Romy, who beamed with pleasure. No doubt she assumed it was shared with her son. "I won't ask you with whom, since I suspect we both know the answer to that."

Lala swallowed hard. Changing the subject, she asked, "Romy, have you met with Paulina recently?"

Romy withered. "No, I haven't had the strength to do anything, or think about business." She strode to the liquor credenza and poured two fingers of cognac. After downing the contents, she refilled her snifter halfway before rejoining

Lala on the velvet settee, part of a suite of furnishings Josef had recently purchased from a Venetian villa. It was complemented by a fine Canaletto painting of the city perched on the wall behind them. A Monet used to hang there; it now resided in Lala's bedroom, a gift from Josef to celebrate her betrothal to his son.

Romy rolled her snifter between her hands. "I presume business is slow at the shop."

"It is, though Paulina has prospered beyond expectations. She has appealed to the women of the village to buy a nice dress to see their men off, then put it aside for when they return home."

"How clever she is," she said in a dull voice before taking another sip of cognac.

Aiming to distract Romy from drinking, Lala pressed on. "And as shrewd about business as she is about style. She's even convinced women to purchase one of her beautiful gowns in their rush to marry."

Romy swirled the contents of her glass around and around. The fumes reached Lala's nose. She leaned away. Romy took the hint and put the glass on the lacquered pedestal side table.

"Was that your idea?" she asked.

"No, why would you think that?"

"My dear, if this war hadn't happened, you would be approaching your wedding day—oh!" Romy clapped her hands and burst into a joyous smile. "We must do something to commemorate the date, something that will cheer you up as well. I know, we'll have a great party, invite everyone we know and celebrate the day in style."

"But—"

"No buts. I won't hear of it. It will be my gift to you. Tell your family and friends and then leave all the plans to me, dear." She looked so happy, Lala didn't have the heart to say no.

CHAPTER FOUR

"A gala ball, in the middle of the war?" Sarah marched back and forth through the kitchen, shaking her head at the idea. "Romy must be losing her mind."

Hilde stopped her scrubbing to listen until Sarah flashed her The Eye, her forceful gaze that unsettled women and withered grown men. The maid gulped and fled the room.

"I don't want it either," Lala acknowledged. "But try to understand. She's grieving."

"But you're not marrying Armin. The time has come to tell her."

Lala stiffened. Her mother was pushing her into a corner. She had already told Romy she didn't want to take any of her jewelry, suggesting she postpone the gift until after the wedding, hoping it would never come to that. Romy had wanted to give Lala one of her pieces as a betrothal present and only agreed to wait because Lala didn't want it to be "tainted" by the war.

"I will tell her, but not until Armin writes home. Perhaps he'll be forthright about our agreement and I won't have to say anything."

"He'll never do it. The boy has mastered hiding the truth."

Lala's temper flared. "As opposed to us?"

Sarah paused. "It's not the same thing. We lied to protect you. Your life was in danger."

"It's exactly the same. He lied to protect himself just like you lied to protect yourself, Mother. You didn't want anyone to know you were the daughter of a servant."

"Are you purposely trying to be unkind?" Sarah's voice cracked.

"No, Mother, honest for a change. Isn't that the real reason we've never told anyone the truth about our past?"

Sarah looked close to tears. "You go out of your way to protect Romy, but you say hurtful things to me without a second thought."

"You're twisting my words."

"What else could it mean?" Sarah sniffled back tears. "Maybe you'd rather live with her than me. Maybe you would rather have her as your mother than me."

Her mother had been experiencing mood swings of late and her tendency to drift toward melodramatic thinking tried Lala's patience. "You're talking nonsense again."

"You seem more attached to her than to me. You certainly have more in common—you're tall and slender, like her, and appreciate fine things like art and antiques, and now you're constantly there spending time with her, comforting her, growing closer."

Aging hadn't helped her mother's mood. She had grown stout, leading her to periodically fast, and her dark wavy hair, which she'd considered her best feature, had begun to gray.

"But Mother, you two have become closer as well since the engagement was announced. Aren't you friends now?"

Sarah swatted away the notion like it was a fly. "She pretends to be my friend to shield her precious son, but you she genuinely likes. She wants to take you away from me."

"No, she doesn't."

"Do you want that, too?" Sarah cried out.

"You're my mother and nothing is going to change that."

"You say that, but you've already changed mothers once, or don't you remember? I wanted you to be my daughter, and it took some time for you to feel the same way, but back then we shared something." Sarah began sobbing. "We were both forthright—'bold girls'—and that began our bond. But now, what do we have in common? I'm old and dowdy, uneducated, unsophisticated. And Romy is trying to get you to grow closer, like I did when I first met you. So why shouldn't you begin to feel about her the way you felt about me?"

Lala felt a pang of guilt. She knew her mother always felt inadequate when compared to Romy. Why wouldn't she interpret Romy's overtures as a personal slight and Lala's deference as abandonment.

Lala fetched a handkerchief for her mother and offered her a chair before sitting beside her. "You may not have given birth to me, and it's true I had a family before you and Father—"

That brought an explosion of tears to Sarah, so Lala stroked her back and waited until her mother calmed down before continuing. "But you loved me and cared for me, raised and educated me. You put up with my nightmares and flashbacks, my resistance to loving you at first, my foolishness, my temper and all my shortcomings. You took me in when no one else wanted me."

She swabbed tears from her mother's eyes. "You are my

mother. Nothing will change that and no one, no one, can ever replace you in my life, or my heart." She extended her arms for a hug.

Sarah fell into Lala's embrace, alternately laughing and crying until her tears abated. "I shouldn't have said that," she mumbled between sniffles.

"No, Mother, I'm the one who must apologize." She kissed her mother on the head, which always amused Sarah. "I know this was a painful episode in your life."

"It never compared to the fear your father and I felt when we left Russia with you. We worried every minute that Cossacks would follow us here to hurt you, or take you away." Sarah borrowed Lala's handkerchief to dry her eyes and then returned it. "Maybe you're right about finally admitting the truth about my mother. Perhaps Romy will be so repulsed she'll call off your engagement to her son."

Lala almost laughed. Her mother's secret would pale in comparison to her own. "Let's maintain our story. We're family now, so it's no longer about protecting ourselves. Revealing the truth at this time will hurt others, and we don't want that."

"You're right, there's a difference between protecting yourself and protecting others." Sarah shooed Lala off to the parlor to await her father's return home from work.

"Let's maintain our story...."

Secrets. For years she and her family harbored many about their past. Lala grew to loathe secrets, yet she could see their necessity, as her mother pointed out. Kind secrets protected others, but what would those that protected self-interest be called?

Lala had two new secrets locked within her. The sham engagement benefitted Armin, but her other secret, her budding romance with Josef didn't feel kind.

At the celebration dinner for Armin in Berlin, Josef spoke to her of the Chinese philosopher Lao Tzu...

"I'm not familiar with him."

"He said, 'To love someone deeply gives you strength'."

She had to find the strength to resist Josef, give up the notion of ever loving him. How remained to be seen.

CHAPTER FIVE

Thoughts of Lala's dilemma faded when the front door opened. Her father had come home early, looking tired and pale, the perennial twinkle in his blue eyes dimmed. The idea of discussing Romy's misguided plan with him faded in light of his physical distress.

Jakob took off his hat and placed it in the coat closet near the entrance. His hair seemed even thinner and whiter to Lala than it had been before their trip.

"Are you unwell?" she asked.

"Other than a touch of heartburn, I'm fine." He undid his tie and removed his jacket, laying them both across the back of the sofa before sitting in his favored wingback chair. Her father suffered from bouts of indigestion, which had worsened since his promotion. He blamed it on the lavish lunches served in the executive dining room, but Lala suspected the strain brought on by the war, and its effect on the factory's business, aggravated the problem.

"Where is your mother?"

"Upstairs taking a nap before dinner. Would you like me to fix you a drink?"

"Water, perhaps." He rubbed his fingers up and down over his chest.

Lala brought him a glass and sat in her mother's slipper chair beside him. "Father, may I ask you something? But you must promise not to get upset."

He eyed her with apprehension. "This sounds worrying already. I'd better get something stronger than water."

"It's not, really."

Nevertheless, he poured himself a small glass of Scotch and took a good sip before returning his attention to her. "I'm ready."

"You know how very proud I am of you, don't you?"

He put the glass down on the satinwood table next to his chair before crossing his arms over his chest. "Now this definitely sounds troublesome."

"Please, just listen. There's no doubt your skill as a cabinetmaker led to your promotion and it was certainly deserved. But you don't seem happy in your new position, and the added responsibility appears to be wearing you down. I wonder if you wouldn't be better off...?"

"Returning to my old department?" He shrugged. "Don't think I haven't thought about it myself, but I can't now. I've hired a young man to take my former position and he's become very capable."

"If he's young, he'll likely be conscripted. A perfect excuse to fill in for him until the war ends."

"He won't be drafted. He injured his leg in childhood when he was thrown by a horse. His right knee doesn't bend, nor can he move briskly." Her father winced and rubbed his chest again. "I should have stuck to water."

***

Her mother had a strict rule of avoiding any worrisome talk at the dinner table, in part to keep mealtime pleasant, but also to avoid upsetting Jakob until he digested his food. Both she and Lala waited to mention Romy's absurd plan until the three settled into the parlor for a post-dinner pot of tea, which had become their habit in place of dessert. Although Sarah baked superb pastries and cakes, she'd ceased ending their meals with sweets, blaming her expanding waistline as well as fear of wartime rationing.

Sarah fixed a cup for Jakob, adding a half-lump of sugar to his tea, and placed it on the table next to his chair. She poured a cup of black tea for Lala and then a half-serving for herself, plunking the other half-lump of sugar into her cup instead of her usual three to four lumps. She took one sip and turned up her nose. "I'll never get used to drinking it like this."

Lala chuckled sympathetically. "Mother, your sweet tooth is legendary."

Sarah put the cup back on its saucer and pushed them aside. "I'm going upstairs. Maybe reading will take my mind off dessert."

"Shall I join you?" Jakob asked with a hint of a smile.

"Lala needs to talk to you first."

His smile faded as Sarah went upstairs. He gave Lala a weary look and said, "I thought I already explained about my old position."

"This is something else, Father. Could you speak with Josef about—"

"Since when do you call Mr. Smetana 'Josef'?"

She'd momentarily forgotten she used his given name

strictly in private. "He asked me to when we were in Berlin."

Jakob tented his fingers, a sign of contemplation. "I suppose if you're calling his wife Romy, then he'd want you to be more familiar with him as well. Are you comfortable with that?"

Relieved that a small part of her pretense could be erased, she nodded. "But not comfortable enough to discuss an issue that has arisen. Romy wants to host a celebration at the mansion, in my honor."

"You mean a luncheon, or a ladies tea, don't you?"

"No, an extravagant party."

"How odd. Did she say why?"

"To commemorate what would have been my wedding day. Father, I don't want to celebrate that, or anything right now, for that matter. I thought if you spoke with Josef, he might convince her that a celebration wouldn't be appropriate now."

His face tightened. "Your mother and I should have that conversation with her. Josef has intimated that he and Romy aren't on speaking terms. She still holds him responsible for Armin's enlistment and may not take heed of anything he says."

At Romy's urging, Josef had arranged a medical deferment for Armin in time to prevent him from being conscripted into service, but Armin volunteered for duty anyway. Lala assumed the mysterious disappearance of his lover the night Germany entered the war provoked Armin's enlistment. She hoped Armin would eventually reveal what happened to Karel, but so far, the whereabouts of both men remained unknown.

Jakob took a few sips of tea before replacing his cup on its saucer. "When we see Romy, I'll explain our hesitancy about a festive gathering in wartime. Life must go on, to be sure, but a gala ball would be unfitting even if you were marrying Armin." He then stared upward, lost in thought. Lala was about to call him back when he turned to her. "Lala, are you still working in Paulina's shop?"

"A good question. There's barely enough business for her, let alone me. I doubt she can keep me on much longer."

Jakob cocked his head. "Hmmm. I think Romy has the right idea."

"You can't be serious, Father. Even if I agreed to appease her, it would be outrageous to throw a lavish party with the war on."

"I agree, but she's right about not letting what has happened interfere with what would have been. Life going on."

"What do you mean?"

"You're forgetting what started this situation with you and Armin."

"Our so-called engagement?"

"No, my dear daughter. You persuaded him to propose to you. Don't you recall why?"

It took a moment for her mind to reel back. "So I could live in Prague and attend the Art Academy."

"You should attend. You've been accepted for fall classes, which start next month. Go to school, study painting. It's what you've always wanted, isn't it?"

"But Mother said you wouldn't allow me to live in Prague alone."

"On that we still agree. But I would allow you to share a flat in the city with Paulina, where a dress shop has a much better chance of succeeding." His face relaxed. "Despite your initial pretense, which I can understand without approving of it, you managed to turn the situation around in a mature and sensible manner. Since you and Paulina have shown yourselves to be responsible young women, I trust you to share quarters when you have classes, but I'd expect you to return home on the weekends to visit your family."

"Oh my, I don't know what to say."

Jakob gave her one of his special smiles, which made his blue eyes twinkle and lit up her heart with love. "Then say yes."

CHAPTER SIX

It took several minutes for Paulina to stop hugging Lala after hearing the good news. Her face shone brighter than usual.

"Having a shop in Prague has always been my dream, but I never thought it would happen so quickly," Paulina cooed.

"Will you be able to run two locations?"

"That's the best part. I won't have to keep my current shop open if it's not profitable. There's a young man working in the factory who's been looking for a place to stay. He asked about renting the apartment over the shop and even offered to lease the entire building if I closed the business. We can take all the furnishings with us to Prague. And the money I'll collect in rent will be enough to tide me over in the new location, which means I can afford to keep you on as well."

Lala recalled the satisfaction of receiving payment for her work. If she could manage a few hours a week helping Paulina, it would minimize her father's need to provide for her financially, as well as the added stress funding her education and living quarters would likely cause him.

"But first I must find a vacant shop in Prague with an

apartment above for us to rent. When shall we begin looking?" asked Paulina.

"As soon as possible. My classes start September twenty-eighth. It's so exciting I can't quite believe it."

"Yes, you're finally going to the Academy. Still, I can't help but think if your parents had allowed you to attend in the first place, you could have avoided that whole mess with Armin."

"Actually, it's more likely I wouldn't have been able to attend at all. It was only Armin's insistence that got me accepted. I almost feel badly about that."

"Don't, my friend. After what he put you through, you deserve this. If he's going to keep you tied to him in the eyes of the world, then you ought to take advantage of that connection. It works both ways." Paulina beamed. "Your classes. You're going to art school, like you've always dreamed, to learn how to paint and now, to create architectural drawings as well."

Lala picked up a popular fashion magazine from Paulina's counter. "And also fashion illustration. Perhaps one day my renderings of your designs may appear in here."

"And we will be sharing a room together, like sisters." Paulina sighed. "I can't believe how brilliantly everything is working out for us."

"We have much to plan. Shall we begin tomorrow morning?"

"No, let's meet in the afternoon." Paulina's happy countenance faded.

"Is something wrong, my friend?"

"Why would you think that?"

"Because I know you too well to believe that forced smile you're wearing."

She made a dismissive shrug. "I haven't been sleeping well, that's all."

"Have you heard from Ivo?"

"I've gotten several letters. He tries to write every week, when he can."

"That's good to hear." Lala still hadn't received any correspondence from Armin, nor had his parents. She wondered if his friend Zigmund might have heard from him, but wasn't sure any contact with the smug man, still bitter after Paulina rebuffed him for Ivo, would be worth it.

Paulina agreed. "This new venture will be a godsend. Staying busy will help distract me from constant worry. So, tomorrow at one in the shop? We can begin packing as well."

"We should speak with Mrs. Smetana about our plans," Lala advised. "She might be insulted if we proceed otherwise."

"Can you do that? She seems to react better to you than to me. After all, you're the woman who's marrying her son. I'm the one draining her bank account."

"I will as soon as I enroll at the academy. I don't want her to try and talk me out of it."

"Could she?"

"No, never," Lala giggled in delight, and the two hugged before she bade her friend goodbye and left the shop. As she pedaled her bicycle toward home, she wondered if Paulina had been honest with her. She could understand a business-related problem troubling her friend, but suspected the concern was over something more personal, like Ivo. The war, which was supposed to end quickly, had expanded into several lines of battle. Ivo had been sent to the Eastern front to fight the Russians.

That had to be it. Lala worried about Armin, even though

they weren't in love. Still, if Paulina received bad news, she wouldn't keep it from Lala.

With all that was going on, it seemed logical that Paulina would have trouble sleeping. But Lala knew her friend too well to believe that was the problem.

CHAPTER SEVEN

Lala's hand shielded her eyes from the sun as she left the relative coolness of the Art Academy for the sultry campus with her parents. A gangly teen dozed under a shade tree, his body stretched out, hands tucked behind his head, a drawing tablet propped against the trunk. Nearby a group of young women surreptitiously sketched him. Lala pictured herself joining them next month and allowed herself a moment to savor the idea. Paulina had said it best—this was a dream come true. It reminded her of Ash Girl, her favorite book from childhood.

Jakob linked his arms with her and her mother and escorted them to Jindrisská Street, a bustling thoroughfare nearby. Lala believed, as many did, that Prague was second only to Paris as a center of creativity. For years she'd dreamt of someday living in the city and now her dream was within reach.

They stopped to look at a vacant shop with a FOR LEASE sign in the window near the corner a block away from the Academy. A convenient location, if she and Paulina could afford it. She caught their reflection in the shop window. Lala stood half a head taller than her father, her diminutive mother a head shorter than her. It sparked a memory of something her father had said recently about their appearance...

"Look at us," commented Jakob. "We look like a staircase."

Lala burst out laughing. She extended her leg and pointed her toes. "It's these Cuban heels."

Her mother eyed the shoes. "No, I keep telling you, you take after my side of the family. I always say, the Hessens are like fir trees —"

"Long branches and short needles," Lala and Jakob recited in unison.

Jakob pulled his wife close and kissed her cheek. "You're right, dear, you always say it."

Her father nudged her affectionately.

"Such a happy occasion deserves a celebration. Where shall we go, to a café for a treat? Or perhaps a museum, to find a spot to hang your work?"

"Oh Father," she laughed. "You're a little premature, aren't you?" Still, his idea appealed to her. He always knew the right thing to say.

They walked at a leisurely pace with no particular destination in mind. As they approached Nekázanka Street, Lala spied an antiques store near the corner. Beyond the store, several women stood in line holding baskets and cloth sacks, their backs to the antiques proprietor who sat outside his shop. Another woman approached and got on line.

"May I stop to look?" Lala asked her parents.

She peered through the window. The shop was filled with eclectic pieces of furniture and bric-a-brac marked down for quick sale, but no customers browsed through the tightly packed aisles. The proprietor, a squat man who seemed overdressed in a fine suit, perked up when Lala approached, but soon his focus returned to the women queued along the street, their faces hovering between boredom and worry. Lala overheard one woman say to another, "Do you think they'll still have anything left by the time we get in?"

Jakob muttered something as they passed the antiques store. Lala couldn't quite make out what he'd said, but knew his comment wouldn't be positive. Work had virtually halted at the factory since the war began. As her father had predicted while in Berlin, people don't buy furniture during a war. With raw materials in short supply and parts suppliers closing their businesses due to mass conscriptions into the military, it had become difficult to produce furniture even if a market still existed.

Sarah urged them on, past the queue of women that snaked around the corner and along Nekázanka Street to a market one block away. The family walked until they reached Wenceslas Square, the central gathering place dividing old and new Prague. The imposing National Museum loomed ahead. She remembered being here four years earlier with Armin and his friends, when they surprised her for her eighteenth birthday. How different it seemed now.

August temperatures often cast a lazy spell on the city, but despite the heat, Lala noticed how people in the square walked with purpose. No one ambled along the street, or dawdled in front of shop windows evaluating their merchandise, or relaxed in sidewalk cafes. Instead, she saw mothers pushing baby carriages or gripping the hands of their young children as they traversed the square. Walking alongside were middle-aged men, newspapers tucked under their arm, and old ones as well, bent over their canes as they hobbled along.

The young men were gone. The war had stolen them away.

Her father gestured ahead. "Lala, you decide where to go next."

"Let's go home."

"Perhaps that would be best." He glanced over his shoulder in the direction of the idle merchant sitting in front of his antiques shop. "I should return to the factory."

CHAPTER EIGHT

Lala volunteered to mind Paulina's shop while her friend went to inspect the vacancy in Prague the following week. She stood until her legs ached, then sat on a stool and waited for a chance to make a sale. From her perch she observed women, mostly factory workers, as they walked by. Some would stop and peer in. One would point at something and nod favorably while her coworkers agreed or enthused over another dress. Only one woman entered the shop and Lala sold her a practical work ensemble. Otherwise she attempted to keep busy by rearranging clothing on the racks, so neat and undisturbed they didn't require straightening.

When Paulina returned with a lease for the Prague shop, Lala was relieved until she saw the paperwork. The deposit alone would wipe out most of the money they'd made.

They would need another loan from Romy.

Lala made arrangements to meet with her a few days later.

***

Lala lifted the engagement photo of Armin and her from the Venetian side table. The picture was taken last June, though it seemed like a century had passed. She placed it back on the table filled with other silver-framed family portraits and once more studied the Canaletto landscape of Venice hanging in the Smetanas' parlor as she waited. The butler had said that Romy would join her momentarily. That was nearly a half hour ago.

Romy finally entered the room looking ragged and pale. She walked with some difficulty to the liquor credenza and helped herself to a generous pour of cognac.

"It's good to see you, my dear." Romy hoisted her glass in Lala's direction and took a good swallow. Fortunately, she didn't offer to pour one for Lala. At least the woman had enough sense to recognize most people would refuse cognac at ten in the morning. "It has been awhile since you last visited me."

Romy's eyebrows arched at that and Lala caught the implication. This was not going to be easy or go well.

"I had to enroll at the Academy, Romy. Classes will start soon."

"How nice to have something to distract you from your troubles…or perhaps not. Where will you stay? And won't you be lonely without Armin there?"

"I would miss Armin no matter where I lived. Fortunately, I will have Paulina for company. We plan to share the apartment over her shop."

Her eyebrows arched again as she swirled her drink. Lala feared that if the woman clutched the crystal snifter any tighter it would shatter in her hand.

"Are you sure you wouldn't feel safer staying close to home until the war ends? Being alone in a big city like Prague would be frightening for a young lady under the best of circumstances. Come to think of it, if you stayed here, I could have Josef find an exciting position for you at the factory, perhaps selecting the upholstery fabrics, or better yet, arranging the furniture for the catalog. You'd like that, wouldn't you? And you could learn more about the factory, so when you and Armin marry, you can take over for Josef when he retires. After you refused my offer to host a party to commemorate your wedding day...."

"I am grateful for the offer, but it would have been too sad to celebrate without Armin present. I'm certain the guests with sons and brothers off fighting the war would agree."

"Yes, your parents made that abundantly clear," Romy said in the dismissive tone usually reserved for servants, but it sweetened when she added, "But you can't refuse me this."

"It's an exciting proposal, to be sure. I won't say no, but...not yet. I'd prefer to wait until I've finished my studies at the Academy and help Paulina establish her business. She's so grateful for your belief in her and wants to return your investment, with interest, as soon as she can, but she'll need a little more help from both of us."

Romy downed the contents of her drink before returning to the credenza to pour another.

Lala silently chastised herself for bringing up the subject after refusing Romy once again. The more the woman drank, the less chance of a successful outcome to their meeting. She pressed on. "And between my studies and working with Paulina, I'm less likely to embarrass you and Josef when I do join the family business, working together with Armin after he's returned."

She thought that might please Romy, but the woman turned glum.

"I still haven't gotten a letter from my son. Have you?"

"No, Romy. I'm certain he's been writing to us both, though."

"I'm surprised. I would have thought you at least, unless he thinks you'll share your letter with me. He wouldn't want that."

Romy must have assumed Armin's letters to Lala would be too intimate.

"I'm sure we'll hear from him very soon, Romy. The War Office has held up mail for censorship."

"That isn't the reason." Romy took another gulp. "My son hates me." She paced the room, her arms held away from her as though she feared that if they came into contact with her body, she would electrocute herself. Her face contorted into a mask of agony.

"Why would you say that? He loves you very much," Lala said, hoping it would calm Romy. "He has never hated you."

A bitter smile slashed across her face as she stared off into the distance. "He does now. He hates me for everything I've done, but I was only trying to protect him. He's still a boy in many ways. He doesn't understand what it means to be a man, a real man." She downed her drink. "He had to go away."

"No Romy, he chose to volunteer for service, to fight in the war, remember?"

Romy looked blankly at Lala. "I made him go away, and now he hates me."

Romy kept babbling that over and over. Lala saw no point in arguing, as the woman was too intoxicated to make sense. Lala rang for the butler and when he arrived, she asked for some coffee. "Would you join me in a cup, Romy?"

"I made him go away." And with that she left the room.

"Would you like some coffee, Miss?" the butler asked.

"No, thank you. I'd best be going."

She gathered her things and when she stepped into the grand hall, the front door opened and Josef entered the house. As soon as she laid eyes on him Lala felt a flutter inside her that spread to every part of her body.

Josef froze in place and gazed at her with surprise, which quickly turned into longing.

"Sir," the butler approached Josef to take his hat. "Madame is not…well this morning. Would you have me call the doctor again?"

Josef slumped. "It won't do any good. Let her sleep it off."

CHAPTER NINE

"It's only me, Paulina," Lala said as she entered the shop. Paulina had brightened when she heard the door open, but her smile tempered when she saw it wasn't a customer. She attempted cheeriness, but couldn't quite succeed. Lala doubted her friend had seen any customers that day, possibly longer, judging by the merchandise filling the racks. All those beautiful dresses, the practical work attire, untouched and unsold, almost frozen in time, thanks to the war that was supposed to be over in a few weeks. In reality it had entered its second month with no end in sight. Paulina had predicted a store in Prague would have a better chance of success. She'd used her last koruny to put a deposit on the vacant shop Lala saw on Jindrisská Street. Unfortunately, after seeing the antique dealer's situation, Lala wondered if business would be any better in the city.

"How did Mrs. Smetana respond to your request?" asked Paulina.

"We didn't exactly, um, speak."

Paulina appeared shocked. "Oh dear, at this hour of the morning?"

"I tried to discuss business but she kept changing the subject. All she wanted to talk about was Armin, if I'd heard from him. Romy kept babbling about how he hates her for what she did."

"What did she do?"

"Probably nothing, but she kept saying over and over, 'I made him go away'."

"Are you sure she meant Armin?"

No, she wasn't. Romy could have meant Josef.

From the corner of her eye, Lala noticed a group of women about to pass the shop. She hurried to the rack near the window and chose two practical day dresses, one in dark red and one made to look like a black skirt and ivory blouse. She held both of them up as though trying to decide between the two. The women outside stopped momentarily and watched with admiring eyes, but their favorable expressions dissolved and they walked on.

Lala replaced the dresses on the rack. She saw Paulina was clearly in distress.

"Excuse me, I must go upstairs," she murmured to Lala before dashing to her apartment.

"I'll watch the store," Lala called out to her. She considered following Paulina upstairs to try and console her, but what could she say? That the war would end soon and every woman in town would buy a dress to celebrate? No, better to let her cry in private.

Lala walked toward the back of the store, where Paulina showcased formalwear. One of Paulina's elegant evening gowns, displayed on a dressmaker's form, caught her eye. A sheer overlay of tulle in a rich shade of terra cotta draped around a sleeveless underdress of almond green silk like a loose robe. The layering produced subtle changes in tone.

Paulina had encrusted the edges of the tulle with crystal beads and sequins in shades of silver and gold, one of her trademarks. She'd added more in swirling lines that flowed from the edges and along the sheer sleeves, which mimicked the soft gathering she'd created in the underdress. Lala recognized some design ideas from French couturiers like Jacques Doucet and Jeanne Paquin, whom Paulina idolized, but the final result before her transcended their influences. The dress was uniquely her friend's and worth more than its lofty price.

Paulina returned, dabbing a handkerchief to her mouth. "Please excuse me for rushing off like that."

Paulina's wan face rivaled Romy's. "No need to apologize, you were upset." Lala went to embrace her friend. "Oh my, you have a blotch on your dress."

Paulina looked down and huffed when she noticed the cloudy stain above her left breast. "Would you be a dear and wait here until I change?" She selected a day ensemble from the rack and slipped into her dressing room. "Do you like that gown?" she called out through the red and white striped curtains.

"It's stunning, Paulina, as beautiful as any in your fashion magazines."

"Then take it."

Lala was sure she misheard. The dress cost three hundred koruny, a giveaway compared to a French couturier gown, but more than a year's salary for her. "You can't be serious."

"I am. I haven't paid you since the war began."

"Even so, I couldn't take it, it's too expensive." But her friend inspired an idea. "Paulina, what about offering it to Mrs. Smetana toward your debt? This dress is worth far more than your weekly payments, and having a lovely gown like this may cheer her up, perhaps get her to stop drinking so much."

"I wish I could, but how can I negotiate with her if she refuses to meet with me?" Paulina emerged from the dressing room carrying the soiled dress, which she stowed behind her counter.

Lala carefully removed the gown from the form. "Let me take care of that."

"That's good of you, Lala, but you needn't. You've done enough."

"Nonsense, my friend. I want to help you."

Paulina took the gown to her counter and folded it into a white dress box. "You're trying to save Romy, and you can't, not if she doesn't want to be saved. And I sense there's more to your motives than you let on."

Yes, Lala acknowledged to herself, there are other reasons.

"Don't misunderstand, I am sympathetic. The woman is despondent about Armin, but it's almost as though she blames herself for him being off to war." Paulina measured out and cut a length of red ribbon.

"From what she said today, I think she does."

"Even if he wanted to punish her, that's awfully extreme." Paulina wrapped the ribbon around the box and tied it into a bow. "If Karel enlisted, I suppose Armin might have thought that by joining up they could be together, but how foolish of him. What guarantee would he have that they'd be sent to the same front, let alone placed in the same regiment?" She handed the box to Lala.

As Lala accepted the box a thought occurred to her—did Armin know something the rest of his family and friends didn't?

CHAPTER TEN

That night, Lala tried to sleep, but Paulina's words came back to haunt her…

"You've done enough…."

Since Berlin, Lala's feelings toward Romy had changed from tolerance to sympathy. While she couldn't condone the woman's excessive drinking, she could see how Armin's continued silence upset his mother. What began as a balm against her son's enlistment worsened when he failed to contact her. He hadn't written to his father, either, or her, much to her disappointment.

"…You're trying to save Romy and you can't…."

Maybe not, but she had to try. For Romy's sake. For Armin, so he wouldn't blame himself for his mother's decline when he finally communicated. For Paulina, who put so much of herself into her business.

And for Josef, who ought to have a wife he needn't pity, one who could be a positive partner in his life. He deserved to have that. Even if it wasn't her.

And what about her?

When she finally pushed the thoughts away, she fell asleep.

***

Several days later, Lala went to see Romy. She arrived at the Smetana mansion early in the day, after Josef left but before Romy could have had too much to drink.

She trailed behind the butler, who carried the box with the gown inside as he escorted her to the parlor. He placed the box on the pedestal table next to the settee and after Lala declined his offer of coffee, closed the doors behind him. Lala passed the time trying to remember the name for that type of three-legged table...gueridon, she thought.

Not long after, Romy entered looking tired and raw, her eyes squinting in the morning light. "Hello, Lala. How good of you to come, but I wish you had informed me in advance. These days I'm not always up to visitors, especially in the morning." She raised one hand to the side of her face to shade her eyes from the daylight as she sat on the settee.

Lala sat next to her. Mercifully, she didn't detect alcohol on Romy's breath. "I apologize, but Paulina and I have good news and didn't want to wait—"

Romy brightened. "Have you heard from Armin?"

"Oh, no, not that. Good news about repayment of your loan, for our business."

Romy slumped.

Lala wondered if she could salvage the conversation. "I brought you something." She gestured to the box on the table.

Romy squinted at it. "What is that?"

"It's something to pay down your loan. Open it and see for yourself."

Her eyes roamed from the box to the liquor credenza.

Lala snatched up the box and handed it to Romy, hoping it would intrigue her long enough to open it before she began drinking. When Romy didn't immediately respond, Lala untied the ribbon for her.

Romy finally removed the lid and lifted the bodice of the dress out of the box. "What is this?"

"Paulina created this gown, Romy. Isn't it exquisite?"

Romy laid the dress across her lap and inspected the detailing along a tulle sleeve. "It truly is, as fine as anything I've seen in Paris."

Her comment buoyed Lala's spirits. "She wanted you to have it as partial payment on her loan," Lala explained, and added a small lie. "She created it with you in mind. The colors flatter you, don't you agree?"

"They're quite lovely." She lifted the sheer sleeve and laid it across her arm. "It—"

The butler interrupted them. "Madame, there is a Mr. Handlanger waiting outside. He has a message for you."

Romy let the dress slip from her hands. It fell to the floor as she extended her hand toward the butler, palm up. He handed her a folded note and stepped a discreet distance away, waiting for a reply.

Romy opened the note and read it, her face tensing with every line. "Tell him if the problem has returned, he must go back and finish it once and for all." She crumpled the note and held it in her outstretched palm for the butler to whisk away before leaving the room. Ignoring the dress, she went directly to the liquor cabinet and seized the nearly empty decanter of cognac. After she poured the splash left into her glass, she rummaged through the cabinet for another bottle. Finding none, she filled her glass with whatever was in the matching decanter. Scotch, judging by the peaty aroma.

Lala picked the dress off the floor and folded it back into the box. "Romy, will you accept this gown as partial payment for Paulina's loan?"

Romy remained at the liquor credenza, her back to Lala. She'd finished her first drink and then poured a second, which emptied the second decanter. As she sipped, she bent over the credenza. Lala heard bottles rattling and clinking together as Romy rifled through the liquor stock, no doubt looking for a decanter with more than a glassful left.

"…You're trying to save Romy and you can't…."

Paulina's admonition was brutally apparent now. Time to set aside the woman's problems and focus on herself. Classes would begin in two weeks. She and Paulina had to find a way to keep financially afloat until the new store could support them.

Before she left the parlor, she took one more look at Romy. The woman held a full bottle of something over her glass as she poured herself another drink. Poor Romy.

And poor Josef.

Josef…

"…you've done enough…."

CHAPTER ELEVEN

"Why did Hilde have to pick today of all days to volunteer at the hospital?" Sarah groused as she mopped the kitchen floor. One of her plum jam jars had slipped from her hand and shattered on the floor, creating a sticky mess along with broken glass everywhere.

Normally Sarah became flustered by her occasional clumsiness, but Lala figured that losing the contents made with precious sugar, which had become expensive, difficult to obtain and very limited in quantity when it could be found, intensified her mother's ire.

"I'll help you clean it up." Lala tried to reach for the broom, but her mother pushed her out of the kitchen.

"No, stay away. I don't want you to cut yourself." Her tone could have cut glass as well. "Go wait in the parlor for your father while I clean up this mess."

The room held a cozy mix of mid-nineteenth century furniture, new pieces and objet d'art acquired through inheritance and gifts, which Lala had combined into a tasteful and cohesive arrangement. Hanging on the walls were paintings, including several of Lala made by Armin.

She looked for a distraction among the items on display in the secretary bookcase and chose a fine arts book, a gift from Josef for her sixteenth birthday.

Josef.

After her disastrous encounter with Romy, Lala decided to stop fighting her urges and allow herself to daydream about him. It brought about pleasurable sensations, which were becoming more difficult to resist.

She settled onto the sofa and thumbed through the book, past pages of art history she'd memorized and photographs of paintings she'd tried to copy. The Corot landscape printed on a full page plate wasn't as fine as the one hanging in the Smetanas' grand hall.

She placed the book on the sofa table at the click of the door latch. "Father, welcome home." She greeted him at the door with a peck on the forehead, damp with perspiration. He'd been in the woodworking shop today; a light film of sawdust coated his skin and several wood shavings accompanied him home.

She waited to take his jacket. As he struggled to remove it, she grabbed the collar from behind and slid it off. He appeared more stooped than usual, especially after the way he'd strolled so proudly through Prague a few weeks ago.

"What's wrong, Father? You look like you're in pain."

"Just tired. I'll be fine." He shuffled into the parlor and sank into his wing chair.

"Can I get you a drink? Some Scotch before dinner?"

"No thank you, Lala, not tonight." He rubbed his chest and grimaced. "I still have a touch of indigestion from lunch. Maybe some water, though."

He ignored the glass she set before him. His eyes swept the parlor, his face pensive.

"I've always loved sitting in this room."

She nodded. "You tell me that all the time."

"I do? As many time as your mother has told you how much you look like her sister Hannah?"

"May her name be a blessing," they said in unison.

"Tread carefully around Mother," Lala warned. "She's not in a good mood."

Her father tried to smile. "What did you do to annoy her?"

She crossed her arms in protest against his insinuation. "What makes you think it has anything to do with me?"

He wrestled out a snicker.

"It was…never mind, Father. How was your day?" He shrugged, but then squirmed in discomfort.

Lala moved beside him. "Are you sure you're all right?"

"It will pass, it always does. Go sit down. Tell me about your day."

"I met with Romy."

"Ah, no wonder your mother is in such a bad mood."

"It has nothing to do with that."

"Don't be too sure." He tented his fingers, which tempted Lala to ask for an explanation, but she worried it would aggravate his heartburn. Another time.

Sarah entered the parlor announcing, "The stew is nearly done. Hello, dear." She bent to kiss her husband and frowned. "Your head feels awfully hot."

"I'm not feeling well," he conceded.

"Dinner can wait. Let's get you upstairs for a nap."

Sarah helped Jakob out of his chair. With arms linked, they slowly walked up the stairs, chatting amiably about the day and other trivial things with great interest.

Lala delighted in seeing her parents so warm and loving

with each other after nearly twenty-four years of marriage. She could picture sharing that level of devotion with Josef. Could they ever share that level of comfort? She shook the fantasies from her head and returned to her art book.

Her mother came down from the bedroom and poked her head into the parlor. "He fell right to sleep. If he naps for an hour, he'll feel better. In the meantime, I'll finish making dinner."

"I'll help."

Sarah began to protest out of habit, but waved her concerns away. "Fine. You can peel the potatoes while I get the water boiling."

She put on an apron and handed one to Lala. Sarah assumed her station at the chopping block while Lala fetched potatoes from the pantry.

"Watching you and Father before was lovely," Lala said as she joined her mother. "It reminded me of how happy two people can be together." She smiled as she ran her paring knife barely under the potato skin the way her mother had taught her. She pictured intimate dinners with Josef. "It gives me hope that someday I'll have that in my life as well."

"You're a loving person, dear. You'll find love, like I did, someday soon." After stirring the stew, she came over to observe Lala's progress. "When you're done peeling, cut them into quarters instead of in half so they'll take less time to cook."

Lala followed her mother's instructions. "But after all these years, you still feel the same way about Father as you did when you first met."

Sarah issued a coy smile as she covered the pot. "I'll let you in on a secret. The key to our relationship is both of us are convinced we married above our station. Now wait until the water comes to a boil, and don't forget to put a good pinch of salt in before you add the potatoes."

Working together, the two had dinner prepared in less than half an hour. Sarah took off her apron and checked her appearance in the hall mirror, patting her hair and tucking a few stray strands in place.

"Can you finish setting the table while I get your father?" she asked Lala.

Lala brought out plates and silverware for three. As she was about to place the last water goblet on the table, an image sputtered in her mind, of Josef and her kissing on a Berlin street, of the overwhelming emotions that sprang forth from that kiss...of the passion, the longing it—

A scream erupted from the upstairs bedroom, filling every corner of the house with pain. The glass fell to the carpet and rolled across the floor, where it came to rest against the leg of her father's wing chair.

CHAPTER TWELVE

The world went gray, like it did once before on a street in Russia, triggered by similarly tragic news. Blurred faces, hollow voices, numb embraces. Murmured words of sympathy that could not penetrate the stone walls of grief. She stood before an open grave, staring down, not at old clothing and memories of the past, but a real coffin holding her father's lifeless body. It jarred Lala as much as the rhythmic scraping of shovels against a dwindling mound of earth.

As she watched his casket disappear beneath the soil, she felt a piece of her heart go with it. Pieces had already been buried long ago, in two unmarked graves in a Russian forest. How many pieces were left?

Lala sat on a hard bench in the rear of the parlor between her mother and her Aunt Naomi. Wife, daughter, sister. Three women dressed in black; three women beset by sorrow. For a moment, she became conscious of how limp her hands felt, curled in her lap. Idle. Words from the distant past came back to haunt her…

"…*when you have nothing to do, it means you have nothing*…."

Lala stifled back a sob and tried to focus on what she still had. Paulina had come to the house as soon as she received the news. Working with instructions provided by the Smetanas, Paulina helped Hilde prepare the Hafstein home for shiva, the weeklong Jewish ritual of mourning. They covered the mirrors, set out benches for the mourners to sit, and put an extra bed in Lala's room for her cousin Esther in anticipation of the Zedek family's arrival the next day. They prepared Lala's parents' room for Uncle Hershel and Aunt Naomi. Sarah had refused to go upstairs since Jakob's death, so another bed had to be set up for her downstairs in the hallway outside the kitchen.

It took several days for the shock to wear off, but once it had, the bone-crippling pain of sorrow hit Lala and knocked her down, over and over like surging waves. At times she could barely move, barely speak, barely breathe, all made worse by the suffering she beheld in her mother, who hadn't stopped crying since finding her husband lying dead in his bed.

Lala clutched her handkerchief, dampened with tears, as she observed guests milling about. Friends, neighbors, and her father's coworkers had flocked to the house to pay their respects. Soft voices drifted in from the dining room where they savored platters of food sent over by the Smetanas. Three days of unseasonably mild weather provided a measure of relief.

The factory's personnel manager, Mr. Strahov, approached the women with a rotund middle-aged man who, despite his fine dress, had an air of tawdriness about him. Strahov bowed and gestured as though he was presenting royalty to Sarah. "Mrs. Hafstein, may I introduce Mr. Anezska, the upholstery manager of the factory."

Anezska clamped one hand over the skullcap perched on his bare scalp as he bent over to take Sarah's hand.

"Allow me to express my condolences to you and your family, Mrs. Hafstein. Jakob was a fine man, a very fine man. He'll be greatly missed."

"Thank you, Mr. Anezska," Sarah said, her voice flat.

"When, may I ask, is the funeral?"

"It was two days ago," Lala informed him.

"Oh, you buried him already? He's only been gone...." He fell silent as Sarah began to wail.

"One day you come home from work, like every other day, and twenty-four hours later you're in the ground," she sobbed.

Lala put a protective arm around her mother.

"It's our custom, Mr. Anezska." She wiped tears from her eyes, which felt puffy from crying. Anezska nodded and backed away, returning the skullcap to a basket near the front door as Josef and Romy arrived. Lala forced her attention from them to her mother, whose emotional turmoil grieved Lala as much as the loss of her father. "Why don't you lie down awhile, Mother? You need to rest."

"No, I don't want to sleep," Sarah moaned. "I just want to be left alone, so please don't...." Her shoulders heaved as she began to cry again.

Naomi leapt up to fetch a small glass from the bar tray and filled it with an amber liquor from one of three matching crystal decanters. "Drink this, it will help."

Sarah reluctantly swallowed the contents. Her nose crinkled in distaste.

"What was that?"

"Whiskey." She sniffed the glass. "Or maybe brandy. It doesn't matter; either will help you sleep. Hershel will take you to your bed—"

"NO, not the bedroom, not upstairs!" Sarah cried out, halting all conversation in the room. Hilde rushed over as Naomi explained, "Sarah, we set up a bed for you down here, remember?"

"I'm so lost without him. I don't know what to do."

Hilde took Sarah's hand as Hershel grabbed her other arm and helped her to stand.

"Thank you, Rabbi, I can manage now." Hilde guided the distraught woman out of the parlor, nodding to Paulina as she approached.

"Have you eaten yet today?" she asked Lala and Naomi. They hadn't.

Paulina pressed her fingers to her mouth as she drew a deep breath. "I'll have Hilde bring you plates of food right away." She grimaced and hurried away.

Paulina's mother had committed suicide that spring, leaving her without family. She'd grown close to Lala's parents in recent months, so the loss had to affect her deeply as well, but something else had been upsetting her, evident in her look of distress. Lala saw her aunt noticed it as well and described her friend's business difficulties to Naomi.

"What with all that, Paulina's beau is fighting on the Eastern front," Lala explained.

"Her beau? She's not married. Ah, no wonder she's upset."

"What do you mean?"

Naomi patted Lala's hand. "My dear, from what I observed, your friend is most definitely with child."

CHAPTER THIRTEEN

More guests arrived to pay their respects.

A white-haired man approached. "Miss Hafstein?"

She recognized the elderly cabinetmaker who had worked for her father and stood up to greet him. "Hello, Mr. Tesar, thank you for coming."

"How could I not? My goodness, look at you. I haven't seen you since you were a child, and now you're all grown...up." His palms rose from his waist to his brow.

Lala had long been teased about her height. "I take after my mother's side of the family. She's always said, 'The Hessens are like fir trees, long branches and short needles.'" She flashed back to her recent trip to Prague and wept.

Mr. Tesar nodded sympathetically. "It's nice to see you again, despite the circumstances. Regards to your mother."

Exhausted, Lala sat down. She glanced across the nearly empty room and noticed one decanter missing from the bar cart. She speculated who would have taken it, then ruefully assumed the likely answer was Romy.

Naomi shifted next to her and stroked Lala's cheek, brushing a tendril of hair behind her shoulder.

"Why does it have to take a tragedy to bring everyone together?" Naomi lamented. "I've always regretted that our families couldn't spend more time together, especially since we live so much closer to you now."

"But with Uncle Hershel's new position, you're also much busier in Warsaw." She caught a glimmer of pride in her aunt's eye.

"Did you know his congregation is three times the size of the one in Russia?"

"You mentioned that last January in your letter announcing Saul's wedding."

Naomi squirmed. "It's a shame more family couldn't attend. It would have been grand to have everyone together under happier circumstances."

Lala issued a polite smile. The newlyweds welcomed a baby last May, making it obvious why Naomi's son and his bride married in the teeth of winter, when few could travel to the ceremony.

"The newspapers keep saying the war will end soon, so we'll have Esther's wedding to look forward to next year," Lala noted.

They both looked across the room at Naomi's petite daughter. She had grown into an attractive young woman, with a pink complexion, fair hair and deep brown eyes.

"She's lovely, Aunt Naomi, but after all, she looks like you."

Naomi acknowledged the compliment with a weak smile, which faded when she said, "I'm sorry Saul couldn't join us, but he's been conscripted and his wife's struggling with our grandson David. He has colic, but otherwise he seems healthy."

The couple named their baby after Naomi's first born,

who died very young of a disease that took their youngest child as well. Anxious to change the topic, Lala said, "Tell me about your new daughter-in-law."

"We weren't too keen on Devora at first, it all happened so quickly, but we're making the best of it. Her family is nice and we get along quite well with them."

"How long had he been courting her?"

Naomi frowned. "He hadn't, in fact, for the past two years he'd been courting another young lady whom he'd known since childhood in Russia. We suspected he would marry her, until circumstances…well, changed." She leaned in to whisper in Lala's ear, "Frankly, I'm pleased he didn't marry that piglet."

"He was going to marry Ruthie Grossfleisch?" Lala blurted. Saul had once told her he wanted to be the richest man in the world. Marrying Ruthie would have accomplished that, but a cruel streak ran through the girl's parents. They would have been horrible in-laws. "Consider yourself fortunate, Aunt Naomi. I wouldn't wish *machatunim* like that family on my worst enemy." The women stifled snickers and embraced, appreciating the momentary respite from grief.

A young man in his mid-twenties limped over, dressed in a rumpled black suit that judging by its boxy cut, might have belonged to his father years ago. He wore a velvet skullcap embellished with braided gold trim. His full beard matched his hair in color and texture, resembling a tan bristle brush, his features plain but not unpleasant. It was then Lala noticed his most unusual eyes, amber around the dark center, radiating out to a golden green and then to blue-gray at the outer edges.

He bowed slightly to the two women. "How do you do. I recently hired on as a cabinetmaker with the Smetana factory, where I had the great, if brief, privilege of working with Mr. Hafstein," he stammered. "In fact, he was the reason I took the job, so I could work with such a master craftsman. Oh, excuse me, but I don't always remember my manners. My name is Gershom Kindemann. I am very sorry for your loss." He bowed again.

"Thank you for those kind words about my father, Mr. Kindemann. I thought I knew all the cabinetmakers. Have we met?"

"I don't think so, that I would have remembered." The tips of his ears reddened before his face followed suit.

"Is that you, Kindemann?" Josef approached with her uncle. Lala looked up as Josef handed Gershom a black prayer book.

"I've found nine men to say Kaddish for Mr. Hafstein, so we're one short for a minyan. Will you join us?"

"I'd be honored, Mr. Smetana."

"Good man. Rabbi, where would you have us say prayers?"

"Over there." Hershel pointed to the hallway connecting the parlor and kitchen.

"Why don't you gather the others and I'll join you shortly."

Hershel and Kindemann escorted the other men to the hallway. Josef removed his silver cigarette case from his breast pocket. His fingertips stroked the Arte Nouveau engraving before he returned it to his jacket.

As Lala gazed at him her eyes misted, blurring her vision with a cloak of tears. She tried to blink them away, but the more that rolled down her cheeks the more tears sprang up to replace them.

"Is your mother feeling better today, Lala?" Josef

asked quietly.

"She's worn down with grief and exhaustion. It pains me to see her like that."

Naomi nodded in agreement. "It's unbearable to watch someone you love suffer."

He took a shuddering breath. "I know." Lala could hear sorrow rattling his voice.

"Give her some time. She's a strong woman. She'll come around, I'm sure of it." His fingertips patted her shoulder with the barest touch, but it sent a quiver through her and she looked down, fighting the desire to reach out and nestle into his body, feel his arms sweep around her.

"I don't want you to worry about her, about anything. Your father was a trusted colleague and friend to me." He paused. "And you're engaged to my son. As far as I'm concerned, you are family now. So, if either of you need anything, don't hesitate to ask."

"Thank you…Mr. Smetana. That's very kind of you to say." She couldn't bring herself to call him Josef now; it would betray all she had kept hidden within her.

"I must join the men in the hall. If you ladies will excuse me."

As he walked away, Naomi leaned toward Lala. "What a shame his son isn't like him. He would have been perfect for you," she whispered.

Voices of men praying in the hall floated into the room. Lala listened to the words being said, words she'd heard a hundred times before without feeling, without truly connecting to their significance. Familiar words, now shards that bored through flesh and bone into her heart…*how many pieces were left?*

As a child traumatized by the loss of her home and

family, she sought comfort in the arms of her aunt. But Lala knew Naomi couldn't provide what she needed now, something beyond comfort. When the last words of Kaddish had faded away she excused herself and went to the hallway as the men were dispersing.

She saw Josef in conversation with her uncle.

"Excuse me, gentlemen. Mr. Smetana, may I have a word with you in the kitchen?"

Josef turned, his lips parted in surprise as he faced her.

"Please go ahead, Mr. Smetana," urged Hershel. "I hear more visitors arriving. We can talk later." He shook Josef's hand before returning to the parlor.

Lala and Josef stood alone in the hallway. "What do you need?" he asked.

"Not here, in the kitchen."

He followed her into the room, empty except for stacks of washed dishes and flatware beside the sink, ready to be set out for the next set of visitors.

"Please tell me," he said, his eyes looking into hers. She struggled to get the words out.

"I'll do anything." He touched her shoulder.

In a faltering voice, she said, "Hold me."

He looked around. "Lala, I wish nothing more, but—"

"Please, put your arms around me and hold me like you did in Berlin. I need to feel something other than grief, even for one moment," she implored. "I need to feel like I'm still alive."

He wrapped his arms around her and drew her into his body. She took in his warmth, the scent of wood and bergamot emanating from his neck, the softness of his silk shirt against her cheek, the firmness of his body beneath. Her breathing deepened as she lingered in his embrace, soothed in the brief cushion from sorrow it provided.

"Lala?" A voice echoed from the doorway.

She immediately broke away from Josef's embrace to face Romy, standing in the doorway with Naomi. Lala's face turned hot as blood rushed into her cheeks.

Naomi tendered a fragile smile. "How kind of you, Mr. Smetana, to offer comfort to my niece, and your future daughter-in-law."

"Why shouldn't he, Mrs. Zedek?" remarked Romy. "He's like a father to her now."

Horrified at the idea, Lala spat out, "He is not my father, and will never, ever be!" She slammed her hand over her mouth, ashamed of her outburst, but more fearful of what her words might have implied.

"I'm sorry, dear. I only meant…." Romy fell silent, then fled the room.

Naomi merely nodded and said, "Please forgive my niece, Mr. Smetana. Grief can sometimes bring about anger."

"I understand, Mrs. Zedek. And no offense taken, for Lala is absolutely right."

CHAPTER FOURTEEN

When Lala and Josef returned to the parlor, Esther told them that Romy had rushed out of the house moments earlier. Josef excused himself and left as well. Lala settled onto the bench, soon joined by her aunt and her mother, who seemed more alert and less weepy after a nap.

By eight o'clock the last guest had bid the mourners good night. Esther had retired an hour earlier. Paulina looked so exhausted after straightening up the parlor Lala insisted she spend the night, offering to share her bed.

Lala divided the stack of condolence letters between her uncle and herself. She sat across from him in the parlor and skimmed through them. She tried to read one sent by Miriam, the woman she met in Berlin, but she couldn't focus. Shock and grief had smothered her since her father's sudden death, momentarily relieved while in Josef's embrace. Though she worried how Aunt Naomi, and especially Romy, might have interpreted what they saw, she had no regrets. At least she felt able to breathe again.

Her head throbbed from too much crying. She left the letters behind to join her mother and aunt in the kitchen, where they pecked at their food while Hilde cleared the buffet.

"Lala, have something to eat," her mother urged.

Lala's appetite had deserted her, but she poured a ladle of soup into a bowl and forced it down to quell her headache.

Sarah passed her the breadbasket. "Romy came and left in a hurry. Hershel said he smelled alcohol on her breath."

"In the middle of the day? Shameful," Naomi exclaimed as she laid her fork on the table.

"Go ahead, have some more." Sarah tapped Naomi's half-finished plate of food. "Hershel said you haven't eaten all day."

Hilde stood in the doorway. "I'm finished, Mrs. Hafstein. May I go home now?"

Sarah nodded. "It's late. Would you like me to ask the Rabbi to escort you?"

"No need, Missus. My father is waiting for me outside."

"Then take some food with you for your dinners."

"May I? Thank you, Missus." Hilde picked up a half-empty platter of sliced meat. "I'll bring the platter back in the morning. Good night."

After Hilde left, Lala heard her uncle's footsteps climbing the stairway, off to bed.

Naomi pushed her plate away. "It's good. I wish I had the appetite to enjoy it." She dabbed a napkin to her mouth. "I'm going to bed. You both ought to as well."

Lala helped Sarah change into her nightclothes next to the cot outside the kitchen.

"Is tomorrow Thursday?" Sarah asked, her voice as pale

as her face in the dim lamplight.

"Friday, Mother."

"I can't keep track of the days anymore."

Lala pulled back the blanket as Sarah got into bed.

"It doesn't matter," Lala murmured as she tucked her mother in.

"Of course it does," Sarah bristled. "We have bills to pay, food to buy, and no money coming in. We have some savings, but not enough to manage without your father's income. I already told Hilde she should take that factory job. She'll make more money and we can't afford a housekeeper anymore." Her eyes filled with tears.

"This is not the time to worry about these things, Mother."

"Then when? *Shiva* will be over in a few days but not the war. Life must go on. Why do you think all those people from the factory showed up here, to pay their respects to your father?"

"Why else?"

"To eat. They knew the Smetanas would be providing food. How would we have been able to feed them?"

Sarah pushed the covers away and sat up. The pallor had left her face. "I don't have the luxury of feeling sorry for myself anymore, and your father wouldn't stand for it if I let everything he worked so hard for slip away. What can we sell? Nobody's buying new furniture now, why would they want our old things?"

"We can sell this house. You can't bear to go upstairs anymore, so—"

"We can't." Her mother turned pale again.

"Why not? It's yours now."

"It never was. It belongs to the factory. Josef provided

the house as part of the hiring agreement when your father accepted the position fifteen years ago. It's not ours to sell." Sarah gasped. "It may not be ours anymore, either. Oh, Lala," she began to sob and fell into Lala's outstretched arms.

Lala knew Josef would never make them leave, but to convince her mother of that she would either have to make up a lie, or tell the truth. She wasn't prepared to do either. "We will not lose our home. Even if we did, we could live in the apartment above Paulina's shop."

Her mother pulled away. "Then where would she live?"

"She still has her house, and when she opens her shop in Prague, she would move there."

Sarah wiped away her last tears. "I could help her. She's always asked me to do embroidery for her dresses—no, there's barely enough work for her now. I could take in some sewing work from the—"

"You won't do anything of the sort." Lala sat on the edge of the cot. "I've made up my mind. I'm going to ask Josef for a job."

"A job? How can you work and go to the Academy?"

"We can't afford the Academy anymore. I'm going to work instead. We need the money, so please, Mother, no arguing. I have to do this. Let me do this."

Sarah reached out to stroke Lala's cheek. "When did you get to be such a wise and mature woman? Sometimes it seems like yesterday you were still a little girl."

"I had to grow up very quickly. You're the only reason I got to be a little girl for a while. Now go to sleep, so I can as well."

"You're right." She patted Lala's hand. "I should listen to you more often."

"Paulina's asleep in my bed by now. Would you like me

to stay with you tonight?"

"No, this little bed won't be comfortable for you. Sleep in your bed, but don't go yet," Sarah pleaded.

Lala pulled back the covers and slipped into the bed. Her mother turned and pressed her back into Lala's. Lala lay there until she heard soft snoring, then eased herself out without waking her mother. She went upstairs to her room. Esther's bed wasn't in there. Lala prepared for bed as quietly as she could so as not to disturb Paulina.

"It's late. Where have you been?" Paulina rolled over to face Lala.

"With my mother." Lala lit the lamp by her bedside table. "I'm sorry if I woke you."

"You didn't. I couldn't sleep."

"Where's my cousin?"

"She thought the room would be too crowded with the three of us, so her father helped us move the bed into your parents', I mean, your mother's room." Paulina sat up against the headboard. "You don't look tired, either. Do you want to talk?" She sidled over to the far side of the bed to make room for Lala.

Lala peeled back the covers on her side of the bed. "Yes, but I'm not sure how to say it."

"My dear, dear Lala. I understand what you're feeling. I'm grieving for your father, too."

"I know." She paused. "We've grown very close," she said as she got into bed.

Paulina reached out to Lala and took her hand. "You're my best friend, my business associate…why, you're more like family to me than anyone else. I love Ivo, but I would never abandon you for anyone."

Paulina's reassuring words did not inspire Lala to

frankness.

"Go to sleep, my friend," Paulina urged. "You need your rest, especially now."

"As do you." Lala turned on her side and propped herself up on her arm. "Paulina, are you expecting?"

Paulina crossed her arms. "Expecting what?"

"Please don't be coy. You know what I'm asking."

Paulina let out a long sigh. "How did you know?"

"I sensed something different about you a few weeks ago, but I was too naïve to figure out what it was. My aunt said you have all the signs."

"I wasn't sure until last week, but now I'm certain about my...condition."

"Does Ivo know?"

Paulina shook her head. "I haven't told him. I'm not sure if I should."

"You must. He deserves to know he's going to be a father."

"Thank you for saying so. I'm sure there are some in town who would wonder about that, given my past."

"Nonsense. Anyone who speaks ill of you will have to deal with me."

Their friendship began in school when Lala overheard several classmates harassing Paulina and defended her, unaware that Paulina was more than capable of defending herself.

"You are a true friend, Lala."

"I hope you still believe that after hearing what I must tell you." Her voice cracked. "I won't be able to attend art classes now. We can't afford it anymore, which means—"

"You won't be able to help me run my shop in Prague."

"I will have to find a job closer to home, to take care of

my mother. I'm so sorry."

"No need. There will be no shop in Prague and probably not one here, either. Mrs. Smetana has cut me off. I can't survive right now without her financial backing and she's not willing to give it to me. She won't even meet with me."

"I can talk to her."

"No, it's best you don't. She's too attached to you right now. It will only make her angrier when she learns you're not going to marry her son. It's better I stay close to home, with the baby coming…oh, Lala. For the first time in my life, I'm frightened, for Ivo, for our child. For the future. I don't know how we can survive."

"Don't worry, my friend," Lala said with a firmness that surprised her. "I have a plan."

"What will you do?"

"It will have to wait until shloshim, the thirty days of mourning, is over," she explained. "But then things will change." She kissed Paulina on the forehead. "Now go to sleep. I'm going outside for some air, but I'll be back soon, I promise."

Lala tiptoed down the stairs, opened the front door as quietly as possible, and stepped outside. Standing on the front step, looking for the moon, she could barely make it out. A sliver, a broken fingernail, a frown turned on its side. The night had cooled and she inhaled until her lungs felt like they would burst. Her breathing had become shallow in grief.

In a few days shiva would end. She would have to put her grief aside and go on.

Her eyes scanned the property around the house. She could still remember the first time she saw it, the day she and her parents arrived by train in Prague. The local railway station hadn't been built yet, so the three of them transferred to a coach and rode north toward the countryside, to begin their lives together...

The sun blazed across a cloudless sky when the coach stopped in a small town, where a smaller carriage with uniformed driver awaited them. It felt good to stretch her legs while their trunks were being loaded into the back of the carriage. Father helped Mother up and Lala climbed in next to her. Her father sat opposite them, his back to the driver, as they rode off.

Soon the carriage turned and began to climb past a wooded area. Lala peered out at a copse of trees ahead, through which she could barely make out some dots of color. As they passed under the shade of the leafy canopy, the temperature dropped several degrees. A gust of wind rode alongside their carriage, lifting spirals of dirt from the road and rustling the leaves until it sounded like applause. The wind died as they entered the clearing, the road smoothed out and the ground cover changed from wild growth to a soft green carpet of young grass sprinkled with wildflowers. Birds sailed across the sky, their voices filling the air with song. God's music—it was back and it filled her heart with a joy she had forgotten....

It had begun with the three of them. Now her father was gone.

For the first time Lala sensed the burden placed on him, the responsibility of providing for their little family ...having a roof over their heads and food on the table, clothes on their backs and much more. With his death, that burden would pass to her. She had to take responsibility for her new family of three, soon to be four, likely for the duration of the war. Lala took another deep breath and slowly let it out.

She was ready.

CHAPTER FIFTEEN

"I'm here to see Mr. Smetana." Lala stood before the desk of Josef's personal secretary Berthe, as stern-looking a woman as Lala had ever seen. She remembered hearing tales about her from Armin for many years. They seemed to bear out his description of a formidable white-haired creature with the face of a cat and the body of a bear.

"Have you an appointment, Miss?" Berthe's intense scrutiny rivaled The Eye, Sarah's cringe-inducing glare.

"Hafstein. Lala Hafstein, and no, I don't, but would you please tell him I'm here?"

Berthe's withering gaze softened at the mention of Lala's surname. "Please excuse me while I see if Mr. Smetana is available. Would you care to wait in our reception area?" She stood and offered Lala a slight nod before escorting her back to the public entrance down the hall.

Lala took a seat in the front room, furnished with factory pieces, their design influenced by the Cubist movement currently in vogue among contemporary architects. She admired the interpretation, the shared sensibility of strong lines and sharp angles, which resulted in furniture that was as practical as it was comfortable.

As she waited she observed the office workers in the adjacent clerical room. It consisted of a double-sided desk and three work tables lined up like soldiers, surrounded by a bank of dark wood cabinets. One mature-looking woman typed forms and stacked them in a shallow box next to her desk. Her matronly desk mate took each form and copied figures from them into a ledger. Then a pretty woman around Lala's age, dressed as dowdy as her coworkers, filed the forms in a wooden cabinet. Each woman repeated her task over and over. Lala visualized herself sitting in art class. A shake of her head dispelled the wishful thought from her mind, though she allowed herself a moment to mourn the dream that died with her father.

When she heard the twelve o'clock whistle, the three women packed away their work and with a courteous nod to her, filed out of their workroom.

Berthe returned from Josef's office. "He will see you now, Miss Hafstein."

"Thank you, Berthe." Lala offered her a smile that was not returned. She stood and with head held high, followed Berthe.

Lala tried not to overreact when she entered the room, twice the size of Josef's home office. She'd never been here, and although she expected it would be superbly furnished, its luxurious appointments caught her by surprise. Wood paneling covered the walls and fine Persian carpets accented the parquet floors. A large picture window behind his desk faced a landscaped courtyard accented with a sculpture of "Venus." Along the left wall, two matching cabinets revealed objets d'art, including a bronze dancer by Degas. To the right was an odd grouping of furniture in no particular arrangement, which she assumed were samples to show prospective buyers.

"What an unexpected surprise, Lala. Please, sit here." Josef held out one of the brocade-upholstered side chairs facing his massive desk. She almost couldn't see him over the paperwork, wood samples and fabric swatches spread across his desk as he sat behind it.

"Thank you, Berthe. That will be all."

Berthe paused, as though unsure of what he meant, but she gave a brief nod and left the room with what Lala interpreted as an air of displeasure.

When the door closed, Josef left his seat and moved to the chair at Lala's side. "What brings you here?"

"I need to speak to you about an important matter." She got up and paced away from him, for although grief had wrung her dry, her ardor for Josef remained. She braced herself to look at him without feeling overcome with yearning as she had days ago in her kitchen. Indulging in life's pleasures had become a luxury she could no longer afford.

"Lala, I would do anything for you." Josef stood and approached behind her, close enough that she could feel his breath on her neck, which sent shivers down her back. She hugged herself and turned to face him.

"Anything," he repeated, staring into her eyes as his hands moved to her shoulders.

She worried his touch would take her breath away. It nearly did. But no matter how she felt about him, he was the head of a household, with responsibilities to his family and staff as well as to his reputation.

And now, so was she.

She looked him in the eye. "First, I want to know what will happen to my home. Will you allow us to continue to live there?"

He seemed taken aback by her suggestion. "It is your home. I would never consider it anything else."

"Thank you," she said and released her breath, more audibly than she intended. "That settles our housing concerns."

"If you no longer want to live there, I'll arrange to have the deed signed over to you so you may sell it and move wherever you wish."

"No, we don't want to leave. It's just...with my father gone, and my tuition money lost...I...."

Suddenly the reality of what she needed to say hit her like a slap, taking her voice, and breath, away. Josef wrapped his arms around her, but she could not yield to him now and fearing she would, slid out of his embrace.

"Tell me," he urged.

"I need a job, Josef. I came here to ask you for a position at the factory. You can tell everyone you want your son's fiancée to learn the family business. And with so many of the men gone you probably need help, so hiring a woman won't seem odd. Romy suggested the upholstery department, or perhaps furniture arrangements for the catalog, but I'll do anything as long as I can earn enough money to support my family."

"Lala, you don't have to do that. I'll take care of you and your mother, for as long as it takes."

"Under what guise, the family of your late friend and employee? You wouldn't do that for any of the other executives' families. And how long can we hide behind the 'Armin's fiancée' excuse? The war won't last forever and the truth will have to come out. I can't let my mother—"

A knock at the door startled them both. "Mr. Smetana?"

Berthe's voice pierced through the door. "Your lunch is ready. I've taken the liberty of ordering a meal for Miss Hafstein."

"Thank you, Berthe. I'll set up in here. Have the kitchen bring it in." To Lala he said, "Is trout to your liking?"

"It's my favorite."

Josef selected two ornately carved side chairs from the odd grouping of furniture and set them near the display cabinets on the other side of the room. He opened one of the middle cabinets and pulled out an extension. Parallel with his desk, it was tall enough to serve as a dining table. He unfurled two legs that reached the floor, then held a chair for Lala as she sat down.

"Are you comfortable?" he asked.

"Yes, this chair is quite comfortable."

"I'm glad to hear that. This is one of our new designs. I've asked some of the secretaries to test it, but none of them are as willowy as you."

Lala noticed that Josef kept his gaze away from her when he said that.

A kitchen worker wheeled in a cart and set up their meals on the table: fried trout and potatoes, without dessert. Josef, like Lala, didn't indulge in sweets.

"What if I spill something?" she asked. "I wouldn't want to damage this new merchandise."

Josef offered a sardonic half-smile as the kitchen worker laid an ivory napkin across his lap. "It doesn't matter, the order has been cancelled. Even if it hadn't been, we couldn't ship the furniture. The War Ministry has requisitioned our trucks for troop and supplies transport."

"I didn't know that."

"You've had your own concerns."

Josef waited until the kitchen worker left before admitting, "You have presented me with a challenge. I will need some time to find a suitable position for you."

"Honestly, I'm not expecting anything choice. I really don't care what I do as long as I can earn a reasonable salary and start straight away."

"You assume there are positions available. Although you're right about the men leaving, many of their positions have disappeared because there's no business right now. If the war doesn't end soon, we won't be able to stay open for more than six months. Unless...." He fell silent, but his eyes darkened.

"Unless the factory is converted to wartime production." She caught him gazing at her, and looked down.

"So you're aware of that."

"I read about that probability in the Berlin newspapers. It stands to reason it would happen in other nations at war."

"It is likely here as well, though our fractured empire isn't as organized as our German counterparts," he said as he filleted his trout. "There, an industrialist has been working with the Prussian Ministry of War to organize control over critical raw materials and production."

"You're speaking of Walter Rathenau, who heads up the company that provides electricity to Germany."

His eyebrows rose so high they creased his forehead. "Yes, the AEG. Your depth of knowledge never fails to surprise me. I ought to stop saying that, you might consider it rude."

"Would you prefer if the government transformed the factory to wartime production?"

"I'd rather keep the factory open and operating. It would certainly provide much needed employment, but it would also be dispiriting to see munitions rolling off the assembly line. Unfortunately, furniture is of little use during a war."

Josef tossed his napkin aside, avoiding the pool of butter sauce on his plate. Lala suddenly became overwhelmed with grief; her father would have sopped up every bit of sauce with bread. She kept her head down and used her talent for pushing bad memories away to hold back her sorrow. All she could manage was to avoid tears, but fortunately, if Josef noticed, he said nothing about it.

"Of course, the War Department needs other products besides munitions, but our metal work is limited," he said. We're set up to manufacture wood furniture, so what could we make that would be considered necessary during a war?"

The answer came to Lala immediately, although she would not say it aloud.

Coffins.

CHAPTER SIXTEEN

After lunch, Josef suggested they tour the factory. Lala wasn't sure why; he still hadn't mentioned a position for her. Perhaps he wanted her to find something on her own, though as likely he wished to discourage her from working at the plant. She'd already considered that possibility and wasn't about to let it happen.

Josef escorted her out of his office through a back door that led to a narrow hallway.

"I had this facility made to my specifications, an elegant façade with a well-built, functional building behind it. Just like my furniture—traditional beauty married to modern technology."

Josef stopped before a framed diagram of the factory floor plan hanging on the wall, illustrating its L-shape with extensions at the upper right and lower left edges. He pointed to the horizontal section along the bottom of the diagram. "The business offices, sales, accounting, and administration are here. Manufacturing is contained within the long corridor to the left, and the extension above is for shipping and receiving. Let's start there."

When they reached the end of the corridor, Josef held the door for her as she entered a cavernous area. One side contained crates in all sizes and stacks of lumber. On the opposite side, several dozen finished pieces of furniture stood in neat rows. Above them hung a sign that read "Cancelled Orders."

"So, this is where it all begins, and ends," she noted.

"Not quite." Josef guided her through a lane of crates. "It actually begins in your father's…" he lowered his head, "the custom furniture department."

The buzz of workers quieted as they acknowledged the presence of the factory owner. Lala mentioned that the men were older than she would have expected.

"Most were foremen before the war," Josef said. "Now they're all that's left to do the labor."

Josef gestured to an interior wall with large sliding doors. One of the workers slid open the doors for them. She and Josef entered another vast room filled with huge machines and littered with wood debris. The noise was almost deafening. Josef led her through the back of the room, pointing out the different machines for cutting wood, shaping it, and finally, sanding the surfaces. When she covered her ears, he motioned her to the next room.

"This is where we apply color to the wood."

Huge vats streaked with brown, ochre and tan filled the room with a harsh odor. Unfinished pieces waited near the vats, while on the other side, stained furniture dried in rows.

"Once the pieces dry, they're finished with a lacquer. I won't take you in there because the smell is dreadful. After that, any hinged pieces get attached."

"Which is anything that moves, such as a door on a cabinet or a drop leaf on a table."

"That's right. After the final assembly, everything is polished and inspected. If it passes, it's ready to ship."

"Where is the gilt work applied?"

"That's only on custom orders. Let me show you where the upholstery work is done."

The room where Paulina had worked before she launched her business was large and utilitarian. Lala counted rolls of fabric, organized by color and pattern, stacked on deep shelves that sloped down in front. She saw the tubes of cloth would slide out much easier that way. Clever. Still, she could not imagine how someone as creative as Paulina could have chosen to work in this department. Then she remembered her own purpose for being here.

"The next stop on our tour would be the custom furniture department. I'll understand if you would rather not go there."

Where her father had worked before his promotion. "No, I'd like to see it again."

"It's a short walk down this hall and around the next corridor."

Lala had never gotten a complete tour of the factory, and it had been over a decade since she'd visited her father at work. She admired Josef's building design. Each department connected to its logical partners. Employees had spacious, well-lit work areas. Even the corridors were designed in a pleasant but functional way, with sand colored walls that reflected light and added warmth.

They walked in silence but not quietly; their heels reverberated against the stone floors.

"Josef, have you ever considered carpeting the hallways?"

"Because of the noise? No, I planned it deliberately. How else will the employees know when their boss is about to make a surprise visit?"

She laughed, which made him smile. Josef's sense of humor could always make her laugh. She loved that about him.... She forced herself to table the thought and focus on her task.

"We're almost there. Does it look at all familiar to you yet?"

They turned right to the second corridor, wider and with more refinement. She recognized one of her father's greatest pieces, a drop leaf desk with an inlay top, which matched the chest he'd given Aunt Naomi as a wedding gift. Above it hung a painting she'd first seen at the art premiere in Berlin.

"What a fine tribute to my father. And paired with Armin's newest painting." She felt close to tears.

He passed his handkerchief to her. "Your father deserved it." He positioned himself to her right at the door.

"Here's what I suggest. I'll take you in, show you around, and answer any questions you have. If at any time you wish to leave," he extended his left arm toward her, "link your arm in mine and I'll escort you out immediately."

She caught her breath as she entered the custom furniture workroom. The only thing missing was her father. Two young workmen wore those customary aprons as they shaved and sanded strips of wood. No one sat at the desk that had been her father's for fifteen years.

"The department is much smaller now that we've introduced the machine-made lines, but to my mind, better," Josef explained as he turned to face her.

A familiar, if preoccupied, man limped into the room with a stack of blueprints under his arm. Gershom Kindemann, whom she'd met when he'd paid a shiva call to her home, blindly walked past Josef and Lala to speak with one of the workers, until the workers pointed out the two visitors to him. Kindemann straightened up, but his sheepish look gave him away.

"Mr. Smetana, sir, I didn't see you." He bowed slightly to Lala and smiled. "Miss Hafstein."

"Mr. Kindemann."

His eyes lingered on her a moment longer before he addressed his boss in full flush. "Sir, despite the problems with the last shipment of mahogany, we're on schedule."

"As much as a half-day ahead, I'm told."

"Yes, sir. The men have been working very hard. They've made all the difference, in great part to honor the memory of your father, Miss Hafstein."

"Have you had a chance to review the product reduction plans?" Josef asked.

"I have, but there's one design I'd like you to see, something I thought of after reading the newspaper. I have it somewhere in my desk."

He went to what had been Lala's father's desk, ripped through one of the drawers and pulled out a handful of sketches. Lala's stomach turned. She slipped her arm around Josef's.

"This is not the time, Kindemann. Send them to my office—I will let Berthe know I am expecting them. Shall we continue to our next stop, Lala?" He escorted her from the room.

She had no right to be upset; it was Mr. Kindemann's desk now, but despite her father's promotion she would always remember him as a master carpenter. The man who made that beautiful inlaid desk she had called "patchwork" as a little girl. How he'd come home with sawdust all over him, or the way she would find the occasional wood shaving stuck to his clothing, something she noticed the first time she'd met him. Seeing her father's work tossed around like that upset her to the verge of tears, but she fought the urge to cry. The last thing she needed was to have Josef try to comfort her.

CHAPTER SEVENTEEN

Grief engulfed her as Josef led her back to the hallway. They walked in silence until they approached a turn, then she suddenly felt his hand along her back. Firm yet gentle, meant to direct her toward the left corridor, Lala gasped at his touch and lost her battle for composure.

Josef's arms encircled her as she buried her face into his chest, her body heaving and shaking with grief. He said nothing as she cried, for which she was grateful, otherwise she could not have prevented herself from planting her mouth on his to silence him. The memory of him kissing her in Berlin played in her mind, the way it turned sadness and fear into something wonderful, something life-affirming. There was nothing she wanted more than to linger in the memory. Except to recreate it. And in that moment of despair, she did.

Her head swirled with pleasure as their lips met, their bodies pressed together. Her hands traveled down from his neck to his chest, feeling the firmness of his body underneath his clothing, slowly moving down to his flat stomach. He responded by lowering one hand, tracing his fingers down the center of her spine, drawing spirals over the small of her back. Desire rose within her at his touch, the sensation intensified by the heady aroma of bergamot and wood that radiated from his body. Then with both hands he explored her back, from her waist to her shoulders, and then slid down to caress her bottom, pulling her into him. A wave of pleasure made her knees buckle, but Josef caught her. Lifting her into his arms, he carried her down the hallway to a room across from the back exit of his office and managed to turn the knob before shoving the door open with his shoulder.

The cozy space inside looked like a sitting room. Josef set her down on the sofa, resting her head against a small pillow, and sat beside her, half-smiling. His eyes met hers. She shuddered as his fingertips danced along the contours of her face, down her neck and arms, gently at first, then with a firmer touch. Lala thought she would faint from pleasure. Then he bent down and kissed her, beginning with her cheeks. Her breathing quickened as he ran his tongue around the curves of her ears and nibbled on the lobes before moving down to her neck, her collarbone. A fever rose in her as her heart pounded faster and faster. She closed her eyes and reveled in each new sensation as his hands and mouth widened their exploration of her body, finding private locales and crevices that brought on shivers of ecstasy.

I love him, more than I ever could have imagined. But something familiar about those words pricked at her.

Paulina had said the same thing in Berlin before she gave herself to Ivo. Though she said at the time she had no regrets, Lala suspected her friend might have one now, a little one, soon to grow bigger.

She bolted up and moved Josef's hand away from beneath

her skirt. "Please forgive me, but we can't do this. I'm truly sorry, but as much as I'm tempted, it's too risky, for both of us."

He looked startled at first, but nodded with sensitivity and, she assumed, intense regret. He moved to the adjacent chair as she attempted to straighten her clothing and smooth her hair.

"There is a washroom to your left," he told her.

"Thank you. I won't be a minute."

She went inside to splash water on her cheeks. As she stood before the mirror, she beheld her face, flushed with passion. She yearned to run back to him, to let him make love to her. But she'd made a promise to support and protect her family, and she would not break that promise for anyone.

Not even herself.

CHAPTER EIGHTEEN

Engulfed by shame for initiating their tryst and letting it go on too long, Lala said nothing as the two returned to Josef's office. Worse, this was supposed to be an enquiry about work.

Josef offered her one of the brocade chairs fronting his desk and sat next to her.

"Fulfilling your request has become more complicated. I told you I would do anything for you, and I meant it. But after what happened earlier, I can't see putting either of us through that temptation unnecessarily."

"I understand. I behaved outrageously. What sort of position could I expect now?"

It took a moment to realize what she'd said, but when she saw Josef struggling to refrain from grinning, she blushed.

"I'll think of some other way." She got up, but he took her hand and urged her to stay.

"I'm not saying no. I need some time to think of something suitable, for both of us. What were your earlier suggestions?"

"They were Romy's. She thought I could arrange

furniture for the catalog."

"There won't be enough business to warrant producing and shipping a catalog until the war ends. What else?"

"Selecting upholstery fabrics?"

"We're not buying any more fabrics now, but there may be other work, like inventorying the stock on hand. I'll talk to Anezska about it."

"Be sure to tell Romy. She'll be very pleased. She's wanted me to work here, learn the business so I could help Armin run it someday."

He pondered that for a moment. "Now that is a spectacular idea. I could arrange for you to be trained in all areas of factory production and then you can help me run the business. You have a superb understanding of design and color. You're organized and intelligent enough to learn the technical aspects. I can certainly justify that with the executives, as well as offer a more generous salary for you."

"It's a marvelous offer. I'm grateful, but are you sure? After all, I'm not going to marry Armin."

"I know. But maybe someday, you and I..." he became wistful. "You and I can find a way to be together. Until then, we can be partners in business. Would that be agreeable?"

She wanted to say yes, but something stopped her. "May I think about it overnight?"

"Take as much time as you need."

She got up and Josef ushered her to the door. Before he opened it, she stopped him. "Can we, Josef? Can we work closely together as business partners?

"Lala, I'm not a beast, and you plainly demonstrated you could, earlier in my private quarters."

Remembering the shameful incident caused her to blush again. "I am truly sorry, Josef. I wasn't trying to be coy, but if we had continued, the consequences could have been devastating for both of us, nine months later."

"You thought the only way to...." He chuckled as he opened the door for her. "My sweet, innocent Lala, you have a lot to learn."

CHAPTER NINETEEN

Rather than go directly home, Lala decided to stop at Paulina's shop in town. Paulina had fortuitously arranged for the store and apartment upstairs to be leased out to one of the factory employees. The steady if modest income would help Paulina provide for her baby and reimburse Romy for the business's seed money. Romy's insistence on payback vexed Lala. There were no guarantees made and Paulina's business would have fared better if it hadn't been for the war.

Lala found the back door open so she entered the narrow hallway and climbed the steps to the apartment. Upstairs she found Paulina packing up crates and boxes of ribbons, buttons, rainbow spools of thread, and other dressmaking materials. She looked avant-garde dressed in flowing trousers and a man's shirt, front tails loosely tied around her waist.

Paulina bent down to lift a box, but Lala took it from her. "Where do you want this?"

"Over there with the rest of the notions." Paulina pointed to the left corner of the room, where six crates were stacked beside the window. She went to pick up another box, but Lala got to it first.

"Lala, I'm not an invalid."

"I know, but I worry about you doing too much."

Paulina took Lala's arm and gave it a gentle squeeze. "I promise if I need help, I'll ask for it." She proceeded to gather remnants of fabric from different piles throughout the room and organize them into a crate. "What did you do today?"

"I went to see Mr. Smetana about a job."

"Really, like that? You look a bit disheveled. Why, your dress is all wrinkled."

Suddenly self-conscious, Lala adjusted her bodice and brushed her hand over her skirt. She hadn't been able to see more than her face when she freshened up after her exploits on Josef's sofa.

Paulina reached out to stroke her cheek. "I'm sorry, my friend. I shouldn't have said that. You're still in mourning. When my mother died, I couldn't care less about how I looked for quite a while."

Lala knew it wasn't true, but said nothing. She kept drifting back to the factory, to Josef.

"Lala, is there something else going on? You have this strange look I've never seen before on you."

For a split second, she was in the hallway again, running her hands over Josef's body. "Jo…job. Mr. Smetana offered me a job."

"Good, I thought he might. Anything interesting?"

"He wants me to help him run the factory."

Paulina leaned back. "Oh my. It's good to be the heiress apparent. Was this Romy's idea, or his?"

Lala's earlier tryst with Josef played in her thoughts, altering time and place until she could feel her back pressing into the sofa cushions, Josef's mouth on her throat, his hands gently stroking her….

"Lala, what's going on? Why are you moaning?"

Lala flinched when she realized Paulina was standing right in front of her.

"Oh! I'm…that is, it's been a strange day. Very strange."

A sardonic smile crept upon Paulina's face. "You're not telling me the truth, are you?"

"I am, it was a strange day."

Paulina folded her arms over her chest. "Lala, I have something to tell you. I'm in love with Ivo Chytry and sometime in late April I will have his baby. Now it's your turn." She grabbed Lala's skirt and shook it. "How did your skirt get so wrinkled?"

Lala thought she could maintain a stoic face, but knew immediately she'd failed when Paulina's eyes widened and her hands clamped around her cheeks.

"Lala! What did you do? And more importantly, with whom?"

Lala could no longer contain her secret. She leaned in and whispered, "Josef."

"Josef? From the dye unit? He's such a…that is, I didn't know you liked him."

"Not him. Josef…from the head office."

She looked puzzled. "Josef…Smetana?" As it registered, Paulina's eyes narrowed and her expression turned fierce. "Did he make unwanted advances toward you?"

Lala erupted into giggles. "No, I did the advancing. And there was nothing unwanted about it."

Lala was afraid her friend would faint from shock, so she urged her sit on the sofa and proceeded to tell Paulina everything, from that passionate kiss in Berlin to her dalliance with him earlier, alluding to what occurred without going into detail.

"He was quite the gentleman about it. Of course, I apologized profusely to him, but I couldn't risk it."

"By 'it' I presume you mean 'this.'" Paulina patted her belly, and Lala nodded. "I never suspected…oh my friend, you certainly have become a master at keeping secrets."

"I couldn't tell anyone, Paulina, not even you. Only Armin knows. He saw us kissing in Berlin. Before he left, he told me that his father was in love with me and he believed I loved Josef. That was why he asked me to wait for him, to keep me connected to his family."

"Now I feel badly for all the awful things I said about him. He was trying to help you, not trap you." Paulina picked up a jumble of lace trim from the floor.

"At times he knows me better than I know myself, like you. I wasn't even aware of my true feelings for Josef until recently."

Paulina twirled the lace into a neat ball. "Since your father's death?"

"I know what you're thinking, this stems from grief. I'm replacing my father with another father figure. But while I'll admit these interludes have eased my sorrow, it's more than that. Much more."

"I'm not saying you're wrong. After all, I met Ivo shortly after my mother died, but much of my grieving had ended by then. It's been barely a month since you lost your dear father, so how can you be sure of anything your emotions tell you?"

Lala anticipated her question. "Because ever since I was a little girl, I have had visions. Most of them provided me with guidance, but shortly after Armin and I became engaged, I had a vision of me in the future, with a husband I knew wasn't Armin, and a baby. When Josef held me in Berlin, I knew what I saw was a prophecy of the two of us. I'm destined to be with him."

"But Lala, he's married. Does he intend to leave his wife for you?"

"It doesn't matter. I would never allow that to happen."

"Then how can you be together, unless you're willing to forego marriage?"

"I know it doesn't make sense, but somehow I know we will be together. Maybe as business partners, maybe as husband and wife. I can't explain it, but I know."

"Sounds like you've already made up your mind about the position he's offered you."

"No, that's what I've yet to decide. If I take the position, I'll have to work closely with him at some point. I don't know if I can hold my feelings in reserve when I'm near him."

"Do you want to, Lala?"

She exhaled loudly. "No, but I have to. I never pictured myself as a paramour. No matter how we feel about each other, he is married. I'd never do anything to hurt him, or Romy."

Paulina raised her hands. "Well then, you have your answer."

CHAPTER TWENTY

The first thing Lala did when she returned home was to slink upstairs to her room and change into another dress. After pinning her hair into place, she went downstairs to find her mother, who was washing the kitchen floor on her hands and knees.

"It's the only way to do it right," her mother said as she struggled to stand. "I thought I'd hate having to do housework again, but at least it keeps me occupied, so I don't have to think too much...." She wiped a tear from her eye and cleared her throat. "Would you mind having leftover roast again tonight?"

"Better than letting it go to waste."

"That's my girl. Let's sit in the parlor while the floor dries."

They left the kitchen, stepping past the foot of the cot that had been forced into the hallway. It reminded Lala of her time with the Zedeks, the little bed Naomi had set up in the storage room when she intended to train Lala for service. Lala hated seeing that shoddy thing, but Sarah still couldn't bring herself to enter the bedroom she shared with Jakob since his death. Lala wished she could think of a way to get her mother back into her bedroom.

As they settled into the parlor her mother asked, "How did your meeting with Josef go?"

"He offered me a job, a very good position, in fact. I should be able to earn enough money to keep us comfortable."

"That's wonderful news. Are you excited?"

"Um, pleased would be more accurate."

Her mother's brow furrowed. "What would you be doing?"

"He wants to train me to help him run the factory." Sarah digested the news without saying anything.

"I would learn about the different departments and eventually—"

"Eventually run the factory, you and Armin, side by side. I heard this idea from Romy months ago. That's what she foresaw would happen once you two married and Josef retired." Sarah tapped her foot on the floor, her habit when she got frustrated. "Do you want to do this?"

"Honestly, mother, I'm not sure. But the money—"

"Forget the money. This is not what you want to do, so you'll turn down the offer. Your father and I told you we won't allow you to sacrifice your life to protect their son, and I certainly won't allow you to do it for a paycheck. You have your own plans for the future."

"Then how will we manage?"

Sarah leaned forward to pat Lala's knee. "I had an idea today. The War Ministry has been looking for residences for their staff. We can rent out the bedroom upstairs. Only to women, of course, I won't have you sleeping next to a room full of men."

"Then where will you sleep?"

"Down here."

Her mother wasn't ready to face the bedroom issue and Lala didn't want to force it without a better solution. "Do you really want strangers in the house? And remember, they took our automobile with the promise of compensation, and we haven't received one koruna for it yet."

"We have to do something. I heard talk at the market today. They think rationing will begin soon. It's a good thing your father and I stocked up on food and supplies as much as we did. They'll last longer now that...." Her voice grew thin. "Don't worry. Your father is watching over us. I can feel it. He'll make sure we get through this."

She hoped her mother was right, for she couldn't see a way out of this right now unless she accepted Josef's offer. "Shall we start dinner?"

"The floor should be dry by now," Sarah said as she stood. "I'll warm the roast while you make potatoes."

"I'm not very hungry tonight. Could we just have some cold meat instead?"

"If you wish. I don't have much of an appetite either."

Sarah sliced the roast while Lala set out plates and glasses on the kitchen table. It brought back memories of her early childhood, before her parents adopted her, when her Russian family ate every meal in the kitchen next to the stove. Although the memories had faded over the years, she could still remember nuggets, like her Mama doing her mending every night after dinner, her Papa telling stories about his travels as a peddler. She marveled at how truly happy they were despite having very little, but they had each other.

Lala suddenly longed to hug her mother, which she did, catching Sarah off-guard. But after a moment, Sarah yielded to the embrace and the two women clung to each other as if no one else in the world existed but the two of them.

When they finally ended the hug, Sarah was near tears. "That was nice, dear. I don't think I've been held like that for a long time. Any special reason?"

"Because I love you so much and I'm grateful to have you in my life."

They both began to cry and hug each other again. Soon the tears abated and they sat down to their meal.

"I can't remember the last time we ate dinner in the kitchen," Sarah observed as she laid her napkin across her lap.

"It must have been when Father…" Lala stopped and put her fork down. On the rare occasions when her father had to work late, she and her mother dined informally. Lala thought the convenience of being steps away from the stove prompted the decision, but now she could see it had also been done to mark his absence.

"I'm sorry, Mother. I shouldn't—"

"No, Lala, you should and you must. In his own way, he's still in our lives and shall be forever. We must get used to talking about him again, even though it's painful now. It will take time…." The words garbled in her throat. "A long time, but someday we'll be able to speak of him without crying, or hearing that hitch in our voice. Now finish your dinner and try to enjoy it. Kosher meat is getting harder to find."

They finished eating in near silence. Lala cleared the table while Sarah put the kettle on for tea, then washed as Lala dried. With so little to do, they finished before the kettle boiled. Sarah spooned tea into the pot and added boiling water. With her fingertip she gathered up every leaf and twig that fell from the spoon and replaced it in the tea canister.

"You mentioned earlier that there may be rationing soon.

Any idea what, or how much?" Lala asked as she set out teacups.

"As much as they want." Sarah plunked a sugar cube into her cup. "Besides, rationing means the government will limit how much you're permitted to buy, but if you can't afford the higher prices, what does it matter?"

"The newspapers say the war won't last much longer. Let's hope they're right."

"I've gotten to trust gossip more than any official report."

"Why is that?" asked Lala.

"You can't believe the newspapers. The Ministry of War oversees everything they print." Sarah added another cube of sugar to her cup. "I've become friendly with the Smetanas' cook, Mrs. Havlik. She told me the Ministry staff censors letters between families and the fighting men. Her two sons and her daughter's husband serve in the army and when they write home, their letters have whole sections blacked out. One son married a Slovenian girl and her son-in-law is Croatian, so they mix in their languages with Czech and German to confuse the censors enough that some information gets through. The four women work together to translate the letters, otherwise they wouldn't know the truth."

Lala poured them each a cup through a strainer. "And what is the truth?"

Sarah waved her hand. "That's enough depressing talk for one night. Let's have our tea in the parlor like…" her voice quavered. "Like before."

They carried their cups into the parlor. The last glimmers of twilight flickered through the clouds. Sarah drew the curtains and sat in her favorite slipper chair.

Lala noticed that her mother kept her head facing away from the wing chair where her father always sat, side by side with his beloved wife. She, too, missed him the most in this room, his presence in that very chair.

But it sparked an idea, of moving around the furniture in the parlor to change its appearance. Maybe she could arrange to trade a few pieces with Paulina for furniture in her shop; they wouldn't have the same emotional effect on her mother. She might even—

A frantic pounding at the door disrupted her thoughts. Her concern rose when she saw a look of terror on her mother's face. Lala got up to answer the knock, her mother trailed close behind. Whatever this was, it couldn't be good news.

When she opened the door, she knew she was right, judging by the tear-stained face she met. But Paulina just stood there, trembling and wordless.

CHAPTER TWENTY-ONE

Lala clutched at her heart. "Oh no, please tell me you haven't heard bad news about Ivo."

Paulina shook her head.

Sarah came to the door, clearly distressed by Paulina's grim face. "Come in, dear," she urged. "Sit down, catch your breath and tell us what happened."

Sarah went to the kitchen to fetch a glass of water for Paulina. Lala guided her friend to the sofa and held her hand until Sarah returned.

"Here, drink this," Sarah said. "Or would you rather have something stronger?"

Paulina sputtered, "N…no thank you."

"Now tell us what has you so upset."

"They've taken my shop."

"Who, the Smetanas?"

"No, the War Ministry. They've requisitioned all the shops that sell non-essential goods, with nothing but a piece of paper stating I will be compensated, but I don't know when or how much."

"I'm so sorry, dear," Sarah said quietly. "I know it's not

123

fair, but the government has that right."

Lala crossed her arms. "They gave themselves that right, you mean."

"Let's not argue over politics now. What are you going to do, Paulina?"

"I don't know. I leased the building to a man who works in the factory—oh dear, how will I tell him what happened? He's already paid for the first month and I gave half of that money to Mrs. Smetana. And now I have to remove all my merchandise and the furnishings in the shop before the fifteenth of October."

"That's tomorrow," observed Lala.

"Hardly enough time, but they'll take whatever I leave behind."

"Try to stay calm, dear," urged Sarah. "I know it's difficult under the circumstances."

"Ivo warned me about this in his letters. He was smart enough to know this would happen. It's why before he left, we worked out a code so that he could write to me without the censors catching on."

"How clever. What do you do?" Sarah asked.

"He can't state what's really happening, especially if the war is not going well. So, he begins with a few pages that sound very personal, to trick the censors into thinking it's merely a love letter, but he hides a code word in the beginning. When he calls me darling, the information in the letter is written in a roundabout way, but if he calls me sweetheart, then what he states is the opposite of what he wants to say. Sometimes he underlines a passage. It's his way of saying read between the lines.

"We have other code words, too. Let me show you." From her pocket, she retrieved a letter and opened it. "He begins with 'Dear Sweetheart', but I'll skip the first two pages," she said with a coy shrug. "Here, listen to this:

"As our mighty army fights the great war against our enemies, my soul is eased by thoughts of home, of your delicious medovnik, and wish that you could bake over a thousand for me to share with my brethren soldiers."

Paulina pointed to Ivo's words. "When he writes *'mighty army,'* it means ill-equipped, *'the great war against our enemies,'* means they're ambivalent, but this bit here about the medovnik? Honey cake is our code for anyone who's against this war. I believe he's telling me that more than a thousand troops have gone over to the other side."

"Wouldn't they be shot as deserters?" Sarah asked.

"Not if they surrendered."

She appeared to ponder that. "Then the rumors are true."

"What have you heard, Mother?"

"Mrs. Havlik told me the Smetanas' housemaid Galina's son was severely wounded and sent home. He said some of the troops had met up with family members and surrendered to the Russians, or defected."

"Has Galina's son recovered?" Lala asked.

Sarah shook her head. "He was shot, which was bad enough. But gangrene set in and he lost part of his right leg. And from what she tells me, it's not uncommon."

Paulina began sniffling again.

"Don't listen to me, I'm passing along gossip." Sarah patted Paulina's hand in sympathy. "Try not to fret, dear. You shouldn't be alone now," she cautioned. "Stay here tonight."

An idea began to percolate in Lala's mind. "Yes, that is a very good idea, Mother. Since you won't sleep in your bedroom anymore, would it be all right if Paulina and I stay there? Then you could sleep in my room instead of the cot.

You'd be more comfortable, don't you think?"

Her mother agreed.

"Then off to bed, you two. I have work I need to do and I don't want to disturb you. Mother, could you show Paulina to the bedroom?"

The women went upstairs, but her mother returned shortly. "Paulina's exhausted, she'll soon be asleep."

As Lala surveyed the room, her mother followed her about. "What do you have to do that's so important you can't come to bed?"

Lala put her arm around her mother's shoulder. "I think I may have a way to solve our problem, and Paulina's."

"What are you planning to do, Lala?"

"'Lala' isn't going to do anything. This is a job for 'the Peddler's daughter. '"

Lala spent the first few hours taking measurements, making notes, and sketching. Then she began moving furniture around, like she did as a little girl in her Aunt Naomi's sitting room. A few pieces went into the hallway to be exchanged with Paulina's furniture. She calculated where to set up work areas for Paulina and herself, and then jotted down notes of what would be needed to finish the décor. After the furniture was set, she worked on the decorative pieces, switching out artwork and display items for others. Combining the pieces in the hallway with what she recalled in Paulina's home and shop, she sat at the kitchen table and redesigned the two upstairs bedrooms, sketching in different furniture. Then she drew a floor plan for the Sipek house, revamped as an inn to comfortably accommodate as many guests as possible.

She surveyed the parlor, the first step in converting her house into something different, something reborn for a new purpose. A new family. She, her mother and Paulina considered themselves family now. And now family they would be. Living together, caring for each other. Working together, pooling their resources to ensure their survival in very unsure times.

Lala reviewed her sketches. She recalled the sofa and two salon chairs she and Paulina salvaged from the dress shop. After Paulina reupholstered the tattered chair seats and Lala's father repaired the split in the sofa frame, the pieces looked as good as new. She added them to her sketch of the parlor, quite pleased with how well they fit the room. The red and white striped curtains she'd used in the shop's dressing rooms would look lovely in a bedroom window. Some of the extra fabric Paulina had could be used to recover older pieces, make them look fresh.

The first rays of dawn poked through the kitchen window when she finished her sketches of Paulina's house as well as hers. Pleased with her work, she went into the parlor. The moment she laid down on the couch she drifted off to sleep, satisfied that she would not only transform their homes, but their lives.

CHAPTER TWENTY-TWO

Lala awoke an hour later feeling chilled. She headed for the kitchen and lit the stove, relishing the warmth as it heated, then prepared breakfast for her mother and Paulina.

As she poured herself a steaming cup of coffee, she heard footsteps coming downstairs followed by muffled words. Curiosity registered on their faces as they entered the kitchen, but Lala asked them to wait until after breakfast for an explanation.

Afterward, Lala ushered them into the parlor. She shivered. "It's chilly in here. Shall I light the furnace?"

"It's only October," her mother said. "We must save the coal for winter. Light the fireplace instead, and I'll bring us something warm to wear."

After Sarah returned with three shawls, she sat on the sofa next to Lala and offered Paulina the slipper chair. "So, are you going to tell us why you moved the furniture about?"

Lala wrapped a shawl around her shoulders. "It's part of my plan. Let me be frank, Mother. We have no income now, unless I take the job Josef offered. And Paulina, without your building, you can't sell your merchandise, nor rent space to your prospective tenant."

"That's true."

"And whatever you don't clear out by tonight will be kept by the War Ministry. How much merchandise do you have left?"

"Most of my supplies are now in my house. All that's left is some furniture and fixtures, but I have no place for them."

"Now you do." Lala brought out her sketches for the women to see. "Here's what I propose—the three of us shall live together, here, and we'll convert Paulina's home into a temporary boarding house for the duration of the war."

"Where will we all stay?" asked Sarah.

"If you're willing to give up your bedroom, then Paulina and I could share your room and you could move into mine. You can't continue to sleep on a cot in the hallway downstairs forever. Did you sleep well in my bed last night?"

"Better than I have in a while, since…your father died."

"But Lala, aren't you forgetting something? It won't be the three of us for much longer," Paulina reminded her.

"I think Lala means until Ivo returns and you two marry," Sarah said. "We wouldn't expect you to continue living with us."

Paulina looked puzzled.

"I haven't told her anything," Lala explained to her friend. "Perhaps you should now, since she'll find out fairly soon anyway."

"Find out what? Have you two already married?"

"No, Mrs. Hafstein, I'm embarrassed to say, especially with what I must tell you now. You see, I'm with child." She lowered her head. "I'd understand if you didn't want me here."

"Not want you? Nonsense," Sarah exclaimed, but her

face registered confusion as if unsure of what she'd heard. When Paulina's confession fully sunk in, Sarah clasped her hands and smiled for the first time since her husband's death. "A baby. How wonderful! To think, there'll be new life in this house." Tears misted her smiling cheeks like a sun shower. "No one can ever replace my Jakob, but having a little one to fill this house with joy again...this would be a good thing. As for the circumstances, I'll wager you're not the only young lady to find herself in the family way...so as long as you're happy, I'm happy for you."

"I'm so glad to hear you say that. Since my mother is gone, I have no one I can talk to about this except you, Mrs. Hafstein. I have so many questions. I seem to get sick every morning now. Did you have this problem when you were expecting Lala?"

Sarah paled. "I, er...."

Paulina waved her hands. "I'm sorry, if you'd rather not talk about it. My mother would have been uncomfortable discussing this, too. I understand." She looked dejected. "It's only that I wouldn't dare mention this to Mrs. Smetana and I don't know anyone else whom I can ask."

"Mother, we have to tell her."

Sarah nodded.

"Paulina, we've kept a secret from you as well."

Lala told her friend how she came to be Lala Hafstein. Paulina looked stunned by the revelation and shocked by the horrific circumstances that brought it about.

"Oh, my," she kept saying. "You were so close I never suspected you were adopted. I can't believe you kept that secret for so long."

"Other than the Zedeks, you're the only one who knows."

"Never mind that," exclaimed Sarah. "I can't believe I never knew your real name was Luska!"

"Hadn't I told you that?" Lala said, half laughing. "Well, now you know everything about my past." Her laughter ceased. "I thought I'd buried Luska long ago in the Russian forest, along with Mama and Papa's clothes. But those memories began to return in the past few months, especially the last thing Mama said to me: 'Follow your heart.'"

Her mother took her hand and gave it a squeeze. "It's why you're here, with us."

Lala dabbed her eyes with her shawl. "We ought to leave the past behind now and talk about the future. Mother?"

"I like the idea of us sharing this house. Paulina, you should not be on your own now. We can help you care for the baby—oh, a baby." Sarah looked blissful every time she mentioned the child, which cheered Lala. Her mother needed some pleasure in her life. They all did.

Lala held up one sketch of the main floor. "I thought we could convert the dining room into a work room for the three of us. There's adequate space for two sewing machines and a place for drawing, plus a spot for the baby to nap while we work."

"Then where will we eat, dear?"

"In the kitchen. It's adequate for four, and I doubt we'll have dinner guests anytime soon." Lala spread the sketches she made across the sofa table. "As you can see, I've planned for a series of areas for us to be together as well as some nooks for when we want more privacy. Mother, you'll have a bedroom to yourself, and although it's not as large as your former room, there's still plenty of space to store away things we won't need for a while, like evening dresses. I also thought we could clear out Father's shed and make it more useful. "

"But if we are going to take care of the house and property ourselves, we'll need tools," Paulina pointed out.

Lala hadn't considered that. "We don't know how to use them."

"I know a little bit about house maintenance."

But not enough. The exterior of Paulina's house appeared quite rundown the last time Lala visited. If not for her father's skill, the elegant sofa she planned for the new parlor décor would have been firewood. No, one of them would have to learn.

"Could we barter something for help with fixing things?" her mother asked.

"Let me worry about that. For now, let's move on to discussing the financial possibilities. Paulina, may I ask how much you were charging to lease your building?"

"Twenty-eight koruny a month for the shop and furnished apartment upstairs. Twenty to cover my cost, three to Mrs. Smetana and the rest for myself."

Lala jotted down the figures. "Do you know if your tenant planned to live alone?"

"He rented part of the space to two other co-workers. It's probably why he didn't balk at the price."

"Do you think he'd be willing to pay more if we included meals and housekeeping?"

Paulina pondered that. "Maybe for housekeeping, but he expressly said he wanted to cook for himself. He's Jewish and keeps kosher."

"I keep a kosher kitchen here," Sarah said. "I could

convert your kitchen as well."

Lala checked her calculations. "What if we offered Paulina's house, with kosher meals and housekeeping, for…twelve koruny apiece for three residents, and ten koruny if there are four or five? Mother, could we feed them for that amount?"

"Unless food gets scarce or too expensive, then yes, especially if we pool that money with ours. And between the three of us, we can take care of both houses, lowering our costs. It would provide almost enough to live on, barring runaway inflation."

"But not quite, Mother. That's why I've decided to take the position in Josef's factory."

"Lala, I thought I made it clear that I would not allow you to sacrifice your life to that family."

"I don't intend to. But we need some income, don't we? And as you said long ago, it's better than some pursuits."

"I suppose so," Sarah finally admitted.

"I've figured it all out. I will agree to train at the factory, starting with construction. This way I can learn enough about tools and fixing things to help out around the house. You each have skills necessary to make our arrangement succeed, so this will be my contribution. If you can take on the cooking, sewing, cleaning and such, then I can do the rest."

Pauline shook her head. "Are you sure that's wise, my friend?"

"I'll only work in departments that will be of benefit to our project. When it's time to move into the corporate office," she looked squarely at Paulina to make sure she understood. "I will resign."

Paulina nodded.

The room had warmed up enough for Lala to remove her shawl. "I'll leave shortly to give Josef my decision, then I'll meet Paulina at the shop to cart away whatever we can."

"You needn't come. The other displaced shop owners have offered to help, so I should go now." She returned her shawl to Sarah. "Thank you again for letting me stay the night, and many nights thereafter." Paulina hugged Lala, then Sarah. "I'm so relieved, now that you know my secret and still want me, Mrs. Hafstein."

"We'll always want you, dear," said Sarah as she returned the hug. "And since you are going to live here, please call me Sarah, or whatever you choose as long as it's not as formal as Mrs. Hafstein."

"You've been like a mother to me for some time."

"Then what about Mama Sarah?"

"I like that. And my child will call you Grandmama."

Sarah broke into sun showers. "I'm to be a grandma. What a joyous secret that is."

"So, we know your secret and now you know ours," said Lala.

Paulina glanced at her. "Then there will be no more."

Lala said nothing, but noticed a faint look of concern on her mother's face. She began to press her but stopped. She still concealed a secret, and likely for the same reason— revealing the truth at this time would cause too much pain, something from which they both needed a respite.

CHAPTER TWENTY-THREE

Lala glanced up ahead at the secretary's desk outside of Josef's office, with Berthe firmly planted behind it. As Lala approached the imposing woman stood and attempted a smile.

"Good morning, Miss Hafstein. Mr. Smetana is expecting you." She escorted Lala to his office. When Josef responded to Berthe's knock with, "Show her in," she opened the door and waited for Lala to enter before seeing herself out.

Josef stood, but clung to his desk. He tried to appear businesslike, reserved, but behind his public face she could see traces of uneasiness, of struggle. Of yearning. It stirred her. She resolved to keep the meeting as brief as possible to avoid weakening.

Lala met his gaze. "After considering your offer, I have decided to accept the position. I want to learn how the factory operates and help you keep it open during the war."

"I'm pleased. I've discussed this with Mr. Anezska in upholstery and he—"

"I would prefer to begin in manufacturing."

"Wouldn't you find working with the fabrics more

interesting?"

"I know a great deal about fabrics, but virtually nothing about how furniture is made and assembled. I want to learn about the machines that cut lumber into usable pieces and then shape those pieces into chair legs and tabletops. The best techniques for joining the pieces and how to determine where to put the hinges, and how many, and..."

He raised his hands. "Stop, I'm convinced. You want to learn the production end first. I'm pleased you're taking this so seriously. I—" A brisk knock at the door interrupted him.

"Not again," he grumbled. "Berthe, I told you I did not wish to be disturbed."

From behind the door Berthe announced, "Mr. Smetana, there is a Mr. Jezek here to see you...from the Imperial Foreign Minister's office."

Josef stiffened. He glanced at the closed door, then at Lala. "You'd better leave."

"Absolutely not."

"Then take that file from my desk, so you appear to be at work." She did as he asked as he called out, "Please show him in, Berthe."

In walked a slight man of average height, with a head too small for his body and an enormous mustache that dominated his face. His hooded eyes flitted around the room, sizing up the office, and he barely glanced at either Josef or her. He set his black leather briefcase on the floor and paused to stare out the window.

She took the opportunity to glance at the papers inside the folder she held, searching for information to justify remaining in the office. Stunned, she realized the file contained what the factory most needed—a way to stay operational throughout the war.

CHAPTER TWENTY-FOUR

Josef broke the uncomfortable silence. "Welcome to my factory, Mr. Jezek. To what do I owe the pleasure?"

Jezek continued staring out the window. "Magnificent statue you have out there, Mr. Smetana. Is that 'Venus' one of Antonio Canova's pieces?"

"It is. May I offer you something to drink? Coffee, or if you like, something stronger?"

"No, thank you." He turned to face them, acknowledging Lala for the first time with a cool glance. "Allow me to introduce myself. I am Felix Jezek, special attaché to Count Hoyos." To Josef he added, "Your secretary can leave us now."

"Miss Hafstein is my business assistant, Mr. Jezek, and my future daughter-in-law. She has taken over the duties of my son, who volunteered for service when the war began."

He smirked at that. "Are you familiar with the War Requirements Act?"

"We have read and complied with all laws of state."

"Then you are aware of our right to conscript personnel and reassign them as we see fit."

"Somehow I don't believe an important man such as yourself is here to tell me I've been drafted."

Lala saw the sarcasm behind Josef's comment was lost on Jezek.

"Count Hoyos reports directly to Imperial Foreign Minister Berchtold. He has been in communication with our allies in Germany, who have created an alliance of industrial and business leaders to oversee the efficient production and distribution of war materials. We want to create such an alliance within our empire. You have been recommended to be part of our coalition, headquartered in Vienna."

Josef appeared to contemplate the offer, really more of a command to Lala's mind. "I'm flattered to be considered for such a prestigious position and I will do whatever I can to help your coalition, but I have a factory to run. My vice president passed away recently so I have no one else to oversee production now."

"Come now, Mr. Smetana. No one is buying furniture at present. You make nothing that's important for the war effort, nor are you equipped to do so. I fail to see why this factory should remain open."

"Excuse me, Mr. Jezek, but I beg to differ with you." Lala's voice came out softly at first, but strengthened with each word. "We are equipped to make a product that's vital to the war effort; in fact, to help our fighting men."

Even Josef looked surprised by her declaration.

She continued. "Our factory can manufacture and assemble medical equipment like stretchers, hospital cots and gurneys. All necessary for the war effort to transport and treat wounded soldiers."

She opened the folder she held and showed the men sketches and plans for those items. She thought whoever came up with this idea was brilliant.

"We already have factories making those products, Miss Hafstein."

"What about crutches?" added a new voice. Lala turned to see Gershom Kindemann standing in the doorway holding several rolls of draft paper under his arm. "And wheelchairs, for those who survive their injuries. And for those who require amputations, artificial limbs."

"Young man, I don't know who you are, but you know nothing about artificial limbs. We don't use wood anymore. The newest models are made of metal," Jezek said.

"The ability to manufacture...may I come in, Mr. Smetana?" Kindemann asked, and Josef nodded. Kindemann continued, "The ability to manufacture prosthetic devices out of metal is not practical in the numbers you will be needing. Metal will be reserved for making weapons, ammunition, planes and vehicles. After all, we can't go into battle with horse carts and slingshots anymore. Wood, on the other hand, is ample, easier to work with and extremely durable."

He sat in one of the sample chairs along the side of the office, reached down, grabbed his right ankle and pulled, removing an artificial leg that extended to the knee. Lala grabbed hold of Josef's desk and took deep breaths to keep from fainting.

"So, you see, I do know firsthand about artificial limbs. This one has served me well for eight years." Turning away from them, Kindemann replaced his prosthetic leg and stood.

Mr. Jezek remained stoic, but he tapped one finger against his voluminous moustache.

"Who are you?"

"Gershom Kindemann, head designer of custom products for the factory." He bowed slightly to Mr. Jezek.

"May I see your plans?" Jezek asked Josef.

"Mr. Kindemann will show them to you." Josef pulled out his extension tabletop and invited Gershom to use it.

Kindemann unrolled his sketches and spread them across the surface. "These are my designs for ambulatory equipment for soldiers who've suffered debilitating injuries to their limbs. For those who will heal, they provide temporary assistance. For those who won't, they offer mobility. In the case of amputation, knowing there is hope after the loss of a limb boosts morale and aids recovery. It is vital to return the patient to a sense of normalcy as quickly as possible, to salvage the spirit as well as the body."

"How did you lose your leg, Mr. Kindemann?"

"A riding accident as a boy. Once I received my prosthetic limb, I felt hopeful for the first time since the amputation, which helped me through the adjustment period."

"I appreciate your candor, Mr. Kindemann, as well as your perspective. I will postpone the closing of the factory until I can review your proposal."

"Thank you Mr. Jezek," Josef said. "I am sure you will see the value of what we can produce to help the war effort, by helping those who have made such a great sacrifice. I know that if my son were injured in battle, I'd want him to have the best chance for a full life."

"That is easy for you to say since your son can never be in that position, can he?"

"I don't understand."

Jezek's smirk returned. "Why do you persist in lying to me, Mr. Smetana? Do you think it will improve your chances of saving the factory?"

"I am not lying about anything, Mr. Jezek."

"Then why do you keep saying your son is fighting in the war when you know very well you obtained a medical exemption for him."

"Because he never used it. He enlisted in the army when my family was in Berlin, shortly after the war began. If you check with the German—"

"I did a thorough check on you, your background and your family as well as your business. There is no Armin Smetana in the military, Mr. Smetana. He registered as physically unfit for service, using the note you obtained for him, and therefore never entered service. I even checked with the German War Office to see if his artistic training led him to join the Ministry of Information. He hadn't."

Mr. Jezek's pronouncement left Josef wide-eyed and silent.

Stunned, Lala exclaimed, "There must be some mistake, Mr. Jezek. I was present in Berlin the day after Germany declared war, when Armin announced he had enlisted in the military."

Josef added, "He said he'd grown fond of Berlin and considered himself a citizen of the city, and therefore wanted to stand up for his new homeland."

"Which 'homeland?' France, perhaps? Because on the same night you say he enlisted, he boarded a westbound train," Jezek declared as if it was common knowledge. "Badly injured as well."

Lala couldn't believe what she was hearing. Was Jezek testing Josef, or deliberately tormenting him?

"That's not possible." Josef sprang forward. "My son wasn't hurt the night he left. Are you sure you have the right person?"

"See for yourself." Jezek opened his briefcase and

removed a photograph, which he laid on the table.

Lala recognized the Anhalter Bahnhof, the central train station in Berlin. In the background, she could see the commotion on Friedrichstrasse as families bid goodbye to their fathers and brothers, sons and sweethearts.

"Is that your son, or isn't it?"

The man Jezek referred to had his left arm in a sling, his nose taped up and a large bandage on his forehead. Even in profile Lala could make out substantial bruising on his face as well as—

She forced a shriek back into her throat, fighting her instinct to cry out. Anything she said now could endanger her life as well as Josef's, for she recognized the man in the photo. It definitely was not Armin Smetana.

It was Karel Palaky.

CHAPTER TWENTY-FIVE

"Is this your son or not, Mr. Smetana?" Jezek repeated.

Before Josef could answer Lala blurted, "Forgive us, Mr. Jezek. We are both shocked by the extent of Armin's injuries, as he had none when he left that night. Do you know how he...?"

"Nationalistic feelings run quite high in Germany," Jezek said. "I wouldn't be surprised if some patriots took offense at seeing a man who appeared able-bodied shirking his duty to his country. After all, having pleurisy is not something visible to the naked eye..." Jezek's index finger tapped his moustache. "...like a missing limb."

"Can you tell us where he is?" Lala asked, controlling her breathing, and not wanting to appear overanxious.

Jezek opened his briefcase and removed a sheet of paper, which he held in his hand. The urge to snatch the paper from him burned inside Lala, but she wouldn't give that pompous man the satisfaction.

Jezek turned back toward the window. "Lovely view. Now let us get back to the business at hand—your transfer to Vienna. You will be ready to leave with me tonight."

"Mr. Jezek, you can't expect me to leave now, with my factory about to be converted to wartime production. I must be here."

"Mr. Kindemann can handle the conversion and Miss Hafstein can assist him in whatever manner she assists you." He picked up his briefcase. "The train to Vienna leaves at nine tonight. Be at the station with your bags packed."

He dropped the paper on Josef's desk. Tipping his hat to Lala, he walked out.

Josef waited until Jezek had cleared the hallway to snatch the paper off his desk. He read it silently, but Lala saw his eyes widen and his mouth open in surprise, or shock.

"Where is 'Armin?'" she asked.

Josef folded the paper. "He traveled to Spain and bought passage on a ship to America. He arrived in New York over a month ago."

"Does it say if he traveled alone?"

"It doesn't."

If Armin wasn't in the military, where was he?

CHAPTER TWENTY-SIX

Lala sat down and took several long, deep breaths. The enormity of her situation began to crystallize—beyond the responsibility of supporting her mother, Paulina and eventually a baby, the entire factory and its conversion to wartime production would now rest on her shoulders.

Her shoulders. Like her family's bundle of laundry long ago…

"Luska, are you sure you have everything there? It looks too small."

"Yes, Mama. I pressed my knees into the bundle so I could wrap it tight, just like you told me. And see how I made a strap out of Papa's shirt sleeve."

Mama cupped Luska's face in her hand. "Ah, how could such a big girl fit inside such a small child? Go, and try to get that stain out of my dress…scrub everything well."

Luska went to the door. "I will Mama. I'll do a very good job. You'll see…."

Where would she find that courage again, now that Josef was leaving her, too?

She snapped back when Kindemann approached Josef. "Mr. Smetana, if Miss Hafstein and I will be managing the factory in your absence, I would be grateful if you could spend as much time as you can helping us prepare."

Josef remained silent, his gaze elsewhere, as removed from Kindemann's presence now as Lala had been moments before.

"Mr. Smetana?" Lala's voice seemed to awaken Josef from his musing with a start. He appeared disoriented for a moment, but it passed quickly.

"Yes, you are right. Kindemann, I thank you for what you've done. You may have saved my factory from ruin, coming to my office when you did."

"I'm embarrassed to admit this now, but I came here because I forgot to put a note with my name and an explanation of my proposal in the file Miss Hafstein is holding."

"Is this what you were searching for in my fath…in your desk yesterday?" she asked.

"It is. Lucky I found it when I did."

Josef shook Kindemann's hand. "We shall all be grateful for that, but now we must make plans." He checked the clock on the shelf of his cabinet. "Almost eleven. Kindemann, any work to do in your department?"

"My assistants can handle it."

"Good." He called Berthe into his office. "Please ask the department heads to come to my office immediately. Then have my chauffeur take you to my home. Arrange to have my bags packed and delivered here for an extended trip to Vienna."

"Sir?"

"Please, Berthe, I need you to do this for me."

The secretary nodded, though for a moment she betrayed a look of doubt. "Yes, sir." She hesitated before asking, "What shall I say to Mrs. Smetana?"

"You needn't tell her anything. I doubt that she'll be …present."

"Then shall I leave word for her?"

"Please do. I won't have time. I'll have to contact her from Vienna."

Berthe nodded once more before leaving.

"Let's move into the conference room. Kindemann, would you direct the department heads there while Miss Hafstein and I prepare the room? And bring one of the secretaries in the front office here to take notes."

"At once, sir."

As soon as Kindemann left, Josef turned to Lala. "The man in the photograph—was it Karel?"

She nodded.

He exhaled loudly. "Then I pray Armin is safe and with him, in America."

CHAPTER TWENTY-SEVEN

Josef escorted Lala to the factory's conference room, located mere steps across the hall from his private quarters where their tryst occurred yesterday. She maintained her attention on her new role in the factory as he unlocked the door; if she kept her eyes averted from the room across the hallway, perhaps her thoughts would follow suit.

The room faced a meadow with a wooded area beyond, offering privacy from all but a mother hare and her three leverets nibbling clover. An oval walnut table anchored the center of the room, surrounded by a dozen of the same cubist-inspired chairs as in the reception area. A pair of art nouveau chandeliers hung overhead and an antique Persian rug lay underneath. Lala liked the mix of traditional and modern styles.

Along one wall a bank of windows allowed the afternoon sun to brighten the room. Directly opposite was a credenza with an empty pitcher and a tray of drinking glasses on top. Above it hung Armin's finest piece from his Berlin show. The cubist-inspired painting contained Lala's manipulated image in the lower left corner of the canvas and one of Karel, his full lips puckered as if ready to kiss, at the top.

Josef carried the pitcher from the room and returned with it filled with water. He set it alongside the glasses, then opened the cabinet door below and brought out a tin of Fidorka sweet wafers, which he opened, then placed the contents on a small tray next to the water.

Lala chuckled; he stopped and looked to her. "What?"

She laughed. "I never expected you to be so…domestic."

He grinned. "So, I too, have the ability to surprise." His smile vanished. "Lala, before I leave tonight, there is something I must say to you—"

"No," she insisted. "We must put everything aside but the factory now."

He cradled her arms in his hands and she trembled. He bent toward her and planted a chaste kiss on her forehead. She could not look at him for fear of succumbing to her emotions.

"Lala, we will spend the entire day planning the factory's conversion. I will make sure that you, Kindemann, and the other executives understand what must be done. But before I go…." He again kissed her forehead. "The last thing I want to do before I leave for the train station is hold you in my arms one more time. Nothing more."

"I can't hear this right now." She stepped back, ending his embrace.

"Then later?"

She nodded.

"What do you want of me?" he asked.

"I don't know yet, but I will tell you when I do."

***

The department heads gathered with Josef, Lala and Kindemann to set out strategies for the factory's conversion. By one-thirty, a few groused about breaking for lunch, so Josef ordered the kitchen to send up sandwiches for everyone while the discussion continued.

"But Mr. Smetana," complained Mr. Anezska, pushing his sandwich to the side. "Can't we stop long enough to eat like civilized men?"

Josef leaned back and crossed his arms. "Isn't your son fighting in the war?"

"Yes, but...." The point must have finally dawned on Anezska. He retrieved his sandwich and bit into it as Josef turned the floor over to his factory foreman.

As hour after hour ticked by, a plan developed, and each person in attendance was given a set of responsibilities and areas to explore further. Josef asked Lala to assist Kindemann with implementing the plan and coordinating each department's duties. Kindemann would design the product line based on his sketches and direct the factory foreman in converting the machinery to produce the necessary pieces. Assembling, finishing, shipping and billing would continue as before, and upholstery would have to take the smaller role of cushioning some of the devices and making, at Kindemann's suggestion, seat and back pads for wheelchairs.

Whenever Lala made a comment, at least one of the executives questioned it. Fortunately, the detailed notes she had gotten from Kindemann supported her answers, and if she wasn't certain, she deferred to Kindemann or Josef.

As daylight began to fade, the secretary rose and switched on the overhead lights before continuing to take notes.

"So, if we follow this plan, the conversion will allow for nearly full employment," Josef concluded.

Lala said, "Afterward some positions will have to be cut, but based on the number of men we've already lost to military service, future conscription should account for nearly seventy percent of the job losses."

Several of the men looked skeptical at that. "Are you sure your figures are correct, Miss Hafstein?" asked the employment manager, his eyebrows raised in doubt.

"I trust your estimates, Mr. Strahov. These figures came from your report."

The management staff reviewed their notes and nodded in agreement. It had taken several hours of thoughtful questions and solid support from Josef, but most of the department heads seemed to finally accept her role in the company, some grudgingly, others more willingly.

Josef adjourned the meeting shortly past six, at which each department head rushed over to shake his hand and wish him well before hurrying out to their homes, and no doubt, their dinner. Their impatience perturbed Lala. She refrained from venting her ire until the secretary finished clearing the room and left, then she clucked her tongue.

"What's wrong?" asked Josef.

"The management staff seems more interested in their meat and potatoes than the company that puts food on their table."

"You mustn't take it personally."

"Why not? Their behavior was ungrateful, even disloyal. If my father was here...."

For the first time since his death, speaking of him did not overwhelm her with sadness, but rather lit a fire in her. She felt her father's indignation over the men's actions as if she shared a spiritual connection with him in his workplace. "If he were here, he'd feel the same way."

Josef and Kindemann stared at her.

"But," she conceded, "he would have the grace not to say it in such a blunt manner."

Josef nodded. Kindemann grinned.

Josef closed the conference room door behind them. "Kindemann, you may go home now."

"Thank you, Mr. Smetana, but I am not sure I have a home to go home to anymore."

"Why not?"

"I had arranged to rent a building in town with my assistant and apprentice, but we learned today the War Ministry has requisitioned it."

"That seems to be happening more and more," said Lala. "My friend's shop has been taken as well...Mr. Kindemann, from whom were you going to rent the building?"

"A Miss Sipek. Why?"

"Then I have some good news for you." Lala explained the plan she'd drawn up earlier with her mother and Paulina.

A relieved Kindemann went out to tell his associates, leaving Lala and Josef alone in the hallway. Lala couldn't resist glancing at the door to Josef's private quarters, but the sound of footsteps approaching obliged her to keep her distance.

Berthe appeared with Josef's chauffeur alongside.

"Sir, all necessary items have been packed for you. The chauffeur has stowed your trunks in the automobile. Shall I ask him to bring them in, so you may check the contents for yourself?"

"That won't be necessary, Berthe. I trust you."

Berthe, unable to speak, blinked back tears at the compliment. She lowered her head and clasped her hands in front of her, as if praying. "Th...Thank you, Mr. Smetana."

She paused, then added in a broken voice, "It has been an honor to work with you, sir."

"Berthe, I'm going to Vienna, not to my deathbed. I will return." He smiled at her. "And you will be needed here. Mr. Kindemann and Miss Hafstein will rely upon you to help keep the factory running in an organized and efficient manner."

"I will do my best, sir."

"I have no doubt you will." He checked his watch. "It's late." To his chauffeur he instructed, "Smolak, take Berthe home, then come back for Miss Hafstein and me."

The chauffeur tipped his hat and bowed before escorting Berthe out.

As soon as they left, Josef took Lala in his arms. She clung to him as he held her, their bodies swaying as if to music. She took in every sensation, from the warmth of his body, the delicate scent of bergamot, the feel of his arms around her. She needed him here, to hold and caress her. She needed him. Tears filled her eyes as she realized why. Her father dead, Armin missing, Ivo conscripted. And now Josef about to leave.

All of the men in her life were being taken away from her.

They stayed locked together for a while, not saying a word, not moving beyond a gentle sway. Eventually he ended the embrace.

She looked up at his face, warm and expressive. "Josef, I…"

He placed his finger to her mouth. "Please, don't say anything more. It will make this even more difficult."

She'd promised to protect her family, respect his marriage, but any doubt that she could be near him without longing for him faded. She knew what she wanted in their last moments together, though it took a moment to gather the courage to voice it.

"I have one request of you before you leave."

"Anything." His fingers stroked alongside her cheek and underneath her chin.

She raised her hand to the back of her head. Slowly, she released the comb that held her hair in place, sending it tumbling over her shoulders and down her back as she opened the door to his private quarters.

PART TWO

THE GREAT WAR

CHAPTER ONE
November 18, 1914

Lala entered the factory's conference room, her de facto office since Josef's departure, to find Kindemann sitting at the table, already at work. Steeling herself, she poured a cup of coffee from the sterling service borrowed from the showroom. "Am I late?" she asked in a neutral tone.

"I came in early." Without looking up, he passed a document to her containing the cost estimates of the conversion project's second phase, which they had finalized yesterday. "I wanted to see if I could eliminate any expenses before we go ahead."

She took a sip of coffee; too hot. She dipped a spoon into her cup and swirled figure eights to cool it down. "I thought we'd already done that, Mr. Kindemann."

"It can't hurt to check again. Whatever we manage to save now will be passed along to the staff."

Her stirring grew more vigorous. "Why not provide a better product for a lower cost?"

One corner of his mouth turned up. "I thought we'd already done that, Miss Hafstein."

In the weeks they'd worked together, Lala had come to learn he enjoyed verbal sparring and would sometimes deliberately goad her. She'd tried flattery, indifference, and combativeness to deflect his baiting, all ineffective, though flattery generated the weakest reaction.

"Everyone at the factory appreciates what you've already done."

"That's because you're so good at explaining it to them." He smiled at her, lingering on her face for what she thought was a moment too long, another attempt to bait her.

She turned her attention to the paperwork. Costs had been cut to the bone, perks eliminated and work hours increased. "The staff will protest this," she said.

"No one will complain. They're grateful for the work." He fumbled through the piles of paperwork surrounding him. "We lost two more workers, though. Anezska's assistant was conscripted, and a foreman was injured repositioning a lathe."

"Oh no. How badly was he hurt?"

"Back fracture. He'll be laid up for months. Two less we'll have to let go."

"But we must do something for the foreman—help him out financially. After all, he was injured on the job."

"How softhearted, but no."

Thus far she had managed to keep her temper at bay, but his remark offended her. "I must insist on this. The man would never have been hurt if not for us. We owe him—"

"We owe him nothing," Kindemann contended. "He neglected to clean up the machine oil that had spilled on the floor, which is what caused him to fall. He has his own carelessness to blame." He dropped his pencil on the table and pushed back against his chair. "If you want, we can provide him with a wheelchair and crutches until he recovers."

"How thoughtful. Why don't we throw a few hellers in

the family's begging cup?"

"Go ahead, as long as those coins don't come out of the factory's budget."

She sought to put an end to their squabbling. "Shall we return to the business at hand?"

"Is that pun intended?"

"What pun?"

"Business...at hand, when we're discussing prosthetics?"

She ignored his pitiful attempt at humor. "Let's proceed, then."

Kindemann unrolled a blueprint with designs for a series of prosthetic devices. "Our greatest advantage over the competition will be mass production coupled with some customization, exactly what made the factory successful when it produced furniture. We must offer the best selection of sizes, not only in length, but width. It's important for the prosthetic to match the surviving limb as closely as possible."

"Why do you think I've been working with Mr. Ruzicka to create a range of dyes to match various skin tones?" She took a calming breath to avoid further reacting to his condescension. More flies with honey, she reminded herself as she exhaled. "Sorry, I did not mean to imply your work needed improvement."

"I know what you meant." He rubbed his eyes. "I'm just tired."

"You've been working hard."

He shrugged it off. "No harder than anyone else."

She crossed her arms. "Your modesty is becoming legendary."

"So is your sarcasm."

"What can I say? At our core we're both artists. We go with what inspires us."

Lala caught him chuckling at that. "Well played, Miss Hafstein."

Lala spent the afternoon with Ruzicka perfecting the special dyes for prosthetics. They agreed on the number of shades needed but not the labeling. Ruzicka suggested using ethnicities, but Lala convinced him using actual skin tones would be more accurate and, judging by the vile comments about some nationalities printed in the newspapers and spread by gossip, less likely to risk offense.

She returned to the conference room to find Kindemann had gone back to the design department to confer with his crew. Lala decided to straighten up the room, which granted her some quiet time alone. She heard the heavy footsteps of Berthe approaching.

Berthe stopped at the door. "You needn't do that, Miss Hafstein. The clerk will put everything away."

"Please don't bother her. A little busy-work is just the thing for me before I leave."

"Shall I call Smolak to drive you home?"

Lala flipped through the paperwork on her desk and found nothing that needed immediate attention. "Yes, would you?"

The chauffeur parked the automobile in front of Lala's home. He escorted her to the front door and waited until she opened it and bid him goodnight.

"Shall I bring the automobile tomorrow at eight

o'clock, Miss?"

A momentary temptation to leave earlier, to arrive before Kindemann, faded as quickly as the twilight. She would not play that game for his entertainment. "Yes, Smolak. Come as usual."

CHAPTER TWO

The moment Lala walked through her front door her mother greeted her with a smile and an empty glass in hand.

"Hello, dear. You're home early. How was your day?"

Lala's position with the factory returned a sense of normalcy and purpose to her mother's life. Sarah had devoted herself to caring for her husband and maintained a routine for when he came home. That routine now transferred to Lala.

Sarah held up the glass. "Shall I pour you a drink before dinner? Some of that cognac you like?"

The notion tempted Lala, but although her father enjoyed a small glass of Scotch most nights, Lala's experience with Romy made her hesitant to develop the habit. She instead opted to reserve cognac for a special occasion rather than a difficult day, difficult having become typical.

"No thank you, not tonight." The aroma of meat cooking led her to the kitchen. "Something smells delicious in here," she said as she spied an iron pot bubbling on the stove.

"I'm stewing mutton." Sarah removed the cover from the pot, releasing a burst of meat and onion scented steam. "I splurged on enough for the two of us." She gave the contents a stir.

"What about Paulina?"

"She's in Prague. She received an invitation to meet Ivo's parents."

"I wonder if they know about Paulina's condition."

"If not, it won't be a secret anymore. Poor Paulina. I wonder how they'll react."

"With any luck, like you did, Mother."

Sarah looked away.

"You were quite happy to hear her news," said Lala.

"I still am, but this is different."

"How so?"

"I wouldn't have been as enthusiastic if you found yourself in that situation."

Lala set the table for dinner while her mother stirred the pot. Sarah poked the meat with a knife tip. "It's not ready for the potatoes. Shall we wait in the parlor?"

Lala settled into the one of the two salon chairs salvaged from the dress shop. The moss green brocade with which Paulina had reupholstered them complemented the meander-striped fabric on the sofa.

Her mother added two quarter logs from the firewood rack to the hearth and poked the embers to get them lit. The room brightened as the wood caught fire, the flickering reflected in the hall mirror. Lala heard the snap and sizzle of the fireplace, sounds that brought a measure of tranquility to her.

"Relax while I finish dinner." Her mother patted Lala's hand before leaving the room.

Lala closed her eyes. She finally understood why her hard-working father favored his wing chair all those years.

Comfortable enough to induce sleep, to absorb the troubles of the day.

Her thoughts harkened back to her latest round of sparring with Kindemann. With all the challenges they faced, he still made the work more difficult with his confrontational behavior as if he took pleasure in needling her, like little boys who enjoy teasing their female classmates.

Why were young men so exasperating? Not only her irritating co-manager but every other one she knew, going back to Armin and his friends. Karel annoyed her with his snide remarks from the moment they'd met. Zigmund's boyishness, at first almost appealing, soon became obnoxious, and Armin? Dear Armin. His mastery of concealment meant their relationship was never as close as she'd believed. Despite promising in Berlin to stay in contact, he hadn't written to her once. Ivo seemed to be the exception that proved the rule. No wonder Paulina felt attracted to him when they first met. He had a maturity that belied his years, a sophistication Lala rarely found in men of his age.

Now older men; that was another story. She smiled. For the first time, she realized part of why she felt so attracted to Josef. She wasn't looking for a father figure, but someone with the kindness, maturity and understanding of men like her father and her uncle. Stable men who knew who they were and what they wanted. She thrashed and stumbled through life enough for two.

Lala heard the front door open. Paulina entered the house and hung up her coat.

"I didn't expect you back so soon," said Lala.

Paulina marched into the parlor and held up her left hand, displaying a gold band on her fourth finger.

Lala leapt out of her chair. "Oh my, Paulina, you and Ivo got married! Did he come home on leave?"

"No, but apparently we did marry; at least, that's what he wrote to his parents. His mother gave me her mother's ring to wear since Ivo didn't have time to present it to me at our 'wedding' back in August."

"That's wonderful."

"Is it?"

"Paulina, it means he thinks of you as his wife."

"I suppose you're right." She grinned. "That is very wonderful."

"Were his parents thrilled about the baby?"

"They certainly were pleased that they didn't have to care for us. It's much harder to find food and provisions in the city than here."

Sarah emerged from the kitchen. "Paulina, you're home. I'd better add more potatoes to the stew."

Paulina repeated her story to Sarah over dinner. Afterwards, Lala cleared the table while her mother filled the washbasin with hot water.

Sarah handed a kitchen towel to Paulina. "If Ivo were here right now and asked you to marry him, would you say yes?"

"Absolutely, and not just because of..." she pointed to her belly. "I do love him and I want to be his wife. We would have married before he left, if time allowed."

Sarah washed the rest of the dishes and stacked them on the counter for Paulina and Lala to dry. "When he returns you can marry quietly and no one will be the wiser."

"In the meantime, I now have to pretend to be Mrs. Ivo

Chytry." She yawned.

"You've had a busy day. Why don't you go to bed?"

Paulina yawned again. "I think I shall."

Lala gave Paulina a playful nudge. "Goodnight Mrs. Chytry."

"Goodnight...no, I can't call you Mrs. Smetana, that would be mean." Paulina giggled as she left the kitchen.

Mrs. Smetana? Not necessarily.

Sarah offered to finish cleaning the kitchen, so Lala decided to take a bath. With three women cohabitating, privacy came at a premium. She now shared what has been her parents' bedroom with Paulina and it was rare when no one else was home. At the factory Kindemann had invaded her office, and she spent a great deal of time working with the managers and supervisors of each department. Other than exclusive use of Josef's private facilities, necessitated by the fact that the executive washroom was men only, she had little time to herself now. The demands of work left her too exhausted to think about anything when she returned home. Work, and Mr. Kindemann.

Her time in the bath, alone, provided comfort. Quiet. Escape. And safety, to think about things she couldn't dare think about anywhere else.

"*...call you Mrs. Smetana....*"

Settling into the tub, the warm water dissolved her cares and enfolded her like a caress. She swirled her fingers in the bath. It stirred up a memory from childhood, of the pond near her childhood home in Russia where she'd been washing laundry the day Cossacks attacked her shtetl. Closing her

171

eyes, she willed her mind silent, free from the pressures of today and memories of yesterday. Her thoughts drifted to Josef. His mouth on hers. His hands tracing the curves and crevices of her body. The memory of their last hours together.

When the bath water cooled, she left the solitude of the tub, donned a nightgown and went to her room. Paulina had fallen asleep so Lala slipped into her bed and soon fell into peaceful slumber, ready to dream of better times.

CHAPTER THREE

When Lala stepped into the conference room, to her relief she found it vacant. The coffee service was gone as well.

Berthe knocked on the door before entering with a cup of tepid coffee. "Mr. Kindemann took the service from the room to his workshop, but I managed to save this for you." She placed the cup and saucer on the table by Lala. "You take your coffee black and unsweetened, is that right?"

"Thank you, that's perfect."

After Berthe returned to her duties, Lala visited each factory head to check on the conversion progress. All seemed to be proceeding on schedule to meet their first deadline on January fourth. Conversion would be completed, raw materials delivered, and the factory ready to start manufacturing their new product line.

After lunch in Josef's private quarters, she returned to the conference room to review her paperwork. She found the cost estimates of the second phase of the factory's conversion, which she'd begun reviewing yesterday. As she read through it, Kindemann entered the room with more paperwork. She involuntarily tensed.

"What have you there?" he asked as he took his preferred seat next to her. The huge conference table allowed plenty of room to spread out. Why did he choose to sit so close to her?

"I'm reviewing the cost estimates, Mr. Kindemann."

"They're no longer correct." He pulled the paper from her hand and dropped one of two folders in front of her. "I want you to cast an admiring eye on my new designs."

She pushed the folder aside. "What do you mean, the cost estimates are not correct? We reviewed them for a week."

"I changed them when I redesigned the wheelchairs. Go, look at them. They're brilliant."

She bit her lip, an old habit that had resurfaced since the war began, and scooted her chair several centimeters away from his, for if he was sitting any closer to her, he'd be in her lap.

He picked up the folder and waved it in her face.

Lala pushed it away. "I wish we could work together in a more cordial way. Must you always try to goad me, Mr. Kindemann?"

"Call me Gershom."

"No."

"Then I won't answer your question."

She rose to get a glass of water from the breakfront, pushing her chair back with more force than she'd intended. She caught him smiling at that and took a breath to calm herself.

She resolved to put a halt to this nonsense once and for all. She returned to the table and set the glass of water by her place. "Why must you always try to goad me...Gershom?"

He smiled. "Because when you get flustered, you crinkle your nose and knit your eyebrows, your eyes narrow and your mouth tightens."

"And that amuses you."

Now he was laughing at her. "Yes, it does, quite a lot."

She fought her temper. "Why should your amusement override our ability to work together?"

"That's the point. It doesn't. You still look appealing in a funny sort of way when I tease you, but not so beautiful that you distract me beyond thinking."

Words of reply failed to form. His confession instilled a vulnerability that disturbed her. She finally sputtered, "Don't say that."

"Why, because it bothers you to know I find you attractive?"

"Yes, it does, a great deal."

He leaned forward toward her, propped his elbow on the table and rested his chin on his palm. Staring directly at her, he grinned. "I'm glad. At least you haven't said it offends you, so I can take it as a sign that you might hold some tender feelings for me, which causes the bother."

"Don't confuse pleasantries with tender feelings." She held up her hand with her engagement ring. "I have a fiancé."

"And do you have tender feelings for your fiancé? I only ask because you've never seemed to before, or even now. You didn't say, 'I'm in love with another man,' or 'My heart belongs to Armin,' but 'I have a fiancé.' How impassive you make it sound."

Lala felt her temper flash. "You have no idea how I feel about anything beyond this factory, for I would never confide my private life to anyone here, especially you. You've done nothing to contribute to a pleasant work atmosphere between us."

"And don't pretend that you are in love with Mr. Smetana's son when you obviously harbor no romantic

175

feelings toward him...unless it's his wealth that's attracted you."

"How dare you even imply something so reprehensible?"

He sat up, still smiling at her, and crossed his arms. "For you, that's as good as a denial. So, you're not marrying him for love, or for money. Then what? To forge a bond between your families...no, that can't be, you're not evenly matched. Do you expect him to become a famous artist someday? Is that why you're marrying him?"

She tried to remain calm, but anger welled deep within her. "You disgust me."

"Or are the rumors true and you're entering a 'mariage blanc?' Whose reputation are you trying to preserve—yours, or the sodomite's?"

Before she realized what she was doing, she slapped him across his face. It shocked her more than him, for he quickly recovered and rewarded her with a sardonic smile.

"I'm not..." she spat out, then fell silent. This conversation had become too dangerous.

He rubbed his reddened cheek.

"So, you're not the innocent maiden after all, unaware of your fiancé's...proclivities."

She gathered her possessions and rushed from the room, wondering how she would survive the next few months.

CHAPTER FOUR

Lala broke her rule and had a small glass of cognac when she arrived home. Her mother must have sensed her distress, for she left Lala alone in the parlor while she finished dinner. Lala sipped her drink, making it last as long as possible, while her fingers traced the contours of the bottle, a poor substitute for what she truly craved.

What had possessed Kindemann to speak to her the way he did? Not only confessing his attraction to her, which she could easily sidestep, but his remarks about her engagement to Armin, which were as inappropriate as they were vicious. She had to bring equilibrium back to their relationship, civility as well, but how? Understanding men was not her strong suit. Fortunately, her best resource for a solution would be arriving home any minute.

When Lala went upstairs that evening, she found Paulina propped up in her bed, rereading her recent letter from Ivo. Paulina's nightgown strained across her bosom, which had grown fuller in the past month. Soon her middle would as well. A memory swept over Lala, of Mama making tea in their shtetl kitchen, her belly, swollen with child, pressing against the buttons of her old dress. Lala shivered involuntarily and the image faded.

Paulina looked up from her letter. "You're cold."

"Not really, just…" She sat on the edge of her bed. "Paulina, have you had any trouble with your boarders?"

"None at all. They pay their rent on time, they're clean, polite, and quite respectful."

Lala nodded and began to undress.

Paulina finished her letter and folded it into its envelope, but her gaze fixed on Lala. "Why do you ask?"

Lala relayed what had happened earlier that day as she changed into her nightclothes.

"You can't blame the man for being attracted to you, especially now."

"Because of Armin?"

"No, because of Josef. You never felt desire for a man before him." Paulina smiled knowingly. "Men like innocence, but they're drawn to passion."

"Why would he say those horrible things about Armin?"

"Not everyone is as broadminded as you, Lala. You know how most people view men like Armin. Try not to take it personally. He meant to be frank, not cruel, and if he's attracted to you, naturally he would prefer that you weren't betrothed. And since he's heard the rumors about Armin, he sees that as an opening, as he knows you cannot be truly…fulfilled." Paulina settled back into her pillow. "I don't know the men well, but I can tell they're not very sophisticated about women. They tend to defer to Mr. Kindemann, and he is unfailingly polite and considerate toward me, especially now that I've asked him to call me Mrs. Chytry."

"So, he's flirted with you as well?"

"I'm not the sort of woman he fancies."

"Because you're not available, Mrs. Chytry."

"No, because I'm not Jewish, Miss Hafstein."

Lala sat on the edge of the bed. "What am I to do? I have to work with the man. How do I keep his comments from damaging our fragile work relationship even more?"

"By understanding why it's been awkward. He's finally admitted what had been concerning him, so leave it behind and move forward." Paulina yawned.

"How thoughtless of me, you're tired and need your sleep." Lala settled under the covers and turned out the light. Within minutes she could hear Paulina's breathing slow and deepen. She laid her head on her pillow and stared at the ceiling awhile, then went to the window for solace from the moon. Rolling clouds obscured it from her view.

Move forward…the words echoed from the past; this wasn't the first time she'd been given that advice. It worked before; it could work again. It would be a challenge, she admitted to herself, and whispered to the hidden moon, "But when have I ever avoided a challenge?"

CHAPTER FIVE

As the chauffeur drove Lala to the factory, she rehearsed to herself what she'd say right off to Kindemann, beginning with a terse greeting, "Good morning, Mr. Kindemann…"

"Call me Gershom."

…Followed by a reminder of their upcoming deadline. She would review their list of tasks, separate duties as outlined by Josef, and then walk away, denying him the opportunity to speak until she'd had her say. Any comments of a personal nature would be rebuffed. She vowed to stay detached, both physically and emotionally, no matter what.

She'd confront him in the design department, where he'd be finalizing the equipment plans with his team. He'd be less likely to raise a fuss with his staff present. And although he might consider the shop his domain, she had a strong connection to the place. Her father had built it from an afterthought to an internationally renowned and respected division. Lala could take strength from that.

Berthe was already at her desk. Lala asked the secretary to accompany her to the department; Berthe's presence would further dissuade Kindemann from misbehaving.

Berthe followed Lala through the hallway, pad and pencil in hand. They reached the anteroom, marked by her father's masterpiece desk. Lala resisted the urge to brush her fingertips over the patchwork of wood. Instead she tapped the frame of Armin's painting, which hung above the desk at a slight tilt, to straighten it. Then with one deep breath for courage, she marched into the room.

Kindemann's assistant, Lew Wachowski, ran a plane over a section of wood. She didn't know him well and suspected no one outside the craftsmen's shop did, either. A quiet and unassuming young man, he said very little, speaking in words and phrases rather than sentences. Of average height and build, his ordinary features failed to distinguish him from other men, particularly his work associate Elia Zacco.

When Kindemann hired on, he brought along his young Italian cousin to train as his apprentice. Elia, small of stature, with a rounded body and tousle of bronze curls, reminded Lala of Rafael's "Cherubini." His eyes, wide and disarming, always sparkled with mischief, his plump cheeks rosy and punctuated by dimples whenever he laughed. The teenager seemed perpetually cheerful, as he did now, sanding what looked like a wooden seat at the far end of the workbench. Neither man noticed her standing in the doorway with Berthe, so she cleared her throat. They still didn't respond.

"Gentlemen?" Berthe boomed, startling the men out of their focus. When they noticed Lala's presence, they leapt from their benches.

"Where is Mr. Kindemann?" Lala asked.

The two men looked at each other, then at her. "He not here, Miss," Elia finally said.

"I can see that. Do you know where he is?" They both shook their heads.

Lala suspected they were trying to cover for their boss's unexplained absence, and wondered if it had anything to do with his loathsome behavior the day before.

"When you see Mr. Kindemann, please tell him to continue whatever he's working on. Berthe, shall we return?"

They walked back through the corridors. Lala stopped at the conference room and tried the handle, but the door was now locked.

"Allow me to open that for you, Miss." Berthe went back to her desk and returned with a key. She unlocked the door, turned the handle and stepped back so Lala could enter first.

There, planted in a chair, his upper body sprawled across the table, was Kindemann. A nearly full bottle of whiskey rested near his head, his hand still wrapped around a half-filled tumbler. Lala heard soft snoring. She walked around the chair to observe the right side of his face pressed against the tabletop, his mouth askew. A strand of dribble hung from his upper lip.

"Dear Lord, he's soused," Berthe murmured. She snatched the bottle from the table. "Will you wake him, Miss?"

"Me? No. Let him sleep it off," Lala whispered back as she and Berthe left the room.

Berthe closed the door. "This is not like him, Miss."

"I agree." Lala worried that their exchange from the prior day might have been the cause. "I wonder what drove him to do that?"

Berthe chuckled. "Whatever it was, it must have been a short drive." She held up the bottle. "By my estimate, he couldn't have drunk more than a thimbleful."

Lala maintained her composure for about two seconds before bursting into laughter, while Berthe managed to resist a moment longer.

***

Lala made her rounds through the factory. Pleased that the conversion was progressing well, she felt ready to return to the design department to finish her intended conversation with Kindemann. On the way, she recalled the first time she made this trip with Josef…

They walked in silence but not quietly; their shoe heels reverberated against the stone floors.

"Josef, have you ever considered carpeting these hallways?"

"Because of the noise? No, I planned it deliberately. How else will the employees know when their boss is about to make a surprise visit?"

She smiled at the memory and considered taking off her shoes. Instead she slowed her pace and walked on tiptoes as she rounded the corner. Standing in the entryway next to her father's drop leaf desk, she observed Kindemann's two assistants at the workbench studying a drawing under the light of a lamp, its shade missing. Elia chattered away, his hands moving as rapidly as his mouth, as Lew listened and gave the occasional nod. Kindemann was nowhere to be seen.

Elia looked up and noticed Lala, for he suddenly stood up straight, prodded Lew on the shoulder, and then flashed her a smile more brilliant than the light bulb.

"Miss Hafstein, we not expect you."

Lew kept his eyes averted. Lala wondered if it was shyness or an attempt to hide something, such as his boss's now conspicuous absence.

As if on cue, Kindemann walked into the shop from the adjacent lumber storage room looking as disheveled as he did that morning, his clothing rumpled, his hair plastered to the right side of his face, his eyes bloodshot. He noticed her and

184

froze.

"Good afternoon, Mr. Kindemann. You'll be pleased to know that the dye and finishing departments are on schedule, and thanks to our hiring of experienced female seamstresses, the cushions and padding for our devices will be completed well ahead of schedule. If you haven't found any problems in your production line, then we're currently on course to meet, and possibly beat, our deadline."

Kindemann blinked a few times but said nothing. Whether it was his reaction to the news or the sunlight streaming through the windows, Lala couldn't be sure.

"I'll take that as a positive sign." She turned to his assistants. "Gentlemen, I'll leave you to your work. I'm going home early today."

CHAPTER SIX
Tuesday, February 9, 1915

Lala arrived at the factory to find Berthe frazzled. Berthe directed her to the design department to locate Kindemann. The door was shut, but through it she could hear rapid footsteps, banging, and voices fraught with alarm. She knocked, but no one responded; she probably couldn't be heard over the near shouting that came from the room.

She knocked once more and was about to turn the knob when the door flung open. Kindemann, clearly agitated, stared at her as though she were a policeman coming to arrest him.

"Come in, quickly!"

Lala heard terror in his voice. "What has happened?"

Before he could answer, Elia shouted from across the room, "I find it!" and held up a drawing.

Kindemann turned away from Lala. "Bring it to Hajek in finishing and tell him to compare the models we've produced with the specifications on this version."

As Elia ran out, Kindemann gestured to his desk and offered Lala a seat. "We've been notified that the War Ministry's purchasing agent for recuperation devices and prosthetics is coming here in three days."

Lala caught the implication, as well as the panic, immediately. "That's over two weeks earlier than they originally said. Where do we stand?"

"The good news is we're about a week ahead of schedule, but when I checked the wheelchair inventory this morning I found a few samples that weren't made to the latest specifications."

"How many?"

"I don't know yet; that's what Elia is checking now. There may only be a few, or an entire lot."

"Are they faulty?"

"No, but they're not as well designed as the others. They may not stand up to our competitors' products."

Lala stood. "I want to see them for myself."

They hurried to the finishing room, where Elia was stacking wheelchairs side by side. Lala could see one set looked smaller and closer to the ground than the other.

"Twenty they make right, but fifty they make like this, not right size." Elia grimaced. "Whata we to do?"

"Fire the fool responsible," growled Kindemann.

Lala waved her hand. "No, we won't. We need to fix the problem. That's all that matters."

"We can't make enough of the right size between now and when the buyer arrives. If we can't impress him with our products, he won't order enough to keep the factory in business. All our work will have been for naught."

"Then how can we fix these units?" She sat in one. "I agree it's too low for someone my height or taller, but perhaps it will accommodate a shorter soldier, or nurse, or civilian child."

Kindemann crossed his arms. "Try wheeling it."

She placed her hands on the wheels and rolled them

forward, but realized what Kindemann alluded to; the small wheels required great effort to travel a short distance. She stood and looked at it again. "Can we put on bigger wheels to raise them up?"

"Then they would be too difficult to reach."

She nodded. "What if we also raised the seat?"

"It would look awkward, like we were hiding a faulty design in the chair, which in fact is what we'd be doing."

"Only if the raised seat served no other purpose." She strode around the chair. "Could we put a box or shelf underneath the seat?"

"What for?"

"Storage, perhaps."

Kindemann appeared to be considering that when he lit up. "Better than that, a commode. Yes, that would be practical for someone in a wheelchair. Why didn't I think of it before?" He beckoned to Elia. "Help me here."

They flipped the chair every which way, taking measurements and spouting ideas in half-sentences, with Elia jotting notes as they spoke. Kindemann looked up at Lala and gave her a relieved smile.

She acknowledged the solution with a nod. "I'll finish the inventory while you and Elia settle this."

As she walked away, Kindemann called out, "We make a good team."

Lala didn't respond. He needed to focus on correcting a problem. This was not the time to tell him that once they completed the factory's conversion, she intended to resign.

Lala found no other errors in the production line, to her

relief. She instituted a round-the-clock schedule, effective immediately, to ensure they would have sufficient product completed when the War Ministry's agent arrived. Some of the workers complained about the longer hours, but Lala sweetened the pot by offering to provide meals during their shifts.

She had Berthe type her notes in anticipation of meeting with Kindemann before their customary end of day review, and was in the process of studying them when he joined her in the conference room. Before he could say anything, she handed him a copy.

"The remainder of our products met our specifications. Our big push early on put us ahead of schedule, and I took care of ramping up production so we'll be ready by our new deadline this Friday."

He scanned her notes. "Thank you."

"There's no need to thank me, it's what I'm supposed to do."

"No, thank you for before. For not making me feel like a bigger idiot than I already do after that blunder. It could have ruined everything."

"But it didn't, so let's move forward."

"I've noticed you say that a lot." He shuffled toward the window and stared out. "I never apologized to you, did I?"

"There's no need. You made a mistake. It can happen."

He kept his gaze on the meadow. "I meant for what I said to you awhile back, about your betrothal. I had no right to say those things, yet you never held it against me."

"We don't have time to feel sorry for ourselves right now." She tapped the edge of her set of papers on the tabletop to straighten them.

He turned to face her, silhouetted against the backlight of

the window bathed in sunlight. "Why, do you feel sorry about something?"

"Who alive doesn't have regrets?" She opened her notes. "Let's review—"

"Let me make it up to you."

"You have, Mr. Kindemann, by coming up with a solution for the—"

"That isn't what I meant. And would you please call me Gershom? Every time you call me Mister I feel like an old man."

"I should think 'Mr. Kindemann' fits your position as the current executive of this factory."

"Co-executive, Miss Hafstein."

She laid her papers on the table. "I might as well tell you now. Once we get the production up and running, I will be leaving my position here."

He stepped forward toward the table, bringing lamplight to his face, etched in distress. "You can't leave now, how will I run the factory without you?"

"You'll manage quite well once everything is in place. It never was my intention to work here any longer than necessary, and I don't see any reason for me to stay beyond next week."

It was as if some invisible weight overwhelmed him, pulling every part of his body down from his brow to his legs, crushing him. She realized her remark sounded like she couldn't wait to leave—true, but insensitive. "Mr. Kindemann, what I meant—"

"Don't patronize me. You meant exactly what you said."

CHAPTER SEVEN

Lala entered her house and found her mother standing in the entryway, tapping her toe. Lala eased her mother's impatience by smiling.

"It went well, then?" Sarah asked as Lala hung up her coat.

"We didn't sell as much as we'd hoped, but enough to stay in business awhile without laying off any of our staff but myself. One more week and I'll have fulfilled my obligation to the factory." She heard an audible sigh, but couldn't tell if it came from her mother, or her.

"I'm glad you're home early. Paulina went to visit the Chytrys. She'll return tomorrow, so I'm fixing a special Sabbath dinner for the two of us to celebrate your good news."

"She didn't mention anything about going to Prague this morning."

"A last-minute decision, thanks to a deal I got at today's market. All they had left was a pork roast, so I traded half of it with Mrs. Havlik's daughter-in-law and gave the rest to Paulina."

"What did you trade for the pork?"

Her mother grinned. "A chicken. It's scrawny, but it will

be tender." She fetched a long, sharp knife from her chopping station.

An odd squawk came from outside, startling Lala. "What was that?"

"Our dinner."

Standing at her bedroom window, Lala felt her spirits rise as the sun dipped behind the bare treetops. The absence of daylight had worn her down this past winter, more so than ever before. Working long hours since November, she went weeks without seeing natural light. Although the days were still short compared to summer, dawn now greeted her when she awoke and the sun bade goodbye as she left the factory. On this cloudless mid-winter day, sunshine flooded the room. It felt warm compared to the parlor downstairs.

She heard squawking again and saw a white chicken run across the yard with her mother in pursuit. Lala almost laughed until the sun glinted off the knife her mother wielded. Her stomach clenched at the thought of what would happen when her mother caught that bird.

When she saw her mother walk back with the chicken under her arm, Lala opened the window and called out, "Mother, are we being shortsighted about this?"

Sarah looked up at her. "How so?"

"If we kill the chicken, we'll have dinner tonight. But if we keep her, she could provide eggs for us."

Sarah shook her head. "My family kept chickens when I was little. It's not so easy. We'd have to build a henhouse with a place to lay eggs, and buy feed until it can scrounge for food."

"I can do it. And if we can find more chickens, we'll have enough eggs to eat and perhaps to trade."

Sarah still looked hesitant. "Chickens attract rodents, and predators. We'll need to find your father's gun."

"We'll build the henhouse near the shed."

"Fine, we'll try it your way. I'll put this pischer back in the crate."

Lala closed the window and went downstairs. Her mother came in, beaming.

"Your plan is working already. Look what I found in the crate." She held up one egg. "Enough for stuffed potato dumplings. How does povidla knedliky sound?"

Lala's stomach rumbled. Her mother had taught her how to prepare the dumplings, though Lala hadn't mastered her mother's technique for making the dough sturdy enough to hold in the plum filling, yet delicate on the tongue. She'd offered to help, but Sarah felt Lala's time would be better spent drawing, so she shooed Lala off to the parlor. Lala spent a half hour practicing her figure drawing until the aroma wafting from the kitchen distracted her.

"Shall I set the table?" she called to her mother.

"Yes, dear. Dinner, such as it is, will be ready soon."

Despite the simple meal, Lala dressed the kitchen table as though for a feast, laying one of her mother's hand-embroidered cloths over the plankwood tabletop and selecting their finest crystal goblets. From the pantry, she fetched one of the bottles of Moravian wine that Paulina had brought with her when she moved in. In lieu of flowers, a crystal bowl holding two napkins folded to look like cabbage roses completed the arrangement.

"Those dumplings smell wonderful, Mother. I can hardly wait to enjoy them."

Lala hoped her comment pleased her mother. Still grieving the sudden loss of Jakob, Sarah became despondent whenever food prices skyrocketed. She worried constantly about providing good meals for her family, but a lack of provisions made it difficult, and rather than attribute it to the war, she blamed herself; she arrived at the market too late, or she didn't make a good enough deal with a neighbor. After years of being able to afford whatever foodstuffs could be bought and serving ample meat or fish every night, she found it difficult to adjust to wartime shopping. To keep her mother optimistic, Lala encouraged her to try meatless dishes. When Sarah did, they usually turned out well.

Lala smiled as her mother put the platter of dumplings on the table, and took her seat.

"Go ahead and eat, dear," her mother urged. "You've worked hard all day."

"I think you'd better take a few first, or else I'll eat them all."

Her mother suddenly grew stern. "That's enough."

"Why are you angry? I meant what I said."

"Don't think I don't know what you're doing. Please don't patronize me."

Lala slammed back against her chair. "Not you, too."

"Me too what?"

"I'm sorry, I shouldn't have said that. It was something that happened at work a few days ago. I don't want to bother you with all that nonsense."

"Why not? Your father used to talk to me about work all the time. He said it helped him. Maybe I can help you, too."

Her gaze fell. "I suppose you discuss this with Paulina."

"I do, sometimes."

Her mother forced a smile. "I'm glad you have someone to share your problems with, and being a business woman, she probably understands better than I can."

"In this case, it's not her business experience that has helped me as much as her, um, nature."

Sarah nodded thoughtfully. "You mean flirting with men. So, which one of you is doing the flirting, you or him?"

Lala laughed out of embarrassment. Her mother's insightfulness caught her by surprise. "It's not me. I don't even like him very much. He's immature, obnoxious, and constantly pestering me."

"It sounds like you're protesting a little too much. Do I know this person you say you don't like?"

"He's the man Father hired to take his place in the custom furniture department."

"Gershom Kindemann? I remember when your father told me about that poor lame boy. I thought he hired him out of pity, but the quality of his work convinced your father to offer him the position."

"You flatter him. His workmanship is not up to Father's levels, but he had the foresight to predict how to adapt to a war economy. Since he co-runs the factory with me in Josef's absence, we have to work closely together all the time."

Sarah refolded her napkin and placed it on the table. "I thought Josef split the factory duties between you and him."

"We still have to meet twice a day to review and share information. I told him today that I would be resigning next week and leave the day-to-day operations to him, but I said it in an insensitive way and offended him. When I tried to rephrase my comment, he accused me of patronizing him,

197

just as you did."

"What did you say?"

Lala repeated the conversation as she gathered the dishes.

Sarah filled the basin with water. "Sounds like a tempest in a teapot. He'll get over it."

"You think so?"

"Absolutely. He likes you and believes he has no chance to win your heart because you're engaged to his boss's son, so he can't do anything about it without risking his job. Take pity on the poor nebbish. Do a kindness for him." She washed a plate and handed it to Lala to dry.

"I won't have to, since I salvaged a production mistake he made, and I didn't chastise him for it, or for a bigger mistake of speaking out of turn." She told her mother about Kindemann's harangue about Armin three months earlier as she finished drying the dishes.

Her mother stacked the tableware in the cupboard. "Sorry dear, but you know most people feel that way. Especially men."

"Paulina said the same thing," Lala conceded. "Shall I make us some tea?"

"Not for me. There's very little sugar left and I'm saving it to make hamantaschen for dessert on Purim."

The traditional cookie, shaped like a three-cornered hat, was a favorite of Lala's. "Is Purim Monday?"

Her mother nodded.

"Good. I can avoid Gershom one more day." She caught her mother smiling. "What has you so happy?"

"I just had a wonderful idea."

"What is it?"

"No, dear, I want it to be a surprise," Sarah chuckled as she left the room.

CHAPTER EIGHT

Monday morning Lala awoke to the smell of cinnamon; her mother was baking. Paulina wasn't in the room. Lala lingered under the covers until the sound of hammering filtered in from outside. She put on her robe and went to the window.

Through the bare tree branches she saw Elia and Lew carrying a stack of wood boards from her father's shed to a makeshift work area outside where Kindemann sat, his back to her. A pair of sawhorses supported planks next to him, while the framework of a small enclosure rested against the south wall of the shed. Two rolls of fence wire leaned against the structure.

The men were building a chicken coop. Paulina must have asked them, but Lala guessed her mother had put Paulina up to it. She could tolerate the presence of a placid fellow like Lew, or Elia; he was quite charming and sweet. But the last thing Lala wanted to do was spend any more time than necessary with Kindemann.

Fuming, she dressed quickly and marched downstairs to confront her mother, intent on telling—no, insisting—that the men leave. That she could build the chicken coop on her own. That her mother had no right meddling in her life like that, bringing the work stress of the factory into her home, her sanctuary.

She heard the rat-a-tat-tat of Paulina's sewing machine coming from the former dining room. Paulina was piecing together a muslin sleeve with a puffed upper arm and tapered forearm. An unusual choice for a contemporary dress, but if anyone could incorporate traditional elements with modern, it was Paulina.

"Aren't you going to your house today?" Lala asked.

Paulina looked up. "They gave me the day off for Purim, so I decided to do some sewing instead. What do you think?"

"Very unique."

Outside the kitchen Lala could hear her mother singing for the first time since her father died. She entered as her mother removed a tray of poppy seed-filled hamantaschen from the oven, her face aglow in a way Lala hadn't seen in months. All of Lala's ire floated away like a twig on the river.

Sarah turned and beamed. "Good morning, dear. Look what I made for our Purim party tonight." She placed the tray on the counter and put a second batch into the oven. "Your friends at the factory were kind enough to bring extra flour, butter and sugar, so I baked plenty. We're going to celebrate together. That nice boy Elia will cook something called saffron risotto, and Paulina is sewing costumes for us all. She will be Queen Vashti, I'll be a kitchen maid and you get to be Queen Esther."

The purpose of the sleeve now made sense. "Did you tell Paulina that King Ahasueros has Vashti executed early on in the story?"

"I did, but she said she didn't care as long as she got to wear a pretty costume."

Lala snatched a cookie. "And I suppose Mr. Kindemann

200

will be the mighty Persian King who's captivated by Esther."

Sarah laughed. "He told me you'd probably prefer him as the wicked Haman."

Lala laughed as well. So, the man had a sense of humor.

Lala sorted through the day's mail. A letter from Aunt Naomi sat on top of the pile. She was about to open it when she noticed the envelope beneath, addressed to her and postmarked in Vienna. She caught her reflection in the entryway mirror, her cheeks flushed with excitement; it had been over a week since she'd received correspondence from Josef. Leaving the remaining mail on the bureau, she rushed upstairs to her bedroom, locked the door and tore open the envelope as she settled on her bed.

My Dear Lala,

Thank you for your recent letter. I'm pleased to hear how much progress you've made in the factory, and that life has not become too challenging. It appears you have ample food and supplies to last through the winter and early spring. I have great faith in our empire and her allies to bring this war to a victorious end.

Lala and Josef followed the Chytrys' tradition of beginning letters with propaganda to satisfy the censors who read the mail. They inserted coded messages to convey what they wanted to keep hidden. Ivo and Paulina openly expressed their love and passion and kept their political opinions private, while Josef and Lala had to maintain secrecy on both counts.

She noted "faith," one of their code words. Josef was not a devoutly religious man, so its usage in the letter implied the opposite—the war was not going well for the Triple Alliance and no end was in sight.

> My search for Armin's friend Karel has proved fruitless. There is no record of him traveling from Berlin by train, or on any ship registers in August. He hasn't enlisted, nor is he working with any agencies in Berlin. Unless he contacts us, we will not know where he is.

"Agencies" meant the War Ministry's propaganda arm. Germany had recruited artists to create war-themed postcards with patriotic images or humorous cartoons. It would have been a logical position for Armin.

So, Josef's search for his son proved fruitless, his whereabouts were still unknown. Armin hadn't switched identities with Karel. Lala's assumption, that he followed Karel to America using a false identity, now seemed credible. It would explain why he hadn't contacted anyone. She read on:

> I miss my home and family, and most of all walking along the Vltava in the spring, to hear the waters rushing along, to delight in the budding wildflowers along its banks, to see how the river sparkles in the sunlight. I yearn to lie beside it and enjoy its beauty, its freshness. I'd run my hand in the swollen water and imagine I could hold it back, and then laugh, for

I could no more restrain its surging than I would wish to do so. I long for the day when I can swim in its bracing water, but for now I must be content to remember how it felt to swirl my fingers and take pleasure in how it cascades.

Her breath became heavy and she laid her head back against the pillow, not wanting to swoon. Before Josef left, he'd told her that the river would be his code word for her. His words brought back memories of their last hour together, alone. She had seduced him and he'd introduced her to one of the pleasures of being a woman. That memory had kept her sane on more than one occasion.

Her mother's voice outside distracted Lala. She watched through the window as Sarah ushered Lew and Kindemann into the house to warm up. Lala folded the letter back into its envelope and stashed it in her jewelry box. She checked her appearance in the dressing table mirror and fixed the pillow knots in her hair before going downstairs.

Elia perched on a footstool in the sewing room, his arms sticking out from his sides, as Paulina fitted a sleeveless emerald and gold robe over his work clothes.

"Who are you to be, Elia?" asked Lala.

He adopted a noble stance, back straight, head high, and thrust out his chin. "I am the King, and a most fortunate king at that." He gestured to Paulina. "This lovely lady is my first wife, and you are my second." He laughed at that and shrugged. "I may not look royal, even in my fine robes, but this is what a king would do."

"I believe you, Elia," she said, and laughed with him.

"All done. You may get down now," Paulina told Elia before turning to Lala. "And your costume is almost ready,

Queen Esther." She made an exaggerated curtsey.

"Thank you, Queen Vashti," Lala said, curtseying as well. "And now I shall take my leave to help the kitchen maid prepare our feast."

At one end of the kitchen table, Lew and Kindemann sat with their hands wrapped around hot cups of tea as platters of her mother's hamantaschen cooled on the other end. Near the platters were some unusual ingredients, including an open sack of tiny white grains and a glass vial containing dark orange threads that emitted a potent, almost medicinal aroma through the cork stopper. A potato peel clung to the side of the chopping board. On the stove, a pot of milky water boiled as nugget sized pieces of potato bobbed on the surface.

"Mother, your potatoes are falling apart."

"Elia says that's what is needed."

As if on cue he entered the kitchen, bright threads clinging to his work clothes like jeweled lint. "Miss Hafstein, Mrs. Chytry needs you for your fitting."

Paulina had a clever idea to create the women's costumes in two simple parts, a frontless jacket and a full-skirted apron covering the bodice. Lala's tied at the waist, while Paulina's featured a high waistline set under her breasts and above her noticeable belly.

Lala stood next to the stool and put her hands on her shoulders as Paulina instructed.

Paulina draped the red and gold apron over Lala's dress. She tied it at the back of Lala's neck and wrapped it around her waist. "Mr. Kindemann made something called 'groggers.'"

"They're noisemakers. When we read the story of Esther, we make them rattle whenever the name of wicked Haman is mentioned," Elia said.

"That sounds like fun." Paulina slipped the jacket on next, tugging the sleeve into place.

"This is beautiful," observed Lala. Her friend had layered strips of red velvet interspersed with braided ribbon of gold foil....

"...*Look at me, dressed like a Queen, like Esther in the Bible....*"

The recollection of that fateful day in Russia came on so suddenly it made her dizzy. She grabbed Paulina's shoulder for balance.

"Are you all right?" asked Paulina as Lala stepped away.

"I got dizzy for a moment. I'm fine now." But the long-buried memory from childhood persisted.

On the table, next to the sewing machine, Lala spied a basket holding the groggers. Kindemann had constructed them from wood rods, with a tuber-shaped piece filled with pebbles extending from its side like a flag. It fastened on top with a rounded cap. When held by the rod and turned, the tuberous piece spun and clattered.

She picked one up and whirled it, watched it rotate round and round, listened to it rattle. She spun harder, forcing it to go faster, louder, not to drown out the name of Esther's nemesis, but her own—Cossacks, who destroyed her village and murdered her family. Images of that day swirled as rapidly as the grogger, of her innocently playing by the pond at the very moment—

The cap popped off, launching the pebble-filled vessel off the rod. It hit the edge of the table and smashed, spilling its contents over the floor. Ancient memories resurfaced and tumbled out, of Papa in the barn, showing Mama the latch he designed. Of him sitting on his rock, carving latches from morning to night.

Lala bent to pick up the pieces from the floor.

"Don't bother," said Paulina, "I'll fetch the broom and dust pan from the kitchen." She passed Kindemann as she left the room.

"I broke one of the groggers," Lala confessed to him. "I'm sorry."

"I thought that might happen so I made extra." He took the napkin from the grogger basket and held it by its corners, making a sling for the rubble. "You needn't apologize."

She stood with pebbles and broken bits of wood in her cupped hand and placed the debris in the napkin. "Yes, I must, not only for this, but for my part in making our situation at work so strained. I must seem ungrateful to you for all you've done, not only in the factory, but today. This celebration has cheered my mother, and I'm very thankful for that. And the chicken coop would never have been finished as quickly, or as sturdily, if I'd built it."

"It's my pleasure, for I don't know of a better way to honor the man who did so much for me than to help his family."

"We appreciate your efforts as well, Mr. Kindemann."

"Then will you please call me Gershom?"

She judged his request to be reasonable. "If you agree not at work unless we're in private conference, and then you may call me Lala."

"Again, it's my pleasure. So, I must ask—are you still exasperated with me, Lala?"

"No, nor should I be. Some of my vexation comes from events in my past that have nothing to do with you."

"What events?"

"Something I must learn to put behind me. So, I

apologize for my part in our professional difficulties."

"Are you telling me that I haven't been an annoying pest?"

Unable to refrain from grinning at that, she tilted her head side to side. "Let's put all that behind us and start anew. Shall we at least be friends?"

She offered to shake hands. He looked at her outstretched palm and hesitated. Lala wondered if she'd misread the situation. But as Paulina returned with a broom, he took her hand in his and said, "At least."

CHAPTER NINE

Lala was pleased with the chicken coop Gershom and his helpers completed shortly before sundown. After they washed up, she had them put on their costumes.

The men took turns reading the Book of Esther. Elia enlivened his passages with dramatic relish and even Lew broke away from his monotone to bring the story alive. When Elia read the section describing the King's proclamation for Vashti's execution, Paulina stood and play-acted a histrionic demise, collapsing into a salon chair, arms splayed, tongue hanging out, her rounded belly pushed upward. Gershom and Sarah giggled at Paulina's theatrics, but it upset Elia enough to cry out, "No, no, no! I change her fate to banishment."

Gershom prodded him. "That's not what happened, Elia."

"I know, but what can I do? I cannot bring myself to put this beautiful woman to death, especially in her condition. So, I make her go away until the child comes, and in the meantime, I find myself another beautiful woman to keep me company." He held up his index finger like a royal scepter. "This is what a king would do."

After the reading, they went into the kitchen. Lala brought out six place settings while Sarah set a second pot of water on the stove to boil for her cheese dumplings next to the simmering potato water. Paulina set the table while Lew gathered wine glasses for Gershom, who opened a bottle of German Riesling.

Elia poured himself a glass before taking his position at the stove while the three women crowded around him to observe how he prepared the risotto. Sarah helped by chopping onions and setting aside a good pinch of the orange spice to dissolve in a bowl with a spoonful of hot potato water.

"I share with you my Mama's secret," he explained as he swirled a knob of butter in a sauté pan. "Some add the saffron to the pot of potato water, but if you do not use it all, you waste it. So, she adds it with the third ladle of potato water."

"Why do you use potato water?" Paulina asked.

"The risotto is supposed to be creamy, so the starch in the potato makes it creamier."

When Elia announced, "Another fifteen minutes to finish," Sarah reached for her bowl with dumpling dough. "Then I'll put the syrove knedlíky in to cook." She rolled each spoonful of the dough into small balls and dropped them into the boiling water.

When the food was cooked, they crowded around the kitchen table, feasted on Elia's risotto and her mother's cheese dumplings, drank wine, laughed, and shared stories about their lives. Elia kept everyone amused with tales about his beloved Mama and his four older sisters living in the Jewish quarter of Venice. Lala learned that Lew's family lived next door to Gershom's in Warsaw and his mother made a similar cheese dumpling called kluski, though he declared Sarah's were more delicate. Lala surprised Elia when she mentioned the Canaletto painting in the Smetanas' parlor.

"Venice is the most beautiful city in the world," he decreed. Then his mouth flew open, he slapped his cheeks and cried, "*Ah, dimenticavo…*I forget to put the nuts and dried fruit in the risotto, to make it more like the Persians."

"I thought it was delicious as is." Sarah reached for the platter and added another spoonful of risotto to her plate. The others asked for more as well, in part to placate Elia. As he helped himself, Gershom reminded his cousin, "The great King Ahasueros doesn't make mistakes, Elia."

"Yes, you are right." Elia took another bite of his dish and raised his hand. "I declare this entire meal…*perfetto.*"

Moving to the parlor after dinner, Lew brought out a bottle of Goldwasser, a Polish herb liquor with flecks of gold in it. He poured some for the ladies before asking Gershom, "Want some?"

Gershom hesitated before answering, "Maybe a little."

"How little?"

Paulina blurted, "A thimbleful!" and began to giggle uncontrollably.

Between Paulina's laughter and Gershom's puzzled expression, Lala had to turn away for fear she'd begin laughing, too. Her mother finished her Goldwasser and said, "Enjoy your drinks while I clean the kitchen."

Elia leapt to his feet. "No, no, Mrs. Hafstein. You sit and enjoy. Lew and I will wash the dishes for you. It is our way to thank you for your most generous hospitality tonight."

Lew gave his friend a mystified look. Elia grabbed Lew by the arm and pulled him out of his seat. "Mrs. Hafstein, I miss my family so far away, but you make it feel like home here."

"How kind of you to say. Come visit anytime you feel homesick."

"Thank you. You remind me a little of my Mama, too, except you are much younger. My Mama, by now she must be over thirty."

At that, Lala and her mother joined Paulina in giggling until tears rolled from their eyes. Paulina tried to stand and couldn't make it out of her chair, so Sarah and Elia helped her up.

"What fun, but I drank too much tonight," she gasped through her laughter. "I had better get to my room now before I behave foolishly...foolisher; no, more foolishly."

Sarah took Paulina's arm. "And I'd better help you prepare for bed."

Still laughing, they bade everyone goodnight and went upstairs.

Lala was fighting back laughter, in part from the lively conversation, but she placed some of the blame on her potent nightcap. "Elia, if you and Lew truly want to wash up, I'll show you where we keep our supplies. Excuse us, Gershom."

She led the boys into the kitchen and handed them the appropriate dishrags and towels for washing dairy tableware. After putting the soiled tablecloth and napkins in the laundry basket, she returned to the parlor to find Gershom standing near the front door, staring at the bureau in the hallway.

"Are you leaving?" she asked.

"I was admiring your father's work."

"You knew it was one of his pieces."

"I'd recognize his masterful work anywhere. This bureau must have been made later in his career."

"How could you tell?"

"It has all of his signatures." He ran his fingers across the top. "He loved to work in satinwood and inlay with ebony. Notice how he rounded the edges along the top and side trim, how it softly curves? If you measure it, you'll find it to be exactly the same on every piece. He grew to like this proportion the best. May I open the drawer?"

When she assented he pulled it out, commenting, "See how smoothly it opens, without tugging or wobbling. That is the sign of expert craftsmanship. And look at the tongue and groove connections. Again, all perfectly measured, cut, and precise. This piece will outlast all of us."

She never doubted Gershom admired and respected her father, but the fondness he expressed touched her. Something they could share, a way toward détente. "I have something else to show you. Wait here."

She ran upstairs and fetched her jewelry box. After removing Josef's letters, she brought it down for him to see.

He studied it from all angles, including underneath where he could read the inscription her father had written.

She saw the admiration in his eyes and felt moved by it. "You may open it if you wish," she told him, but he shook his head.

"I don't need to see what's inside. No matter how many jewels it contains, nothing could be more precious than this."

And then he leaned toward her and kissed her, a slow lingering kiss that didn't flare her passion, but felt effortless, as comfortable as slipping into a well-worn shoe that fits every contour of the foot. It generated warmth rather than heat, and despite her surprise she did nothing to dissuade him, nor end the encounter. When it did, she attempted a neutral reaction, but his crestfallen look said she'd failed.

She rubbed her cheek.

"Trying to wipe me off?"

"Gershom, your beard tickled, that's all."

"I'd almost prefer that you'd have slapped me again."

"You caught me off-guard. What did you expect?"

"Something other than indifference. But I had to try, even though I knew a woman like you would never be interested in a man like myself." He turned to leave when she took his arm.

"Earlier, when you asked me about my past, I couldn't talk about it, but I will now."

She led him into the parlor and sat beside him on the sofa. "You remind me of a man I knew long ago; he, too, lost his leg. Not in childhood, but as a husband and father with a family to support. He almost died from his injury and it left him unable to pursue his work. So, he figured out a way to use his woodworking skills to make something that people needed and managed to support his wife and child for…his whole life."

"Who was he?"

A part of her wanted to confess, but she said, "It doesn't matter."

"Yes, it does."

"Why should it?"

"Because whoever he was, you loved him very much."

He was right. She became overwhelmed with emotion as memories of her dear Papa resurfaced. "I did, but he died when I was young. I hardly think about him anymore, but he's a part of me in ways I can't even explain."

"You don't give your heart easily."

"Only to three men in my life."

"And when you do, it's sincere," he acknowledged with

sadness in his eyes. "Mr. Smetana is a lucky man."

She knew he meant Armin, so she merely smiled.

"I won't bother you any more." He bowed and walked away from her.

CHAPTER TEN

Berthe stood by as Lala finished gathering folders, paperwork and receipts, ready to be filed away.

"There, I'm finally done," Lala exclaimed as she handed the stack to Berthe. "It's hard to believe how much we achieved in such a short time, but with everyone's help, the factory is now safe from closure."

"It couldn't have been done without you, Miss Hafstein," Berthe noted. "I speak for the entire staff when I say you have our gratitude. This town would be a sad place indeed if the factory had closed."

"How kind of you to say that, but you deserve much of the credit. I couldn't have accomplished half of what I did without your knowledge and assistance. Mr. Smetana has always held you in high esteem. In these three months, I've seen why."

Berthe looked close to tears, so Lala changed the subject. "Mr. Kindemann thought I should address the entire staff before I go, but I would prefer to do that one department at a time, with you beside me to signal continuity when I leave. In which department do you think I should begin?"

Without hesitation, Berthe said, "The design shop. It is where this all began for you, when your father ran the department. And this way Mr. Kindemann may choose to join you as you bid your farewells."

Lala had planned to go there last, but Berthe's point was well taken. As they made their way through the corridors, memories of the past few months flooded her thoughts. She would miss some of this, the sense of accomplishment, the hope she helped provide for the town as well as the wounded who would use the factory's new product line.

They approached the design room and Berthe stepped ahead to knock three times on the door before opening it. When Lala entered, each of the factory executives and foremen gathered before her applauded.

Caught by surprise, she cried, "Oh my, I never expected…thank you. Thank you all."

Elia pushed through the crowd and handed her a small plaque with a bouquet of flowers carved into it. The inscription below read: "To Miss Lala Hafstein, with our thanks The Staff of the Smetana Furniture Factory 1915."

She didn't expect to become emotional, but her eyes welled up and she couldn't find the words to respond. Fortunately, the continuing applause gave her a moment to compose herself.

"Speech, speech!" Elia shouted above the din.

Lala cleared her throat as the applause died away. "I'm flattered, but I couldn't have accomplished anything without each of you, your knowledge of the factory, your skill, and your hard work."

"Some harder than others," someone in the back shouted, which led to a few guffaws and even more shushing.

She continued, "We have security now that wartime production has begun, and we've set up plans to convert back to manufacturing furniture as soon as it's possible. Our product line has been successful, so we can look forward to staying in operation not only throughout the war, but long after it ends. I wish you all continued success, with full confidence that you will achieve it."

She gestured to the assemblage with a sweep of her hand. "So now, I shall leave you to your work, and I will return to my home knowing the factory will continue to prosper."

"You can't leave yet," she heard Gershom call out, followed by a loud pop. He emerged from the crowd holding a bottle of champagne, Elia and Lew behind him carrying trays of glasses. Gershom poured while Berthe distributed the champagne to the staff, beginning with Lala. When the entire staff had a glass, Gershom toasted, "We owe you a great debt for your tireless efforts despite many problems, both mechanical and mortal." He issued a sly grin at that as he raised his glass. "To our colleague, and our champion."

Cries of "Hear, Hear!" echoed through the room. She took a sip of champagne and walked through the crowd, greeting each foreman and executive by name and thanking them for their department's efforts. She ended her tour where it began, by Gershom's side.

"Whose idea was this send-off; yours, or Berthe's?" she asked.

"Modesty prevents me from revealing that," he said, and grinned.

She took notice of his multi-hued eyes, which had fascinated her when they first met. She stared at them for a moment too long, she decided, and looked away.

He took one sip of champagne before putting the glass down. "Aren't we being civil."

She laughed. "It's about time, don't you think?"

"I've always wanted to be friendly. You put me off."

"You acted like an annoying pest, Gershom."

"I suppose I did, but for a good reason. How else would I have burrowed into your thoughts?"

She crossed her arms. "Did it ever occur to you that being pleasant and easy going would have been more effective at winning my friendship?"

"Naturally, but I wasn't after your friendship."

"Gershom, you—" She became aware of the Smetanas' chauffeur standing behind her. She turned to greet him, but immediately noticed concern on his face.

"Miss Hafstein, forgive me for interrupting."

"Smolak, you're early. Is there a problem?"

"Yes, Miss. Trouble at the house."

"What sort of trouble?"

"Madame received a letter today from America. I believe it may be from young Mister Smetana, but the news made her very upset and I don't know what to do. Perhaps if you spoke with her…?"

"Yes, of course I'll go. Berthe, would you be kind enough to bring my things to the entrance. I'll meet you there."

"I shall, Miss."

She asked Smolak, "Did Mrs. Smetana say Armin was wounded, or ailing in any manner?"

"No, Miss."

"What a relief."

So, Armin finally wrote. If the letter came from America, he must have met up with Karel, as she assumed he would. Lala smiled inwardly, glad that Armin was safe and hopefully reunited with the man he loved. He deserved to be happy and free from the dangers of war. She stepped away from the others and beckoned Smolak over.

In a low voice she asked, "Has she been drinking?"

He didn't hesitate. "No more than usual, Miss."

"And when you say she's 'upset', is she crying and wringing her hands, or yelling and throwing things?"

"Both. It seems to change minute by minute."

The chauffeur escorted Lala from Gershom's department, past her father's inlaid desk and Armin's painting, askew once again. She tapped the frame to straighten it on their way out.

As they walked through the corridors she mentally prepared for her encounter with Romy. Lala wasn't surprised that Romy reacted to the letter with hysteria. The woman never approved of her son's relationship with Karel. Lala wondered if the news would lead to even heavier drinking, if that was possible. Perhaps her presence would calm Romy enough to see the bright side of this; Armin finally contacted his family and chose his mother above all others.

Berthe met them at the entrance, Lala's coat and purse in hand.

"Thank you Berthe."

"It was no trouble, Miss."

"No, thank you for all you've done for me during the past few months. And I will be sure to tell Mr. Smetana his trust in you was well-placed."

She gave Berthe a quick hug, which the woman accepted with grace, and was about to leave when Gershom called out, "Wait!"

He hurried to her side. "I didn't want you to leave without giving me a chance to say goodbye."

"Gershom, I'm not going far. Passover is a little over a week away and my mother has already invited you to lead the Seder."

"I also wanted to say…." He fell silent and offered a sheepish grin.

"What?"

"It sounds like you've received news from your fiancé. I'm happy for you. You deserve to be happy, more than anyone I know."

She almost felt like hugging him, but knew it wouldn't be proper under the circumstances. She took his hand in hers, as he had done on Purim, and said, "So do you, Gershom."

CHAPTER ELEVEN

The chauffeur drove faster than usual to the house, which Lala attributed to his wish for her to mediate the situation with "Madame." He brought the vehicle to an abrupt stop in the Smetana driveway. Too impatient to wait for his assistance, Lala exited the vehicle and rushed toward the wide-open front door to the mansion. From inside the house she could hear the echo of Romy's voice; it sounded angry. Why wasn't she **thrilled to have finally received a letter from Armin, and not as concerned with the motive behind it?** She had to be intoxicated.

Lala crept through the darkened grand hall, keeping watch for the irate woman whose shouts and cries seemed to move around the house, listening for warning sounds like objects being thrown or shattered. She looked over her shoulder toward the entrance, expecting to see Smolak approaching, but he was heading back to the car.

She followed him outside. "Aren't you coming with me?"

"I'm sorry, Miss, but Madame ordered me to fetch Mr. Handlanger."

The name sounded familiar. It took Lala a moment to place it. He had come to see Romy the last time Lala was there, though he never entered the house. The butler had given "Madame" a message from him...

Romy opened the note and read it, her face tightening with every line. "Tell him if the problem has returned, he must go back and finish it once and for all."

How strange that the cryptic message and Romy's odd reaction to it had slipped her mind. Then she remembered why: her father had died later that day.

Lala returned to the house. The Aubusson rug was missing from the grand hall, as were several paintings, including the Corot landscape. She flinched at the sound of glass breaking somewhere. Moments later a housemaid skittered toward the parlor, a broom and dust pan in hand, her heels clacking on the checkerboard marble floor. Lala followed her into the room.

Clutching an envelope and papers in her left hand, Romy paced back and forth like a caged beast, mumbling words of rage, her face a palette of negative emotions. What shocked Lala more was Romy's appearance. She still wore her bathrobe. Her hair hung down in feral strands and her waxen face lacked make-up, all made worse by the lighting. She'd strewn lampshades across the floor, and with the draperies closed, the naked bulbs of the lamps cast garish light throughout the room. Lala noticed all the family photographs were missing from their perch on the side table as well.

The maid tiptoed to the pile of shattered crystal and swept it up as Romy caught sight of Lala, giving the maid a chance to escape. Romy froze in place, but her nasty expression softened.

Lala took advantage of the calmer moment. "Hello Romy, I came as soon as I heard the news about the letter. How wonderful—"

Romy's anger resumed. "Wonderful? Do you know why

he wrote? He wants my money."

Lala smelled liquor on her breath. "I'm sure that's a small part of what he wrote to you. What else does he say? Where is he? What is he doing? Is he in good health?"

"Why should I care?"

"Romy, he's your son." Lala hoped her bluntness would pierce the alcohol haze that had fogged Romy's thinking, but she appeared even more shocked.

"How could you say such a thing about that, that animal, who wants nothing more than to devour my son and take my money!"

She was too drunk to make sense. "Let me see your letter from Armin."

Romy's head darted around at the sound of her son's name. "Armin? Did Armin write a letter? Where is it?"

"You're holding it. Would you please give it to me? I would like to read it for myself."

She looked at the papers in her hand. "You mean this? It isn't from Armin. It was sent here, addressed to Armin. From that beastly man in America." She pried the envelope from the papers and passed it to Lala. It was addressed to Armin Smetana at his parents' address. A U.S. stamp was affixed to the upper right corner of the envelope and its postmark read "New York City." The handwriting looked familiar, but the florid spiral on the A in Armin was unmistakable. Identical to letters she discovered secreted in a lockbox hidden in the Smetana garden last summer, sent from Berlin.

Letters written by the person whose name appeared in the return address: Karel Palaky.

Lala had presumed the men were finally together. If Karel was writing to Armin here, then not only was her assumption that Armin had joined him in America wrong, but it also meant that Karel didn't know of Armin's whereabouts, either.

Almost six months had passed without word from him, and now her last clue to locating him had fallen through.

Where on earth was Armin?

CHAPTER TWELVE

"Madame? Mr. Handlanger," the chauffeur announced before stepping aside.

A tall and brawny man lumbered into the parlor. Handlanger stood with shoulders hunched and gloved hands clenched into fists, as though ready to fight. His face bore the brunt of violence from his misshapen nose to the nasty scar that ran from his ear to his eyebrow. That welt was partly hidden by a weathered Homburg, its brim worn low enough to obscure his forehead. His eyes canvassed the room in a slow sweep, his expression cautious but unconcerned. If he was the thug Lala suspected him to be, he certainly looked the part.

His gaze stopped at her. Lala bit her lip. "Who's she?"

"Someone you can trust," said Romy. "My son's fiancée."

His smirk exuded disbelief. He turned to Romy. "What do you want this time?"

She poked her finger in the air toward him. "I want you to finish the job I gave you."

"I thought our business was done. So, unless you want to pay me more money, you had better tell me why you summoned me here."

"You failed in your assignment. I paid you a large sum of

money to warn Mr. Palaky off."

"I did, good and hard. Broke his arm, a couple of ribs, even broke his tiny little nose. It wasn't tiny anymore after I warned him off, I can tell you." He chuckled.

Lala choked back a gasp, but Romy didn't even blink. Lala recalled the photograph of Karel, battered and bandaged, leaving Berlin. So, it wasn't "patriotic fervor" that caused Karel's injuries.

Something Romy had told her began to make sense…

"He hates me." A bitter smile slashed across Romy's face as she stared off into the distance. "He does now. He hates me for everything I've done, but I was only trying to protect him. He's still a boy in many ways. He doesn't understand what it means to be a man, a real man." She downed her drink. *"He had to go away."*

"No Romy, he chose to volunteer for service, to fight in the war, remember?"

Romy looked blankly at Lala. "I made him go away, and now he hates me."

She'd misinterpreted what Romy had meant. It wasn't Armin whom she made "go away." She wanted Karel out of Armin's life, which was why Romy believed Armin hated her and refused to correspond. Lala couldn't blame him, if it was true.

Romy began pacing again. "But he didn't leave, did he?" Handlanger shrugged it off. "I told you he came back, but I returned and warned him off again, as you ordered."

"Once and for all." Romy nodded. "And you say you did, good and hard."

"Very good. And much harder. Like I said, his tiny little nose wasn't tiny anymore when I went back. The animal was thinner too, after the pounding I gave him."

"Unfortunately, it was neither good nor hard enough. Did

you threaten him as to what would happen if he reappeared in my family's life again?"

He raised a fisted hand and rubbed it with the other. "More than threatened."

Lala stiffened as a chill ran down her back. What had Romy tried to do?

"Then why is this man writing to me now, from America?"

He looked puzzled. "That can't be. I did what you told me."

"How seriously did you threaten him?"

The room felt colder when he answered, "All the way to the bottom of Lake Wannsee."

Lala raised her hand to her mouth. When she pulled it away, she saw blood; she'd bitten through her lip.

The implication of his answer seemed to elude Romy. She threw the letter at Handlanger. "Then how do you explain this? It arrived from New York earlier today, written by the man you say has been at the bottom of Lake Wannsee for months. How does a dead man write a letter?"

Lala felt her knees buckle. She grabbed a chair back and took deep breaths to remain standing, but a sense of foreboding crept through her. Karel had two brothers. "Mr. Handlanger, how did you identify the man you say is, or was, Karel Palaky?"

"I went to his apartment on Monbijoustrasse and asked for him."

"When was that?"

"The first time, on August first. Easy day to remember now."

Germany had declared war on France that evening. It was also the opening reception for Armin's art exhibit, which finally explained Karel's absence that night. Lala continued, "And what about the second time, when Mrs. Smetana sent you back. She instructed you to 'finish it once and for all' on September fourteenth."

"How would you know that?" Romy asked.

"It was the same day my father died." She turned to Handlanger. "Easy day to remember. When did you confront Mr. Palaky the second time?"

"The following evening, so the fifteenth of September."

"And you recognized Mr. Palaky that night?"

"His face looked different, though like I said, you would expect that after my first visit. But I asked if he was Mr. Palaky and he said yes."

"Mr. Palaky," Lala repeated. "And how did he react when he saw you standing in his doorway a second time?"

Handlanger hesitated. "He let me in."

"But wouldn't he have recognized you?" Lala asked him. "Shown fear after the thorough thrashing you gave him back in August?" Her voice grew louder.

He tugged the brim of his hat down further. "Maybe he didn't remember me."

Lala glared at him. "Maybe it wasn't Karel Palaky!"

Romy shouted back, "We all know that now. What we don't know is who Mr. Handlanger encountered."

"He said he was Mr. Palaky. I found him ready to leave and almost let him go until I saw his train ticket. He meant to come here."

"To my house?" Romy asked.

"Why else would he travel to this town?"

"He wanted money," Romy said. "But why would someone pretend to be him?"

Lala couldn't breathe as pieces of the puzzle swirled

through her mind...

"... *Your son never enlisted in any army, Mr. Smetana...on the same night you say he enlisted, he boarded a westbound train...badly injured...."*

"*That's not possible.*" Josef sprang forward. "*My son wasn't hurt the night he left. Are you sure you have the right person?*"

"*See for yourself.*" Jezek opened his briefcase and removed a photograph, which he laid on the table for them to see. "*Is that your son, or isn't it?*"

The acrid odor of smelling salts brought Lala back to consciousness. She found herself lying on the floor and tried to get up, but Romy stopped her.

"Stay down for now, dear. You fainted." To Mr. Handlanger she said, "All this talk is upsetting her."

"Then send her home."

"No, I will not leave! I'm disgusted by what you tried to do, Romy, but now I'm more frightened of what you may have done."

"Don't concern yourself with it, my dear. Even if Mr. Handlanger didn't take care of that pansy, I'm sure that whoever was there that night was an animal like Palaky."

Lala got up from the floor. "Romy, your son is no different than Karel Palaky."

"How dare you say that!" she snarled. "That animal led him astray."

"No, you're wrong. In fact, when Armin and I announced our engagement, Karel left Armin and went to Berlin to give him a chance to make a life with me, but it was Armin who ran back to Karel the first chance he could. They were in love and nothing was going to change that. That's why Armin—oh dear God, what have you done?"

"Go home, Lala. Leave this to Mr. Handlanger and me to sort out."

"Romy, you didn't know, did you?" Lala began to tremble.

"Know what?"

"Armin never entered military service."

"Of course he did. The night of our last dinner in Berlin, he told us he'd enlisted in the military, don't you remember?"

"But he didn't. He must have found out about Karel's beating before the dinner and decided to protect him."

Romy shook her head. "What are you going on about?"

"Armin gave Karel his medical deferment. The War Office has a record of Armin Smetana leaving Berlin for Spain and sailing to America, but the photograph is of Karel Palaky. If Karel took Armin's identity...."

She felt faint again and grabbed hold of the sofa arm to steady herself. "Romy, do you have a recent photograph of Armin?"

"There's one in the brochure from his gallery opening. It must be here somewhere." She searched through bureau drawers and tabletops until she found it.

Lala took the brochure from her and opened it to the page with Armin's photo. She handed it to Handlanger and asked, "Have you ever seen this man before?"

As soon as he looked at the picture, Lala knew the answer. The man lying at the bottom of Lake Wannsee, a mere twenty-five kilometers southwest of Berlin, was Armin Smetana.

CHAPTER THIRTEEN

Lala heard the screech of automobile brakes outside. She rushed to the parlor entrance. Through the open front door, she saw three uniformed men exit a police vehicle and hurry toward the house. Handlanger grabbed a chair, bashed it twice against the window, and leapt through to the terrace in back. Two of the policemen gave chase as Handlanger tried to flee. Lala stood aside as Smolak escorted a middle-aged police officer with heavy jowls and a bulbous nose, dressed in the uniform of a sergeant, into the parlor.

"What is all this?" cried Romy.

"Madame, when I overheard the conversation earlier," Smolak said, "I took the liberty of calling the police to come arrest Mr. Handlanger."

One of the policemen entered the parlor and gave a hand signal to the sergeant.

He nodded. "They have him in custody now." He turned to Smolak. "Very clever of you to disable your vehicle so he couldn't escape in it."

"Thank you, sir. If you will excuse me, I must replace the parts I removed."

Romy threw up her hands. "Will someone please tell me what is going on?"

The officer introduced himself as Sergeant Novotny. "Mrs. Smetana, what can you tell me about this man who has committed murder."

Sergeant Novotny's questioning of her began with gentle prodding, but gradually turned more pointed as it became obvious that she had been involved in the death of the victim. She became irritated, but showed no remorse.

"We are getting nowhere here, Mrs. Smetana. I want you to come down to the station—"

"It's all a mistake, Sergeant," Romy stated, waving her hand. "I thought Mr. Handlanger killed someone named Karel Palaky, but the man is still alive."

"I don't believe that to be the case. After your chauffeur called our department, I contacted Berlin *Landespolizei*. They'd found the body of a man by that name floating in Lake Wannsee months ago."

She scowled. "That's impossible. Mr. Palaky just wrote me from America."

"Let me see that." He read through the letter. "Judging by the date, the victim couldn't have written this letter. Are you sure this was written by Mr. Palaky?"

"Yes, Sergeant," Lala volunteered. "I recognize the handwriting."

"Then if Mr. Palaky is alive, do you know whose body was dumped into the lake?"

"I think I do," Lala blurted. "I believe it may be Mrs. Smetana's son, Armin. When the war began the two men exchanged identities. Mr. Handlanger thought Armin was Karel and…."

She couldn't bring herself to say Armin had been murdered, likely beaten to death and sent to the bottom of a lake, or possibly thrown in alive and drowned. Lala began to weep, softly at first, but soon in streams. She cried out, wounded by anger, savaged by pain—someone she loved was murdered because of hatred, like her Russian family. Another man dear to her had been taken away. The thought sickened her, but not as much as the reason behind it—Romy wanted to control his life. Deny him what he wanted most. And now she'd destroyed what she wanted most. Her son, alive and well.

The Sergeant helped her to a seat. She looked to Romy for an explanation, but the woman gazed back with a puzzled expression and asked her, "Why are you crying?"

Lala couldn't contain herself anymore. "Don't you understand? The man you had Mr. Handlanger kill was Armin. Your son, Romy. It was Armin."

"No, it couldn't be. I wouldn't hurt my boy." She shook her head. "No, not Armin."

Smolak brought one of the policemen into the room. The officer took Novotny aside and handed him the gallery brochure as he whispered. The Sergeant listened and nodded, casting a glance at Lala momentarily. The policeman left and Novotny returned to Mrs. Smetana.

"Mr. Handlanger confessed to killing a man he believed at the time was Karel Palaky, on your orders. He indicated that you paid him a sum of money to commit the act. Is that true?"

Romy pursed her lips and said nothing.

"He also said that the man he killed was not Karel Palaky, but was the man whose picture is in this brochure."

The finality of that statement brought about a fresh round of tears to Lala's eyes, but Romy waved the brochure in her hand. "No, no, the photograph I showed him was of my son, Armin." She turned to the page with Armin's photograph and pointed to it.

"Yes, Mrs. Smetana. That is a picture of the man who Mr. Handlanger said he killed at your behest."

The reality finally pierced Romy's haze of alcohol and denial. Her eyes registered silent terror before she covered her face and shrieked. Part of Lala wanted to go to her, but she couldn't bring herself to comfort the woman, to forgive her for what she'd tried to do, and especially for what she'd done.

Romy bolted from the parlor. Lala followed after her, Novotny steps behind, as she ran up the stairs. Romy fled into Armin's bedroom and locked it. Lala pounded on the door, shouting, "Romy, open the door. Open the door!"

Novotny called for the other officers to come upstairs.

Together they pushed against the door, but it didn't budge.

"The chauffeur seems to be in charge here. Ask him if there's another key. If not, find something to break down the door," Novotny instructed one officer.

"Yes, *Wachtmeister* Novotny." The officer went downstairs and returned with a ring of keys. Novotny tried them all, but none worked on the lock. Another officer found a fireplace poker and a large fire log in an adjacent bedroom. Together the three policemen pried the lock and battered the door until it smashed open.

The two junior officers rushed into the room. Sergeant Novotny held Lala back until the officers stopped at the rear of the bedroom and indicated it was safe to enter. Lala followed Novotny in. They found Romy lying on the floor, curled up in a ball, catatonic.

"No sense bringing her to the station in this state."

Novotny asked one officer to fetch a doctor, the other to stand watch outside her room.

He asked Lala, "Is there anyone we should contact?"

"Yes, in Vienna. Armin's father, Josef Smetana."

Josef. For months, she'd longed to see him, to have him return home. Now he would, under unspeakably tragic circumstances. She could not imagine how he could survive such heartbreaking news.

But she knew how.

After all Josef had done to educate her, as a girl growing up, as a young lady wanting to study art. As a woman in love. Now there was something she could teach him.

How to endure the sorrow brought about by hatred.

CHAPTER FOURTEEN

Lala awoke with a start; she'd fallen asleep on the settee in the Smetana's parlor, fully dressed except for her shoes, which she vaguely remembered taking off last night. The draperies had been drawn and the door closed, so she had no idea what time it was, or if anyone knew she was here. Someone must, though. A blanket had been laid over her.

Remembering how much shattered glass there'd been on the floor, she put her shoes on before getting up to open the draperies. Unfortunately, she picked the window that Mr. Handlanger had broken last night. Cold air invaded the room, so she pulled the brocade lengths closed and left the parlor.

The sound of running water guided her to the far end of the house. She traced it to the kitchen, where Mrs. Havlik was wiping the table. Of similar height and build to Lala's mother, the woman's downturned eyes, which always conveyed a sense of sadness, today looked reddened and grieved.

She stopped when Lala entered. "Good morning, Miss Hafstein. I took the liberty of sending a message to your mother last night. She returned with Mr. Smolak to bring you home, but as you had already fallen asleep she said to leave you be. I put her in a guest room."

"Thank you, Mrs. Havlik. Is my mother awake?"

"Yes, Miss. I made her breakfast. Would you like some?"

"No thank you, though I'd be grateful for some coffee."

Mrs. Havlik poured a cup for her in the Smetanas' finest Bavarian china. Lala heard a clock chime the eight o'clock hour.

Out of habit, Lala sat at the table. She noticed Mrs. Havlik seemed uncomfortable, likely because in this house only servants ate in the kitchen.

"I can take my coffee in the breakfast room if you wish, Mrs. Havlik."

"No, Miss. I…." She bowed her head. "I wanted to express my condolences to you, about young Mr. Smetana. He was such a fine young man. There is so much tragedy nowadays."

Lala swallowed hard. "Thank you, I couldn't agree more." She heard activity upstairs.

"An ambulance will be arriving any minute to take Madame to Bohnice Hospital in Prague. Your mother has graciously offered to accompany her, along with the police."

"What sort of hospital is it?" asked Lala.

Mrs. Havlik paused before answering, "The sort that can treat Madame."

An asylum. "Did the police authorize this?"

"No, Miss. They sent word to Vienna. After the authorities there notified Mr. Smetana, he made the decision as a way to avoid something more…scandalous."

Prison.

Lala heard the crunch of gravel as the ambulance rounded the driveway and parked. She hurried to the grand hall as Smolak opened the front door for the two attendants who carried a stretcher. How many had she seen come off the assembly line at the factory?

The attendants went upstairs and came down soon after carrying Romy, who lay silent and unmoving, her eyes half opened, her mouth slack. Lala wondered if strapping Romy down was a precaution or a necessity. Two police officers followed the attendants down the curved staircase and Lala's mother trailed behind.

Sarah rushed to her daughter and embraced her in silence.

Lala began crying again. "Why are you going with Romy? She doesn't deserve it."

"I'm not doing it for her, but for Josef. He shouldn't have to see her now, while he's grieving for his son. Josef did so much for us when your father died, and long before that. This is one way to repay him."

"May I come too?"

"No, go home, get some sleep," her mother urged. "Have Paulina stay with you, and I will return as soon as I can."

"But I want to do something to help him."

Sarah patted Lala's hand. "Then stay here, show the housekeepers how to prepare the house for shiva tonight. You know how to do that now."

As her mother left, Sergeant Novotny entered, studying the pad he used to jot notes. He approached her.

"Miss Hafstein, I'm checking into something Mr. Handlanger told us. Perhaps you can help."

"I'll try, Sergeant."

"I understand you were going to marry Armin Smetana."

Lala did not want to lie. "We were betrothed."

"But he hadn't contacted you or his family since Berlin." He studied his notes again. "And you're sure your father passed away on September fourteenth of last year?"

"I wouldn't forget that."

"Mr. Handlanger said the man he murdered had a train

ticket to come here. He saw it as an act of defiance, which led to his, shall we say, actions that resulted in Mr. Smetana's demise. Do you think he might have planned to come here for your father's funeral?"

Lala's knees locked. Could she be the reason why Armin was killed?

CHAPTER FIFTEEN

Lala asked Galina, the last housemaid left in the Smetana's employ, to please stay until they finished preparing the mansion for Josef's arrival as well as for shiva. As they went from room to room, the house looked bereft, as if it mourned the loss of its family—one dead, one gone mad, one grief-stricken. A feeling of emptiness came over Lala. It went beyond the tragedy. Some of the furnishings were missing and many fine works of art had been replaced with inferior pieces.

"Galina, do you know what happened to the Aubusson rug that was in the grand foyer?"

"No, Miss. I came to work one morning and it was gone."

She would ask Smolak about it.

Lala found out Romy and Josef each had their own bedroom ever since Armin was little when the maid casually mentioned it, as if it was perfectly normal for a married couple to live such separate lives. Somehow it tempered Lala's guilt to discover the Smetanas' separation began years before she and Josef initiated their romance.

As they replenished the rooms with fresh bedding and towels, Lala recalled how her mother, who for years expected her daughter would marry Armin, had prodded her to learn how to manage a household with servants. Despite outwardly rejecting her mother's assumption, she must have absorbed her instructions, for they came instinctively to her now.

After covering the mirrors throughout the house, Lala asked Mrs. Havlik to prepare several platters of food for Josef's arrival as well as any family, friends, or employees who might come to pay their respects. How many was uncertain. After almost seven months of battle, few families hadn't been at least touched, if not devastated, by loss. The death of a son ceased to be unique, even though the circumstances were. Once again, her mother's advice rang in her ears—they'll come for the food.

"Miss," Galina said, "I've prepared Mr. Smetana's bedroom for his arrival, as well as three of the guest rooms." Lala thanked Galina and gave her the rest of the afternoon off before returning to the parlor to wait. Wait for Josef to return.

A crystal tumbler on the credenza caught her eye, tempting her to pour herself a cognac, but she could not bring herself to drink in this house. It wouldn't ease her sadness, merely mask it, and after witnessing how that affected Romy, she dismissed the idea.

Would Romy have done what she did if it hadn't been for the alcohol? What irked most was that Lala believed the answer was "yes." Romy might have been more cognizant of her actions, but she wouldn't have regretted them, not without knowing that her victim wasn't Karel, or one of his affairs, but Armin.

Armin. Part of her still couldn't believe what had happened, that he was gone forever. Learning that he was about to return home on the day of her father's funeral made the death more personal, more painful, if that were possible.

After all that had occurred between them—their misguided attempt to marry, his deliberate withholding of his nature, his deception about entering the military, and his silence until his demise—he still cared enough to risk everything to be with her as she mourned. The notion grieved her, but it couldn't stir up tears. Why? Had she become hardened to death?

She heard a car in the driveway and her heart began to race. Despite the circumstances, she longed to see Josef even though she would have to submerge all affection and tenderness beyond daughterly. She became flustered, wondering what to do; should she sit on the settee and wait for them to enter, or meet them at the door? Fetch one of the trays of food Mrs. Havlik had prepared? She spent a moment rearranging the vases and statuettes she'd placed on the bare tables in place of the lamps Romy had damaged, then made haste to the grand hall.

The door partially opened and her mother entered, carrying a small satchel. She opened the door wider to reveal Smolak with a large trunk in each hand. He set them down on the floor and turned to the doorway, offering his arm. Moments later, a stooped figure tentatively stepped across the threshold, head lowered, shoulders slumped. Josef, a broken man detached from his surroundings. She wanted to run to him, embrace him, but he looked so fragile she feared he might crack into a thousand pieces, falling and scattering across the floor to be swept up like the broken glass in the parlor. She bit her lip and waited.

"May I take your coat and hat, sir?" Smolak asked. Without responding Josef removed his hat. Streaks of white radiated from his temples, and much more gray threaded through his once dark hair. When he took off his coat, Josef's body appeared even leaner than before.

It pained her to see him like that, but more so to know that she could do nothing to ease his suffering. No one could.

"Shall I have Mrs. Havlik prepare some food for you, Josef," Sarah asked.

He shook his head.

"I understand how you feel right now, but you must eat something," Sarah prodded.

"Please, Josef," said Lala.

Josef turned to her and for an instant their eyes met before he looked away. Lala felt sickened. She didn't see love, or longing, or passion in his eyes. There was no sadness. Just pain. Sheer, intense pain at the sight of her, so unbearable he had to turn away. She fled to the kitchen before her emotions could betray her, and sat at the table and cried.

Her mother entered and placed a hand on her shoulder. "Don't take it personally, dear. He still thinks of you as Armin's fiancée. Seeing you reminded him of what he lost, and what he believes you lost as well."

Her mother believed that, but Lala knew it couldn't be true.

"Where is he now?"

"The chauffeur put him to bed. He should rest until dinner."

Smolak provided Sarah with contact information for Josef's family, which consisted of two distant cousins who lost interest once they learned there would be no financial benefit, and Armin's friends. Most of them were away fighting except for Zigmund, who'd moved away and left no forwarding address. Lala wrote to Karel using the Smetanas' stationery and sent it to the New York address printed on his letter.

Lala asked Smolak about the missing rug. He tactfully implied Romy traded some of the furnishings and artwork for cognac, which could only be obtained on the black market due to the war, and some went to pay Handlanger in addition to cash.

"The police have inventoried Mr. Handlanger's apartment and will provide a copy to Mr. Smetana. He should be able to reclaim his property."

"Somehow, I doubt Mr. Smetana will want anything connected with his son's murder, no matter how valuable," said Sarah. She glanced at the clock. "Smolak, would you kindly check on Mr. Smetana? Perhaps you can suggest he join us for a light supper in an hour."

He nodded and left.

"Lala, will you see that the table is set while I speak with Mrs. Havlik?"

Lala decided the dining room felt too elegant and cold. An informal supper in the breakfast room would be preferable, especially after she lit a fire in the fireplace. She laid a pale blue cloth on the table and set it with porcelain dishes without gilded borders, paired with the plainest silverware she could find. Flowers seemed unfitting, so she asked Mrs. Havlik to bring some fruit from storage, which Lala placed in a bowl hand-painted with folk art. She set Josef's place at the head of the table, her mother to his left and she to his right, leaving the seat opposite him empty.

As soon as she finished setting the table she began to second-guess herself. Should he face an empty chair? Would it be better if he faced her? Her mother? She switched the place settings around several times, agonizing over what would be best. She decided to leave both ends of the table empty, and have Josef sit on one side facing Lala and her mother. Once she adjusted the settings, doubts arose once more.

"Pardon me, Miss." Smolak stood in the doorway. "Mr. Smetana has asked me to extend his regrets, but he is very tired and not feeling up to dining downstairs tonight. He will take his supper in his room."

"Thank you, Smolak. Please notify Mrs. Havlik."

"I already have, Miss. Mr. Smetana also wanted me to ask you and your mother if you would consider spending the night. Your mother has agreed. She believes it would not be advisable to leave him alone in the house tonight."

"I will stay as well."

"Very good, Miss. I will inform Mr. Smetana immediately."

Josef wanted her to stay overnight. Her reunion with him would be a late-night rendezvous. She could not take away his grief, but she could offer him comfort and ease his sorrow as he had done for her when her father died. In her loving embrace, soothed by her nearness. Remind him that despite everything, he was still alive.

CHAPTER SIXTEEN

Unable to sleep, Lala lay in the guestroom bed, her eyes focused on the door, her ears listening for footsteps in the hallway. She glanced away to the window, searching for where moonlight fell to guess the hour. It had to be past midnight.

Was Josef unable to sleep as well? Was he tossing in bed, longing to bury some of his grief in her embrace? Seek consolation in her arms? Despite his earlier demeanor, she believed he needed comforting as much as she wanted to provide that comfort. That soon she would hear his footsteps approaching, see him open the door and walk into her room. She would hold him as he cried for Armin, or raged against Romy's evil plot. She would offer him whatever he wanted, for she loved him that much. If he desired her, she was willing to give herself fully to him, if it would help ease his pain, provide solace from the nightmare that his life had become. She knew all too well how sudden, overwhelming tragedy could deplete the soul and how tenderness could ease it for a few precious moments.

Waves of expectation and nervousness kept her awake, wondering what Josef would do, and when.

She became aware of a rhythmic sound cutting through

the darkness and sat up to pinpoint what it was—the ticking of a mantle clock perched above the marble fireplace. The fire hadn't been lit and the room felt cold. She arose and went to check the time. Nearly two-thirty. Lala went to the door and listened for activity, but heard only ticking and her heart pounding. She opened the door to the dimly lit hallway and peered out. No one stirred. She shivered as the chill penetrated through her thin nightdress and found a shawl to wrap around her shoulders.

How broken Josef appeared when he arrived home. So weakened by sorrow. How could he manage to leave his bed? She left her room and tiptoed down the hallway to the last door, Josef's bedroom. With a cautionary glance over her shoulder, she turned the knob bit by bit until the door yielded. She paused to catch her breath, then entered his room.

It took a moment for her vision to readjust to the dark. Moonlight streamed into the room and fell across his bed. She allowed her eyes to rove over his form beneath the plush covers, from his legs up to his face. He didn't look peaceful, which upset her. She knelt by the bed, wondering how he'd react when he realized she was beside him.

Josef began to stir, murmuring little cries of grief. Lala reached up to stroke his cheek. He flailed and then opened his eyes.

"Josef," she whispered. "I'm with you."

He scrambled to the other side of his bed and leapt out. "No, Lala, you mustn't be here."

"It's all right. No one saw me come in."

But he looked frantic. "You have to leave at once."

She stood, confused by his reaction. "But why? I can't bear to see you suffering—"

"Lala, everything has changed. We cannot be together."

"Don't say that."

He threw his robe on and wrapped it around his body. "This has to end now."

"Because of Romy? You can't possibly remain married to the woman who murdered your son."

"I have no choice. Whether she is declared insane or tried for murder, I cannot divorce her because neither insanity nor imprisonment is legal grounds. And where would that leave us? My physical absence is the only reason our relationship has yet to be consummated. Were you planning on becoming my mistress? Because I will not allow that."

"But Josef, I love you and I know you love me."

"That cannot matter anymore. Do you know what people call a woman who becomes the mistress of a man in my circumstance? Horrible names that would not only ruin your reputation, but also the good name of your family. I cannot take that risk, no matter what our feelings may be. Now please leave me and go back to your room." He paused. "You must not think of me in that way anymore"

She stood by the side of his bed. "So, I don't have a say in this?"

"No, because you do not know what will happen, but I do." His voice turned gentle. "I can't allow you to give up a chance at happiness for me. You'd eventually hate me for ruining your life."

"I could never hate you, and I don't know how to stop loving you."

"In time you will. You'll meet someone else and feel that sense of joy with him. You'll marry and raise a family, live the happy life you deserve." He gestured to the door. "The last thing I ever wanted to do was hurt you, but this is how it

251

must be." He looked away.

Had she heard him? His voice had sounded muffled and far off, or was it a vibration echoing in her ears that filtered out his words? And was she still standing on solid ground? Was she still standing? Too stunned to cry, she remained in place, unable to accept what he'd said, shutting herself down, wanting to close her heart to protect herself from pain. She felt like a child again. Back then her Uncle Hershel had told her, *"No matter how much it may hurt when you love, when you cannot love, it hurts more."* Now it sounded like platitudes to bolster a fragile child's spirit. *"No matter..."* It hurt either way.

She tried to turn away with dignity, but her legs betrayed her. Trembling, she shuffled to the door and left the room, clutching her shawl, but she couldn't feel anything, not the chill in the hallway, or the sorrow over Armin's death, or the pain of losing the only man she ever loved. All she felt was adrift... *"Like a petal in the wind."*

As she closed Josef's door, Lala heard a gasp and looked up. Standing in the hallway, glaring at her in shock, was her mother.

CHAPTER SEVENTEEN

Lala almost walked out when she entered the breakfast room at eight o'clock and saw her mother already seated at the table, drinking coffee.

"Come in, Lala. Sit down," her mother said in a clipped voice layered with frost.

Mrs. Havlik had her coffee poured before she sat.

Lala had spent a restless night wondering which was going to be worse, living without Josef, or living with her mother. She knew her mother would hold her tongue until they returned home, but as much as she dreaded the wrath she'd face later, her mother's coolness set her teeth on edge. Dread built up inside her, alongside overwhelming sorrow.

Mrs. Havlik set a plate with a boiled egg and toast before Sarah. "May I make you the same, Miss Hafstein?"

"Yes, thank you."

"A sensible decision," said her mother without looking up from her plate.

After breakfast, Lala and Sarah helped Galina close up

the extra bedrooms. Sarah had brought a mourning candle, which she placed on the parlor mantle. Galina fetched a box of matches from the outer hearth and withdrew a match.

"Here, I'll do it," Lala volunteered as she reached out for the match, but her mother interceded.

"No, that's not something you should be doing for Mr. Smetana. Galina, light the wick and let it burn continuously until sundown on Friday night, when the Sabbath begins."

Lala took a deep breath to suppress her growing ire. "Then what should I do, Mother?"

Sarah surveyed the room. She turned to Lala and in a tepid tone said, "Why don't you remove the cushions from the settee so Mr. Smetana can sit there to mourn."

Lala did as her mother asked.

They returned to their rooms to pack. It was close to noon when they finished so they accepted Mrs. Havlik's invitation to stay for lunch before Smolak drove them home. Neither spoke more than a few words to each other.

When Smolak dropped them, Sarah and Lala entered the house and hung up their coats. As soon as she saw that Paulina wasn't there, Lala exploded.

"No one's here, so go ahead, shout at me, tell me how wicked I am. I don't care anymore."

Sarah momentarily recoiled at Lala's outburst. "I have no intention of yelling at you. Yes, seeing you leave Josef's room shocked me. It was such a foolish thing to do. But you're so clever, I tend to forget you're still young and naïve. I'm sure your heart was in the right place, but nothing you can say will bring comfort to a man who's lost a child. I watched my mother go through that agony when my sister died and believe me, it's not the same as losing a father. Why would you think I would call you wicked for that?"

"Coming out of a man's bedroom in the middle of the night?"

Her mother waved her hand at the notion. "Don't be silly, Lala. I know you had no untoward intentions with Josef, and I doubt he would be so vulgar as to try and seduce you. Why, the man could be your—"

"Don't you dare say that!" Lala cried.

"Why are you getting so upset?" Her mother seemed puzzled. "Fortunately, no one else saw you entering or leaving. I presume Josef was asleep, or he would have sent you away."

"He did!" She burst into tears.

Sarah reached out to her. "Lala, what happened in there?"

Between sobs she bawled, "Nothing. Absolutely nothing." She bolted from the room and ran outside.

Sarah followed her. "Lala, what on earth…? Get in the house, you'll freeze to death out here."

"I don't care. He broke my heart." Her sobbing grew louder. "What's wrong with me? All the men I've ever loved have been taken away from me, and now this. I should have never opened my heart."

"Lala!"

Her mother's voice trailed behind her as she fled the front yard to the road. She kept running, past the meadow that filled with wildflowers every spring to the unpaved stretch that cut through a forested area, where she stopped to catch her breath. In all the years she'd lived here, she'd never entered the woods. It reminded her of the forest in Russia, where she'd wandered for days after the pogrom, frightened

255

and alone. Where her parents had dug a ceremonial grave for her Mama and Papa. Where she'd left the little orphan girl Luska behind and become Lala.

Wrapping her scarf around her shoulders for warmth, she took a few tentative steps into the wooded area. Still winded, her breath came out in frosty puffs. Her feet sank into the mulch-layered ground as she trod deeper into the forest, her senses alert to danger. Birds rooting for food rustled the dead leaves, intruding on the silence. She caught movement out of the corner of her eye; turning, she watched a hare scoot away. Above she could glimpse an overcast sky through the bare tree limbs. With each step, her apprehension eased and her long held fear of the woods dissipated. It was, she decided, a calming place, the isolation comforting. Peaceful.

After walking about twenty meters she spied a rock large enough to sit upon. She bent over to run her hand across the surface, which triggered a memory of how her Papa used to sit on a rock much like it to carve. How uncomplicated her life seemed back then, living in the shtetl.

Lala sprang up as the sound of gunshots in the distance echoed through the forest. She ran back to the road and followed it home, where she promptly locked the door. She allowed her mother to think she was brooding, so Sarah left her alone while she sat by the window looking out, watching the daylight fade as memories of past and present horrors invaded her thoughts.

Hours must have ticked by when Lala heard the doorknob turn, followed by knocking.

"Why is the door locked?" Paulina called through the

door. Lala let her in. Paulina threw her arms around Lala and hugged her tightly.

"Oh, my dear, my dear, what heartbreaking news. I am so sorry for your loss. I wish I could have been with you yesterday, but I'm here now." She released Lala and stroked her cheek.

"I'm all right. It's Josef who's shattered."

"I can't imagine how awful this must be for him. Armin didn't deserve his fate, no matter what."

"No, he didn't. Neither did Josef."

"He's devastated, no doubt. To learn your only child was murdered is horrific enough, but the circumstances? I can't imagine he'll ever speak to Romy again."

Lala told her of Romy's fate. "No punishment can ever be enough for what's she's done."

"She'll sober up, and when she does she'll have to live with that knowledge every day of her life. As for Josef, they say time heals all wounds, and he'll have you."

Lala's eyes filled with tears. "He doesn't want me."

Paulina clasped Lala's shoulder. "What happened, my friend?"

Lala took a breath and calmed down enough to tell her. "All I wanted was to hold him, comfort him."

"I'm sure he wanted that as well, but he couldn't risk hurting you."

"Oh yes, tossing me aside without regard to my feelings is far less hurtful."

Paulina looked profoundly sad. "Lala, when did you become so cynical?"

"When he ended our romance. I suppose it's a blessing, really. If I don't care it won't hurt as much."

Paulina shook her head. "You truly don't understand, do

you?"

"What's to understand? I lost my oldest friend and the love of my life in one day."

"And he lost his only child at the bidding of his son's mother. He had to leave his factory to others while he wasted time in some absurd organization that's of no benefit to anyone. All he had left was you, but still he let you go so you wouldn't be sullied by the tragic muddle of his life. And do you know why? Because he loves you. Don't you remember the gossip that followed me for merely flirting? Imagine what would have happened if you became known as his mistress. Josef is right. You cannot be together."

She hadn't thought she could shed another tear, but they flowed relentlessly. "Oh Paulina, why did you have to say that? It only makes me love him more."

CHAPTER EIGHTEEN

Lala dreamed of her eleventh birthday, the day Armin had clipped the bud of her romantic interest in him when she saw his naked drawings of a manservant. She hadn't understood what it meant at the time, but their conversation moments before, long forgotten, played in her dream…

"Here is my birthday present for you."

She opened it to find a portrait of her painted in oils and set in a gilt frame.

"Oh, Armin, it's magnificent. When did you start painting?"

"A few months ago. I am glad you like it."

"I like everything you do," she gushed.

"You have always thought I was grand. I told Father that. He said you were my muse."

"What is that?"

"Someone who inspires you."

"Inspires?"

"Makes me a better artist, or want to be one." She beamed. "Do I do that?"

Would she ever inspire anyone that way again?

***

259

She had dressed for work before remembering she wasn't working anymore. A part of her rued her decision to leave the factory. It would have taken her away from the house, and her mother's hovering, for the day. No matter. Unlike the factory, her home didn't carry constant reminders of Josef. She would make herself useful to her family, provide for them any way she could, as she had vowed after her father died. At the time, everyone believed the war would end in a few months, but she intended to keep her vow.

She opened the walnut dowry chest at the foot of her bed to check her nest egg, the money she'd saved during her employment at the factory. A stack of Josef's letters tied together with red ribbon sat on top, tempting her like a mythical siren. The words that filled every page had excited her more with each successive reading. Her hands trembled as she lifted the stack and brought them to her lips. A trace of his signature scent lingered on the paper. She inhaled it deeply and with a kiss, buried them at the bottom of the chest before her resolve weakened.

Underneath the linen tablecloth her mother had embroidered for Lala's engagement lay the satin drawstring bag she sought. She emptied its contents onto her bed and counted it twice. After stowing the money away, she went to her writing desk and made some calculations. Less than a quarter of her salary had been needed to supplement Paulina's earnings. Her calculations showed that if inflation didn't go beyond twenty percent, she'd saved enough for the three of them to survive through spring. By then Paulina would have had her baby and could help out again. By then the war could be over.

She went downstairs, prepared to meet her mother, but instead found Paulina at her sewing machine. "What a nice surprise. I didn't expect to see you until dinner," Lala said.

"I'll be here all day, working on my layette." Paulina held up an undershirt that nearly fit in the palm of her hand.

Lala smiled at the sight. All those tiny undershirts, day and night caps, and gowns her friend had created lifted her spirits. Paulina's baby was due in two months, and the reality had become tangible now that preparations were underway.

Paulina put the folded undershirt in a basket at her feet. "Your mother will be caring for our boarding house until I've given birth. She thinks it's too much work for me and feels my time would be better spent here, helping you and preparing for the baby. She's convinced Mr. Kindemann and the other gentlemen that she can cook for them as well as keep house."

"Then I will take over maintaining this house. I'd appreciate some guidance, though." Lala glanced around. "What would you suggest I do first?"

"Change your clothes, my friend. If you're going to clean, cook, feed the chickens and chop wood, you don't want to wear such a fine outfit."

As Lala scrubbed the kitchen floor on her hands and knees, she couldn't help but observe how different this was going to be from working in the factory. It had been, she decided, a more interesting life than housework. She had to laugh when she remembered telling her mother last year that she might not want servants when she married.

Leaving the kitchen floor to dry, she put on her coat and went outside to feed the two chickens; her mother had traded some of Jakob's winter clothing for a second pullet. Lala entered the coop, blanketed with a thick layer of straw, wood chips and dried leaves, and peered at the hens nestled on their roosts inside the henhouse. She used a pitchfork to turn the mulch before filling the feed and water dishes. That mulch, combined with chicken droppings, would be invaluable in the vegetable garden this spring.

Next Lala chopped wood until the cold penetrated her hands and she couldn't hold the axe safely. She stacked the split logs in two neat piles before returning to the house for a cup of tea to warm her sore hands, then went to the root pantry for onions and potatoes. After a half hour of peeling and chopping, sautéing in butter and simmering in water, she filled a bowl for Paulina and took a ladle for herself before calling her friend into the kitchen for lunch.

Paulina must have been famished, for she ate so heartily she didn't notice that Lala ate very little. "That was really delicious," Paulina exclaimed as she finished her bowl.

Gratified, Lala said, "Don't sound so surprised." She whisked the dishes away to wash. Standing at the washbasin, a sensation ran over her, of hands caressing her body. She closed her eyes and took deep breaths, waiting for the phantom feeling to pass. She had been through so much hardship and heartache in her life; she would not allow this to conquer her.

Twilight had begun when Lala finished sorting the laundry. She arched her back, sore from bending and scrubbing, chopping and carrying. Three months of working in the factory left her ill-prepared for this level of physical labor. Perhaps a soak in the tub later would help, unless her mother had the same idea.

"Lala, you must be exhausted," Paulina called from the parlor. "I'll make dinner tonight."

"Fine, but let me help," Lala said as she returned to the workroom.

Paulina covered her sewing machine. "You could set the table," she suggested as she packed up her fabric scraps.

"Meat or dairy tonight?" Lala asked.

The front door opened and her mother entered carrying a covered bowl. "Hello, girls. I made a big pot of soup today and brought some back for us."

Paulina beamed. "Perfect timing, Mama Sarah. We were about to start dinner."

"What are we having?" asked Lala.

"Potato and onion soup."

Lala hoped her forced smile looked more genuine than Paulina's. She set the table while her mother warmed the soup. As Lala passed behind her, Sarah reached out and took her hand.

"You look worn down, dear."

Lala shrugged. "I'm not used to physical labor. I'll adjust."

"I know you will. It takes time, but it will get easier."

"Are we still talking about housework?"

Sarah stirred the soup pot. "You tell me."

Paulina called from the parlor, "Mama Sarah, Smolak is here to see you and Lala."

Sarah took off her apron and went to the front door, with Lala following behind.

"Hello Smolak. What brings you here at dinnertime? I trust it's nothing serious."

"Good evening, Mrs. Hafstein. Please forgive me for interrupting your meal, but Mr. Smetana wanted to know if you had another mourners candle."

"I'm sure I do," her mother responded. "Did something happen to the other one I brought? If the flame went out, it's perfectly all right to relight it."

"No, Ma'am. He asked me to tell you that he's decided to light two candles."

Sarah's brow furrowed. Then she must have understood what Smolak meant, for she put her hand to her mouth and nodded. "I'll get you another." She asked Paulina to bring one from the pantry.

Paulina brought the thick candle to Sarah, who gave it to Smolak. "Please tell Mr. Smetana that we will come tomorrow morning at ten o'clock to pay our respects."

"Allow me to bring the automobile for you." He thanked her and bid them all good night.

Her mother closed the door with an audible sigh.

"Why do you think Josef wanted two yahrzeit candles, Mother?"

"He's going to sit shiva for Romy as well as Armin."

"Oh my, does that mean she's dead?" Paulina asked.

Sarah looked grim. "She is to Josef."

CHAPTER NINETEEN

Lala awoke suddenly. Had she heard something outside? She saw nothing except for a light dusting of snow on the outer windowsill. It was early morning, still dark, but dawn hinted. Not wishing to disturb Paulina she dressed downstairs. Enough embers still burned in the fireplace for her to relight the fire by adding several small pieces of wood. Once they caught, she positioned the last two logs in the house on top of the flames before putting on her coat to check the henhouse. Twilight had lightened the sky as snowflakes continued to fall. A coat of snow covered the ground, but the gentle snowfall did not threaten to accumulate much depth.

She checked the brown speckled hen's nest for eggs and found none, but had better luck with the white hen, a single egg. "Good girl. Perhaps you can teach your friend how to lay." She gave the mulch a few tosses with the pitchfork and used the handle end to break through the veneer of ice covering the hens' water dish. "I'll return soon with warm water and more food."

Shivering, she nestled the egg in her pocket, closed the henhouse behind her, and walked toward the woodpile. Halfway there she stopped. Before her, barely visible in the

265

dim light, she saw a trail of prints in the snow…human footsteps, too big for her, or her mother, or Paulina. Judging by the snowfall, they were relatively fresh. They seemed to go in the direction of the woods. She followed the tracks back to the woodpile. Yesterday she had cut enough wood to stack two sections over half a meter high each. Now one section dipped below a quarter meter. She guessed four split logs had been taken, too heavy for her to carry. But a man could.

She brushed away cobwebs as she entered the shed. Many of her father's tools were stored there, along with gardening implements and supplies. A film of dust covered his bare workbench. A hatchet for chopping wood and a saw for cutting limbs rested against a shelf with a sharpening stone to hone the blades. She didn't see the rifle he'd inherited from his father, waiting for the hunting trip he never took. Lala welled up as she recalled how every spring and fall he would sit outside and tell her stories about his boyhood as he cleaned the weapon.

She rummaged through a few shelves and drawers until she found the embossed leather box she sought. Inside laid her father's six shot Reichsrevolver, an old military sidearm that he'd bought after moving into the house. He'd used it only once, to dispatch an injured animal. Lala closed the box, slipped it under her coat and returned to the house. Lights glowed on the upper floor. She would decide what to do with the gun later. Right now she had to figure out how to feed three people with one egg.

Sarah poured coffee for Paulina, who had taken her seat at the table, and then for herself as she glanced at the pan

Lala was removing from the stove. "What's this?" asked her mother.

"It's called 'pain perdu'," Lala said as she plated breakfast for three. "I soaked some stale bread in milk mixed with an egg and fried it in butter. Try it with some jam spread on top."

"It sounds delicious. Where did you learn about this?"

Josef had told her about having enjoyed the dish in Paris, how the French had a knack for taking simple ingredients and turning them into something marvelous. She remembered thinking that someday the two of them might go there, the most romantic city in the world.

Lala swallowed hard. "I had it once at the factory." She divided her portion between Paulina and her mother. "I'm not hungry this morning."

Sarah slid her portion onto Paulina's plate. "Paulina, after you've eaten, would you mind washing up?"

"Not at all," she answered with a faint smile that said otherwise.

"Lala, let's go upstairs," her mother said.

Lala had known this moment would arrive, when her mother would confront her for being in Josef's bedroom. They left the kitchen and went upstairs.

"Please sit," her mother instructed as they entered Lala's room, so Lala perched on the edge of her bed. She wondered if her mother would be angry, or upset, if she'd shout, or cry.

"You need to change your outfit."

Lala looked down at the dark blue dress she had on. "Why? It's simple, muted, suitable for a shiva call."

"I've seen you wear it to the Smetanas before."

"I doubt anyone will notice."

"Is it a favorite of Josef's? Because if it is, you should not wear it."

The dress wasn't but the color was. She searched for a hint of where this conversation was heading, but her mother's stoicism gave nothing away. "Mother, you have yet to say a word about what you think you saw that night, or what I told you the next day. How much longer are you going to make me wait for the lecture?"

She thought her comment might bait her mother into finally scolding her, but instead Sarah sat beside her on the bed and patted her hand. "I know you are grieving for Armin, though not in the way others will assume you are. Guests will think you're grieving for your beloved fiancé, just as they'll think Josef is grieving for Romy as well as Armin."

The unexpected gentleness of her mother's tone confused Lala.

"But now I know you're mourning another loss and from what you've told me, Josef may be as well," Sarah continued. "That makes this shiva call very complicated. There's a part of me that doesn't want you to go, but unfortunately you must make an appearance. If you didn't, you would come off poorly, as if your loss was greater than his father's."

Sarah began to pace. "I want to help you, but I don't know how without knowing more. Will you tell me what happened between you two?"

"It began in Berlin. I became frightened at the sight of violence. He tried to comfort me and it led to a kiss."

"Just a kiss?"

Lala, unwilling to lie but unsure of what to reveal, hesitated before answering. "I did not want to find myself in Paulina's situation, if that's what you're asking."

"Did you accept the position at the factory with the idea

of being close to him?"

"No, quite the opposite. I wanted to avoid being near him as much as possible to prevent any unsuitable behavior. That became easier when he was sent to Vienna."

Sarah stopped pacing. "Are you sure what you feel for him is love?"

"Perhaps you don't understand."

"You forget that I'm not a stranger to that emotion."

"I'm so sorry, Mother. Of course you understand." She took a calming breath. "Yes, I did...do love him. How do I stop?"

"You don't, any more than I have stopped loving your father. You just put it in its place. Do you remember when you were a little girl, I told you to keep a place in your heart for your Mama and Papa? This is the same thing. You learned how to love from them, and when you lost them, you took that knowledge and learned how to love your father and me. You'll do the same thing one day, with another man."

"Then what do I do now?"

Sarah sat beside Lala. "Hold on to that feeling, dear. Don't ever forget it. You're still young. You have a chance to recapture it with someone else. It might not be the same, but it can be as exhilarating and joyous in its own way. I know you better than anyone. You tend to close your heart when you're in pain. Don't. I know it's hard, but be patient. You will be rewarded."

Sarah went to Lala's closet and opened it. "Now let's find something else for you to wear."

CHAPTER TWENTY

Smolak drove Lala, her mother and Paulina to the mansion. Mrs. Havlik greeted them at the front door. "Please come in."

"May we help you with the guests?" asked Sarah.

Smolak signaled an elderly footman to take the ladies' coats, which the man whisked away with quiet efficiency. "How kind, Mrs. Hafstein. Fortunately, several of the dismissed staff returned to work." Smolak glanced across the room at two maids as they replenished food and drink on a table that had been brought into the hall. He took Lala and Sarah aside. "The police will keep the circumstances of young Mr. Smetana's death private. The announcement states that he was murdered months ago and his body was recently identified. The shock of her son's death sent Mrs. Smetana into catatonia, which is why she has been institutionalized."

"We won't say a word," Sarah assured him.

When Smolak excused himself, Lala leaned in close to her mother's ear. "So, no one will know that Romy was responsible for Armin's death. She'll have everyone's pity."

"Don't be harsh, dear. It's to protect Josef, not Romy." To Paulina she said, "Come, let's get you something to eat."

Lala heard someone call her and turned to see a teary

eyed Berthe clutching a handkerchief.

"Miss Hafstein, no words could ever express how saddened I was to hear the news. Poor Mr. Smetana. What a terrible loss. And my deepest sympathies to you, Miss."

"Thank you, Berthe. It's good to see you again, despite the circumstances."

"I must return to the factory. Again, my condolences."

Lala recognized most of the guests who milled around the grand hall, people she'd worked with for the past few months. She chatted with many of them briefly and thanked them for their condolences to her. The tone was hushed despite the number of visitors. She ruefully acknowledged that having paid their respects to her family after her father's death, the factory workers were more familiar with the Jewish custom.

She heard *Kaddish*, the mourners' prayer, being recited in the parlor; words that stirred sorrowful memories for her. She approached the room and peered in. Ten men stood in a circle, prayer shawls draped across their shoulders, bowing back and forth as they prayed. The room had been restored to its former appearance except for the settee without its cushions.

She spotted Josef among the praying men. He looked thinner, but wasn't as stooped as he had been the day he returned home. The lapel of his jacket had been torn on the left side, over his heart, and he wore no shoes, as was traditional for a man in mourning. Upon the mantle, two candles burned side by side. One for a dead son, one for the woman who was now dead to her husband. Lala returned to the grand hall before he could see her.

Paulina approached, carrying a plate filled with food. "What a feast. Mr. Smetana must expect a lot more guests."

Sarah joined them. "Mrs. Havlik cleared out the pantry for this. Once Josef leaves, the house will be closed up until he can return. Mrs. Havlik will take on the responsibilities of housekeeper as well as cook for the remaining staff, and Smolak will be promoted to house steward once a replacement driver is found."

"Hello, Lala," a soft voice called from behind her. She turned to see who here would address her by her given name.

Gershom stood before her wearing the same ill-fitting suit he wore when he paid a condolence call to her family. One lapel lay askew. He greeted her mother and Paulina, then returned his attention to her.

"I want to express my deepest sympathies." He shook his head. "Such a tragic loss. I never met Armin but I know how much you loved him. If there is anything I can do to offer you comfort—I cannot imagine how you must feel, but I'm keeping you and your family in my prayers and thoughts."

"Thank you, Gershom. That's very kind of you."

"It's not kindness. It saddens me to think of you grieving once again. So much suffering in someone so underserving of it." He patted her hand. "We will talk again when the time is right, but please call on me if you need anything, a shoulder to cry on, a sympathetic ear. Anything."

"I will, Gershom." She reached over and smoothed the lapel of his suit with her hand.

At her touch, he gazed at her with a tenderness she'd never seen from him. For a moment, she was lost in his eyes, drawing her in with their beautiful colors.

He raised her hand toward his lips, then with a subtle bow, walked away.

Gershom's sudden charm caught Lala by surprise.

Paulina approached and broke her reverie.

"I trust he didn't say anything upsetting."

"Not at all. He offered his condolences. Actually, he was quite considerate. Why would you think he would say something that would upset me?"

Paulina hesitated. She drew Lala aside where they could talk privately. "I overheard him tell his roommates that once the mourning period ends, he intends to court you. I thought he might have grown impatient and asked you now."

Lala chuckled. "He doesn't know that the death of my 'fiancé' won't change my feelings toward him."

"Perhaps not, but other factors might."

"Such as?"

"You're unencumbered now. So is he. And he is very fond of you. I don't doubt that he has an immature side, which caused his silly behavior toward you, but he's not like that with others. And I suspect from what you've told me he's learned his lesson. Take some time to grieve your loss. Then why not allow him the chance to court you?"

Sarah joined them. "The men have finished Kaddish. We'll pay our respects to Josef and then leave."

CHAPTER TWENTY-ONE

Sarah had readied the boarding house for Passover a few days early, which allowed her to get a head start on preparing the special dishes to be served at the two Seders. It had fallen to Lala to prepare their home for the holiday. With Paulina's help, they'd begun cleaning on Wednesday, dusting, sweeping, and washing every surface and corner.

"What do we do when it's finished?" asked Paulina.

"We make sure no forbidden food contaminates the area. Certain foods, called chametz, cannot be eaten during Passover. Every speck must be removed from the house before the holiday begins."

"Chametz?"

"It's leavening, or any food that leavens or swells, like bread, noodles, pastry and beans."

Thursday had been dedicated to cleaning the kitchen and searching for chametz, which Lala put aside on one shelf.

"There's not much left," she observed. "We can finish most of it before the holiday, but once Sabbath begins we won't be able to have it in the kitchen until Passover ends."

"Then where will we eat during Sabbath?" Paulina asked.

"If it's not too cold, outside. Otherwise we could put a bench in the hallway outside the kitchen."

"What fun. It will be like picnicking. But what about Friday?"

"It would be simpler to have everything ready a day earlier, so we can relax on the Sabbath. I'll ask Mother if we may. If so, we'll pack up the dishes and kitchen utensils before sundown and replace them with our Passover sets. Then whatever crumbs are left must be burned."

"So, everything will be fresh and new, like spring."

Lala had been concerned that the strict rules of living in a kosher home would frustrate Paulina, but her friend seemed more fascinated by the rituals than put off. She hoped that would continue once the baby came.

"Paulina, your cheerfulness is just the tonic I need."

"It's good to see you smile again." She patted Lala's cheek. "Doing things differently seems to be an important part of Passover. Shall we move my sewing machine and your art equipment to the kitchen for the holiday? Then we could eat our meals in the dining room."

"That's a marvelous idea. We'll all be more comfortable in there."

The tradition for the Hafsteins and the Smetanas had been to celebrate together at the mansion on the first night and for each family to hold their own Seder the second night. Lala had thought Gershom and his roommates would need to take their meals with her family. Her mother revealed that Josef had kindly supplied the men with Passover kitchenware and dishes. He had accepted an invitation to stay at the home of a Jewish art dealer in Vienna during Passover. Lala was glad he had somewhere else to spend the holiday. To her mind, sitting in the Smetana dining room, haunted by memories of the past, would be as distressing as dining in a graveyard.

Lala and Paulina finished the last of the bread and some of Sarah's cherry preserves for breakfast on Friday. Lala carefully gathered all the crumbs in a rag when one corner flopped over. The contents spilled on the floor.

"Oh dear, I'll have to clean this again." As she fetched the broom and dustpan, she heard a knock at the door. "Would you see who that is, Paulina?"

Lala swept the crumbs up into the dustpan and emptied it into some old newspaper. She heard two sets of footsteps approaching.

"Please bring it into the kitchen," Paulina said as Smolak entered. He unloaded a huge basket filled with carp and pike fish, several ducks, beetroot, horseradish, a dozen potatoes, onions, nuts, and dried fruit. After emptying the basket, he took it back to the automobile and returned with two bottles of red wine and a cloth bag containing matzo that Josef ordered every year from Prague.

"Mr. Smetana asked me to bring this to you for your Seder, Miss."

"How generous. Please thank him for us."

"At what time should I bring him tomorrow?"

"Bring him? Here?" She turned to Paulina, who looked as surprised as she.

"Yes, Miss. Your mother invited Mr. Smetana to join you tomorrow night before he returns to Vienna on Sunday."

Why would her mother do that? Didn't she realize how

difficult it would be? Then she remembered her vow to teach him how to bear the sorrow brought about by hatred. She could endure this act of kindness for one evening.

"Tell him to be here an hour before sundown."

CHAPTER TWENTY-TWO

Lala stared at the bare dining table, flooded by memories. She'd stacked Passover dishes on the hand-carved sideboard made by her father, ready to be set as soon as she chose a tablecloth. This would be the first time her father wouldn't be reading the Haggadah, recounting the story of the Exodus. And being the youngest, Elia would read the Four Questions, not her, as she had since childhood. She reflected on the first question: Why is this night different from all other nights....

"...everything will be fresh and new...."

She went to her room. There she removed her engagement ring, given to her by Armin, worn to symbolize her future, not with him, but with his father. After stowing it in her jewelry box, an impulse seized her. She opened her dowry chest, searching for a relic from her past, hidden inside a tablecloth. The yellow crystal goblet she'd rescued from her shtetl. It still felt heavy in her hands, still glowed in the lamplight...

...like sunshine in summer. "It's pretty, Papa."

He kissed the top of her head. "You should have pretty things, my little Lala, more than your poor Papa can give you. But someday you will."

She replaced it with care. It had served as a beacon when

she was a child in Russia. She wished it could guide her through this different night.

An hour later she opened the front door to allow a procession of food and guests into the house. Her mother, followed by Elia, Lew and Gershom, carried platters, pots, baskets and bowls of food to the kitchen.

Her mother immediately took charge. "The pot of soup goes on the stove. Put the roasted ducks and potato kugel nearby to keep them warm until we eat. Lala, where is the Seder plate?"

"On the kitchen table."

"Did you remember everything?"

"I have the roasted shank bone, the egg, horseradish, and slices of potato to dip in salt water. Then there's the three matzos wrapped in a napkin on a separate plate. All I need is the charoses."

"It's in this basket." Sarah removed a bowl with finely chopped apples and walnuts, honey, cinnamon, and wine mixed together to resemble mortar. "I may have put too much wine in it."

"No one will object, Mrs. Hafstein," said Elia with a toothy smile as he uncovered a deep iron pan filled with shredded potatoes, onions and eggs. "Your kugel smells wonderful. My mama makes it every year with rice."

"We don't eat rice at Passover."

"Yes," Elia noted. "No rice, but you eat dairy and chocolate and we do not. No matter, we happy to be here, celebrate together like Purim. Thank you for inviting us."

Sarah smiled as she spooned the charoses onto the Seder

plate. "You and your friends are always welcome, especially when you do the dishes."

"Mother, don't make them think they have to clean up."

"I'm not," her mother said, "but if they offer, I won't say no." She handed the Seder and matzo plates to Lala. "Please put these on the dining room table for me, dear."

Lala passed Gershom in the parlor as he added a log to the fireplace. She laid the ceremonial plates on the table and joined him in the parlor. "Are you cold, Gershom?"

"No, but I thought I'd get the fire going now so you don't have to fuss with it once the Seder begins." He stood with some difficulty. Lala tended to forget about his missing limb. She had become accustomed to his limp and never thought about the underlying reason.

He gazed at her with concern. "You've been crying." He reached into his breast pocket and offered her his handkerchief.

"I'm fine, Gershom. It's from grating horseradish. We must have our bitter herbs."

"I wish you could be spared from bitterness. You've had your share."

"That's kind of you to say." She hesitated. "I should finish setting the table."

"It looks beautiful. So do you."

She fell silent.

Gershom turned toward the front door at the sound of an automobile in the driveway. "Are you expecting other guests tonight?"

"My mother invited Mr. Smetana." Lala opened the door to find Josef, his arm raised, about to knock. An image flickered in her mind of him standing in her doorway, posed the same way, when they arrived home from Berlin last

August. How flustered he had become by the sight of her. How aroused she'd felt by his presence. She willed the image to go away, but it refused.

She stepped back to let him in.

Josef proffered a basket filled with crocuses and primroses. "I brought these for you, for your home."

She took the flowers. "They'll make a lovely centerpiece. Thank you."

Sarah came out of the kitchen to greet him. "Welcome, Josef. We're so glad you could join us." As she took his overcoat and hat she noticed the basket in Lala's hands. Her brow knit.

Lala held them away from her body. "Mr. Smetana was thoughtful enough to bring flowers for the table."

Her mother's brow relaxed and she invited Josef into the parlor.

He put on his silver embroidered yarmulke and followed Sarah into the room. As he entered he took notice of a drawing of Lala on the wall, one Armin had made when they were teenagers. Armin had posed her kneeling in his family's rose garden on a misty April afternoon. Her face appeared to float above a tangle of bare thorny branches. The way Josef stared at it made Lala wonder if he was thinking about his son, or her.

His gaze floated through the room. "You've changed the furniture."

Sarah nodded. "Lala's idea. She switched a few pieces around to make our home more comfortable for three women. She's so talented that way...." She flushed. "Josef, I've set a place in the kitchen for Smolak, if you'd like for him to stay."

"How kind of you, Sarah. I'll let him know."

Josef went to the car and returned with Smolak. Sarah showed him into the kitchen and invited everyone else to the table. "Josef, would you do us the honor of leading the Seder?"

Lala kept her attention on her Haggadah and the words recited throughout the Seder. She drank wine and ate the ceremonial foods with the others. Gershom and his companions acted subdued, which Lala attributed in part to the presence of Josef, their employer, but the silence felt more acute. The war, the absence of family members, and the recent tragedies all contributed to the somber mood. She looked toward Paulina to make sure her friend seemed comfortable with the unfamiliar rituals and foods. Paulina sat quietly and partook when everyone else did.

Lala's occasional glance in Josef's direction revealed a man, once confident and assured, who now seemed uncomfortable in his own skin. Her heart went out to him. For all his authority and accomplishments, he lacked her fortitude.

How markedly different he seemed from Gershom. Gershom's solicitousness toward her did not go unnoticed. He seemed to anticipate her every need, whether it was to refill her wine glass or help her read a Hebrew passage.

When the readings were done, the dinner commenced. Courtesies were exchanged between courses, polite inquiries made about family and mutual acquaintances at the factory, though no one talked of business. The men complimented the ladies for their wonderful food, but it felt stilted to Lala. She recalled a dinner at Paulina's home last summer when both Ivo and Zigmund, rivals for Paulina's affection, showed up. She could understand how her friend must have felt. Lala struggled through each course, for she couldn't find an appetite sitting at the same table with the man she wanted to love and the man who wanted her love.

Three hours after they began the Seder, the guests had finished their dessert. Elia and Lew offered to clear the table, which Sarah accepted. Gershom helped Paulina out of her chair and escorted her and Lala into the parlor while Josef accompanied Sarah. Josef offered Gershom a cigarette, which he declined.

Gershom stood when Elia and Lew returned from the kitchen. "We should be taking our leave," he said. He thanked Sarah and Paulina and shook Josef's hand, wishing his employer a safe trip back to Vienna, before turning to Lala.

"Goodnight, Lala," he said, taking her hand. "We miss you at the factory."

"How kind, but I'm sure you're managing splendidly without me there."

He bowed toward her hand before looking directly at her. "It isn't the same without you." He turned toward the parlor. "Goodnight ladies. Until tomorrow."

Lala closed the door behind the men and returned to the parlor.

Josef remained seated. "If you ladies are not too exhausted, may I stay awhile? I'd like to discuss some matters with you."

"You're more than welcome, Josef," said Sarah. "Is there

anything you need us to help you with?"

"No, this is more of a personal nature."

Paulina stood. "I should leave you to talk."

"No, please stay. I would like to speak with you as well."

Paulina looked puzzled as she sat.

He addressed her first. "Miss Sipek—I beg your pardon, I should be calling you Mrs. Chytry now. Mrs. Chytry, I understand that you had a partnership with my, with Romy. A dressmaking business. Is that correct?"

"In part, Mr. Smetana. The business also included a shop here, which I purchased, and one in Prague, which I leased but never opened due to changing circumstances. And I intend to pay back every koruna I borrowed, no matter how long it takes."

"I appreciate that, but it won't be necessary. I intend to forgive your debt."

"Forgive?"

"Cancel it. I've read your business proposal. It's quite good. I believe your business would have succeeded if given a fair chance." Josef called for Smolak to come in.

Paulina nodded. "Yes, sir, the war has made everything more difficult."

"More than the war. You needed adequate financing to launch your venture, which was denied to you when Romy became distracted by…" he paused. "By other endeavors. So, you see, I must find a way to make that wrong right. Forgiving your debt, and also doing what I can to help you make your enterprise successful again." He asked Smolak, "Where is the box?"

"In the kitchen, sir." He returned holding a white dress box tied with red ribbon.

Josef took the box from Smolak. "I believe you gave this

gown to Romy as part of your debt payment. She never wore it, never even took it out of the box. I want you to have it back. I may know nothing about ladies' fashion, but I recognize excellent design and workmanship. Something as beautiful as this should be treasured, not hidden away." He handed Paulina the box.

"Mr. Smetana, your generosity is beyond what I could have ever expected."

"Your proposal stated that you planned to take existing garments and modify them."

"Yes, as a way to bridge the gap between couture and mass-market clothing."

"There are many more garments hanging in Romy's closet, some never worn. You're welcome to them, to use any way you see fit. Smolak will pack them up and bring them to you after I return to Vienna."

Paulina's mouth flew open. "I'm…."

"Speechless?"

She nodded. "Mr. Smetana, you're too kind."

"Normally I wouldn't get financially involved in something I know little about. But I can recognize a business with good potential when I see it. Your concept is similar to mine when I took over the factory. I don't know if your plans have changed now that you're married and starting a family, but if you do decide to continue your business, I would be very interested in taking Romy's place as a silent investor."

The good news brought a glow to Paulina's face. "This business has been my dream for as long as I can remember. How can I ever thank you?"

"By doing what you do best." He turned to Sarah. "Much like your dear husband Jakob. I'd always respected and admired him from the day we met, and in the years we worked together I came to think of him as a good friend. I miss his humor, the calming effect he seemed to have on me, and most of all his wise council, especially now."

Sarah's eyes misted. She said quietly, "I feel that way every day."

"I know you do. That is why I couldn't bear to part with the few pieces of his I own. But awhile back your daughter reminded me of something that I feel now needs to be changed." He reached into his breast pocket and handed Sarah a folded document. Lala guessed by the shocked look on her mother's face it was the deed to their house, now signed over to them.

Sarah looked at Josef with her mouth open and quivering. Tears filled her eyes and spilled onto her cheeks.

"I've apparently left you speechless as well." He smiled. "Please know this is more than my fondness for Jakob, though that would be reason enough. But I'm so grateful to you for all you've done to help me this past week, most especially handling the transfer of Romy to Bohnice Hospital. I doubt that I…"

"Nor should you have, Josef. I was glad to help," Sarah said. "You're right. Our families have long been close."

"And I hope despite what happened we will remain so."

She nodded. "You need to focus on yourself now. Grief takes so much out of us."

"Grief eventually eases. Does the pain?" Sadness creased his face. "I wonder if I might have a moment alone with Lala."

Sarah hesitated, and then said, "I'm not sure that would be…wise."

Lala said, "It's all right, Mother. Why don't you straighten

287

up the kitchen and I'll join you shortly."

"I'll take this box to our room," Paulina said as she headed toward the stairs.

Sarah nodded and left the room.

"Smolak," said Josef, "Please wait in the automobile for me."

When Smolak left, Lala held up her hand. "Josef, before you say anything, please don't apologize again or worry about me. I understand your situation and what you had to do." She swallowed hard. "I can accept it."

"I'm relieved to hear that."

"If there is—"

"Lala, I want you to keep the ring."

"No, Josef, I can't. Not now."

"Please," he implored. "It would help to preserve Armin's memory as a man happily in love, for we both know he was. Besides, as I told you in Berlin, I have no one to pass it on to. You don't have to wear it, but I can't think of anyone I would want to have it more than you."

She pondered his request. "I will keep it, in Armin's memory."

"Thank you. I also want you to keep the painting I gave you. For the same reason, if you prefer. And there is a piece of jewelry that Romy wanted you to have."

"No, I won't accept that."

"I understand." He removed his yarmulke and ran his hand over his hair, which looked even more silver than the night he returned home.

"I have one question," she said. "What about Armin's portrait of me?"

A look of terror crossed Josef's face for an instant. "I was hoping to keep it."

"Why would you want it now?"

"It's the finest piece my son painted, and since there will be no more from him, I would like to have it, at least for now. Would that be agreeable?"

Lala considered it...

"...He thinks it's a masterpiece."

"Not my painting, Lala, you. You are the masterpiece...."

She thought it odd to have him staring at it, a replacement for her, but if it brought solace....

Tension filled every line on his face as he waited, until she responded, "For now."

CHAPTER TWENTY-THREE

Morning brought sunny skies and dispositions. It thrilled Lala to see how Josef's gifts to her mother and Paulina lifted their spirits. Paulina volunteered to prepare the kitchen and dining room for the second Seder that evening and, with guidance from Lala's mother, set about cleaning, setting the table, and keeping the dinner Sarah prepared warm on the stove.

Lala went outside to tend to the chickens, which now numbered three after bartering for a gold and white bird with Paulina's neighbor who was moving to Prague. After feeding the hens, she checked the woodpile and saw nothing was missing. She walked to the entrance of the shed, tied with rope. It wouldn't prevent an intruder from breaking in, but it would slow someone down, perhaps enough to dissuade him from attempting robbery.

Her yard chores finished, she entered the house. Laughter trickled from the kitchen. There she found her mother touching Paulina's distended belly, the two of them giggling.

"I felt it again!" Sarah exclaimed. "My, that baby's active. Does it happen all the time?"

"Fortunately, no, but I've been feeling more movement in the past few weeks."

Sarah noticed Lala in the doorway. "Want to feel Paulina's baby move?"

Lala stepped forward and rested her palm against Paulina's belly. She waited a moment. "I don't feel anything."

"You will."

Lala kept her hand there. Suddenly, she felt something like a bump rolling around underneath. "Oh my."

Paulina giggled. "Isn't it something?"

"Have you decided on the baby's name?" Sarah asked.

"Not yet. I'm leaning toward Eirene if it's a girl, but I can't decide on a boy's name. Ivo said I should pick any I like as long as it isn't Ivo, so I'm open to suggestions."

"It's our tradition to name babies after beloved family members who have passed away. Have you considered naming your child after your father, mother, or brother?"

"My father's name was Otmar, and my brother was Dusan."

"Both nice. It would be a tribute to name your child after either of them." Sarah said. "Do you care if it's a boy or a girl?"

"Not really, but a boy would be nice for Ivo."

"They say there's a way to tell."

"How's that?"

"By dangling a wedding ring from a chain over your belly. If it swings back and forth, it's a boy, but if it moves in a circle, it means you're having a girl. Do you want to try it?"

Paulina laughed. "No, I think I'd rather be surprised."

"Have you made anything new for the baby?"

"Oh yes, Mama Sarah. Let me show you." The two went to the sewing basket, relocated to the back of the kitchen during Passover. Sarah cooed when Paulina brought out a nightgown with a scalloped hem, which Sarah offered to embroider. Smiling, Lala left the women and returned to her household chores.

Gershom, Lew and Elia arrived an hour before sunset for the second Seder. Sarah asked Gershom to lead and gave him the seat at the head of the table. The meal progressed more smoothly than the night before. The men seemed less guarded than when their employer sat at the table. After the soup and meat courses were finished, Lew and Elia cleared the table as Sarah prepared a pot of tea and a platter of meringue cookies. She brought both to the dining table.

Elia helped himself to three cookies. "*Delicioso*, Mrs. Hafstein. And without flour."

"I must confess I hid my flour canister in the shed until after Passover. I couldn't bear to throw food away." Sarah took a cookie for herself. "Have you heard from your families back home?" she asked the men.

"My mother is well," said Gershom in a clipped manner that left more details unspoken.

"She is joining my family for Passover," Lew said.

"How lovely," Sarah said as she passed the cookie platter around again.

Paulina took one more. "I received a letter yesterday from Ivo. He sends his best wishes."

"Is he well?"

"Thankfully, yes. Of course, he doesn't say where he's fighting, but he sounded optimistic."

"He may be near Bukovina," said Gershom. "I hear that our forces have taken it back from the Russians."

Sarah took another cookie. "You've been quiet, Elia."

"I no like the war, but I must remain, how you say, *imparziale?*"

"He means neutral," said Gershom.

"*Sì*, neutral."

"Why?" asked Sarah.

"Because I am Italian and my country declare itself neutral."

Gershom refilled his teacup. "I never understood how Italy could do that when they're part of the Triple Alliance."

"My country agrees to alliance only for defense. Italy not attacked so we do not fight." Elia stared at the remaining cookie on his plate. He offered it to Lew.

"I hope the war ends before I turn eighteen in April, or I'll be drafted," said Lew.

Lala laid her spoon by her saucer. "The war wasn't supposed to last more than a few weeks. Then the gossip was it would be over by last Christmas. And here we are two months into a new year and the war continues with no end in sight."

"Mama begs me, 'come home.' I want to, but I am afraid," said Elia. "The war does not go well for empire, many more men will be needed. You think they will allow Italy to stay out any longer? No, they will come for the men when they need more."

Sarah patted his hand. "You wouldn't have to fight anyway, Elia. You're sixteen. By the time you turn eighteen the war will be over."

"You no think it can last till nineteen seventeen?"

"No, they'll settle it long before then."

Gershom set his empty cup on its saucer. "I agree. Germany just declared the English Channel to be a war zone. A total blockade of Great Britain will accelerate our victory."

"We're making progress in the fighting," Lew pointed out. "It could end soon."

Elia shook his head. "I no want to scare Mrs. Chytry, but I not sure. Russians take Bukovina, then we take it back, but Russians will not give up. They will fight back and forth."

"They want to win this war as much as we do," observed Paulina. "And from what Ivo implies, sometimes it's not clear whom we're fighting for, or against."

Sarah raised her hand. "Perhaps we should change the subject."

Lala rose to clear the table. "How sad that tonight, when we relate the story of the Exodus, the freeing of the Israelites from their oppressors, we find ourselves living under the thumb of another empire." She put the dishes back on the table. "I forgot to bring in more wood for the fireplace. I should do that now."

Gershom stood. "I'll help you."

She was about to say no, but "All right" came out.

The moon was close to new; only the house lights shining through the windows illuminated the pathway to the woodpile. Frozen grass crunched under their feet as they walked.

"What's this?" Gershom asked as they passed the cobbled closure on the shed.

"We may have a scavenger in the forest." She told him of her findings.

"Whoever stole your firewood must be lazy rather than desperate. It's not hard to find wood around here." He tugged on the rope securing the shed latch. "What you need is a way to lock the door and open it with a key. I can fix that for you. I should also strengthen the chicken coop and build a locked enclosure for your woodpile."

"You're very kind to offer, but—"

"It's more than kindness, Lala." He stopped and took her hand. "May I speak freely?"

She nodded.

"I have tried to keep my distance out of respect for your betrothal to Mr. Smetana's son. I admit I haven't always succeeded, so it should come as no surprise that I hold tender feelings for you."

"Gershom, this is not the right time. I'm still reeling from Armin's death."

"I'm saddened by your loss, but there comes a time when we must put our grief aside and, as you often say, move forward. Return to life. When that time comes, I would like your consent to ask your mother for permission to court you."

His fingertips began stroking her hand. Lala had to admit it felt pleasant.

"I've grown very fond of you," he continued. "Whatever difficulties we've had in the past have been settled. We've both accepted part of the blame for that. And I sense that you like me. Doesn't this bode well for our future?"

"My grief can't be rushed. You know I cannot consider marrying until a year has passed from my father's death. That's seven months away. Why not wait?"

"To marry, of course, but when it comes to courting, I may need more time to convince you after my behavior at the factory. If I start soon, that will give me plenty of time to win your heart."

"I need time as well, to consider this."

He released her hand. "Then we will not speak of this again until you tell me you are ready."

CHAPTER TWENTY-FOUR

The day Passover ended, Lala noticed her mother seemed listless. The next morning, Sarah's voice turned husky and she coughed a great deal.

"Back to bed," Lala insisted. "You must rest so you don't get worse."

"I'll be fine," Sarah said.

"Do you want to risk getting Paulina ill?"

That convinced her mother to return to bed. "But you must do the marketing today, and you'd better leave soon, or there'll be little left."

Lala wrote out a shopping list and hurried to the market.

Over a hundred women stood on line ahead of her. She found her place and waited for the market to open at noon. To fight boredom, she listened for snippets of conversations while waiting. Most revolved around family, either fighting in the war or struggling at home. She overheard one exchange that revealed several alternative food sources, such as how certain farmers were forced to slaughter their cows when corn and oats were in short supply.

Shortly after noon, the line began to move slowly. It took over an hour for her to reach the market. By then many of the shelves that stocked staples were nearly empty so she went directly to the man behind the counter.

"Have you any kosher meat today?"

"Miss, at this hour, we have no meat left."

"What about fish?"

He chuckled. "Is this your first time here?"

"Well, what do you have?"

He brought out a half empty five-kilo basket holding potatoes, shriveled and full of eyes. "You can buy up to one kilo."

"How much?" The price horrified her. "No thanks, I'll find something on the shelves." She turned to see what could be had.

But the shelves were now totally bare. Lala returned to the counter. Three women had picked through the basket of potatoes. A market worker stood in the doorway and shouted down the line, "We're sold out. Come back tomorrow."

Dejected, Lala walked home empty-handed. Her failure at the market would mean dinner that night would be meager. Paulina might have to forego sending food to Ivo that week. She vowed to never allow that to happen again.

As the weeks passed, Lala fell into a routine of home maintenance. She devoted one day to laundry and at least two for marketing. In between she cleaned the house, cooked what food could be had, and cared for the chickens. She chopped wood and stacked most of it on the woodpile, bringing in the rest to keep the house warm and the stove cooking. Every muscle in her body ached for the first week, but after that the soreness subsided into occasional discomfort.

The ceaseless boredom wore her down as much as the physical exertion. She neglected her artwork, lacking both the energy and the inspiration to draw. She could not bear to sketch her family for it reminded her too much of Armin, and everything else seemed too upsetting, or so ordinary it couldn't enthuse her. Instead she spent some time designing a new vegetable plot. With spring approaching, Lala intended to expand her mother's garden.

At the beginning of each week she withdrew her bag of savings from her trunk and counted out her weekly budget, which she added to the rent received from Gershom and his roommates. The agreed upon sum had been recently cut in exchange for labor the men provided. Every Sunday they would make repairs and improvements to both houses, hunt for geese, duck and pheasant, or search out locations to forage when spring arrived.

It worked well for all, most of the time. While Gershom installed a lock on the shed door, Elia found a honeycomb in a nearby tree. Lala didn't know whether to laugh or cry when she saw him. His cherubic cheeks reddened and swelled even more from bee stings. She treated his wounds, which seemed to hurt his pride more than him. At Lala's urging he presented the comb to Sarah, which delighted her, or more accurately, her sweet tooth.

Lala'a skill in negotiating at the markets and with farmers in the region developed quickly. She'd learned her lesson and queued up early, bartered for whatever necessities could be found, kept what her family needed, and traded what couldn't be used. Non-kosher meat would be swapped for pantry staples or non-food items like coal, or given to the Chytrys in Prague, where supply shortages were more acute. Being the Peddler's daughter proved handy.

She had no doubt they all could survive. However, between the lowered rent and the increased prices at the market, which could rise daily, she found it necessary to take out a few more koruny every week. The garden became her priority. If she grew enough to see them through the summer months and put some food aside for the following winter, it would lessen their dependence on goods purchased from a constantly fluctuating market, if the war carried on. So would combing the land for additional foodstuffs to supplement each household's larder, though it became more common for the locals to hunt and forage. And not just locals, as Lala observed. Every weekend, trains from Prague would bring men and women to find food to bring back to the city.

Letters from Ivo hinted that the military had access to food in their conquered lands, but would not allow any to be sent home, so Paulina stopped sending food packages to him. Her attention began to rest solely on her unborn child and Ivo. She and Sarah grew closer as Paulina's due date drew near and the idea of a baby became more real. At dinner, talk centered around Paulina and her child, the one cheerful topic left. Still, the approaching birth, and the added responsibility it carried, weighed heavily on Lala.

The lengthening daylight and rising temperatures that promised spring relieved some the drudgery of washing and scrubbing. Standing hours in line. The stress of caring for her family tempted her to drift away into fantasy, as did the monotony of her duties. At night, thoughts of Josef invaded Lala's sleep. During the day, she could fight the urge to daydream, focus on finding food or scrubbing out a stain. But in the middle of the night he visited Lala in her dreams, where she relived their encounters. The best Lala could do was to separate the pleasurable feelings the visions brought from the provider. She reminded herself of her mother's advice, to hold onto the feelings and look to recapture them with another man. It would be possible, her mother insisted, but Lala had doubts. What if no one else could make her feel the way Josef did?

Then morning would dawn. She would arise and set about her daily chores, day after day. Day after day after day.

Those moments of phantom pleasure became harder to resist.

CHAPTER TWENTY-FIVE

"Are you sure you have everything?" Lala asked as she once again attempted to button Paulina's coat over her swollen belly.

Paulina stood on the train platform, suitcase in hand. "Let's see. A week's worth of clothing, including a new dress for the family reception, a nightgown and robe, my hairbrush, some toiletries, a side of pork and a bottle of Moravian wine."

"How nice to spend some time with the Chytrys before the baby comes. How many people are they inviting?"

"They promised to keep it small, Mr. Chytry's brother and sister-in-law and a few cousins." She shooed Lala away. "Leave it unbuttoned, it's pleasant outside." She lifted her face toward the sun. "This Sunday will be the first day of spring, but it feels like it's already here."

The train to Prague entered the station. Lala kissed Paulina on both cheeks. "I miss you already. Have a wonderful visit and then come home safely to us."

Paulina smiled and waved. "I will be back next Friday before the Sabbath begins."

Lala watched her friend climb aboard. As the train pulled away, a dark memory crept into her thoughts, of saying goodbye to her Mama before leaving her shtetl to do laundry. She never saw her Mama alive after that. Lala shook the memory from her head, but a sense of foreboding stayed with her. She did not want to walk home alone, especially past the woods that reminded her of Russia.

The clock in the train station indicated it was a quarter past eleven. She could be at the boarding house before noon, help her mother finish her chores early. Then the two of them could walk home long before sundown.

Lala didn't expect to find her mother sitting in the parlor, knitting, her feet up on the table. Sarah jumped and clasped her chest when Lala shut the door. Her yarn tumbled to the floor.

"You scared the daylights out of me." She took a moment to catch her breath. "What are you doing here?"

"I'm sorry I startled you, Mother. I didn't want to walk home alone from the train station, so I came here to help you." She chuckled. "It appears you don't need help."

Sarah shrugged. "A small house like this doesn't take much time to clean, and cooking for three men is no different than cooking for three women, except I make a little more. So when I have spare time I knit." She picked up the ball of wool she'd dropped on the floor.

"That looks like a baby blanket."

"It is, but don't tell Paulina. I want it to be a surprise."

"You'll have a whole week to finish it. Shall we walk home?"

"I've left their dinner warming on the stove. Let me add water to the pot first so it doesn't dry out."

***

The sun peeked between clouds as Lala and her mother climbed the hill toward their house. Lala stepped on a pebble and winced. She inspected her shoe. The pebble had broken through her worn sole.

"Oh dear. These were my most practical pair. I'd hate to waste money on new shoes. I wonder how much it would cost to repair them?"

"You could take a pair of your father's shoes and have the cobbler use them to replace the soles," her mother suggested.

"He'll want something for his labor. Maybe I can do the repair myself."

They reached the wooded area before the clearing. Although she heard no gunfire, Lala's pace quickened.

"You're still afraid of the woods," her mother observed. "Ever since you were little."

"It brings back dark memories, especially now."

"Why so?"

"I've been hearing gunfire."

Sarah stopped to catch her breath. "It's not the war. What you've been hearing is hunters looking for meat. They're shooting hares, wild boar, ducks, practically anything that moves. If this war goes on much longer there won't be a living creature left. Come to think of it, I should find your father's gun."

"I have it in my room."

Sarah started walking again. "Why?"

"Three women living in an isolated house near the woods." She didn't mention the prowler for fear of upsetting her mother. "We need it for protection."

"But you don't know how to use it. You should ask

Gershom to teach you."

They reached the newly greening meadow that led to their house. With the frost gone, wildflowers would be blossoming soon. So would plants to forage. At the end of the road the path to their house began. Lala spotted a few crocuses popping up underneath the bare rose bushes surrounding the house. Elia had told her the flower stamens were very flavorful. She also noticed a few cracks in the exterior window frames that needed fixing.

Once home, Lala took off her coat before going upstairs to change into old clothes. Sometimes the women dressed for dinner if they weren't too tired, but despite Sabbath approaching, tonight didn't feel festive enough to bother.

Lala went to the kitchen to prepare dinner for the two of them. Sarah offered to help, but Lala insisted on handling the cooking alone.

"You could set the table, Mother."

Sarah laughed. "We've really switched places, haven't we?"

Twilight approached as they finished their meal.

"Mother, you've been quiet all through dinner and you look like you lost your best friend."

Sarah shrugged. "I wish Paulina was joining us tonight."

"So do I. She always enlivens everything. She'll be home in a week."

Lala suspected it was more than Paulina's absence that had her mother so glum. Then it occurred to her why. "Father's birthday is next week."

Sarah nodded with sadness. "Yes, on Monday. We'll have

to light a yahrzeit candle for him. Do we have any more?"

Lala assured her there were several memorial candles left. Her mother turned teary. "He would have been fifty-three." She put her fork down. "Sometimes I still forget that he's gone."

"Only from our presence," Lala told her.

Sarah nodded. "I like that. 'Only from our presence.' Not from our past, or our future."

Lala didn't correct her mother. Instead she thought of a way to cheer her up by reviving a tradition her father had started. "Let's have a treat tonight."

Her mother brightened. "Yes, a treat would do nicely. What do we have?"

"Wait in the parlor and I'll surprise you."

Smiling, Sarah hurried out, leaving Lala to figure out how she would come up with a special dessert with little time and even less ingredients.

Minutes later Lala emerged from the kitchen with what looked like a small layer cake.

"That looks beautiful. What is it?" asked her mother.

"It's my version of a jam tart, except I used bread instead of cake and filled each layer with a different flavor of jam. There's cherry, apricot and plum."

"How clever of you." She held out her plate. "I'll have a big slice."

Now Lala felt tears coming. "You sound just like Father."

After dinner Lala went outside to gather more firewood, holding a torch to illuminate the path on a moonless night. As she carried an armful of quarter logs back to the house, she noticed a dent in the fencing around the chicken coop and stopped to inspect it. Shining her torch on the dent, she saw a small cut in the wire, enough to put a hand through. After depositing the wood by the fireplace, she fetched the key to unlock the shed.

She went to fetch the roll of baling wire and wire cutters on the workbench in the rear of the shed, and felt a sharp object underfoot. She bent down and picked up a ragged-edged pebble. Wondering how it could have gotten in the shed, she noticed shards of glass on the workbench. Her gaze followed a path to the window, one pane broken.

She snipped off a length of baling wire and locked up the shed before weaving the wire around the cut section in the coop. As she twisted the ends closed, the feeling of being watched suddenly seized her. Alarmed, she leapt up and spun around, moving the bulls eye lens of her torch across the black void, trying to catch the culprit. A pair of eyes of some small animal shined back before disappearing into the darkness.

Lala swallowed hard. Perhaps that's all it was. Perhaps.

CHAPTER TWENTY-SIX

Lala missed Paulina, her friend's companionship, her sage advice, having someone to discuss things she wouldn't dare say to her mother. She also had failed to appreciate how much energy and joy her friend brought to their household. After Paulina had her baby she would not be as free as she had been. Her focus would be on the child. Lala would have to respect that.

Her mother seemed particularly despondent in Paulina's absence, or more accurately in the absence of the child she carried. Sarah had begun to think of the much-awaited baby as her grandchild and became very animated every time it was mentioned, which Paulina encouraged. Lala could see the new life would bring many changes to their family, which included losing her mother's attention in favor of the new honorary grandbaby. None of that compared to the burden of responsibility that Lala had taken upon her shoulders. At times, it became so acute it gnawed at her insides, making it difficult for her to eat. She worried constantly, about having enough food, enough coal to heat the house, enough protection for them from predators of all varieties. Their prowler had returned. Several more logs disappeared from the stockpile.

Meanwhile the war raged on without an end in sight. Supplies continued to dwindle in availability, quality; all ways other than price, which seemed to rise almost daily. Despite careful planning, Lala was no longer sure her income would carry them through to the end of spring.

Gershom's interest remained in the back of her thoughts, but as the days dragged by, the idea of courtship grew in appeal. She reminded herself that boredom was no reason to give her consent. Leading him on would be monumentally unfair. But he had the capacity to charm. Perhaps there could be something between them, beyond a distraction from the hardship of life during wartime. She would wait until Paulina returned on Friday and discuss it with her first. Paulina always seemed to understand these matters better than anyone.

It had been awhile since her mother had given Lala "The Eye." A dampened version bore up at her during breakfast on Friday as Sarah asserted, "I'm going with you to the station and that's that."

Her mother had grown impatient for Paulina's return. Despite her duties at the boarding house, Sarah insisted on accompanying Lala to meet the afternoon train. Sarah spoke only of Paulina and the baby from the moment she and Lala had left their house until they mounted the station platform. They waited where the second-class passengers would disembark.

Sarah glanced at the station clock. "It's nearly three. The train should be here any minute." She began to fidget. "I don't know why I'm so excited."

At that moment, a train whistle echoed in the distance,

and two minutes later the train from Prague entered the northbound platform of the station. Four middle-aged men carrying hunting gear got off one of the cars and walked in the direction of the woods. Lala checked up and down the station for Paulina, but did not see her.

A porter stepped down from the first-class car and put a familiar looking suitcase on the platform, then turned back and offered his hand. Lala smiled, knowing he must be helping her friend down from the train. Even with child, Paulina could dazzle and charm the best out of men.

Moments later Paulina appeared, holding a small white bundle in her arms. The porter took her elbow and helped her down to the platform.

Lala grasped her mother's arm. "Paulina's had her baby!" She rushed to Paulina, who looked tired but happy.

With a smile, Paulina held up her bundle. Inside Lala saw a tiny pink face with a smattering of dark hair poking out from a cap.

"Lala, meet my son."

Lala melted. "He's beautiful."

Sarah caught up. She stared incredulously at the baby. "He? Oh, how wonderful, a little boy. He's a bit early though. Is everything all right, with him and with you??"

"He's got all of his parts and is healthy. I went into labor last Monday night. Fortunately, one of Mrs. Chytry's neighbors is a midwife and was able to help. He was born early Tuesday."

"The day after my Jakob."

"Was it difficult?" Lala asked her friend.

"The pain of contractions was excruciating. It felt like my insides were on fire. I was so terrified, I thought I was going to die and all I wanted was to see him. The midwife guided me through and once he came out, the pain seemed to fade away. She said I was fortunate the baby didn't go to full-term, or it would have been even worse. He weighed almost four kilos at birth."

Lala took a deep breath. "Four kilos! Let's take him home. You must be exhausted." She picked up Paulina's suitcase.

"I lost a lot of blood. The midwife said I should stay off my feet for the first week, but I can walk home."

"Wait," cried Sarah. "You haven't told us his name."

"I decided to take your advice, Mama Sarah, and name him after someone dear who has passed away." She let Sarah cradle him in her arms.

Sarah beamed at his sweet face and asked, "So did you name him for your father, Otmar, or Dusan, after your brother?"

Paulina leaned over and kissed her son's forehead. "I named him Jacub."

CHAPTER TWENTY-SEVEN

Little Jacub did not sleep for more than a few hours without waking and crying. Lala helped as much as she could, but Paulina had to nurse him frequently. Twice a week Lala and her mother switched beds so that each could bring the baby to Paulina while the other got some sleep. It was the first time Sarah had slept in the room she'd shared with her husband since his death. She resisted leaving the house each morning, always wanting to spend as much time cuddling the baby as she could.

One night, shortly after Paulina had nursed him, Lala heard Jacub fussing. Paulina had fallen asleep. Lala went to his cradle, picked him up and held him close, gently bouncing him and rubbing his back to calm him. His cries subsided into soft whimpers, then he let out a bubble of air. She could feel him relax in her arms after that. She took him back to his cradle.

After kissing him on his forehead, she laid him down and went back to bed. She dreamed of Josef, as she often did. He seemed to come to her in her sleep whether she wanted him to or not, but the pleasurable feelings it gave her were hard to deny, or resist. She finally relented to them and reminded herself that dreams were fantasies, pleasant but not real.

313

In her dream, he began kissing her, caressing her, replaying their encounter in his private quarters at the factory. Desire welled within her, growing stronger with each touch of his lips, each stroke of his hand. Stronger and stronger...

She bolted awake, surging with unfulfilled yearnings. She hurried to the washbasin to splash water on her face to calm down. This had to stop. Now there were two men keeping her up at night.

Lala awoke early. After checking on Jacub, she dressed and went downstairs to prepare a breakfast tray for Paulina. Her mother joined her in the kitchen.

"Will you make coffee while I see to Paulina's breakfast?" Lala asked.

"All right. Let me take it up to her."

Lala smiled inwardly as she fetched the bread. "Jacub is still asleep."

They worked in silent rhythm. Lala savored the aroma of coffee as it brewed. It had become frightfully expensive.

Sarah brushed stray strands of hair from Lala's face. "You look tired. How many times did the baby wake you?"

"Once or twice." She cut three slices of bread. A memory of her Mama doing the same flickered in her mind, but she pushed it away.

"It's good for you to see what it's like being a mother. Then someday when you have your own children, you'll know what to do."

"If I ever have children."

Sarah looked horrified at that.

"Don't pay any attention to me. I didn't sleep well." Lala

314

put a plate with bread, jam and cheese on the tray for Paulina. "Do you think this is enough?"

"Better to give her small meals more often." Sarah took the tray. "Have you made a decision about Gershom's request?"

"Paulina will be hungry. Take that up to her and we'll talk afterward."

As Sarah went upstairs, Lala nibbled on her slice of bread and sipped her coffee. She had little appetite lately and often gave some of her food to Paulina.

Her mother returned with Paulina's untouched coffee, which she poured back into the pot. She then took the last slice of bread, cut it in two and put one half on Lala's plate. "I'm taking part of my slice up to Paulina. You eat the other half."

"Then what will you have?"

"I can stand to skip a meal, but you can't. Don't think I haven't noticed you giving your food to Paulina. While it's noble of you, it's also foolish." She tugged on Lala's dress. "Look how this hangs on you now. You've lost weight and you're too thin, while I can afford to lose a kilo or two."

Lala began to protest, but her mother held up her hand. "Eat. Men like a woman with some meat on her bones."

Sarah returned to the kitchen awhile later with the empty dish and tray. "I kept her company while she nursed Jacub. That baby is so good, he hardly ever fusses."

Lala washed the remaining breakfast dishes. "When are you going to the boarding house, Mother?"

"Soon." She poured herself a cup of coffee, plunked in a

lump of sugar and stirred it long after the sugar dissolved.

Lala chuckled as she dried the dishes. Her mother had no intention of leaving anytime soon. "I know how fond you've grown of Jacub, but you must let Paulina tend to him. She's his mother and they need to bond."

"Did she complain about me interfering?" Sarah put her coffee on the kitchen table and sat down.

"No, she's grateful for your assistance, and mine, but we must let her focus on him and help out only when it's needed."

"And what are you focusing on?"

"Laundry today, then the garden." Lala wrung out her dishrag and hung it over the washbasin to dry.

"You know that's not what I meant. What about Gershom?"

Lala wiped her hands, noticing how calloused they'd become. "I don't know yet."

"Can you say for certain you're not interested in him?"

"No."

"So, what have you got to lose?"

"What if I decide I don't want to marry him?"

"Then don't. That's why you court."

"That's easy for you to say." Lala poured the remaining coffee into her cup. "You probably fell in love with Father the instant you met him." She sat down opposite her mother.

"I thought he was a very nice gentleman."

"That's all? No shivers?"

"Shivers?" Sarah put her cup down and laughed. "You mean love at first sight. Not at all, at least not for me. I was cautious."

"About what?"

"I had to find out whether he truly liked me or wanted

something less honorable. After all, a servant's daughter was beneath his class. It took time to learn that didn't matter to him."

"How long?"

She smiled. "Awhile. I wasn't perfect, either. I enjoyed the attention. It's nice to be wanted, and when it's by a fine, decent man like your father, you take notice. So, after a few weeks I agreed to meet with him. We had to do it in secret, for his family disapproved of his interest of me. Then one day my feelings for him changed."

"How so?"

Her mother's cheeks reddened. "I don't want to talk about it. I'm going to work."

Lala chuckled under her breath, for she understood all too well what her mother meant. She wondered if it were possible for her to develop such feelings for Gershom. With Josef, it happened suddenly, with that first kiss. When Gershom kissed her, she didn't experience that same sense of exhilaration. She didn't want to lead him on. Then again, a few months ago she could barely stand him, and now their relationship was cordial, even warm.

She recalled how unsure she'd felt about bonding with her parents when they wanted to adopt her, until her uncle gave her some advice: *"...no matter how much it may hurt when you love, when you cannot love, it always hurts more."*

"Mother," Lala called, "I have a message for Gershom."

Her mother opened the front closet and put on her spring coat. "What is it?"

"Tell him I'm ready."

CHAPTER TWENTY-EIGHT

The open closet door blocked Lala's view of her mother and Paulina as they hunted through her wardrobe. She sat on her bed absorbing their commentary as they evaluated each unseen outfit and tried to picture which dress they were talking about.

"What about this?" Sarah asked Paulina.

"It would flatter her complexion, but that's all. We can do better."

Lala heard the scrape of hangers moving across the wood pole. The sound stopped.

"What about this?"

Lala didn't expect selecting a dress to wear for Gershom that night would prove so challenging. Paulina insisted on having a say from a fashion standpoint and her mother wanted final approval to insure Lala wore something appropriate. If dressing was going to be such a problem, she couldn't imagine what went into planning the menu. Sarah, having cooked for the men, knew Gershom's tastes. She directed Lala to splurge on a half-kilo of meaty beef ribs for the occasion and save enough flour and sugar for his favorite dessert, crispy twice-baked mandelbrot, which Elia called biscotti.

Her mother insisted on preparing dinner that night so Lala could spend more time on her appearance, which had been neglected since she left the factory. Rough hands had to be sloughed and oiled, her face refreshed with Paulina's fancy cold cream, her hair brushed and pinned just so. Sarah insisted on adding a touch of rouge to Lala's cheeks and lips to bring color to her fair complexion, which had become pallid of late.

Gershom showed up shortly before five wearing his best suit, which Paulina had altered for him. Lala had to admit he looked more presentable than she recalled from work. Wearing the rose-pink dress that all three women agreed looked best on her, she greeted him at the door and offered him a drink, which he prudently declined.

"Please come into the parlor, Gershom."

They sat side by side on the sofa. For an uncomfortable moment, neither said a word until Lala started to giggle.

"What's so funny?" he asked.

"Us. We never had trouble talking before, but now it feels awkward."

"You mean awkward again. We had some difficult times at the factory. Fortunately, they're behind us."

She nodded.

Her mother called from the kitchen, "Hello, Gershom. Dinner will be ready shortly."

Paulina came downstairs with Jacub in her arms. "Good evening."

Gershom stood as she entered. "Hello, Mrs. Chytry. And congratulations."

"Thank you, but we're all friends here. Please call me Paulina." She nestled into a salon chair and laid her son across her lap. "And this is Jacub."

"I haven't seen many infants. Are they all that tiny?"

"At almost three weeks they are. Would you like to hold him?"

Gershom froze. "I, er, I could, if you show me how."

Paulina looked to Lala.

So, this was a test of Gershom's suitability as a father, as well as Lala's ability to care for a child. She smiled inwardly. Gershom displayed tact and wisdom with his answer. Lala explained how to cradle his head and bottom before lifting him. Gershom followed her instructions and took the baby for a moment.

"He's a handsome boy. Your husband will be pleased," he told Paulina before returning the infant to his mother's arms.

Lala knew dinner would be a trial for her as much as for Gershom. Tense with self-consciousness, she yielded to her mother, who led their conversation around the factory, local events, anything but the war. Sarah managed to probe Gershom about his family. His answers were more forthcoming than in the past. Lala knew he had no siblings, but learned it was due to the death of his older brother and toddler sister to pneumonia. His mother never recovered from the losses, but rather than turning morose like Paulina's mother, she became hardened, much like Aunt Naomi before she brought Lala into the family. It explained his reticence to talk about his childhood.

They finished a meal of soup made from the ribs, studded

with tiny flour dumplings and chunks of beef, followed by boiled potatoes with braised cabbage, and the mandelbrot with tea for dunking. Shortly before seven, Paulina excused herself to nurse Jacub and put him to bed.

Lala tried to clear the table, but her mother stopped her. "Leave that to me, dear. There's nearly an hour of daylight left. Why don't you two take a walk, perhaps watch the sunset?"

"Would you like that, Gershom?"

"Yes, very much."

They put on their coats and went outside.

"Shall we walk toward the meadow? The first wildflowers have bloomed," she said.

They strolled side by side down the path toward the road, accompanied by gusts of wind that carried the promise of rain. A sheet of pale gray covered the sky. As they passed from view of the house, Gershom asked, "May I take your hand?"

"All right."

They continued to walk without speaking, holding hands. It felt odd to Lala at first, but gradually she became more comfortable with it and grew to like the simple contact with him.

He interrupted the silence. "I took your advice and appointed Strahov and Hajek to help me run the factory. This way I can share the burden, plus they can take over if I'm drafted."

She chuckled. He had a good sense of humor.

"You must be happy to be away from all that," he said.

"I must confess I thought I would, but I do miss being there."

That brought a contented smile to Gershom.

"I never understood how physically exhausting housework can be," she continued. "I sometimes wish I could be back at work, which was never boring, instead of washing and scrubbing and…"

"You don't like keeping house?"

She realized she'd gone too far. What man wanted to hear a woman complain about being a homemaker? "It's probably different when you're married, though."

She could smell the herbaceous scent of new grass and wildflowers before they reached the meadow, now green with patches of dandelions and stalks of bright yellow rapeseed. Tall lacy heads of wild carrot blossoms danced in the wind that ruffled the field. She pointed to thick stems poking up from the grass. "Those marsh orchids won't bloom for another month." She could picture the spiky pink petals beside the vibrant blue of late blooming cornflowers. Every spring she would bring armloads home to arrange in vases, study their structure and form while sketching. Now she wondered if any parts of the plants were edible.

Twilight approached as clouds began to gather overhead, which further darkened the sky. "We ought to go back. I wouldn't want you to get caught in the rain on your way home," she said.

He took her other hand in his. "As you wish, though it would be worth it to spend another minute with you."

He plucked a rapeseed flower and handed it to her, then gestured to the road leading back to her house. As they walked on, hand in hand, Lala thought about this unseen side of Gershom. She could grow fond of this man.

CHAPTER TWENTY-NINE

Lala's workload eased when, at her friend's insistence, Paulina resumed housekeeping duties at the boarding house. Sarah balked until Paulina reminded her that while Gershom was courting Lala, it wouldn't be prudent to have her mother scrubbing his floors.

Lala invited Gershom to join her family every week for Sabbath dinner. He would arrive dressed in his suit. Sarah had Lala cook the meals to show off her culinary skills, though she would often prepare a special dish herself or supervise Lala's preparations. Meals were as lavish as they could afford, complemented by their best table linens and Lala's creative table décor. Sarah always joined them at the table, as did Paulina, who helped chaperone the couple. Conversation in the parlor always followed dinner.

After their third meeting, Gershom stole a kiss when the other women were out of the room. Lala smiled and blushed; she hadn't expected it. When he was about to leave, she gave him a cordial peck on the cheek in full view of her mother and Paulina.

After she closed the door, her mother said, "That looks promising."

Lala shrugged. "It seemed appropriate."

"No shivers?"

"Not yet. I'm going to change out of this dress." She heard Jacub's cries from upstairs.

"I'll tend to him," said Paulina. She gave Lala a look that said, "Let's talk."

They walked upstairs together.

"Wait until we've closed the door to our room," whispered Paulina.

She lifted Jacub from his cradle and checked his diaper. "He's wet." As she changed him, she said to Lala, "So no shivers. Will you keep seeing him?"

"I suppose so."

"What are your feelings toward him after that kiss?"

"It was just a peck."

"I meant the one he gave you."

"So, you saw that." Lala took off her dress and hung it in the closet. "Fond would best describe it." She decided the trousers Paulina had made for her would be more comfortable. She paired them with an oversized sweater.

"One needs to be more than fond of a husband to have a happy marriage." Paulina rewrapped Jacub in his swaddling blanket and sat in the chair to nurse him. "You look *tres chic* in that."

Lala sat on her bed. "I doubt Gershom would agree. He's so traditional. Now, Armin would have loved it." The memory brought tears. "I miss him so much. I wonder if I'm trying to replace him with Gershom."

"I don't see how, they're so different."

"As men, yes, but in my life, they seem to serve a similar purpose. I loved Armin, but like a brother, a friend, a confidante. I sometimes think that's how I feel about Gershom."

"Can you talk to him about anything like you could with Armin?" Paulina asked.

"Not yet, but I hadn't confided completely to Armin, either. He never knew about my past, or my suspicions about his romantic interests. Perhaps I couldn't be completely honest with him because deep down I knew he wasn't forthright with me."

"That's very perceptive. You are growing wise about men, my friend."

Her next Sabbath dinner with Gershom was a bittersweet occasion. They celebrated Lew's eighteenth birthday, but it arrived with induction papers, so they had to bid the young man goodbye. Elia searched for more honey and managed to find a quantity without getting stung, and Sarah contributed flour and eggs to make a small cake. Lala foraged with Paulina for young dandelion greens, ramps, bear's garlic and sorrel to stretch their larder for six people.

After a bracing sorrel soup, foraged salad and Lew's favorite cheese dumpling, they sang Happy Birthday to Lew and enjoyed Sarah's medovnik made with Elia's honey. Lew brought out his bottle of Goldwasser. Sarah poured some for everyone and offered a toast, followed by a teary Elia and Gershom.

Lala felt warm after three shots of the potent liqueur.

"When do you leave?" Sarah asked Lew.

"On Monday."

"We'll all go to the train station to see you off."

"Yes, we will," said Lala. The warmth she felt from the Goldwasser began to extend toward Gershom. She licked a sweet drop from her lips and smiled at him. "I should bring in more wood for the fire."

"It won't be cold tonight, dear," her mother pointed out. "You can wait until morning."

"Then I should check the chicken coop and wood pile." She stood cautiously, feeling a little giddy from the alcohol. "Gershom, would you join me?"

Outside, lacy clouds fanned across the night sky to reveal a full moon that softly illuminated their faces like candlelight. The heady scent of flowering bushes and fruit trees perfumed the air, and the rustling of birds in their nests was the only sound she heard. As soon as they were in a blind spot she wrapped her arms around his neck and drew him in for a kiss. It must have surprised him, for at first, he didn't respond, then he slid his arms around her waist and held her tenderly as she pressed her lips against his. He jerked when her tongue began to probe his mouth, but did not resist. Despite an initial awkwardness he soon caught on and followed her lead.

She became lost in his embrace. The sensation of his body pressed against hers sent a shockwave of urges through her. Time ceased to exist as starlight descended from above and swirled around them like a sparkling ribbon, drawing their bodies closer together. Her head spun as waves of joy flowed through her until she suddenly broke off the kiss.

"That was nice," he purred.

It was more than nice. It had been thrilling for a moment, when the man she was kissing wasn't Gershom, but someone else.

CHAPTER THIRTY

Lala lay silently in bed, close to tears. Three rounds of Goldwasser may have prodded her to initiate that kiss earlier, but rather than unveil the possibility of a new romance with Gershom, it brought back the specter of the past.

Josef. If she couldn't overcome her desire for him, it would ruin her chance to create something good with Gershom. She would not consent to marry him unless she could give herself to him body and soul. Five months remained until she could wed. She had to find a new direction with him, a different way to gain closeness. Tenderness. Love. Or know for certain she couldn't.

The brightness of the moon drew her to the window to gaze out, looking for answers. Sometimes the moon lit the way for decisions, literally and figuratively. *Body and soul.*

Jacub let out a muffled whimper so soft it didn't wake Paulina. Lala went to his cradle and rubbed his back until he fell asleep. She returned to bed, knowing he'd wake again soon, and Paulina as well.

Body and soul. If her body longed for someone else, then she would focus on her soul. Intimacy went beyond the physical. Throughout her life, the secrets that families hid from their neighbors, children hid from their parents, friends hid from each other, when finally revealed, brought closeness. Or closure.

The ultimate intimacy was truth.

Elia became so emotional at Lew's sendoff at the train station that Gershom gave him the rest of the month off to visit his family. As Lew boarded the train, Elia kissed the young man repeatedly on both cheeks, which might have alarmed him more than leaving for battle. The entourage stayed to watch the train leave the station.

Lala kissed Elia's cheek and waved goodbye as she wished him a safe journey home.

"I return on first of June," Elia promised as he left the platform to go home and pack. Sarah went along to help.

Lala wondered how Gershom would react, losing his closest friends and work assistants, and at home going from two roommates to none. At the station he responded admirably, offering encouragement to Lew and consolation to Elia. Not quite commanding, but she could see how much Gershom had grown into the role of man-in-charge, a quality he'd developed when he assumed the helm at the factory. Perhaps it had always resided within him, waiting for the right opportunity to emerge.

At home Lala changed into old clothes to work in her garden. The four-by-six meter plot had sprouted over the past few weeks. She crouched to pluck seedlings and thin the rows. From the corner of her eye she saw a large slit in the fence around the chicken coop and went over to inspect it. The three hens were still there, and the two chicks that Paulina had bought at Easter. However there had been no eggs in the henhouse that morning, and only one the day before, as opposed to the three or four she'd found almost every morning for the previous week. Someone or something had gotten into the compound.

She fetched the key to the shed to cut more of the baling wire. While in the house, she wrote a note on stationery explaining the problem. She folded it into an envelope addressed to Gershom and left it on the front bureau for Paulina to take to the boarding house the next day, before changing her mind. She removed the letter and added at the end, *I need you.*

CHAPTER THIRTY-ONE

As promised in response to her note, Gershom arrived mid-morning Sunday dressed in his factory work clothes. He met Lala in the yard and greeted her with a peck on the cheek.

"Where is the cut in the fence?" Gershom asked.

Lala showed him the spot adjacent to the shed wall. He deposited his toolbox on the ground, bent over and pulled at the loose wires.

"Whoever did this used wire cutters. I can repair this, but that won't stop the culprit from doing it again."

"Then what should I do? I can't guard the coop all night."

"I can build a large henhouse out of wood and lock it, like the shed. Your chickens will be safe, but they won't lay as many eggs."

"We need the eggs. Anything else?"

He stroked his beard, which made Lala smile. She remembered her Uncle Hershel used to do that when contemplating.

"If I could get my hands on some heavier gauge wire fencing, like we have around the factory, that might solve the problem, but where could you find that now?"

"There's an abandoned farmhouse about two kilometers from here. We could walk there after lunch. Together."

It took a moment for him to catch the implication of "together."

"Yes, we'll do that. I'll work on the cracked window frames now."

Lala left him to his labor while she tended the garden, pulling weeds and clearing debris. She put in stakes to support the peas and beans, then added mulch to the plot to keep down weeds and hold moisture in.

Flushed from the sun, she went to the house for water and brought a glass to Gershom. He'd been sanding the window frames, leaving him covered in sawdust. He gulped down the water, wiped his mouth with the back of his hand and returned the glass with a thank you.

A sense of déjà vu struck her. Working on their projects side by side, she felt close to him and wondered if what drew her to him was a familiar coziness. It brought back faint memories of her Mama and Papa, working in the yard, sitting together in the kitchen at night, each with their projects. Had they enjoyed a grand passion? Lala never saw it, but she knew they had love by the way they shared life's joys and troubles, the little things they did for each other, the looks on their faces...

Mama sat in the kitchen as she did most nights, humming to herself as she mended clothes. Papa sat beside her. She touched her belly and gazed at him, her face soft, her eyes bright with love.

Papa looked at Luska and said, "Do you know why I married your Mama?"

"No, Papa, tell me."

"Because she was the most beautiful girl in Moscow." Mama smiled

and her face lit up like the sun....

Lala leaned over and with her hand brushed sawdust off his shoulders. "When did you decide you liked me, Gershom?"

The question stopped him. "The first time I set eyes on you, which unfortunately was during shiva for your father."

"I doubt that. I cried almost nonstop for days. I must have looked awful." She knelt on the grass by his feet.

Gershom closed the lid of his tool chest and carefully eased himself down on it. "You were devastated, but I could see beyond that."

"And what about now?"

He gazed at her. "Your beauty is what first attracted me, but as I got to know you better, first at work and then at home, I've come to realize you're much more than a pretty face."

"How so?"

"You're strong in character, shrewd, and capable. I admire how you've been able to manage during these difficult times. Not many people who've lived privileged lives can."

"My life hasn't been that privileged. You know we aren't rich."

"But you were connected to wealth, yet you never put on airs. You seemed to have adjusted to the war economy with grace and skill. I've heard tales of your bargaining prowess. You're a force to be reckoned with, they say."

"Life hasn't always been comfortable. There were times when I struggled."

"Don't you mean your family?"

She paused at his question. It opened a portal to a more intimate level of conversation. "Do you remember last Purim when I said that you reminded me of someone in my past whom I loved very much?"

"I hoped you would tell me who he was someday."

She took a deep breath for courage. "That man was my Papa."

He scowled. "Now you're toying with me. I remember you said the man lost his leg."

"I don't mean Jakob, my father." She sat on the grass and tucked her legs under her. "I was orphaned as child and adopted by the Hafsteins. Although they are my parents, I had a Mama and Papa before them. We lived in a shtetl in Russia, in the Pale of Settlement.

"Papa was a peddler. Cossacks attacked him when he was away, but he managed to escape due to a cart latch he designed, which could instantly separate a cart from its horse, allowing the rider to escape. Unfortunately, one Cossack stabbed his leg. By the time he returned home, the wound became infected and his leg had to be amputated at mid-thigh. But he continued to produce his cart latches and sell them to other peddlers and travelers, to support his family."

"What happened to him?"

"A band of Cossacks found out where he lived. They came to the shtetl and destroyed it, and killed everyone except me."

The color drained from his face. "How did you manage to survive?"

"My Mama had to send me to the river to do laundry. I was far from the shtetl when the attack occurred and returned to find..."

Gasping for breath, she entered the shtetl. Heat shimmied from the ashes and shattered the air above like broken glass. Everything ahead looked bent and folded, from the buckled ruins along the main road clear out to the meadow beyond.

No birds chattered, no horses whinnied, no chickens screeched, no men shouted for their wives, no women screamed for their children, no babies cried for their mothers. An ungodly stillness blanketed the village, save for the crackling of torched wood.

She snapped back when he asked, "Who knows about this?"

"No one other than my family. Not even Armin knew. But there's more."

She told him everything, from finding a dying Mr. Chelmsky in the ruins, to escaping into the woods and wandering for days before she was brought to the nearest city. After being rescued by a peddler whose life was spared by her Papa's latch, she was taken in by the couple that became her aunt and uncle.

"My parents made me promise to keep my past a secret because they feared that the Cossacks would harm me if they knew I was alive. Eventually that threat passed, but by then everyone knew me as Lala Hafstein, so that's who I became. My real name was Luska."

"No wonder you bear up so well in adversity. All this must pale in comparison to what you've been through."

"Are you disappointed?"

"No, but I'm stunned, as much by your honesty as by your past."

"Is there anything you would like to ask me?"

"A question about your engagement. Were you aware that Armin was, um, how shall I put it?"

"Attracted to men." She shook her head. "Not at first. I knew he didn't womanize, but neither did my father, or my uncle, so that didn't seem unusual to me. When I finally learned the truth about him, I chose to end the engagement.

Fortunately, his decision to remain in Berlin gave us a way to call it off without jeopardizing his privacy, or mine. Then when he enlisted, I agreed to carry on the sham as a way of protecting him."

"But when you learned the truth, weren't you angry that he proposed?"

"He didn't propose, I did."

"So, you were in love with him."

"I wasn't, not in the way you mean. I proposed because as his wife, I could have lived with him in Prague and attended the Art Academy. That's why I wanted to marry him.

"My affection for Armin was based on a long and abiding friendship, not unlike my relationship with Paulina. I thought it would be enough, but I quickly learned it wasn't. I yearned for something more than companionship. My parents loved each other with great passion, tenderness and devotion. That's what I want in my life and I won't settle for anything less."

"If you're trying to scare me off, it won't work."

"I'm trying to be honest with you, Gershom. I would rather not marry at all than to commit to a man who hasn't won my heart."

"I can win your heart, Lala, if you let me. But I want a real wife, not what you proposed with Armin. I, too, want what your parents had, except perhaps a few more children. Can you see that for yourself?"

"I can, Gershom."

He kissed her hand. "Then we're in agreement."

They were. Each wanted the same thing. All Lala needed to determine was whether they could have that with each other.

CHAPTER THIRTY-TWO

With only one boarder, the workload at the boarding house eased, so Lala suggested Sarah split her days between the two houses. She had her mother cook meals for all in their home kitchen and deliver one portion for Gershom in the afternoon, where she could watch Jacub while Paulina tended to the boarding house. It freed Lala to concentrate on the outdoor chores, which were more difficult for her mother to do.

By the middle of May, rows of healthy green stalks and leaves filled Lala's garden. She estimated she could harvest peas in a few weeks, with beans following in late June. Once they were finished, she planned on replacing them with winter-hardy vegetables. Over in the henhouse, the two chicks had doubled in size. They would be old enough to lay eggs by winter.

All three women looked forward to Friday night, when Gershom would visit. Even Paulina began to appreciate having a day of rest when her only duty was tending to her baby.

***

Sarah was upstairs helping Paulina bathe Jacub when Lala heard a knock at the door. She opened it to find Gershom with a basket holding aromatic cloth bags and two liter-sized metal cans.

"What a nice surprise. What's all this?" asked Lala as she let him in.

"Some food that Elia left behind."

"None of this should spoil anytime soon. Why not keep it for his return?"

His grim face revealed an unpleasant answer was forthcoming.

"You haven't heard," he said. "Italy announced it has broken the treaty with the Alliance and will side with the French and British. They declared war on our empire yesterday."

The news brought on tears. "I would have kissed and hugged him more if I knew it would be the last time I'd see him." She invited Gershom into the kitchen where they unpacked two half-empty tins of olive oil, several small bags filled with dried herbs, and a burlap sack marked *Riso Vialone Nano* filled with tiny pearls of rice. "I'll use some of this for our next Sabbath dinner to remember him by."

After Gershom left, she turned out the lights downstairs before going up to her room. The news weighed heavily on her heart. Such a delightful young man. She'd miss his cheerful countenance and funny stories. She hoped the war would end before Elia reached the age of conscription. Still, it took him away, likely forever.

Her father and Armin dead. Ivo, Lew, and now Elia gone. Even Josef had to leave because of this horrible war. Only Gershom remained. Gershom, who would never be conscripted, never taken away from her. She took comfort from that.

A cry woke Lala in the middle of the night. She bolted upright as Paulina was rushing toward the cradle.

"It wasn't him," she said. "He's fast asleep."

"It sounded more like it came from the outside." Lala put on her robe and slippers. "I'll go check and you watch from up here."

"Be careful, my friend."

"I'm not going out there alone," Lala whispered as she opened her desk drawer. She felt around until her fingers touched metal. "I'm taking this with me." She held up her father's revolver.

"Do you know how to use that?"

"It's not loaded."

"What animal will be chased off by the sight of a gun?"

"The human variety."

Lala, torch in one hand, gun in the other, stepped outside. Her robe couldn't ward off the night chill, tempting her to return for her jacket, but if she did, she might not have the courage to go back out. Proceeding with caution, she stepped along the path, rustling her mother's rose bushes as she passed to scare off any prowlers in the yard. She heard no other sounds in the immediate area.

She shined her torch on the chicken coop to find a gaping hole cut in the side. After checking the immediate area for lurkers, she hurried to the coop. She spotted the two chicks huddled together in one corner of the henhouse. The gold and white hen acquired from Paulina's neighbor sat on its nesting box at the far end next to the brown speckled hen. The third nest was vacant, the white chicken missing.

Stealing eggs was bad enough, but now the thief had taken a healthy laying hen. Her grip on the revolver tightened. She needed to learn how to use it, without delay.

CHAPTER THIRTY-THREE

Lala baked a challah for Friday's dinner without egg yolks. The theft of their hen put the other chickens in a state of shock; there'd been no laying since the night their roost mate disappeared. Adding a pinch of Elia's saffron to the dough replicated the characteristic golden color that yolks provided, but failed to yield the right texture to the bread. She hated to waste her ration card for bread flour on substandard loaves.

At dinner, Lala tore off a chunk before passing the loaf around the table. As she chewed on the piece her disappointment grew with each bite.

"Gershom, do you know anything about shooting guns?"

Sarah dropped her fork. "Lala, what kind of talk is that on the Sabbath?"

"Practical talk when there's a thief prowling our property. He's stolen firewood, then eggs and now a laying hen. Who knows what he'll want to take next if we don't stop him."

Sarah picked up her fork. "He's probably hungry."

"Then let him come to the door and ask for food. That I would give willingly."

Gershom wiped his mouth with his napkin. "To answer your question, Lala, I have hunted since I was a boy. What do you want to know?"

"Can you teach me how to use my father's Reichsrevolver?"

"I wouldn't recommend using it. They're fine for close range shooting, like dispatching a wounded animal, but not for protection. They're difficult to aim correctly when you're in a panic situation and the recoil alone would overwhelm you."

"What would be better for protection, then?"

"A husband, of course."

Sarah nodded and laughed with him. Lala turned to Paulina, who shrugged.

Lala flinched again as the sound of gunfire echoed through the hills. On Sunday mornings, hunters from all over the region sought prey in the forest. She'd suggested that her mother and Paulina make Sunday laundry day for both households at the boarding house, leaving Lala home alone to do her yard work, followed by a relaxing bath.

She waited as long as she could before going out to tend the chickens. The noise unnerved her, but she dreaded the possibility of finding another hole in the fence, and another chicken missing, even more. Thankfully the coop hadn't been breached since she repaired the hole. With the summer solstice approaching, the long hours of daylight would motivate the chickens to lay more eggs. Hopefully enough to make up for the missing hen until the chicks were older.

She laid her egg basket on the ground and filled the hens' water dish as they pecked through the grass. A search of their roost found two eggs. Better than nothing. A menu for dinner came instantly—potato latkes fried in olive oil, maybe some spring greens if she could find any in the woods once the shooting stopped.

A sunbeam glinted off something metallic laying on the ground outside the coop. Lala left the eggs in the basket and went out to see what it was.

A pair of wire cutters. Were they hers, or left behind by the thief? No matter, she wouldn't leave them out for him to use. She got the key to the shed and unlocked it. As she opened the door, she felt a sharp thrust against her back, pushing her into the shed and almost knocking her down. Lala turned around to face a man in scruffy clothes, not much taller than she. Something about his boyish face, smeared with dirt, his ragged mop of curly brown hair plastered on one side of his head, rang familiar. His large blue eyes glared at her and his mouth twisted in displeasure.

"Hello, Lala. Remember me?"

CHAPTER THIRTY-FOUR

A chill ran through her. He knew who she was. It took several moments to recognize him.

"Zigmund! What on earth are you doing here?"

"I've come to pay my respects. Where is Paulina?"

"Why would you think she'd be here?" She slowly moved her hand clenching the wire cutters behind her.

"Come now. I know she lives here. How fun, just the two of you."

"That's not true."

"Quite right. Your old mother lives here, along with Paulina's little bastard. And she thought she was too good for me."

"She and Ivo are married now. Let her be, Zigmund. She made her choice."

"She made the wrong choice!" he shouted, then calmed down. "What does it matter, I never wanted to marry her, only have a little fun. Nothing wrong with that."

"Then find someone else to have your fun with, Zigmund."

He raised his eyebrows in that lecherous manner that had always disgusted her. "What about you, then? How much fun do you have with your pansy fiancé?"

347

"Please don't talk about Armin that way. He was murdered last year." She thought that would soften him, but it only made him angrier. "I tried to contact you when we found out, but you had moved and left no forwarding address." She inched to her right, hoping to dash past him and flee through the open shed door.

"Yes, well you can't very well get mail delivered to the forest, now can you? At least your old rifle came in handy for hunting." He pivoted left, blocking her escape route. "So he was murdered. Can't say I'm surprised, given his penchant for male flesh."

He took a step closer to her and she backed away. Beads of sweat gathered along her brow. She took deep breaths to stay calm while she calculated how to get away from him.

"I always wondered about you, what you saw in Armin." He moved closer, but her back was pressed against the wall. "You never seemed the type to go for money. Did you like the idea that he wouldn't touch you? Are you as cold as Paulina was fiery? Or perhaps, like Armin, you prefer the bestial arts." Standing centimeters away, he flashed an evil grin. "Either way, the cure is the same."

Lala's throat almost closed with panic. She made a run for the door, but Zigmund grabbed her above her wrist and squeezed until she dropped the wire cutters. He kicked them away and strengthened his grip until she feared her bones would snap.

"Stop it, Zigmund, you're hurting me."

"Stop? I'm just getting started."

She struggled against his grip, mustering every bit of strength she had. A knee to his groin dropped him to his knees and he released her. She ran to the door, but he grabbed her ankle and pulled her down. The two wrestled on the floor of the shed, but she thrashed around, kicking, biting and scratching as furiously as she could. He pinned her down with his left forearm and then struck her across the face with his right hand. She tasted blood.

"So, you're not cold after all, you little animal. Then I'll treat you like the animal you are!"

When that slap didn't subdue her, he punched her in the stomach. She wheezed and lost air long enough for him to grab her by the hair and pull her to her feet, shrieking.

"Scream all you want, no one will hear you."

Standing behind her, he wrapped his arm around her neck and, grabbing the back of her blouse, violently shoved her toward the workbench, tearing the blouse from neckline to sleeve.

"You like rough play? Well, so do I!"

He forced her upper body to flatten across the workbench, grabbed her neck and pressed his forearm into her spine with enough force to bruise her ribs. She wanted to kick him, but couldn't get her legs to move with him pinning her from behind. When she felt her skirt being lifted, she fought him with all her might, to no avail.

"No, no, NO!" she screamed over and over, crying and twisting, trying to break free. She felt his hands searching along the back of her calves, then her thighs, then pressure at the small of her back as she heard the sound of fabric ripping.

"Don't do this. You don't want to do this," she wailed as his hand sought her most private regions.

"Oh yes I do."

Two explosive noises rang through the shed. She felt his hands leave her body as she heard him collapse to the floor. She bolted upright to find him lying on his side with blood oozing out of two holes in his back, through and just below his left shoulder. She heard him gasp. Red froth bubbled from his mouth. He jerked and let out a breath, then stopped moving. She thought she would collapse from fright. What had happened? She looked up.

Standing behind Zigmund's dead body, holding a smoking gun, was Gershom.

CHAPTER THIRTY-FIVE

Gershom stepped over the body and came to her side. "Did he hurt you, Lala?"

Lala trembled so hard she couldn't move, couldn't speak. Her stomach and ribs ached, but she knew what Gershom was asking and managed to shake her head no.

"Let's get you out of here," he said, slipping his arm around her shoulder to guide her. She involuntarily flinched at his touch. He released her and offered his arm. She took hold as he led her around the body.

She caught her breath. "Oh, Gershom. It's a miracle you showed up when you did, and with a gun."

He held up the pistol. "I brought this for you, for your protection like you asked."

"It worked. I'll never be able to thank you enough."

When they stepped outside, she wanted to run to her house, strip off her clothing and wash the nightmare from her body. But he began to weep.

"Gershom?"

"I heard you screaming and tried to run, but I couldn't. I tried, though, I truly tried."

"Don't cry, Gershom. You saved me."

"Not soon enough, though. Not soon enough."

She eased his distress with a tender kiss. It calmed them both.

"We must get rid of the body," she said. "Let's bury him in the forest."

"Leave it to me. Where do you keep your wheelbarrow?"

Lala told Gershom to wait in the parlor once he buried the body so she could take a bath and wash that monster's presence off her body. She undressed next to the bathtub as it filled with hot water, holding on to the side for support. Bending felt too painful; her lower ribs were injured when Zigmund forced her down against the workbench. She tried to will the images of her attack away, but they plagued her like the memories of the pogrom had years ago. She caught a reflection of herself in the mirror; her lower lip split from being slapped, abrasions along her face and arms, purple bruises developing along her lower ribcage and where he'd squeezed her arm. Piling her torn dress and undergarments by the door for burning later, she stepped into the tub and eased herself into the water. That's when her tears began flowing. Taking the bar of soap, she scrubbed her body over and over and tried to forget, knowing she never would.

She dressed and lingered upstairs, waiting until Gershom returned, wondering how she could show her gratitude. She would ask him to hold her, knowing he would be gentle. That might delete the memory of that morning and replace it with something kinder, as had another embrace almost a year ago in the streets of Berlin.

A knock at the front door startled her. Warily she crept downstairs and opened the door to face two hunters. A man of about sixty, with a fringe of white hair around his cap, nodded to her while his younger pipe-smoking companion stood back.

"Pardon me, Miss. Have you seen a strange man lurking around your property?" He proceeded to describe Gershom.

Lala bit her lip. "No, I've been here all day and haven't seen a soul. Why do you ask?"

He looked to his companion, who nodded. "Well, Miss, I don't want to scare you, but about an hour ago we saw this fellow in the forest trying to bury a dead body. It might have been a hunting accident, but he didn't look like a hunter to me."

His companion added, "He could be a local who resented us city folk for hunting here."

"He must have done something bad to be hiding a body in the forest like that. Yours is the closest house to where we found him. We wanted to warn you and your neighbors, in case he's a madman or if any of your men are missing. A girl like you alone—"

"I'm not alone. My father and brother work the night shift at the Smetana factory," she said quickly. "They're asleep upstairs. And we have guns."

"That's good," said the hunter. "We'd best be off to report this to the police. Sorry we scared you."

"That's all right, I appreciate the warning."

She waited until they left to close the door. Leaning against it for support, she tried to catch her breath. Gershom's life was in danger now. If the police found him, he'd be charged with murder and executed. She had to get

353

him out of the city, as far away as possible, no matter what it took.

She'd drawn solace knowing Gershom was the one man who would never leave her. Now she had to send him away.

America. He'd be safe there. With his talent, he could easily find work. She could write to Karel, ask for his help in settling Gershom into a new life. Unfortunately, Gershom couldn't follow the route that Karel took. That would require land passage to Spain, an impossibility now that the war had advanced to engulf most of the continent. He'd have to travel to Germany and try to cross the border into a neutral country like Denmark or Holland. Even if he booked passage on a ship sailing to America, the danger from crossing the North Sea through the German blockade could prove deadly. She couldn't imagine how much it would cost.

One miracle had already happened. Now she had to secure a few more.

She filled her wash bucket with hot water and soap, and draped a washrag over the side to clean the blood from the shed. As she stepped outside she noticed the shed door was closed.

"Gershom, is that you?" she called.

The door slowly opened and he stepped out. "How long have you been hiding in there?"

"Since I got away from those hunters."

"Come into the house. You'll be safer there."

She brought him to the kitchen and fed him, but he had little appetite. She told him of her plan while he picked at his food.

"Will you come with me?" he asked with pleading eyes.

"I can't, Gershom. It would be too dangerous. Besides, I must stay here and care for my family."

"I won't go without you, Lala."

"You must. Go, get established in America, and I will come when I can."

"Do you love me?"

"How can you ask a question like that today?"

"When will you join me?"

"When the war ends. I will come then."

He relaxed. "May I have a picture of you to keep?"

"Of course. I'll get one for you."

She chose the photograph taken for her engagement almost a year ago. She looked more robust then. How she'd changed in that short time. How the world had changed.

She sent him home promising to meet him at the train station that evening. Then she went upstairs. She took her savings bag and counted out enough koruny to pay for his ticket and a few meals. He would have to rely on his own money for the rest of his expenses in Prague, but she would cover the cost of transportation north and passage to America. She wished she'd accepted Josef's offer of Romy's jewelry. That she'd gladly part with. Knowing Romy's taste, the piece would have fetched a great deal, unlike her engagement ring.

The only possession she had that would likely sell and raise enough money was the Monet painting Josef had given her...

"I can't think of anyone I would want to have it more than you."

Nor could she, but after what Gershom risked to save her, she had no choice.

CHAPTER THIRTY-SIX

She almost didn't recognize Gershom at the train station. His face looked common without his beard, though like many men he kept his mustache intact. Only his walk gave him away. She nodded with approval at his appearance. Toting a canvas bag stuffed with some clothing and food, and dressed in a belted Norfolk jacket, clean work pants, and newsboy cap, he looked like a hunter and would easily blend in with the men crowding the platform.

She took him aside and gave him an envelope. "Here is some money to help you get by until I can raise more."

He refused to take it. "You'll need it more than I will."

"Do you know how much passage on a ship will cost?"

"Two hundred thirty-five koruny for second class. I checked."

"And where will you get that much money?"

"I'll work in Prague until I earn enough to continue on my journey."

She lowered her voice. "You can't risk waiting any longer than necessary." She passed him a sheet of paper. "Take this, then. It's a classified advertisement for you to place in the Deutsche Zeitung Bohemia."

He read the message. His eyebrows rose at the last line.

"Five hundred koruny for a painting?"

"If I'm lucky to find a buyer. It's worth at least that much, maybe more."

The train pulled into the station. She kissed him. "Be careful."

"I'll meet you in front of Paulina's abandoned shop on Jindrisská Street at noon next Thursday." He waited until the train stopped, then with his head lowered he melded into the throng and got on board.

For an instant, she felt like following him onto the train. It passed. Leaving with him would not abate the fear that coursed through her whenever moments of the violent attack flitted in her mind. Nor would leaving fulfill the sense of obligation she felt toward him for what he'd done. Nothing would.

She'd ruined the man's life. Joining him would make it worse.

Lala stood watching until the train departed, then hurried out of the station and walked briskly toward the road to her home. Twilight approached and she wanted to return before dark.

CHAPTER THIRTY-SEVEN

"Drink this, Mother," Lala insisted.

Even with carefully couched words, her mother and Paulina were shaken by what had happened in their absence. Paulina blamed herself for Zigmund coming to their house, which Lala vehemently denied. Sarah couldn't stop crying for over an hour. Lala finally had to give her a glass of cognac to calm her down.

"Let me take her upstairs." Paulina handed Jacub to Lala and took Sarah's arm. "Let's get you to bed, Mama Sarah."

Lala sat on the sofa and laid Jacub across her lap, his head resting on her knees. He'd grown even cuter, if that were possible, and more alert. His eyes, more open now than when he was newborn, searched around his environs. He wriggled and pumped his little arms and legs, and made gurgling sounds. She watched him with fascination, marveling at how much he'd changed in such a short time. One hand reached out toward her and she moved her fingers closer to him. He grabbed one finger and squeezed, then looked directly at her. She couldn't help but smile. When he smiled back, her heart melted.

She started imitating the sounds he made, which got him smiling and wriggling more. When she heard Paulina coming down the stairs, she lifted Jacub into her arms and met her friend at the entrance to the parlor.

She kissed Paulina's cheek and handed her the baby. "Thank you, my friend. That was exactly what I needed."

The newspaper advertisement ran in Monday's afternoon edition. No response came that day, or the next, but on Wednesday morning she received a note from an agent representing a collector in Prague asking to come see the painting that afternoon. Lala agreed to meet him at her home. She asked her mother to stay behind. She also kept the Mauser pistol Gershom had given her nearby, fully loaded, just in case.

At precisely three o'clock an automobile parked in front of the house. Sarah opened the door as a man approached, dressed in a flawlessly tailored business suit. He appeared to be slightly taller than Lala, of medium build, with a poised carriage that implied good breeding. With multiple creases etched in his forehead and steel gray hair visible under his English-style Derby, Lala placed him well over fifty.

"Good afternoon. I am Emil Cerveny." He handed Sarah his calling card, which she passed to Lala. It showed him to be an art consultant and advisor to private collectors, with an office across the Vltava River in the Mala Strana section of Prague.

Sarah invited him into the parlor. He took a seat on the salon chair next to Sarah. She offered him a drink, which he politely declined. "My daughter Lala owns the painting," Sarah explained.

"May I see it?"

"I'll bring it to you," Lala said. "May I ask who you're representing?"

"My client prefers to remain anonymous and will maintain your anonymity as well. I assure you it's not uncommon under these circumstances."

She brought the painting from the dining room, where she'd stashed it earlier, and propped it on the sofa directly across from him.

He inspected the canvas, first from his chair and then standing before it. "Ah, it appears to be an early painting from the series Claude Monet created of the Cathedral in Rouen. I'd estimate this to be 1892." He lifted it up and checked the signature, then spent several minutes scanning every square centimeter of the canvas. "Early morning version, quite good. Only very minor visible damage. Original frame as well." He put the painting down. "It's definitely genuine. My client will be very pleased. I've been authorized to purchase this at once for the agreed upon sum." He removed a billfold from his jacket pocket and began to count out fifty-koruny banknotes into a neat pile. "I trust larger denominations won't be a problem?"

That night Lala dreamed of the painting she'd sold. She observed it on the floor of Josef's home office, rising like an angel from a cloud of torn paper. Josef had wanted to commemorate her engagement with a gift. She assumed it was Armin's portrait of her until she unwrapped it...

Her reaction pleased him, judging by his smile. "I can still remember how taken you were with it the first time you came to my home."

She continued to stare at the Monet painting that used to hang in the parlor.

"You had a very sophisticated eye for art, even as a child," he continued. "Fortunately, Armin shares your admiration for Monet, as do I. It took some hard bargaining to find the right replacement for this piece, though." He gestured to a deep alcove opposite his desk. She stepped over and peered in. There hung "She."

She awoke to darkness. Selling the painting couldn't sever her connection to Josef. Would anything?

CHAPTER THIRTY-EIGHT

Sergeant Novotny came to the house shortly after breakfast, inquiring about the murder that had taken place on Sunday. Acting on witness reports, the police found the burial site and dug up the body, which left no doubt of foul play. The man's wallet was missing. Novotny seemed particularly concerned that the victim had been shot in the back, which ruled out self-defense. He called the shooting "a cowardly act."

Lala's forthrightness in the investigation into Armin's death seemed to have made an impression on the Sergeant. He took her denial of any knowledge of the crime at her word. Lala knew Novotny had a distinct disadvantage, being unaware that he was questioning a master of concealment and secrecy.

"I don't like the idea of you traveling by yourself to Prague." Sarah hadn't stopped fretting over Lala since learning of the attack, and the police investigation further unnerved her. "It's too dangerous," she insisted.

"Mother, I must. I owe everything to Gershom, the

sacrifice he made for me."

Sarah's shoulders slumped. "And I'll always be grateful to him for what he did." She eyed the large sack Lala carried. "What's in there?"

"A few things Gershom will need, money and food, and a few small personal mementos. No one will suspect. People will think I'm returning to the city with supplies."

She cupped Lala's face. "I can't help but worry for you."

"There should be no danger on the train and Gershom will protect me in the city." She patted the bag. "Besides, I'll have Father's revolver until I give it to Gershom."

"Where is the gun he gave you?"

"In the front bureau drawer next to the torch. Why?"

"If you're not back before dinner, I'll take it with me to Prague to find you."

Lala stepped out onto Wilsonova, the busy boulevard that fronted Prague's railway station, and crossed to a park. She clutched her handkerchief, ready to dab away perspiration from her brow brought on by the warm June day, or tears along her cheeks when she said her goodbyes.

Walking along a tree-lined path, she passed groups of women on benches watching their children at play. Young mothers pushing baby carriages promenaded alongside and elderly men tottered in slow motion, or sat in pairs ruminating over a game of chess. She also spotted a few soldiers home from the war, with shiny medals and ribbons fastened to their uniforms. Young men all, limping on damaged legs aided by canes or maneuvering on crutches, many with missing limbs discreetly camouflaged by hollow pant legs and pinned back sleeves. Loud voices pierced the subdued chatter as group of men reprimanded a boy who was feeding bread to the pigeons.

She continued northeast into the Jewish Quarter and wandered until she reached Jindrisská Street at the appointed time. Up ahead she saw Gershom waiting for her and hurried to join him.

He took her arm and guided her away from the empty shop. "Let's go to a café. We'll attract less attention there."

As they walked, Lala noticed his limp had worsened. "Are you hurt?" she asked.

"I'm exaggerating my limp so people will think I've been injured in the war." He gestured to a café around the corner of Panska Street and led her inside.

Gershom held the chair for her as she sat. "Two coffees, please," he told the waiter. When the man had his back turned to them, Lala pushed her sack over to his side of the table.

She leaned in and whispered, "I sold the painting. There's enough money to pay for your trip and get you started in your new 'home,' plus my father's revolver for your protection."

"Don't you want it for yourself?"

She smiled. "You said the Mauser pistol would be better for me. Besides, I'd like you to have the revolver as a remembrance of my father."

"I'm touched." He wedged the sack between his ankles. "I trust you kept some of the money for yourself."

"Enough," she lied.

They paused their conversation until the waiter had served them coffee and walked away.

Gershom leaned toward her. "When will you come join me?"

"I told you, not until the war ends. I can't leave my family with no means of support."

"Then bring them with you. We can settle in New York and marry next fall." His face bore earnestness, mouth tightened, eyes pleading. Those beautiful eyes. She looked away.

"It's too dangerous."

He nodded. "Of course, you're right. You must wait. There is no guarantee that I will survive the sailing, let alone the journey to an open port."

She took his hand. "I put a memento in your sack to help you with that. It's wrapped in a towel, but be careful. It's very fragile."

He rummaged through the sack until he brought out a small object encased in linen. He placed it on the table and unwrapped it.

"What's this? A yellow glass?"

"It's a Bohemian crystal goblet. It belonged to my family long ago. When I lost them, this goblet served as a beacon that led me to a new life. I want you to have it. Let it lead you safely to your next home."

He wrapped the goblet in the towel and returned it to the sack. "I will treasure this."

The waiter began to hover so they limited their conversation to small talk while they finished their coffees. Gershom paid the check and escorted Lala out of the café.

They returned to Jindrisská Street. "You must go now or you'll miss your train." He draped the sack over his shoulder.

"What about you? What are your plans for escaping?"

"I have it all worked out, including several fallback plans.

It would be much better if I don't tell you."

"Better? How can you say that? I'll be beside myself with worry."

"Safer, then. If you don't know you won't have to lie about it."

Lala felt tears coming on. "I'm so sorry, I ruined your life."

He took her hand. "You didn't ruin my life. I had no life after my riding accident. My older brother had died, and then my little sister, leaving my parents bereft. Then I lost my leg and became damaged in their eyes. My father felt so shamed by my disfigurement that he fell ill and died shortly afterward. My mother grew cold toward me, as if my injury was meant to spite her."

His faraway gaze returned to her. "Your father was the first person who saw me as more than a lame man, and it crushed me when he died. And then I met you. I had no reason to believe you would even look at me, yet here we are, together. In love." He kissed her hand. "You didn't ruin my life, Lala. You gave it back to me."

He leaned in for a kiss. She clung to him for as long as she could until he released her. Lala watched as he walked away. She touched her lips. That kiss would have to last a long, long, time.

PART THREE

Late February, 1917

CHAPTER ONE

"Antila, Antila."

Lala opened her eyes and found herself on the floor; she must have fainted again, the second time this week. Jacub squatted next to her, poking her cheek with his finger, his eyes fixed on her; big and blue, like his mother's.

"Wake up, Antila."

"I'm awake, Jacub." She sat up but felt lightheaded, so she lowered her head until the feeling passed. She hadn't eaten since last evening. At least this time she passed out in the center of the parlor, where there was no furniture. She had moved the sofa and chairs around the fireplace for warmth when the weather turned bitter and coal became unobtainable. The bare rug had protected her from serious injury. She checked the clock on the mantle. Half past noon. Only four and a half more hours until she could eat again. If there was anything left to eat.

Jacub stood, still staring at her. She reached up and ruffled his dark brown hair.

"Promise you won't tell Grandmama I fell down again?"

He put his finger to his lips and shushed. "Our secret."

Lala bit her lip. She swore to herself she would never do that to her nephew. As he toddled off, she called him back.

"Yes, Antila?"

"Forget what I said."

Jacub nodded. "I get Mama." He put on the coat Paulina had fashioned out of a moth-eaten blanket, then the scarf and mittens Grandmama had knit for him, and went outside. When he'd begun talking, the boy was told to call her "Auntie Lala" by his mother. He couldn't pronounce it so she became "an-TEE-la."

Lala got on her feet and rubbed the bruise on her elbow, a souvenir of the last time she fainted. With faltering steps, she went to the kitchen stove and poured a cup of hot water. She took it to the table and sipped it slowly, imagining it filling her stomach. The heat from the stove warmed her as much as the beverage. She'd brought Paulina's mattress downstairs when freezing temperatures took hold in winter. Paulina slept with Jacub near the stove to stay warm. Lala and her mother slept by the parlor fireplace.

Jacub led his mother into the kitchen. "You fainted again?"

Lala saw the concern on Paulina's face. She looked at her friend with sadness, more for Paulina than herself.

Paulina had been a robust woman with a Rubenesque figure, bouncing blonde curls and a round face. She weighed seven kilos less now, leaving her as slender as Lala had been before the war. Her cheeks sunk, her pink complexion looked waxy, her hair dull. Like Lala, she'd ceased menses last year. Always meticulous about her appearance and dress, Paulina had stopped caring and it reflected in her attire. Garments hung on her lean frame as if she wasn't in them.

"This has got to stop." Paulina turned to her son. "Jacub, go find Grandmama. She should be near the forest gathering wood. Ask her to come here."

After the toddler left, Paulina crossed her arms. "We have practically no food left and little chance of buying any at the market. You are going to eat something now, and then while your mother watches Jacub, we are going to find more food no matter what."

"Which means the Black Market."

"What other alternatives are there? Unless you ask—"

"No."

"Lala, I'm sure—"

"Absolutely not. You know how hard it is to get by in Prague, and it's worse in Vienna. I can't ask him for help."

"If he can afford to keep his wife in Bohnice…."

She raised her hand to halt the conversation, as her mother used to do. "That's his choice. Now let's focus on what we have to trade and come up with a plan."

Lala held the end of her shawl against her face for protection from the wind gusts that bit into her. She hadn't acclimated to the subfreezing weather that arrived in January and continued into February. She fought the temptation to wear her winter coat. It would have been warmer, but it was all she had of real value left to trade. She'd have to cope with the wool sweater, boiled wool jacket and shawl she was wearing until spring, longer if the weather stayed unseasonably cold, so might as well get used to it straightaway.

Paulina, similarly underdressed, shivered against the frigid temperatures. She switched the suitcase she carried to her other hand. Despite the cold, neither she nor Paulina could manage a brisk pace. Lack of food had sapped their energy as well as their strength.

At the bottom of the hill they turned onto the main road that led into town. Although a half-kilometer away from the market, they spotted the end of the line ahead. As they walked along, Lala heard no gossiping, no strategizing, no conversations. The people in queue huddled in groups to keep warm, their haggard faces barren of expression.

Lala turned away and said, "Let's play 'happy times.'"

She and Paulina invented the game to distract themselves from the harshness of their current lives by recalling moments of joy before the war.

"I'll go first." A smile crept onto Paulina's face. "I remember one Christmas when I was six and my father and brother were still alive. I had so wanted a doll, but as you know dolls are expensive, so I didn't expect to get one. But my mother made me a doll out of cloth stuffed with rags. She sewed buttons on for eyes, embroidered a nose and lips, and used yellow yarn for her hair. And do you know what the first thing I did was? I made a new dress for her. Something pretty. A bridal gown, as I recall, from a damask napkin."

"That's sweet, Paulina. You win a point. My turn now." She thought a few moments until something came to her. "My parents brought me to Bohemia by train. I'd never seen a train before, let alone ridden in one. I wasn't used to being their daughter yet, so we all walked on eggshells. Then my father suggested we go to the restaurant car for cake. My parents also ordered coffee and asked me what I wanted to drink. I was about to say tea, but instead I asked for milk. I was seven years old, but for the first time in my life, I realized I was a little girl."

"We're tied for now."

They followed the queue to the market, then trudged past the train station and the row of storefronts beyond, including Paulina's former shop, which the government used to store spare parts for war ships and planes. In all the years Lala stood in line outside the shop, she never saw anything go in or out, nor did the quantity or arrangement of merchandise ever change.

Continuing several blocks farther, they reached a farrier's barn. Lala knocked on the door and waited until an elderly woman gawked through a window.

"What do you want?"

Lala held up her coat and Paulina cracked open the suitcase she carried for a peek. The door opened and the woman ushered them in. Gold filigree earrings hung like chandeliers from her earlobes and a strand of fat pearls adorned her wizened neck.

The barn was empty except for a reclaimed workbench and what looked like a hand-carved Jacobean chair near a working wood-burning stove, inadequate for heating the space.

"My son-in-law will be right with you. Wait here." She hobbled across the straw covered ground to the chair and sat.

Before long a squat middle-aged man wearing a fine double-breasted frock-coat entered the barn. A newsboy cap obscured his silvered hair; hooded eyes and a thick nose defined his face. He strode to where Lala and Paulina waited. "What have you got for me?"

Lala showed him the winter coat. He held it up to inspect it. "Good condition, no moth holes. Fine quality as well, not that it matters much anymore," he noted. "Food, coal, or medicine?"

"Food, mostly non-perishable."

He snickered. "You say that because you think you'll get enough in trade to last awhile. I can give you a loaf of K-brot and two tins of herring."

"No K-brot. If I want to eat 'war bread' made with sawdust and ashes I'll go to my fireplace and get it for free. What else can you give me besides the fish? Do you have flour, or butter? Eggs? Potatoes?"

He scoffed. "Don't waste my time. Go home."

"No," interjected Paulina. "We can sweeten the deal."

"Paulina!" cried Lala. To the man she said, "If you make us a serious offer, that is."

"What else do you have?"

Paulina opened her suitcase to show him two of Romy's evening gowns. "These come from Paris, made by some of the finest couturiers in the world." She showed him the labels. "Look at the workmanship. Any woman would prize these. A nice gift for that special lady?"

"My wife doesn't need a fancy gown, Miss. Even if I was inclined to barter, I wouldn't need two."

"Perhaps I should ask your wife's mother if that's so," Lala said in a low voice.

The marketer asked his mother-in-law to return to the house. When she left, he barked, "I don't need two evening gowns for my wife—"

"Of course not, Mr. Bruzek," Lala said, "and certainly not in different sizes. We thought you might give the larger dress to your wife Lydie and the other one to your mistress, Radka Novotnova." Lala smiled. "Whose husband is Wachtmeister Novotny of the local police." She flashed the calling card the Sergeant had given her.

Bruzek blanched. "Wait here." He went around the back of the barn and returned with a filled sack. "There's two tins

376

of herring, a kilo of flour, a half kilo each of butter and potatoes, and a dozen eggs." He snatched the coat and the gowns from them. "Now go away and don't ever come back!" He showed them outside and slammed the door.

As soon as they were out of earshot, Paulina began laughing. "Despite your reluctance about dealing with the black market, that was a brilliant plan, my friend."

"You performed your role flawlessly, Paulina. You'd make quite an actress."

"How did you know about Bruzek's mistress?"

"You may not get much food on the market lines anymore, but you can still obtain valuable gossip."

CHAPTER TWO

In the kitchen, Sarah ran a hand over her gray hair as Lala showed her the dozen eggs.

"How many should we use for dinner?" her mother asked.

She looked thinner than Lala could recall. Her ashen complexion made the dark circles under her eyes more pronounced.

"I'd say four, so we could have a decent meal," Paulina suggested as she tied an apron around her waist. Enough length remained for her to wrap the ties around to her front and fasten them into a bow.

"But three would give us one more meal," Sarah observed.

"Make six," said Lala. "With a potato. Then none of us will go hungry tonight."

They devoted dinnertime to teaching Jacub his table manners and working on his words. Spending all his time with adult women, he showed an advanced vocabulary and a real interest in learning. Afterward Sarah and Paulina took him to the parlor to play in front of the fireplace.

Lala excused herself. "I'm going upstairs."

"You'll get too cold," her mother warned.

"I won't be long." She wrapped a blanket over her and went to her room.

With no coal to heat the house, Lala decided to abandon the upper level except the toilette and keep everyone downstairs, where they could burn wood in the stove and fireplace.

Lala sat at her desk with a blank sheet of stationery before her, ready to write to Gershom in America. For his protection, she'd been contacting him through Karel, with whom she occasionally corresponded since Armin's death.

Lifting the pen, she wrote:

My dearest friend,

I trust you are well and have grown accustomed to living in New York, which must be so different from where you used to live. I am pleased to hear that your cabinetmaking business is thriving and you now have an apartment of your own. I so enjoy reading about all the interesting places that surround you. It must be very exciting.

I wish I had some good news for you. The past six months have been more dreadful than the previous three years. While the war continues, the weather turned abysmal after last summer. Torrential rains ruined the harvest, followed by the coldest winter in memory, which still lingers. With much of the crops destroyed, grains are limited and potatoes fell to a fraction of a normal harvest. We pray for spring to come, and soon.

Between the weather and further rationing instituted last year, securing adequate food is a challenge. Nowadays only the first few people on line can buy anything at the markets with their ration cards, assuming they have the money. The joke is that often the only place you'll see the item of food is on the ration card. Sadly, it's led to a thriving black market, which makes it harder to buy items legally. Stories abound of people trading valuables like jewelry and silver for a loaf of bread, women selling their bodies to feed their children.

The regular migration of city folks to the country to find food and supplies continues. They've even named it "hamstering." It's became so widespread that many have stopped bartering and simply steal what they need.

The sound of gunfire from the forest has decreased with little left to hunt. The echo of rifles has been replaced by the sound of timber falling as people cut down trees to heat their homes. Coal is almost impossible to find.

Once winter set in and the chickens couldn't find food on their own, I made the grim decision to slaughter them over the course of a month. The birds were so scrawny we could barely get two meals out of each. I've kept the coop in case we can buy more chickens this spring. Seeing it reminds me of you.

I shall finish this letter with my hopes for your continued progress. Until we meet again.

Yours, as always, Lala

She read the letter through. Then, as always, she tore it up and prepared for bed.

CHAPTER THREE

"…and they lived happily ever after." Lala closed the book and basked in Jacub's smile. She'd finished reading him her old *Ash Girl* book, which he loved as much as she had. Her mother and Paulina huddled with blankets on the sofa in front of the roaring fire in the hearth.

Lala added more wood to the fireplace and stepped back. The logs crackled and spit, having been recently cut and given little time to dry. It had become such a struggle to keep up with the demand, she'd ceased storing firewood outside.

Paulina scooped Jacub in her arms. "Who do you want to sleep with tonight?"

He usually picked his mother or Sarah. To Lala's surprise he announced, "Antila!"

Paulina passed him to her.

"Then let's go to bed." She carried him to the kitchen, laid him on the mattress set near the stove, and covered him with a blanket. She got into the bed and snuggled with him. After a few minutes, he fell asleep. Lala eased out of the bed and rejoined the women in the parlor.

"It doesn't feel as cold tonight," said Paulina. "Maybe we'll have an early spring."

"It can't come soon enough for me," observed Sarah.

"Are you girls ready for bed?"

"I'm not tired," said Paulina.

Lala curled her feet under her. "What shall we do?"

"Let's play that game you like, 'happy times.'"

"We were only twenty-two when the war began, Mama Sarah. We've run out of stories."

"Then let's pick our favorite day from last year. Paulina, you go first."

"Normally I would have chosen March twenty-third, Jacub's first birthday, but it would have to be June seventh, when Ivo returned home on leave to surprise me. How wonderful he looked when I saw him standing in the doorway." Her eyes filled with tears. "I shall never forget the look on his face when he first held Jacub."

"What about your marriage the next day?"

Paulina twirled her wedding band. "The icing on the cake." She chuckled. "He still writes about that cake you baked, Mama Sarah. I'm glad you taught me how to make it." Smiling, she turned to Sarah. "What about you?"

Sarah beamed. "That's easy. February sixteenth, the first time Jacub called me 'Grandmama'. Not even a year old. Such a bright child." She sighed. "Lala, it's your turn."

Lala thought about it. "It would have to be July twelfth, my birthday. A sunny day as I recall. I felt inspired for the first time in years and made that sketch of Jacub."

She drifted back to that day. "I remember inviting Berthe to join us for tea and cake, how happy she was. And her gift, that lovely book she made of native plants to forage for food and medicine, folklore handed down from her mother. How many times have we used it since?" Sadness rattled her voice. "She didn't look well, but I had no idea she was dying."

"Dear, these are supposed to be happy memories."

"I'm happy I could spend that day with her. She certainly enjoyed it." Lala felt herself drifting into gloominess.

"And what a feast we had," Paulina added. "It began when you bartered with that fisherman for trout, remember? Then Berthe picked those delicious mushrooms in the forest and Mama Sarah cooked them together with the last of Elia's olive oil."

"Don't forget the cake," Sarah added.

"Yes, your famous burnt sugar cake, which took months of hoarding to make."

The memory cheered Lala. "And you baked real bread, too. None of that K-brot to soak up the juices of the fish."

"What luck your finding that trout. Otherwise I would have spent the last of the money from the sale of your painting to splurge on fish. Instead we could stock up on staples. If I hadn't, I doubt we would have survived this winter."

"Mother, you always said Father would watch over us."

Paulina nodded. "How fortunate we were to have that art agent buy your painting. Wouldn't it be wonderful to have a benefactor make a second appearance in your life?"

"Paulina," Lala admonished. She would not let their talk drift into fantasy, especially about Josef.

"You mean a third appearance," Sarah said as she yawned. "That would be too much to ask for."

Paulina stared at her with shock. Sarah flinched. "I'll check on Jacub."

Her mother's horrified look puzzled Lala. "What do you mean by a third appearance?

Clearly flustered, she said, "I can't tell you."

"Mother, I thought we decided no more secrets between us."

"You agreed they should be maintained when revealing the truth will hurt others." Her mother got up and walked away.

"And who would this secret hurt?"

Before Sarah left the room, she answered, "You."

CHAPTER FOUR

Lala followed her mother into the kitchen, shadowed by Paulina. She waited until Sarah checked on the boy, then whispered, "Tell me."

Sarah backed away, cowed like a defenseless animal. Lala pointed in the direction of the parlor and followed her mother out. She repeated her question.

Sarah shook her head. "I can't. You'll hate me for the rest of your life."

"Mama Sarah," Paulina blurted. "Saying that won't suppress her curiosity. Maybe you should tell her. After all, it happened so long ago."

Lala's temper flared. "So, you confided in Paulina but not me?" She took a deep breath to calm down, to little avail.

"If you promise to stay calm and not get angry at me, I will tell you."

"I can't promise that."

Sarah began to cry.

"Now see what you've done," scolded Paulina. "Why must you be so hardhearted?"

"Spoken like the favorite child," Lala said. "How can I compete with the mother of her grandson?"

"Please, both of you, stop!" cried Sarah, bawling.

387

"Shhh, you'll wake Jacub," Lala said, chastened. "Mother, sit down and try to calm yourself." She led her mother to the sofa and helped her sit. Paulina went to sit next to Sarah, but instead chose the chair and offered Lala the place beside her mother. Lala apologized to her friend, which Paulina accepted with a hug. Then Lala turned her attention to her mother.

Sarah wiped her eyes. "Don't be angry with me."

"I can't unless I hear your secret, but I promise I won't hate you, no matter what."

Her mother took a deep, shuddering breath. "Your father and I kept this from you for many years. We felt we had to, but only to protect you."

"I believe you. Go on."

"Do you remember the last night we spent in Russia, when we told you that you would have to keep your past a secret?"

"To protect me from Cossacks. Yes, I remember."

"That wasn't entirely true."

"You didn't think they posed a danger to me?"

"They may have, but we learned from your Uncle Hershel you faced a greater danger."

"From what?"

"Not what, who." Sarah exhaled loudly, as if her breath could expel demons. "The day before we left the country, thirteen people showed up at your uncle's synagogue, new to the city and desperate for help. They came from a shtetl that had been attacked several days earlier and managed to escape into the forest. They followed the river to a pond in a clearing and spent the night there. The next day they returned to their shtetl to bury their dead and salvage what they could, then set out on foot to the nearest city."

Lala felt her mouth go dry as memories of that day

resurfaced…

…returning to the forest, she hastened toward the small clearing where trees ringed the pond. As she approached, loud voices and horses snorting disrupted the silence.…

"I was there. I heard them, but thought they were Cossacks, so I ran away."

Sarah grabbed her hand. "It's a good thing you did, dear." Sarah's weeping had ceased, but the painful memory creased her face like a crumpled letter. "They were quite angry about the pogrom, placing the blame squarely on someone in the shtetl who had angered the Cossacks. They cursed his name and his family. Then they heard from members of the congregation about the little girl who'd mysteriously arrived at the Rabbi's house only days earlier. They assumed her to be the Peddler's daughter and vowed she'd never know a day of happiness.

"We knew without a doubt these villagers came from the same shtetl as you. At first, your father and I dreaded that you'd want to go off with them if you knew they'd survived. But when we heard the venomous words with which they spoke about the family whom they blamed for the attack.…" Sarah began weeping again. "We feared that if they found you.…" Her body heaved with sobs.

"Mother, how could you ever think I would hate you for protecting me? You made the right decision."

"I'm glad you feel that way, but your father and I can't take all the credit. Your uncle said a mysterious benefactor showed up at his office the next day and offered to give each survivor a sum of money if they left the city immediately."

"Who was it?"

"He never said, but we believed it must have been your Aunt Naomi. Who else would have had that kind of money? I thought it was her way of atoning for the horrid plans she had for you before your father and I took you in. It's also why I forgave her for her callous treatment toward me before then."

"Lala, you were indeed fortunate to join such a kind and loving family," Paulina said. "No matter what else happens in this crazy world, you have that."

"Yes, I am fortunate," said Lala, glancing at her mother. She'd stopped crying, but Lala could see her mother had held something back, and she suspected what it might be.

"So, you believed Aunt Naomi was my 'mysterious benefactor.'"

Her mother attempted an agreeable look, but Lala knew better. Even long ago when she was Luska, she could detect a lie, and her mother was lying now.

Her face smiled, but her eyes didn't.

CHAPTER FIVE

Lala prepared to leave for the market line before midnight. Her mother planned to join her until Lala said, "Why don't you stay here and watch Jacub, while Paulina and I go." She put on her boiled wool jacket over her sweater, draped a shawl over her head, and tied a blanket around her like a cape.

"I'll get ready," said Paulina. "Mama Sarah, would you share the bed with Jacub?"

Sarah nodded with delight.

Lala's torch had given up long ago. On this early March night, a nearly full moon illuminated the road from behind a veneer of clouds. With no wind, the lingering cold didn't sting as much. Still, they didn't chat, preferring to save their energy for the walk and their conversation for the long wait.

The women carried cushions from an old sofa in their marketing bags to have something to sit on while they waited for the market to open at noon. They walked carefully through the darker sections of the road until they reached their destination. Fortunately, only one woman had arrived before them, so their chances of finding food were fairly good. They began a line by setting their cushions on the sidewalk and sitting down. Lala covered herself with her blanket. Paulina did the same. By the time they had settled in for the night, three more women joined them in queue.

Lala nudged Paulina. "When did my mother tell you that story?"

"Awhile back, when we worked together at the boarding house." She whispered in Lala's ear, "Before Gershom left. But she swore me to secrecy."

"Did she tell you the same lie she told me?"

"Lala, please don't put me in the middle of this."

"Then you know what she has yet to admit."

"And what would that be?"

"Who gave the money to the survivors. It certainly wasn't my aunt or I'd have known about it long ago."

Paulina shifted in her seat. "What makes you think it wasn't her?"

"I love Naomi dearly, but she's a braggart. She would never have kept this to herself for all these years."

Paulina heaved a sigh. "All right, you might as well know the truth. Your mother spoke to your aunt about it during shiva for your father. She admitted she didn't supply the money, but she didn't know who your 'mysterious benefactor' was, or why he offered to pay the survivors to resettle elsewhere."

"He?"

"A man they didn't recognize. He had an accent so they assumed he wasn't from the area. That is all I know, and now that you know as well, perhaps you should leave it in the past. It can't make a difference now."

"But it does," Lala insisted. "Another thirteen people

survived the pogrom. Thirteen people who blamed Papa for what happened, and me by extension. They hated my family enough to put a curse on us, on me, to be deprived of happiness.

"And look at what's happened to every man in my life. My father died suddenly and too soon, leaving his family with financial difficulties. Armin was murdered as he prepared to come home to see me. Josef ended our romance because his wife caused his son's death and went mad, and Gershom had to flee the country because he came to my aid. Every man I've cared about is dead, or had his life ruined. It certainly seems like I'm cursed."

"That's utter nonsense. Think of what you do have. Your mother. A darling nephew who loves you. A roommate who's now a sister as well as a friend. Things are not as bleak as you portray them."

Unconvinced, Lala stood. "Take my marketing bag and ration cards."

"Where are you going?"

"We have no food left in the house. If we can't get any today, we could all starve before the market reopens in three days." Lala knotted her blanket around her. "I'm afraid I'll ruin our chances so I'm going home. I don't feel very lucky right now."

CHAPTER SIX

Purple tinged the sky to the southeast as Lala passed the meadow near her home. Dawn would arrive soon, but it couldn't lighten the darkness that had set upon her soul, nor lift the sense of impending misfortune from her heart. Never one to believe in superstitions, she couldn't ignore how one aspect of her life had seemed cursed. Did the sin of the father fall upon the child?

Lala brooded for three days, alone in her room, barely able to leave her bed. She couldn't eat and spent hours sleeping during the day, only to toss and turn at night. Even Jacub couldn't bring her cheer. Her world had been turned upside down, night to day, hope to helplessness.

On the third night, she dreamed of Josef for the first time in over a year. He cradled her in his arms as he did in Berlin and again when her father died, as if willing her to break free of the melancholy that had beset her.

When she awoke, she pulled herself out of bed and promptly fainted from hunger. When she came to, she undressed to bathe, noting her naked body in the mirror. A wan, skeletal figure was reflected back; ribs and hipbones protruding from her concave belly, her breasts almost flat, her shoulder blades prominent. Hollowed cheeks and sunken eyes encircled with skin so dark it looked shaded in charcoal. Anyone who saw Armin's painting, "She," would never know it was Lala. Good that Josef kept the piece. Better he remember her like that than as she looked now.

After bathing and dressing she went downstairs, where she was greeted with a big hug from Jacub.

"Antila, I miss you. All better?"

"I am now, Jacub, thanks to you. Where are your mother and Grandmama?"

"In the garden."

She felt dizzy and teetered for a moment.

Jacub reached up for her hand. "No fall down, Antila." He tugged her over to a chair. "Sit, sit. I get Mama."

As he went outside, she began to cry. She'd worked herself into such a state she had to rely on her toddler nephew to rescue her. Lala clung to the chair until Paulina came in.

"I'm so sorry," Lala cried. "I've been behaving like an idiot. Please help me up."

Paulina took her arm and brought her into the kitchen where she fixed Lala a slice of K-brot, cut into quarters, each topped with a slice of hard-boiled egg.

"There were eggs at the market?"

"They're not from the market." Paulina filled a glass with water. "I borrowed your pistol to hunt. I shot two hares and traded one for the eggs and some dried fruit. I kept the other hare for Jacub and myself." She put the glass on the table by Lala's plate. "Now eat slowly or you won't be able to keep it down."

"I'll be all right. No more feeling sorry for myself."

"Good."

"I refuse to believe Papa was responsible for the pogrom, or that I'm cursed," she said, to convince herself as much as Paulina.

"Even better. How could you be cursed if a complete stranger saved your life by sending the villagers away? Now eat."

Lala took a bite. As she chewed, Lala thought about the mystery man.

"*...Your uncle said a mysterious benefactor showed up at his office the next day and offered to give each survivor a sum of money if they left the city immediately....*"

How was it that no one knew who he was? And what would prompt someone to provide aid to so many strangers? Kindness? How times had changed. She couldn't imagine anyone doing something like that now.

...if they left immediately...."

Thirteen people could have easily settled somewhere in the city. Paulina was right. By requiring the villagers to leave, the stranger had saved her life.

CHAPTER SEVEN

"Jacub, time for your nap," his mother called.

Jacub bounded into the room, full of energy for the first time in months. Lala could swear the boy looked a few centimeters taller than last month, a positive sign. Before that he hadn't grown at all in six months.

The long winter famine had eased somewhat with spring days away. Paulina hunted and the women foraged, guided by Berthe's book, which revealed less-known edible plants. They still hadn't enough to eat, but they weren't starving.

Lala and Sarah kissed the boy before Paulina took him upstairs.

"We have yahrzeit coming up for your father in two days," Sarah noted.

Fortunately, the memorial candle to commemorate the birth date of her father would coincide with a happier candle lighting. "And Jacub's second birthday," she reminded her mother.

"How time flies. Seems like yesterday when he was a babe in the cradle. I wonder if we can manage a cake."

"He's your grandson. He won't care as long as it's sweet."

399

"Nothing is sweeter than that boy." Sarah turned her head toward the front door. "Do you hear someone outside?"

Lala opened the door as a familiar woman dismounted from a bicycle.

"Mrs. Havlik." Lala's stomach clenched, fearing bad news. "Please come in."

Mrs. Havlik offered her a warm smile. "Thank you, Miss Hafstein."

Sarah greeted her from the parlor. "How nice to see you. What brings you here?"

The woman's smile faded, causing Lala's stomach to tighten more.

"A message was sent to the house from Bohnice Hospital." She fell quiet.

"Please go on," Sarah urged.

"Mrs. Smetana is gravely ill."

"Is Mr. Smetana aware of this?" asked Lala.

"Yes, Miss, but he's given me no instructions." She wrung her hands. "Given the circumstances I'm not sure of what to do."

"Allow me to be frank," Sarah said. "He has been paying for her care, but has essentially cut her out of his life."

Mrs. Havlik nodded.

"Then I wouldn't concern yourself with this, Mrs. Havlik. He's already marked her passing. She has no other family or friends, so let the hospital take care of the matter when the time comes."

Relief washed over her face. "Thank you, Mrs. Hafstein."

"Thank you for telling us," said Sarah. "I'll show you out."

Lala went to the kitchen. So, Romy was dying. Josef would finally be free of her. Josef would be free.

Her mother came in. "She's relieved to be free of that responsibility."

"Don't be naïve, Mother. I doubt that's why she came here."

"That's very perceptive. You are growing wise about men, my friend."

Lala was.

CHAPTER EIGHT

Lala fought exhaustion every day to prepare the garden for planting. Although still colder than normal, daytime temperatures finally rose above freezing. She rarely could work more than a few hours a day without adequate food, but she forced herself to go on. Playing a version of "happy times" helped.

Her current favorite occurred two weeks earlier...

"Blow out the candles, Jacub."

"Antila help me."

Lala rubbed his back. "You're a big boy now. You can do it all by yourself."

With one big whoosh, the two-year-old extinguished all three candles, which earned him a round of applause from his mother, Grandmama and Lala.

"I did it!" he cried with pride.

With flour unobtainable, Lala had made him a custard of egg yolks flavored with foraged honey and sweet violets from the meadow instead of a cake. He didn't mind. Or share.

His favorite gift turned out to be the drawing she'd made of him dressed like the prince in her *Ash Girl* book. It brought back sweet memories of her own childhood, when Armin used to give her a drawing for her birthday every year, until her eleventh, when Armin presented her with his first painting…

"Oh, Armin, it's magnificent."

"You have always thought I was grand. I told Father that. He said you were my muse."

"What is that?"

"Someone who inspires you."

She'd ceased to inspire anyone long ago, but took pleasure in beginning this tradition anew.

That happy memory also mollified less pleasant thoughts. Disturbing dreams had plagued her since Mrs. Havlik's visit. Memories of her past resurfaced almost every night, of Armin's death, of Romy and Handlanger plotting. Of Josef crying.

Josef.

What did he expect she would do when she learned of Romy's deteriorating health? Run to him, beg him to love her again? Much of what she'd called love seemed too starry-eyed to be real now. She'd proven to herself she could live without him. Her mother may have been right; Josef introduced her to love, and now she had to find it with someone else. She had thought it might be Gershom. If only he didn't have to leave, if they'd had more time, if….

No. She cared for him deeply but could not say she loved him in that all-encompassing way. After they parted in Prague, she worried about him constantly. When he wrote to inform her he'd arrived safely in New York, her concern changed to curiosity about his life in America. But not once did she long to leave her home and join him. She felt grateful to him for saving her from Zigmund. Absolutely responsible to ensure Gershom didn't suffer for his actions. If the war ended tomorrow and she saw him standing in the doorway to her house, she'd be happy, smile, give him a big hug. But unlike Paulina when Ivo returned home, she wouldn't feel a current of joy coursing through her, run into Gershom's arms and wish to be held, caressed. Loved.

Life in wartime had hardened her. She became accustomed to being the one person everyone relied upon. She helped Paulina launch her business. She gave up her dream of studying at the Art Academy to support her mother after her father's death, and oversaw the factory's conversion to wartime production. She took in Paulina and converted her home into a profitable boarding house, while making her own home livable for three women and a toddler.

She'd worked and saved money, shopped and bartered to keep food on the table and a roof over their heads, cooked and cleaned, chopped wood and raised chickens, dug and tended a vegetable garden. She sacrificed food from her plate to see that Paulina and her child had enough to eat, took on the heavy labor her mother couldn't perform, even sold her Monet to fund Gershom's getaway and new life. She did so willingly, but it took its toll.

All she wanted was to have someone in her life that wouldn't add to her burden, but take on a share of it. Someone who could see value in her beyond what she could do for them, but in who she was. Someone who could make her feel cherished again. With a world drenched in war, she doubted someone like that could even exist.

CHAPTER NINE

Lala passed through the gate and entered her shtetl. Ahead lay the stretch of shops and tradesmen's homes that lined the main road. She recognized Mr. Chelmsky's butcher shop. Its weatherworn door swung open. He stepped out and pointed toward villagers queued up ahead as three women in patched dresses hurried to get in line.

She walked past a row of familiar faces that extended as far as the eye could see. Sophia, the midwife. Bella Vichenko, the farrier's daughter, holding hands with Lev Radovich. The barelegged little girl. Their eyes were empty. They must all be dead.

"Why are you here?" she asked, but no one responded. Silently they moved a few steps forward, then stopped before advancing again. The line snaked around a corner and continued beside tumbledown shacks pushed together like rotting teeth.

The queue ended at a huge steaming cauldron by the well. There stood a figure shrouded in black, its back turned to Lala.

She moved nearer.

The cloaked figure ladled food into bowls and handed one to each villager on line. As soon as each took a bowl, that person vanished.

"Who are you?" Lala cried. The figure stopped serving.

It slowly turned toward her, but mist obscured its face. "Show yourself," she demanded.

The fog began to clear. The face was Romy's.

Lala sprang up in bed, gasping for breath. Was Romy dead like the people in her nightmare? Was she seeking Lala's forgiveness for what she'd done? Or did she have an important message for Lala?

Why would Romy be helping the villagers? She had nothing to do with Lala's mysterious benefactor. They hadn't even met until Lala's seventh birthday, well after she and her family had left Russia. But Lala trusted her visions.

Armin's disappearance and murder, Josef's isolation, Paulina's shop closure. Everything linked back to Romy. Maybe the woman held the key to unlocking this mystery, maybe not, but one thing was sure.

There was only one way to find out.

Bohnice Hospital was located north of Prague's center. After walking through the city streets, she continued on an unpaved road that cut through open fields. A church bell tolled the noon hour. She spotted its source ahead—an art nouveau church adjacent to the facility.

The nine-kilometer walk from the railway station to the hospital fatigued Lala. Her mother had insisted she take food with her. She unwrapped the napkin in her purse to find two slices of bread and a small wedge of cheese, exactly what she'd been given as a starving child in trade for clothing. The irony struck her. She sat on a bench in the garden fronting the hospital and ate her meal. She then took her engagement ring from her purse and slipped it on the fourth finger of her left hand before entering the facility.

***

A mature nurse escorted Lala through the hallway of the hospital to Romy's room, unlocked the door and opened it. Before she entered, Lala asked, "Is she restrained?"

"Yes, Miss, but not to worry. It's to prevent her from injuring herself. You will be safe."

Lala stepped into the room. Romy laid in bed, covers up over her chest, her dull eyes fixed on a blank wall. Her hair, which had been cut very short, had turned silver. Parchment skin stretched across the contours of her face and her exposed hands. Her nail beds had turned white.

"Can she hear me?" Lala asked the nurse.

"We believe so, although she's not responsive."

"Is she ill?"

"Let me call the doctor." The nurse excused herself.

Lala stood in the doorway, unsure of what to say. She'd planned it all in her head, but now that she was here the words wouldn't come to her. Seeing the once indomitable woman withered and unresponsive left her wondering what could be gained by her visit.

"Romy," she finally whispered, then repeated it a little louder. She got no reply.

The nurse returned. "Miss, may I present Dr. Gund."

Lala turned to greet the tall, slender doctor. With his dark hair and eyes and aquiline nose, he startled her. "Forgive me, you look so much like my...like her..."

"Armin Smetana?"

"You must hear that all the time from her visitors."

"You are the first."

"To see the resemblance?"

"To visit Mrs. Smetana. She calls me Armin all the time. It calms her to think he's still alive."

"Why does she look yellow like that?"

409

"Jaundice. She'd been taking a complexion tonic for years, laced with arsenic."

"Arsenic? Isn't that poisonous, Doctor?"

"In large enough quantities, yes, but Mrs. Smetana's tonic contained minute amounts, insufficient to poison her outright."

"Why would she do that?"

"These elixirs leave the skin pale, a quality favored in her circles, but they work by inducing anemia. They also deprive the internal organs of oxygen."

"So, she's been slowly poisoned."

"Yes. Her organs are beginning to shut down. She is dying."

"How much time does she have?"

"Optimistically, a few months." Another nurse entered the room and handed him a board with a paper clipped to it. He scanned the document and initialed it before returning it to her. "I have another patient to see. If you will excuse me?"

All the questions she wanted to ask came roaring back…did Romy want Karel killed to ensure Lala and Armin married? Did she think she could change her son's nature? But what did it matter now?

Lala's mother had warned her she could gain nothing by seeing Romy. Whether acknowledging that her murderous actions tormented her, whether she rued destroying so many lives. Whether she suffered the flames of hell or survived through blithe indifference, nothing would change. Why did Lala come here? Romy had no answers.

Romy wasn't even the person she wanted to see…

"…*To love someone deeply gives you strength'.*"

She knew that to be true in her own life. "*And what if you're loved deeply by someone?*"

"It gives you courage...."

Lala wilted. What little strength she had didn't matter. She lacked courage.

She started to leave, then turned back to Romy laying there, and said her final goodbye.

Voices drifted in from the hallway. A woman's voice...

"Dr. Gund is busy with a client, sir. I am authorized to take payments and issue receipts."

A male voice responded, "I trust larger denominations won't be a problem?"

Lala stiffened. She peered into the hallway to find that her suspicion was right. Standing at the nurses' station, counting out koruny into a neat pile was her benefactor's agent, Emil Cerveny.

CHAPTER TEN

Lala ducked into the room and waited until she heard Cerveny leave. She approached the nurses' station, staffed by a young woman with an egg-sized port wine stain on her left cheek.

"Nurse, would you please check on Mrs. Smetana? I think she's in distress."

When the nurse stepped away, Lala went behind the desk and found the copy of Cerveny's receipt. It showed that he paid Romy's monthly bill on April sixth, and listed an address in Prague. Lala checked the calling card Cerveny had given her. The address wasn't the same. She jotted it on the back of the card and left before the nurse returned.

By midafternoon she'd crossed the Charles Bridge to the Mala Strana and found the place she sought nearby. U Luzichkeho Seminaire was a quiet street of mixed century dwellings, with a small park at the far end. Lala stood in front of number sixteen, a three-story building with small balustrades below the upper floor windows. She glanced up and down the street as she wondered what to do next. What did she expect to find?

She crossed to the other side of the street and gazed up at the building. Opened draperies bordered most of the windows. She scanned them one by one, looking for a clue, when on the third floor she spied part of a painting through a window.

Lala knew she was being ridiculous when she entered the building and climbed to the third-floor landing, but her instincts told her to continue. There were four apartments, with a toilette at the end of the hall. She determined which door had to correspond with the window outside. She pressed her ear to the door, listening for activity inside, then knocked and waited. She heard chair legs scraping against a wood floor followed by approaching footsteps.

A thousand questions rushed through her as she waited. Lala swallowed and stopped breathing as the doorknob turned. The door slowly opened. She released her breath when she looked up and saw him standing before her.

Josef.

CHAPTER ELEVEN

He looked thinner than the last time she saw him, but who didn't nowadays? More of his hair had turned silver and she saw prominent lines etched around his eyes, which had opened wide in surprise at the sight of her. Other than that, he looked the same, distinguished and dashing, even dressed in black trousers turned shiny with wear, a white shirt unbuttoned at the collar, and a charcoal gray wool cardigan a size too big.

"Lala. What are you doing here?"

"A good question. I could ask you the same thing."

He leaned his head out of the doorway and checked the hall. Finding it empty, he stepped aside. "Please, come in."

She entered a sparsely appointed flat with worn furniture. A small settee and a wingback chair sat at right angle, an amateurish side table at the juncture. The parlor faced the street. Afternoon sun reflected off the building across the way. A niche in the wall opposite the windows served as a kitchen, fitted with a sink, ancient stove, a few cupboards and a small round table barely big enough for two. A few fine paintings interrupted the busy pattern of wallpaper faded with age. She recognized one canvas—the marvelous Ludwig Meidner street scene she'd seen in Berlin. The artwork

415

seemed out of place with the surroundings.

"Would you like to sit down?" he asked.

"I'm not sure I'll be staying."

He nodded. "You're wondering what I'm doing here. When news of Romy's placement came to light, my participation in the consortium was no longer required."

"So, you chose to live in Prague."

"I couldn't go back to that house. How did you find me?"

"I've developed a talent for detective work. Are you the anonymous client who bought the Monet?"

"I am. Would you like to see it?"

"I already have."

"You're angry with me."

"No. I want to know why you bought the painting."

"I knew you had to have placed the ad in the newspaper. You loved that painting, so there could only be two reasons why you'd sell it. Either you were desperate for money, or it reminded you too much of me. I presumed the former explanation, otherwise you would have sold it long before. I trust it helped you survive during these difficult years?"

"I didn't keep the money. I gave it to someone else."

"Gershom Kindemann?"

"So you know what happened."

"Only that he disappeared suddenly, didn't show up at the factory one day and no one has heard from him since. I feared something terrible must have happened. Is he all right?"

She felt she could trust him. "He's in America. Most of the money went to pay for his passage."

"Why did he leave so suddenly?"

"He did something to help me, but it put his life in danger."

Josef appeared to mull the possibilities. "Will you join him?"

She shook her head. "I can't now."

"If it's money, you can sell your painting again. I always intended to return it to you. You can take it with you."

She wondered if he'd buy it back, but looking at his living quarters, she doubted he could.

"No, I can't leave my family. They depend on me. Why would you assume I would join Gershom?"

"I may be old, but I'm not a fool, Lala. During the Seder, I could see he was in love with you. If you love him, then don't deny yourself the opportunity to go there, make a life together. Time has a way of slipping by until you realize there's nothing left but memories and regrets. Please don't let that happen to you."

"It's really not your concern anymore." She regretted her remark immediately.

His eyes filled with sadness. "Lala, why are you here? Is it to hurt me? Because nothing you can say or do can make me feel worse than that night when I sent you away. But sometimes you must think of others above yourself."

"That has become my life, Josef. Since my father died I have had to put everyone else before me." She walked across the bare plankwood floor. The adjacent room held a bed, chest of drawers, a small table and a wood chair. Hanging on one wall was the sketch Armin made of her kneeling in the rose garden, which became the drawing on display in her parlor. She noticed "She," Armin's painting of her, leaning against a bare wall...

"*...not my painting, Lala, you. You are the masterpiece....*"

"I really don't know why I'm here, Josef. I'm trying to find answers."

"To what?"

She turned to face him. "To my life. Do I serve a purpose other than to serve others? I am at the bottom of the pile. I've become a stranger to myself. I used to be my father's daughter. Armin's muse. A woman who only wanted to go to art school. Now who am I?"

"You are everything, Lala."

"Everything? Certainly, the primary breadwinner, negotiator, shopper, and home maintainer."

He started to say something, but swallowed the words back. Instead, he went into the bedroom and brought out a canvas, wrapped in paper.

"Here is the painting."

"Just like you gave it to me the first time."

The room darkened as the sun dipped below the rooftops across the street.

"Where are my manners? You must be hungry. Shall I fix something for you?"

She was hungry.

"I have trout," he said quietly.

Her favorite. "How did you find it?"

"I know a fisherman who provides me with a steady supply. Will you stay?"

She took off her jacket. "For a while. The last train leaves at six-thirty."

He hung up her jacket before going into the kitchen. "You take your coffee black."

"Yes, you remembered…you have coffee?"

"From Vienna. I rarely drink it anymore, but it would be good with fried trout."

"Since when do you cook?"

"Since I had to."

In spite of herself, she laughed.

They sat at his tiny table. She told him about Jacub, how he had brought joy into their lives despite the hardships, as they ate their trout with surprisingly good K-brot and coffee. Lala cleared the table when they were done.

"How are you faring, Josef? Paulina's in-laws say it's harder to find goods here than in the country."

"I have my sources."

She decided not to pursue that. "It must be very different for you, living here."

"My situation should change shortly."

She presumed he meant Romy. "Will you sell the mansion and find a house in Prague?"

"It's likely."

"I hope everything works out for you, Josef. I truly do."

Sadness filled his eyes again. "I thought it might, but now I'm not very confident it will."

He was still in love with her. After all this time.

"Josef, I wish it could be like it was before, but I've been broken into a thousand pieces. I need to make myself whole again."

"It pains me to hear that. All I've ever wanted for you was to be safe and happy."

"I'm sorry you didn't get your wish."

CHAPTER TWELVE

"What time is it?" she asked.

Josef checked his silver pocket watch. "Half past five."

"I should leave if I'm to catch my train."

"May I walk you to the station?"

"Thank you for offering, but it won't be necessary."

He brought her jacket and helped her put it on. She studied the Meidner painting again.

"I bought it after hearing your impression of it," he said. "It does represent what I remember seeing in Berlin that summer. I had intended to present it to you as a special gift."

"For what?"

"July twelfth, when you celebrate your birthday. I wasn't sure you'd have accepted it."

"No, I probably wouldn't have."

She should have left, but something kept her there, some unanswered question hidden so deep within her she didn't even know what to ask. "I should go," she said, more to convince herself. "I'll leave the Monet here for now."

"Then you'll return?"

"Perhaps."

She forced herself out the door. Should she have kissed

him goodbye? No, it only would have confused the situation. Better to leave it as is.

She stood outside his door, expecting something to happen, though she didn't know what. Words from her past led her to believe...

"...it may be something he says, or does, that means something special to you, but you'll know...trust your heart."

He didn't come after her. Nothing pointed to her returning to him other than a vague feeling that a piece of the puzzle was missing. She would return home and remember this last time with him fondly, talking about Jacub over a trout dinner...

"...I know a fisherman who provides me with a steady supply. Will you stay?"

As she walked down the stairs, one thing he said nagged at her.

"...July twelfth, when you celebrate your birthday..."

He remembered her birthday. She smiled. It was sweet, but...

"...July twelfth, when you celebrate your birthday..."

He phrased it in that peculiar way. Most people would say, 'July twelfth is your birthday.' Then it occurred to her. It wasn't, not really. Her parents had changed her birth date when they adopted her because she was actually born the year before they married, and in mid-August, though the exact day was unknown. But how could Josef had known that?

She mulled that as she left the building, sparking other unanswered questions...

"All I've ever wanted for you was to be safe and happy." He said safe, even before happy. It had to be the war. *"...safe and happy."*

Her pace slowed as she recalled all that he'd done for her

family, for her…

She looked for a distraction among the items on display in the secretary bookcase and chose a fine arts book, a gift from Josef for her sixteenth birthday…

"…why do you think all those people from the factory showed up here to pay their respects to your father? They knew the Smetanas would be providing food. How would we have been able to feed them…"

"…all he had left was you, but still he let you go so you wouldn't be sullied by the tragic muddle of his life…"

…he handed Sarah a folded document. Lala guessed by the shocked look on her mother's face it was the deed to their house, now signed over to them…

…all he'd done, whether she knew it or not…

"…what a feast we had that day when you bartered with that fisherman for trout…"

"…my client prefers to remain anonymous and will maintain your anonymity as well.…"

And much more. He had always been there for her, for her family, without anyone having to ask, without expecting anything in return…

"All I've ever wanted for you was to be safe and happy."

Was she looking for an excuse to go back to him? Her gratitude didn't constitute a reason, any more than she felt obligated to marry Gershom for rescuing her. But as she neared the Charles Bridge, the sense that all the puzzle pieces lay before her grew stronger, the answer was at hand, if she knew where to find it.

She gazed at the antique ring she wore, a lovely pearl surrounded by six diamonds set in gold. She had seen herself wearing the ring in her vision, before she fell in love with him.

He'd asked her if she wanted his son to present it to her the same night he gave her the painting. The ring had belonged to Josef's mother, who died when Armin was young. Josef's father died not long after…

Josef glanced away. "I suppose that could be interpreted as a sign of devotion, one not being able to survive without the other."

"I'm so sorry," Lala said. "It must have been dreadful for you, losing both of your parents in such a short time…"

Like she lost Mama and Papa…

…she could see he was fighting back words. Finally, he nodded. "It was a long time ago. At least they were older and died peacefully in their bed. I'm sorry, Lala. I hope I didn't ruin the evening for you by bringing up sad memories."

"Not at all, Mr. Smetana. I understand. Your parents were old and lived a long life."

He seemed to fumble for a response, but said nothing more and neither did she….

Something about that conversation struck her again…

"…I hope I didn't ruin the evening for you by bringing up sad memories…"

"…at least they were older and died peacefully in their bed…."

Lala gasped. It had been there all along and she never saw it.

"You are everything, Lala."

She turned and started walking back to Josef's flat, heart pounding and tears streaming. Her steady pace quickened, faster and faster. She ran the last block to his building and dashed up the stairs. Breathless, she pounded on the door until he answered.

"Lala, what is it?"

"…Trust your heart."

She looked into his face. All the long-unanswered questions and mysteries suddenly seemed clear, as clear as the devotion she saw reflected in his eyes. Like two lanterns of love.

"Josef. You knew."

CHAPTER THIRTEEN

"You knew all about my past. My life in Russia. How—"

"Come in first," he insisted, and shut the door behind them. "My agent, Cerveny."

"How did he find out?"

"I sent him to follow your father."

"Why?"

"You have to understand, I'd just hired him and he asked to delay until he and your mother went to Russia. I didn't know him well enough, so I tasked Cerveny to ensure he'd been truthful and wasn't pitting me against another offer. Cerveny found out about an orphaned girl who survived a pogrom, looking for help. I couldn't imagine how you survived your ordeal, the fortitude you showed. I considered taking you in myself, but Cerveny said your parents wanted to adopt you. When I learned about the survivors, how they threatened to harm you, I authorized him to offer each one a lump sum of money to help them relocate in exchange for their promise to never harm you." He fetched a metal box from his desk and opened it. "I kept the letters they signed as a guarantee." Inside was a stack of yellowed papers.

"May I see them?"

He gave the box to Lala. "I worried that when the newspapers printed your engagement announcement with a photo, someone from your past might recognize you, so I retrieved them from my vault."

She looked through the letters, recognizing a few names—Mr. Vichenko, the farrier. Mrs. Radova, whom everyone called Radovich, the widow with the cow.

"So you see, my fascination with you began even before I met you. It pleased me to learn that Jakob and Sarah were going to adopt you. That is why I invited your family to our home for your birthday.

"When I met you for the first time, standing in my parlor, staring at the Monet, I was enchanted. The way you studied it, the look on your face, of curiosity and pleasure. I watched you awhile. I'd purchased it because Romy thought it would impress our guests, but after that day I began to look at it with new eyes, to see the beauty in it, the story it told. It changed the way I viewed art from then on."

His fingers brushed a tendril of hair from her face. It made her shiver.

"You've always had a wonderful curiosity for things, never afraid of something that was different. You judged things on their own merit, even as a child. How remarkable that is."

"Why didn't you tell me this before?" But she knew it wouldn't have mattered if he'd told her. She had to find out for herself, or it would have meant nothing.

"I had no way of knowing if what you felt for me was truly love or merely infatuation, and I did not want to impose on you because of the way I felt, especially with my recent complications."

She moved so close to him she could feel his breath.

"And how do you feel about me, Josef?"

"I love you. I always have. You've captivated me since childhood, and as I watched you become a woman, those feelings of admiration and love deepened. I've never stopped loving you, Lala. Never. I never will."

He wrapped his arms around her in an embrace. She felt his ribcage through his sweater as her cheek pressed against his chest and detected the faintest hint of bergamot and leather, the scent of his aftershave. Yet it didn't matter as they stood together, enfolded, each of them as much a muse as a creator of this moment. Of all those moments they'd shared before. The kisses, the passionate embraces, the tender stroking and exploration of their bodies, none could compare to the reawakening of devotion. She kissed him, a long, lingering kiss that set her aflame. Standing here, with Josef's arms around her, she'd found her place. Her purpose. Her reason to be. She'd tried to right a wrong and instead righted herself.

When the kiss ended, he stroked her cheek. "You must leave now if you're to catch your train."

"I'm not going anywhere tonight except to bed with you."

"Lala, your family—"

"I don't care if there's hell to pay tomorrow. Make love to me."

CHAPTER FOURTEEN

Sunshine streaming through the window woke Lala. She rolled over in bed and saw Josef lying next to her. A perfect ending to a perfect night.

She borrowed his sweater, rolling up the sleeves past her wrists, and went to the kitchen to make coffee. As it finished brewing she heard him stirring. She poured two cups and brought them back to bed.

"You're spoiling me," he said, wiping the sleep from his eyes.

"Get used to it." She kissed him.

He took his cup and then hers, and put them together on the nightstand. He playfully stroked her back. Lala curled up next to him as his fingers began to explore her body. She sighed deeply and arched her back. No hot coffee this morning.

After they dressed, Lala fetched two place servings from the cupboard as Josef sliced bread and cheese for breakfast.

"I'm concerned about your mother's reaction when you get home today," said Josef. "If she suspects where you've been, she will certainly object."

"I don't care," she said, setting the table. "I'm too happy."

"What if I went back with you?"

"Have I ever told you about The Eye?"

Josef brought two plates of food to the table. "I see your point. Still, I'd rather be honest and face her wrath."

"All right. We'll go together. Will you stay the night?"

"Let's not tempt fate."

"You could stay in Paulina's house. You'd be more comfortable there than here, and this way we can pool our resources until your situation changes."

"It's a thought. Once the war ends, we could live there together once we're married."

Startled, Lala dropped the silverware. "Josef, no. You can't say that, not yet. It will put a hex on us."

Her good mood faded. She'd stepped over the line last night, but hearing Josef propose marriage while still technically married upset her. Still not convinced the curse had been broken, Lala sensed a sign confirming or disproving her fears would be forthcoming.

She put on her jacket. "We should leave now if we want to return before lunch."

The sun on her face felt pleasant, countering some of the morning chill in the air. As they walked arm in arm toward the Charles Bridge, Lala wondered how much the coffee, sugar and other staples she carried in her bag would fend off her mother's ire when she returned home with Josef. Not much. Then again, the war had changed them all. Paulina was a wife and mother, Sarah the doting grandmother of a boy named in honor of her late husband. And she, who a few years ago thought only of art, oversaw the conversion of a factory to wartime production. She could now run a household, grow her own food, raise chickens, and care for a child, as well as draw.

A throng gathered at the far end of the bridge. Lala could make out some people walking away as others pushed their way into the crowd.

"What's going on?" she wondered aloud. "Let's see."

They walked toward the crowd.

"It's a newsstand," Josef said. "Something very important must have happened."

Lala swallowed hard. If the news were bad, especially today, it would prove that she was cursed. That despite everything Josef had tried to do for her, the villagers were right. The Peddler's daughter would never know happiness.

As they approached, Lala observed people as they left the newsstand. A few looked resigned, but most appeared grim. Fearing the worst, she stopped.

"Josef, please find out what happened."

He went to the newsstand and soon disappeared into the throng. She struggled to breathe normally, for as hard as she tried to fight the notion of being hexed, the more it frightened her.

As the war dragged on, rarely a day had passed without reports of another horrific battle with thousands dead, each side fighting over the same patch of land for months on end. Lala tried to remain impassive, but her imagination took her into dangerous territory. What if another village had been overrun by enemy soldiers, its population exiled, persecuted, slaughtered? If yet another starving community had held a demonstration somewhere in the empire or Germany, which led to rioting? Or looting, which often seemed to target Jewish shopkeepers as the hatred fomented by war rekindled anti-Semitism.

She had even heard talk of expanding the conscription age to children as young as fifteen and men up to fifty, leaving Josef vulnerable. After all they'd been through, she couldn't bear the thought of them being separated again. It would shatter her to find that the villagers' curse extended to him.

She closed her eyes and silently prayed that it not be tragic news.

Josef emerged from the crowd and hurried toward her, a newspaper tucked under his arm. "What is it?" she begged.

"The Americans have declared war on Germany." He showed her the headline.

"What do you think that will mean for us?"

"Now that they have joined the war, I expect the Allies will be victorious." Josef skimmed the front page of the newspaper. "So much death and destruction, and the war will have been for naught."

Defeat might be demoralizing, even humiliating, Losing the war would likely cause the empire to crumble. Was that bad news? Lala wasn't sure. What would defeat mean to Bohemia? Karel had written of Czech and Slovak nationalists in America, gathering support for a new independent nation. Would they achieve that support? Or would America punish the nation-states of the empire for bringing about this war?

She took the newspaper from him and tossed it in the garbage. "The war has been for naught since the beginning, hasn't it?"

He nodded. "Let's hurry or we'll miss our train."

As they walked, Josef took her hand in his. A natural

gesture. His touch sent an unexpected wave of serenity through her.

Was the war news the sign she sought? She could not tell. Did she carry a curse? Maybe, maybe not. No matter, she thought as she held Josef's hand. Life would go on, as she observed at the beginning of the war, on the night she left Berlin. The sun would rise and set, the moon would wax and wane. The war would eventually end, perhaps sooner now that the Americans had joined the fight. It didn't matter anymore which side declared victory, only when. No one would win. No one outright.

On the day it all began, the day they fell in love, Josef had taught her a valuable lesson…

"To love someone deeply gives you strength."

She knew that to be true in her own life. "And what if you're loved deeply by someone?"

"It gives you courage…."

She would take her strength from loving. And I have the courage to go on as well, she thought. Courage that derived from being loved.

In a few hours she would return home with Josef to face her mother's wrath, but she knew it stemmed from worry. From caring. From love. Eventually her mother would forgive her and when Josef was finally free, all would be forgotten. Paulina would scold her in public and express her joy in private. And little Jacub, a product of love, would look up at her, with his mother's features and his father's coloring, and remind her of the wonder children bring to families.

She thought back to her darkest hour and recalled Paulina's words to her…

"Think of what you do have. Your mother. A darling nephew who loves you. A roommate who's now a sister as well as a friend. Things are

435

not as bleak as you portray them."

And now Josef. Her muse and mentor, as much as she'd been his. She smiled and her heart lightened. Like a nearly full moon, she'd seen a sign of change on the horizon, only it wasn't in the news. It was in herself.

She could feel hope once again. For peace. For independence.

For love.

ACKNOWLEDGEMENTS

I couldn't have completed this book without the help and support of many people. Many thanks to Heather Ames, Bonnie Schroeder, Terry Carr, and Chris Page of the Pacific Online Writers Group, who got me through my first draft. Appreciation to the many writers in Whidbey Island Writers Group who helped me polish my second draft.

Special thanks to my beta readers, Hanna Rhys Barnes, Linda Pease, and Bonnie Schroeder for their input and advice, and to Mike McNeff for his many contributions from start to finish.

A big thank you to Renee Le Verrier, a multi-talented woman whose poppy painting graced the original book cover. I'm grateful to the readers of my earlier books, who have been so encouraging. And as always, thanks to my husband Allan.

ABOUT THE AUTHOR

Miko Johnston first contemplated a writing career as a poet at age six. That notion ended four years later when she found no "help wanted" ads for poets in the classified section, but her desire to write persisted. After graduating from New York University, she headed west to pursue a career as a television and print journalist before deciding she preferred, to paraphrase Mark Twain, the more believable realm of fiction. Her first novel, *A Petal In The Wind*, was published in 2014, and *A Petal in the Wind II* in 2015. Her short story, "By Anonymous," was published in the Sisters in Crime anthology *Last Exit To Murder*. Two short stories are featured in the anthology *Write Around Whidbey*, and two more have been published in *Whidbey Landmarks*. Miko lives with her rocket scientist husband Allan on Whidbey Island in Washington.